The Portygee

by
Joseph C. Lincoln

The Portygee
by Joseph C. Lincoln

Copyright © 2024

All Rights reserved.

No part of this publication may be reproduced, stored in a retrieval system, or transmitted in any form or by any means, electronic, mechanical, photocopying or Otherwise, without the written permission of the publisher.
The author/editor asserts the moral right to be identified as the author/editor of this work.

ISBN: 978-93-65789-38-6

Published by
DOUBLE 9 BOOKS
2/13-B, Ansari Road
Daryaganj, New Delhi – 110002
info@double9books.com
www.double9books.com
Tel. 011-40042856

This book is under public domain

ABOUT THE AUTHOR

Joseph Crosby Lincoln was an American novelist, poet, and short story writer, with many of his works situated on a fictional Cape Cod. Lincoln was born in 1870 in Brewster, Massachusetts, on Cape Cod, and after his father died, his mother relocated the family to Chelsea, Massachusetts, an industrial community outside of Boston. Lincoln's writing career extolling "old Cape Cod" can be viewed as an attempt to return to an Eden that he had fled due to familial sorrow. Lincoln's work was frequently featured in renowned journals like The Saturday Evening Post and The Delineator. Lincoln was aware of contemporary naturalist writers like Frank Norris and Theodore Dreiser, who utilized American literature to delve into the depths of human nature, but he rejected the creative exercise. Lincoln stated that he was content "spinning yarns" that made readers feel good about themselves and their neighbors. His work served as the basis for six films and a short.

CONTENTS

CHAPTER I	7
CHAPTER II	25
CHAPTER III	38
CHAPTER IV	59
CHAPTER V	74
CHAPTER VI	92
CHAPTER VII	101
CHAPTER VIII	121
CHAPTER IX	141
CHAPTER X	157
CHAPTER XI	177
CHAPTER XII	196
CHAPTER XIII	200
CHAPTER XIV	219
CHAPTER XV	236
CHAPTER XVI	249
CHAPTER XVII	259
CHAPTER XVIII	270
CHAPTER XIX	283
CHAPTER XX	296

CHAPTER I

Overhead the clouds cloaked the sky; a ragged cloak it was, and, here and there, a star shone through a hole, to be obscured almost instantly as more cloud tatters were hurled across the rent. The pines threshed on the hill tops. The bare branches of the wild-cherry and silverleaf trees scraped and rattled and tossed. And the wind, the raw, chilling December wind, driven in, wet and salty, from the sea, tore over the dunes and brown uplands and across the frozen salt-meadows, screamed through the telegraph wires, and made the platform of the dismal South Harniss railway station the lonesomest, coldest, darkest and most miserable spot on the face of the earth.

At least that was the opinion of the seventeen-year-old boy whom the down train—on time for once and a wonder—had just deposited upon that platform. He would not have discounted the statement one iota. The South Harniss station platform WAS the most miserable spot on earth and he was the most miserable human being upon it. And this last was probably true, for there were but three other humans upon that platform and, judging by externals, they seemed happy enough. One was the station agent, who was just entering the building preparatory to locking up for the night, and the others were Jim Young, driver of the "depot wagon," and Doctor Holliday, the South Harniss "homeopath," who had been up to a Boston hospital with a patient and was returning home. Jim was whistling "Silver Bells," a tune much in vogue the previous summer, and Doctor Holliday was puffing at a cigar and knocking his feet together to keep them warm while waiting to get into the depot wagon. These were the only people in sight and they were paying no attention whatever to the lonely figure at the other end of the platform.

The boy looked about him. The station, with its sickly yellow gleam of kerosene lamp behind its dingy windowpane, was apparently the only inhabited spot in a barren wilderness. At the edge of the platform civilization seemed to end and beyond was nothing but a black earth and a black sky, tossing trees and howling wind, and cold—raw, damp, penetrating cold. Compared with this even the stuffy plush seats and smelly warmth of the car he had just left appeared temptingly homelike and luxurious. All the way down from the city he had sneered inwardly at a one-horse railroad which ran no Pullmans on its Cape branch in winter time. Now he forgot his longing for mahogany veneer and individual chairs and would gladly have boarded a freight car, provided there were in it a lamp and a stove.

The light in the station was extinguished and the agent came out with a jingling bunch of keys and locked the door. "Good-night, Jim," he shouted, and walked off into the blackness. Jim responded with a "good-night" of his own and climbed aboard the wagon, into the dark interior of which the doctor had preceded him. The boy at the other end of the platform began to be really alarmed. It looked as if all living things were abandoning him and he was to be left marooned, to starve or freeze, provided he was not blown away first.

He picked up the suitcase—an expensive suitcase it was, elaborately strapped and buckled, with a telescope back and gold fittings—and hastened toward the wagon. Mr. Young had just picked up the reins.

"Oh,—oh, I say!" faltered the boy. We have called him "the boy" all this time, but he did not consider himself a boy, he esteemed himself a man, if not full-grown physically, certainly so mentally. A man, with all a man's wisdom, and more besides—the great, the all-embracing wisdom of his age, or youth.

"Here, I say! Just a minute!" he repeated. Jim Young put his head around the edge of the wagon curtain. "Eh?" he queried. "Eh? Who's talkin'? Oh, was it you, young feller? Did you want me?"

The young fellow replied that he did. "This is South Harniss, isn't it?" he asked.

Mr. Young chuckled. "Darn sure thing," he drawled. "I give in that it looks consider'ble like Boston, or Providence, R. I., or some of them capitols, but it ain't, it's South Harniss, Cape Cod."

Doctor Holliday, on the back seat of the depot wagon, chuckled. Jim did not; he never laughed at his own jokes. And his questioner did not chuckle, either.

"Does a—does a Mr. Snow live here?" he asked.

The answer was prompt, if rather indefinite. "Um-hm," said the driver. "No less'n fourteen of him lives here. Which one do you want?"

"A Mr. Z. Snow."

"Mr. Z. Snow, eh? Humph! I don't seem to recollect any Mr. Z. Snow around nowadays. There used to be a Ziba Snow, but he's dead. 'Twan't him you wanted, was it?"

"No. The one I want is—is a Captain Snow. Captain—" he paused before uttering the name which to his critical metropolitan ear had seemed so dreadfully countrified and humiliating; "Captain Zelotes Snow," he blurted, desperately.

Jim Young laughed aloud. "Good land, Doc!" he cried, turning toward his passenger; "I swan I clean forgot that Cap'n Lote's name begun with a Z. Cap'n Lote Snow? Why, darn sure! I . . . Eh?" He stopped short, evidently struck by a new idea. "Sho!" he drawled, slowly. "Why, I declare I believe you're . . . Yes, of course! I heard they was expectin' you. Doc, you know who 'tis, don't you? Cap'n Lote's grandson; Janie's boy."

He took the lighted lantern from under the wagon seat and held it up so that its glow shone upon the face of the youth standing by the wheel.

"Hum," he mused. "Don't seem to favor Janie much, does he, Doc. Kind of got her mouth and chin, though. Remember that sort of good-lookin' set to her mouth she had? And SHE got it from old Cap'n Lo himself. This boy's face must be more like his pa's, I cal'late. Don't you cal'late so, Doc?"

Whether Doctor Holliday cal'lated so or not he did not say. It may be that he thought this cool inspection of and discussion concerning a stranger, even a juvenile stranger, somewhat embarrassing to its object. Or the lantern light may have shown him an ominous pucker between the boy's black brows and a flash of temper in the big black eyes beneath them. At any rate, instead of replying to Mr. Young, he said, kindly:

"Yes, Captain Snow lives in the village. If you are going to his house get right in here. I live close by, myself."

"Darned sure!" agreed Mr. Young, with enthusiasm. "Hop right in, sonny."

But the boy hesitated. Then, haughtily ignoring the driver, he said: "I thought Captain Snow would be here to meet me. He wrote that he would."

The irrepressible Jim had no idea of remaining ignored. "Did Cap'n Lote write you that he'd be here to the depot?" he demanded. "All right, then he'll be here, don't you fret. I presume likely that everlastin' mare of his has eat herself sick again; eh, Doc? By godfreys domino, the way they pet and stuff that fool horse is a sin and a shame. It ain't Lote's fault so much as 'tis his wife's—she's responsible. Don't you fret, Bub, the cap'n'll be here for you some time to-night. If he said he'll come he'll come, even if he has to hire one of them limmysines. He, he, he! All you've got to do is wait, and . . . Hey! . . . Hold on a minute! . . . Bub!"

The boy was walking away. And to hail him as "Bub" was, although Jim Young did not know it, the one way least likely to bring him back.

"Bub!" shouted Jim again. Receiving no reply he added what he had intended saying. "If I run afoul of Cap'n Lote anywheres on the road," he called, "I'll tell him you're here a-waitin'. So long, Bub. Git dap, Chain Lightnin'."

The horse, thus complimented, pricked up one ear, lifted a foot, and jogged off. The depot wagon became merely a shadowy smudge against the darkness of the night. For a few minutes the "chock, chock" of the hoofs upon the frozen road and the rattle of wheels gave audible evidence of its progress. Then these died away and upon the windswept platform of the South Harniss station descended the black gloom of lonesomeness so complete as to make that which had been before seem, by comparison, almost cheerful.

The youth upon that platform turned up his coat collar, thrust his gloved hands into his pockets, and shivered. Then, still shivering, he took a brisk walk up and down beside the suitcase and, finally, circumnavigated the little station. The voyage of discovery was unprofitable; there was nothing to discover. So far as he could see—which was by no means far—upon each side of the building was nothing but bare fields and tossing pines, and wind and cold and blackness. He came to anchor once more by the suitcase and drew a long, hopeless breath.

He thought of the cheery dining room at the school he had left the day before. Dinner would be nearly over by now. The fellows were having dessert, or, probably, were filing out into the corridors, the younger chaps to go to the study hall and the older ones—the lordly seniors, of whom he had been one—on the way to their rooms. The picture of his own cheerful, gay room in the senior corridor was before his mind; of that room as it was before the telegram came, before the lawyer came with the letter, before the end of everything as he knew it and the beginning of—this. He had not always loved and longed for that school as he loved and longed for it now. There had been times when he referred to it as "the old jail," and professed to hate it. But it had been the only real home he had known since he was eight years old and now he looked back upon it as a fallen angel might have looked back upon Paradise. He sighed again, choked and hastily drew his gloved hand across his eyes. At the age of seventeen it is very unmanly to cry, but, at that age also, manhood and boyhood are closely intermingled. He choked again and then, squaring his shoulders, reached into his coat pocket for the silver cigarette case which, as a recent acquisition, was the pride of his soul. He had just succeeded in lighting a cigarette when, borne upon the wind, he heard once more the sound of hoofs and wheels and saw in the distance a speck of light advancing toward the station.

The sounds drew nearer, so did the light. Then an old-fashioned buggy, drawn by a plump little sorrel, pulled up by the platform and a hand held a lantern aloft.

"Hello!" hailed a voice. "Where are you?"

The hail did not have to be repeated. Before the vehicle reached the station the boy had tossed away the cigarette, picked up the suitcase, and was waiting. Now he strode into the lantern light.

"Here I am," he answered, trying hard not to appear too eager. "Were you looking for me?"

The holder of the lantern tucked the reins between the whip-socket and the dash and climbed out of the buggy. He was a little man, perhaps about forty-eight or fifty, with a smooth-shaven face wrinkled at the corners of the mouth and eyes. His voice was the most curious thing about him; it was high and piping, more like a woman's than a man's. Yet his words and manner were masculine enough, and he moved and spoke with a nervous, jerky quickness.

He answered the question promptly. "Guess I be, guess I be," he said briskly. "Anyhow, I'm lookin' for a boy name of—name of—My soul to heavens, I've forgot it again, I do believe! What did you say your name was?"

"Speranza. Albert Speranza."

"Sartin, sartin! Sper—er—um—yes, yes. Knew it just as well as I did my own. Well, well, well! Ye-es, yes, yes. Get right aboard, Alfred. Let me take your satchel."

He picked up the suitcase. The boy, his foot upon the buggy step, still hesitated. "Then you're—you're not my grandfather?" he faltered.

"Eh? Who? Your grandfather? Me? He, he, he!" He chuckled shrilly. "No, no! No such luck. If I was Cap'n Lote Snow, I'd be some older'n I be now and a dum sight richer. Yes, yes. No, I'm Cap'n Lote's bookkeeper over at the lumber consarn. He's got a cold, and Olive—that's his wife—she said he shouldn't come out to-night. He said he should, and while they was Katy-didin' back and forth about it, Rachel—Mrs. Ellis—she's the hired housekeeper there—she telephoned me to harness up and come meet you up here to the depot. Er—er—little mite late, wan't I?"

The Portygee | 11

"Why, yes, just a little. The other man, the one who drives the mail cart—I think that was what it was—said perhaps the horse was sick, or something like that."

"No-o, no, that wan't it this time. I—er—All tucked in and warm enough, be you? Ye-es, yes, yes. No, I'm to blame, I shouldn't wonder. I stopped at the—at the store a minute and met one or two of the fellers, and that kind of held me up. All right now? Ye-es, yes, yes. G'long, gal."

The buggy moved away from the platform. Its passenger, his chilly feet and legs tightly wrapped in the robes, drew a breath of relief between his chattering teeth. He was actually going somewhere at last; whatever happened, morning would not find him propped frozen stiff against the scarred and mangy clapboards of the South Harniss station.

"Warm enough, be you?" inquired his driver cheerfully.

"Yes, thank you."

"That's good, that's good, that's good. Ye-es, yes, yes. Well—er—Frederick, how do you think you're goin' to like South Harniss?"

The answer was rather non-committal. The boy replied that he had not seen very much of it as yet. His companion seemed to find the statement highly amusing. He chuckled and slapped his knee.

"Ain't seen much of it, eh? No-o, no, no. I guess you ain't, guess you ain't. He, he, he . . . Um . . . Let's see, what was I talkin' about?"

"Why, nothing in particular, I think, Mr.—Mr.—"

"Didn't I tell you my name? Sho, sho! That's funny. My name's Keeler—Laban B. Keeler. That's my name and bookkeeper is my station. South Harniss is my dwellin' place—and I guess likely you'll have to see the minister about the rest of it. He, he, he!"

His passenger, to whom the old schoolbook quatrain was entirely unknown, wondered what on earth the man was talking about. However, he smiled politely and sniffed with a dawning suspicion. It seemed to him there was an unusual scent in the air, a spirituous scent, a—

"Have a peppermint lozenger," suggested Mr. Keeler, with sudden enthusiasm. "Peppermint is good for what ails you, so they tell me. Ye-es, yes, yes. Have one. Have two, have a lot."

He proceeded to have a lot himself, and the buggy was straightway reflavored, so to speak. The boy, his suspicions by no means dispelled, leaned back in the corner behind the curtains and awaited developments. He was warmer, that was a real physical and consequently a slight mental comfort, but the feeling of lonesomeness was still acute. So far his acquaintanceship with the citizens of South Harniss had not filled him with enthusiasm. They were what he, in his former and very recent state of existence, would have called "Rubes." Were the grandparents whom he had never met this sort of people? It seemed probable. What sort of a place was this to which Fate had consigned him? The sense of utter helplessness which had had him in its clutches since the day when he received the news of his father's death was as dreadfully real as ever. He had not been consulted at all. No one had asked him what he wished to do, or where he wished to go. The letter had come from these people, the Cape Cod grandparents of whom, up to that time, he had never even heard, and he had been shipped to them as though he were a piece of merchandise. And what was to become of him now, after he reached his destination? What would they expect him to do? Or be? How would he be treated?

In his extensive reading—he had been an omnivorous reader—there were numerous examples of youths left, like him, to the care of distant relatives, or step-parents, or utter strangers. Their experiences, generally speaking, had not been cheerful ones. Most of them had run away. He might run away; but somehow the idea of running away, with no money, to face hardship and poverty and all the rest, did not make an alluring appeal. He had been used to comfort and luxury ever since he could remember, and his imagination, an unusually active one, visualized much more keenly than the average the tribulations and struggles of a runaway. David Copperfield, he remembered, had run away, but he did it when a kid, not a man like himself. Nicholas Nickleby—no, Nicholas had not run away exactly, but his father had died and he had been left to an uncle. It would be dreadful if his grandfather should turn out to be a man like Ralph Nickleby. Yet Nicholas had gotten on well in spite of his wicked relative. Yes, and how gloriously he had defied the old rascal, too! He wondered if he would ever be called upon to defy his grandfather. He saw himself doing it—quietly, a perfect gentleman always, but with the noble determination of one performing a disagreeable duty. His chin lifted and his shoulders squared against the back of the buggy.

Mr. Keeler, who had apparently forgotten his passenger altogether, broke into song,

> "She's my darlin' hanky-panky
> And she wears a number two,
> Her father keeps a barber shop
> Way out in Kalamazoo."

He sang the foregoing twice over and then added a chorus, plainly improvised, made up of "Di doos" and "Di dums" ad lib. And the buggy rolled up and over the slope of a little hill and, in the face of a screaming sea wind, descended a long, gentle slope to where, scattered along a two-mile water frontage, the lights of South Harniss twinkled sparsely.

"Did doo dum, dee dum, doo dum

Di doo dum, doo dum dee."

So sang Mr. Keeler. Then he broke off his solo as the little mare turned in between a pair of high wooden posts bordering a drive, jogged along that drive for perhaps fifty feet, and stopped beside the stone step of a white front door. Through the arched window above that door shone lamplight warm and yellow.

"Whoa!" commanded Mr. Keeler, most unnecessarily. Then, as if himself a bit uncertain as to his exact whereabouts, he peered out at the door and the house of which it was a part, afterward settling back to announce triumphantly: "And here we be! Yes, sir, here we be!"

Then the door opened. A flood of lamplight poured upon the buggy and its occupants. And the boy saw two people standing in the doorway, a man and a woman.

It was the woman who spoke first. It was she who had opened the door. The man was standing behind her looking over her shoulder—over her head really, for he was tall and broad and she short and slender.

"Is it—?" she faltered.

Mr. Keeler answered. "Yes, ma'am," he declared emphatically, "that's who 'tis. Here we be—er—er—what's-your-name—Edward. Jump right out."

His passenger alighted from the buggy. The woman bent forward to look at him, her hands clasped.

"It—it's Albert, isn't it?" she asked.

The boy nodded. "Yes," he said.

The hands unclasped and she held them out toward him. "Oh, Albert," she cried, "I'm your grandmother. I—"

The man interrupted. "Wait till we get him inside, Olive," he said. "Come in, son." Then, addressing the driver, he ordered: "Labe, take the horse and team out to the barn and unharness for me, will you?"

"Ye-es, yes, yes," replied Mr. Keeler. "Yes indeed, Cap'n. Take her right along—right off. Yes indeedy. Git dap!"

He drove off toward the end of the yard, where a large building, presumably a barn, loomed black against the dark sky. He sang as he drove and the big man on the step looked after him and sniffed suspiciously.

Meanwhile the boy had followed the little woman into the house through a small front hall, from which a narrow flight of stairs shot aloft with almost unbelievable steepness, and into a large room. Albert had a swift impression of big windows full of plants, of pictures of ships and schooners on the walls, of a table set for four.

"Take your things right off," cried his grandmother. "Here, I'll take 'em. There! now turn 'round and let me look at you. Don't move till I get a good look."

He stood perfectly still while she inspected him from head to foot.

"You've got her mouth," she said slowly. "Yes, you've got her mouth. Her hair and eyes were brown and yours are black, but—but I THINK you look like her. Oh, I did so want you to! May I kiss you, Albert? I'm your grandmother, you know."

With embarrassed shyness he leaned forward while she put her arms about his neck and kissed him on the cheek. As he straightened again he became aware that the big man had entered the room and was regarding him intently beneath a pair of shaggy gray eyebrows. Mrs. Snow turned.

"Oh, Zelotes," she cried, "he's got Janie's mouth, don't you think so? And he DOES look like her, doesn't he?"

Her husband shook his head. "Maybe so, Mother," he said, with a half smile. "I ain't a great hand for locatin' who folks look like. How are you, boy? Glad to see you. I'm your grandfather, you know."

They shook hands, while each inspected and made a mental estimate of the other. Albert saw a square, bearded jaw, a firm mouth, gray eyes with many wrinkles at the corners, and a shock of thick gray hair. The eyes had a way of looking straight at you, through you, as if reading your thoughts, divining your motives and making a general appraisal of you and them.

Captain Zelotes Snow, for his part, saw a tall young fellow, slim and straight, with black curly hair, large black eyes and regular features. A good-looking boy, a handsome boy—almost too handsome, perhaps, or with just a touch of the effeminate in the good looks. The captain's glance took in the well-fitting suit of clothes, the expensive tie, the gold watch chain.

"Humph!" grunted Captain Zelotes. "Well, your grandma and I are glad to have you with us. Let me see, Albert—that's your right name, ain't it—Albert?"

Something in his grandfather's looks or tone aroused a curious feeling in the youth. It was not a feeling of antagonism, exactly, but more of defiance, of obstinacy. He felt as if this big man, regarding him so keenly from under the heavy brows, was looking for faults, was expecting to find something wrong, might almost be disappointed if he did not find it. He met the gaze for a moment, the color rising to his cheeks.

"My name," he said deliberately, "is Alberto Miguel Carlos Speranza."

Mrs. Snow uttered a little exclamation. "Oh!" she ejaculated. And then added: "Why—why, I thought—we—we understood 'twas 'Albert.' We didn't know there was—we didn't know there was any more to it. What did you say it was?"

Her grandson squared his shoulders. "Alberto Miguel Carlos Speranza," he repeated. "My father"—there was pride in his voice now—"my father's name was Miguel Carlos. Of course you knew that."

He spoke as if all creation must have known it. Mrs. Snow looked helplessly at her husband. Captain Zelotes rubbed his chin.

"We—ll," he drawled dryly, "I guess likely we'll get along with 'Albert' for a spell. I cal'late 'twill come more handy to us Cape folks. We're kind of plain and everyday 'round here. Sapper's ready, ain't it, Mother? Al must be hungry. I'm plaguey sure *I* am."

"But, Zelotes, maybe he'd like to go up to his bedroom first. He's been ridin' a long ways in the cars and maybe he'd like to wash up or change his clothes?"

"Change his clothes! Lord sakes, Olive, what would he want to change his clothes this time of night for? You don't want to change your clothes, do you, boy?"

"No, sir, I guess not."

"Sartin sure you don't. Want to wash? There's a basin and soap and towel right out there in the kitchen."

He pointed to the kitchen door. At that moment the door was partially opened and a brisk feminine voice from behind it inquired: "How about eatin'? Are you all ready in there?"

It was Captain Snow who answered.

"You bet we are, Rachel!" he declared. "All ready and then some. Trot her out. Sit down, Mother. Sit down, Al. Now then, Rachel, all aboard."

Rachel, it appeared, was the owner of the brisk feminine voice just mentioned. She was brisk herself, as to age about forty, plump, rosy and very business-like. She whisked the platter of fried mackerel and the dishes of baked potatoes, stewed corn, hot biscuits and all the rest, to the table is no time, and then, to Albert's astonishment, sat down at that table herself. Mrs. Snow did the honors.

"Albert," she said, "this is Mrs. Ellis, who helps me keep house. Rachel, this is my grandson, Albert—er—Speranza."

She pronounced the surname in a tone almost apologetic. Mrs. Ellis did not attempt to pronounce it. She extended a plump hand and observed: "Is that so? Real glad to know you, Albert. How do you think you're goin' to like South Harniss?"

Considering that his acquaintance with the village had been so decidedly limited, Albert was somewhat puzzled how to reply. His grandfather saved him the trouble.

"Lord sakes, Rachel," he declared, "he ain't seen more'n three square foot of it yet. It's darker'n the inside of a nigger's undershirt outdoors tonight. Well, Al—Albert, I mean, how are you on mackerel? Pretty good stowage room below decks? About so much, eh?"

Mrs. Snow interrupted.

"Zelotes," she said reprovingly, "ain't you forgettin' somethin'?"

"Eh? Forgettin'? Heavens to Betsy, so I am! Lord, we thank thee for these and all other gifts, Amen. What did I do with the fork; swallow it?"

As long as he lives Albert Speranza will not forget that first meal in the home of his grandparents. It was so strange, so different from any other meal he had ever eaten. The food was good and there was an abundance of it, but the surroundings were so queer. Instead of the well-ordered and sedate school meal, here all the eatables from fish to pie were put upon the table at the same time and the servant—or housekeeper, which to his mind were one and the same—sat down, not only to eat with the family, but to take at least an equal part in the conversation. And the conversation itself was so different. Beginning with questions concerning his own journey from the New York town where the school was located, it at length reached South Harniss and there centered about the diminutive person of Laban Keeler, his loquacious and tuneful rescuer from the platform of the railway station.

"Where are your things, Albert?" asked Mrs. Snow. "Your trunk or travelin' bag, or whatever you had, I mean?"

"My trunks are coming by express," began the boy. Captain Zelotes interrupted him.

"Your trunks?" he repeated. "Got more'n one, have you?"

"Why—why, yes, there are three. Mr. Holden—he is the headmaster, you know—"

"Eh? Headmaster? Oh, you mean the boss teacher up there at the school? Yes, yes. Um-hm."

"Yes, sir. Mr. Holden says the trunks should get here in a few days."

Mrs. Ellis, the housekeeper, made the next remark. "Did I understand you to say you had THREE trunks?" she demanded.

"Why, yes."

"Three trunks for one boy! For mercy sakes, what have you got in 'em?"

"Why—why, my things. My clothes and—and—everything."

"Everything, or just about, I should say. Goodness gracious me, when I go up to Boston I have all I can do to fill up one trunk. And I'm bigger'n you are—bigger 'round, anyway."

There was no doubt about that. Captain Zelotes laughed shortly.

"That statement ain't what I'd call exaggerated, Rachel," he declared. "Every time I see you and Laban out walkin' together he has to keep on the sunny side or be in a total eclipse. And, by the way, speakin' of Laban—Say, son, how did you and he get along comin' down from the depot?"

"All right. It was pretty dark."

"I'll bet you! Laban wasn't very talkative, was he?"

"Why, yes, sir, he talked a good deal but he sang most of the time."

This simple statement appeared to cause a most surprising sensation. The Snows and their housekeeper looked at each other. Captain Zelotes leaned back in his chair and whistled.

"Whew!" he observed. "Hum! Sho! Thunderation!"

"Oh, dear!" exclaimed his wife.

Mrs. Ellis, the housekeeper, drew a long breath. "I might have expected it," she said tartly. "It's past time. He's pretty nigh a month overdue, as 'tis."

Captain Snow rose to his feet. "I was kind of suspicious when he started for the barn," he declared. "Seemed to me he was singin' then. WHAT did he sing, boy?" he asked, turning suddenly upon his grandson.

"Why—why, I don't know. I didn't notice particularly. You see, it was pretty cold and—"

Mrs. Ellis interrupted. "Did he sing anything about somebody's bein' his darlin' hanky-panky and wearin' a number two?" she demanded sharply.

"Why—why, yes, he did."

Apparently that settled it. Mrs. Snow said, "Oh, dear!" again and the housekeeper also rose from the table.

"You'd better go right out to the barn this minute, Cap'n Lote," she said, "and I guess likely I'd better go with you."

The captain already had his cap on his head.

"No, Rachel," he said, "I don't need you. Cal'late I can take care of 'most anything that's liable to have happened. If he ain't put the bridle to bed in the stall and hung the mare up on the harness pegs I judge I can handle the job. Wonder how fur along he'd got. Didn't hear him singin' anything about 'Hyannis on the Cape,' did you, boy?"

"No."

"That's some comfort. Now, don't you worry, Mother. I'll be back in a few minutes."

Mrs. Snow clasped her hands. "Oh, I HOPE he hasn't set the barn afire," she wailed.

"No danger of that, I guess. No, Rachel, you 'tend to your supper. I don't need you."

He tramped out into the hall and the door closed behind him. Mrs. Snow turned apologetically to her puzzled grandson, who was entirely at a loss to know what the trouble was about.

"You see, Albert," she hesitatingly explained, "Laban—Mr. Keeler—the man who drove you down from the depot—he—he's an awful nice man and your grandfather thinks the world and all of him, but—but every once in a while he—Oh, dear, I don't know how to say it to you, but—"

Evidently Mrs. Ellis knew how to say it, for she broke into the conversation and said it then and there.

"Every once in a while he gets tipsy," she snapped. "And I only wish I had my fingers this minute in the hair of the scamp that gave him the liquor."

A light broke upon Albert's mind. "Oh! Oh, yes!" he exclaimed. "I thought he acted a little queer, and once I thought I smelt—Oh, that was why he was eating the peppermints!"

Mrs. Snow nodded. There was a moment of silence. Suddenly the housekeeper, who had resumed her seat in compliance with Captain Zelotes' order, slammed back her chair and stood up.

"I've hated the smell of peppermint for twenty-two year," she declared, and went out into the kitchen. Albert, looking after her, felt his grandmother's touch upon his sleeve.

"I wouldn't say any more about it before her," she whispered. "She's awful sensitive."

Why in the world the housekeeper should be particularly sensitive because the man who had driven him from the station ate peppermint was quite beyond the boy's comprehension. Nor could he thoroughly understand why the suspicion of Mr. Keeler's slight inebriety should cause such a sensation in the Snow household. He was inclined to think the tipsiness rather funny. Of course alcohol was lectured against often enough at school and on one occasion a member of the senior class—a twenty-year-old "hold-over" who should have graduated the fall before—had been expelled for having beer in his room; but during his long summer vacations, spent precariously at hotels or in short visits to his father's friends, young Speranza had learned to be tolerant. Tolerance was a necessary virtue in the circle surrounding Speranza Senior, in his later years. The popping of corks at all hours of the night and bottles full, half full or empty, were sounds and sights to which Albert had been well accustomed. When one has more than once seen his own father overcome by conviviality and the affair treated as a huge joke, one is not inclined to be too censorious when others slip. What if the queer old Keeler guy was tight? Was that anything to raise such a row about?

Plainly, he decided, this was a strange place, this household of his grandparents. His premonition that they might be "Rubes" seemed likely to have been well founded. What would his father—his great, world-famous father—have thought of them? "Bah! these Yankee bourgeoisie!" He could almost hear him say it. Miguel Carlos Speranza detested—in private—the Yankee bourgeoisie. He took their money and he married one of their daughters, but he detested them. During his last years, when the money had not flowed his way as copiously, the detest grew.

"You won't say anything about Laban before Mrs. Ellis, will you, Albert?" persisted Mrs. Snow. "She's dreadful sensitive. I'll explain by and by."

He promised, repressing a condescending smile.

Both the housekeeper and Captain Snow returned in a few minutes. The latter reported that the mare was safe and sound in her stall.

"The harness was mostly on the floor, but Jess was all right, thank the Lord," observed the captain.

"Jess is our horse's name, Albert," explained Mrs. Snow. "That is, her name's Jessamine, but Zelotes can't ever seem to say the whole of any name. When we first bought Jessamine I named her Magnolia, but he called her 'Mag' all the time and I COULDN'T stand that. Have some more preserves, Albert, do."

All through the meal Albert was uneasily conscious that his grandfather was looking at him from under the shaggy brows, measuring him, estimating him, reading him through and through. He resented the scrutiny and the twinkle of sardonic humor which, it seemed to him, accompanied it. His way of handling his knife and fork, his clothes, his tie, his manner of eating and drinking and speaking, all these Captain Zelotes seemed to note and appraise. But whatever the results of his scrutiny and appraisal might be he kept them entirely to himself. When he addressed his grandson directly, which was not often, his remarks were trivial commonplaces and, although pleasant enough, were terse and to the point.

Several times Mrs. Snow would have questioned Albert concerning the life at school, but each time her husband interfered.

"Not now, not now, Mother," he said. "The boy ain't goin' to run away to-night. He'll be here to-morrow and a good many to-morrows, if"—and here again Albert seemed to detect the slight sarcasm and the twinkle—"if we old-fashioned 'down easters' ain't too common and every-day for a high-toned young chap like him to put up with. No, no, don't make him talk to-night. Can't you see he's so sleepy that it's only the exercise of openin' his mouth to eat that keeps his eyes from shuttin'? How about that, son?"

It was perfectly true. The long train ride, the excitement, the cold wait on the station platform and the subsequent warmth of the room, the hearty meal, all these combined to make for sleepiness so overpowering that several times the boy had caught his nose descending toward his plate in a most inelegant nod. But it hurt his pride to think his grandfather had noticed his condition.

"Oh, I'm all right," he said, with dignity.

Somehow the dignity seemed to have little effect upon Captain Zelotes.

"Um—yes, I know," observed the latter dryly, "but I guess likely you'll be more all right in bed. Mother, you'll show Albert where to turn in, won't you? There's your suitcase out there in the hall, son. I fetched it in from the barn just now."

Mrs. Snow ventured a protest.

"Oh, Zelotes," she cried, "ain't we goin' to talk with him at ALL? Why, there is so much to say!"

"'Twill say just as well to-morrow mornin', Mother; better, because we'll have all day to say it in. Get the lamp."

Albert looked at his watch.

"Why, it's only half-past nine," he said.

Captain Zelotes, who also had been looking at the watch, which was a very fine and very expensive one, smiled slightly. "Half-past nine some nights," he said, "is equal to half-past twelve others. This is one of the some. There, there, son, you're so sleepy this minute that you've got a list to starboard. When you and I have that talk that's comin' to us we want to be shipshape and on an even keel. Rachel, light that lamp."

The housekeeper brought in and lighted a small hand lamp. Mrs. Snow took it and led the way to the hall and the narrow, breakneck flight of stairs. Captain Zelotes laid a hand on his grandson's shoulder.

"Good-night, son," he said quietly.

Albert looked into the gray eyes. Their expression was not unkindly, but there was, or he imagined there was, the same quizzical, sardonic twinkle. He resented that twinkle more than ever; it made him feel very young indeed, and correspondingly obstinate. Something of that obstinacy showed in his own eyes as he returned his grandfather's look.

"Good-night—sir," he said, and for the life of him he could not resist hesitating before adding the "sir." As he climbed the steep stairs he fancied he heard a short sniff or chuckle—he was not certain which—from the big man in the dining-room.

His bedroom was a good-sized room; that is, it would have been of good size if the person who designed it had known what the term "square" meant. Apparently he did not, and had built the apartment on the hit-or-miss, higglety-pigglety pattern, with unexpected alcoves cut into the walls and closets and chimneys built out from them. There were three windows, a big bed, an old-fashioned bureau, a chest of drawers, a washstand, and several old-fashioned chairs. Mrs. Snow put the lamp upon the bureau. She watched him anxiously as he looked about the room.

"Do—do you like it?" she asked.

Albert replied that he guessed he did. Perhaps there was not too much certainty in his tone. He had never before seen a room like it.

"Oh, I hope you will like it! It was your mother's room, Albert. She slept here from the time she was seven until—until she went away."

The boy looked about him with a new interest, an odd thrill. His mother's room. His mother. He could just remember her, but that was all. The memories were childish and unsatisfactory, but they were memories. And she had slept there; this had been her room when she was a girl, before she married, before—long before such a person as Alberto Miguel Carlos Speranza had been even dreamed of. That was strange, it was queer to think about. Long before he was born, when she was years younger than he as he stood there now, she had stood there, had looked from those windows, had—

His grandmother threw her arms about his neck and kissed him. Her cheek was wet.

"Good-night, Albert," she said chokingly, and hurried out of the room.

He undressed quickly, for the room was very cold. He opened the window, after a desperate struggle, and climbed into bed. The wind, whistling in, obligingly blew out the lamp for him. It shrieked and howled about the eaves and the old house squeaked and groaned. Albert pulled the comforter up about his neck and concentrated upon the business of going to sleep. He, who could scarcely remember when he had had a real home, was desperately homesick.

Downstairs in the dining-room Captain Zelotes stood, his hands in his pockets, looking through the mica panes of the stove door at the fire within. His wife came up behind him and laid a hand on his sleeve.

"What are you thinkin' about, Father?" she asked.

Her husband shook his head. "I was wonderin'," he said, "what my granddad, the original Cap'n Lote Snow that built this house, would have said if he'd known that he'd have a great-great-grandson come to live in it who was," scornfully, "a half-breed."

Olive's grip tightened on his arm.

"Oh, DON'T talk so, Zelotes," she begged. "He's our Janie's boy."

The captain opened the stove door, regarded the red-hot coals for an instant, and then slammed the door shut again.

"I know, Mother," he said grimly. "It's for the sake of Janie's half that I'm takin' in the other."

"But—but, Zelotes, don't you think he seems like a nice boy?"

The twinkle reappeared in Captain Lote's eyes.

"I think HE thinks he's a nice boy, Mother," he said. "There, there, let's go to bed."

CHAPTER II

The story of the events which led up to the coming, on this December night, of a "half-breed" grandson to the Snow homestead, was an old story in South Harniss. The date of its beginning was as far back as the year 1892.

In the fall of that year Captain Zelotes Snow was in Savannah. He was in command of the coasting schooner Olive S. and the said schooner was then discharging a general cargo, preparatory to loading with rice and cotton for Philadelphia. With the captain in Savannah was his only daughter, Jane Olivia, age a scant eighteen, pretty, charming, romantic and head over heels in love with a handsome baritone then singing in a popular-priced grand opera company. It was because of this handsome baritone, who, by the way, was a Spaniard named Miguel Carlos Speranza, that Jane Snow was then aboard her father's vessel. Captain Lote was not in the habit of taking his women-folks on his voyages with him. "Skirts clutter up the deck too much," was his opinion.

He had taken Jane, however, not only on this voyage, but on that preceding it, which had been to Rio. It was Captain Lote's belief, and his wife's hope, that a succession of sea winds might blow away recollections of Senor Speranza—"fan the garlic out of her head," as the captain inelegantly expressed it. Jane had spent her sixteenth and seventeenth years at a school for girls near Boston. The opera company of which Speranza was a member was performing at one of the minor theaters. A party of the school girls, duly chaperoned and faculty-guarded, of course, attended a series of matinees. At these matinees Jane first saw her hero, brave in doublet and hose, and braver still in melody and romance. She and her mates looked and listened and worshiped from afar, as is the habit of maidenly youth under such circumstances. There is no particular danger in such worship provided the worshiper remains always at a safely remote distance from the idol. But in Jane's case this safety-bar was removed by Fate. The wife of a friend of her father's, the friend being a Boston merchant named Cole with whom Captain Zelotes had had business dealings for many years, was a music lover. She was in the habit of giving what she was pleased to call "musical teas" at her home. Jane, to whom Mr. and Mrs. Cole had taken a marked fancy, was often invited to those teas and, because the Coles were "among our nicest people," she was permitted by the school authorities to attend.

At one of those teas Senor Miguel Carlos Speranza was the brightest star. The Senor, then in his twenty-ninth year, handsome, talented and picturesque, shone refulgent. Other and far more experienced feminine hearts than Jane Snow's were flutteringly disturbed by the glory of his rays. Jane and he met, they shook hands, they conversed. And at subsequent teas they met again, for Speranza, on his part, was strongly attracted to the simple, unaffected Cape Cod schoolgirl. It was not her beauty alone—though beauty she had and of an unusual type—it was something else, a personality which attracted all who met her. The handsome Spaniard had had many love affairs of a more or less perfunctory kind, but here was something different, something he had not known. He began by exerting his powers of fascination in a lazy, careless way. To his astonishment the said powers were not overwhelming. If Jane was fascinated she was not conquered. She remained sweet, simple, direct, charmingly aloof.

And Speranza was at first puzzled, then piqued, then himself madly fascinated. He wrote fervid letters, he begged for interviews, he haunted each one of Mrs. Cole's "teas." And, at last, he wrung from Jane a confession of her love, her promise to marry him. And that very week Miss Donaldson, the head of the school, discovered and read a package of the Senor's letters to her pupil.

Captain Zelotes happened to be at home from a voyage. Being summoned from South Harniss, he came to Boston and heard the tale from Miss Donaldson's agitated lips. Jane was his joy, his pride; her future was the great hope and dream of his life. WHEN she married—which was not to be thought of for an indefinite number of years to come—she would of course marry a—well, not a President of the United States, perhaps—but an admiral possibly, or a millionaire, or the owner of a fleet of steamships, or something like that. The idea that she should even think of marrying a play-actor was unbelievable. The captain had never attended the performance of an opera; what was more, he never expected to attend one. He had been given to understand that a "parcel of play-actin' men and women hollered and screamed to music for a couple of hours." Olive, his wife, had attended an opera once and, according to her, it was more like a cat fight than anything else. Nobody but foreigners ever had anything to do with operas. And for foreigners of all kinds—but the Latin variety of foreigner in particular—Captain Zelotes Snow cherished a detest which was almost fanatic.

And now his daughter, his own Janie, was receiving ardent love letters from a play-acting foreigner, a Spaniard, a "Portygee," a "macaroni-eater"! When finally convinced that it was true, that the letters had really been written to Jane, which took some time, he demanded first of all to be shown the "Portygee." Miss Donaldson could not, of course, produce the latter forthwith, but she directed her irate visitor to the theater where the opera company was then performing. To the theater Captain Zelotes went. He did not find Speranza there, but from a frightened attendant he browbeat the information that the singer was staying at a certain hotel. So the captain went to the hotel. It was eleven o'clock in the morning, Senor Speranza was in bed and could not be disturbed. Couldn't, eh? By the great and everlasting et cetera and continued he was going to be disturbed then and there. And unless some of the hotel's "hired help" set about the disturbing it would be done for them. So, rather than summon the police, the hotel management summoned its guest, and the first, and only, interview between the father and lover of Jane Snow took place.

It was not a long interview, but it was spirited. Captain Zelotes began by being what he considered diplomatic. Having assured his wife before leaving home, and the alarmed Miss Donaldson subsequently, that there was to be no trouble whatever—everything would be settled as smooth and easy as slidin' downhill; "that feller won't make any fuss, you'll see"—having thus prophesied, the captain felt it incumbent upon himself to see to the fulfillment. So he began by condescendingly explaining that of course he was kind of sorry for the young man before him, young folks were young folks and of course he presumed likely 'twas natural enough, and the like of that, you understand. But of course also Mr. Speranza must realize that the thing could not go on any further. Jane was his daughter and her people were nice people, and naturally, that being the case, her mother and he would be pretty particular as to who she kept company with, to say nothing of marrying, which event was not to be thought of for ten years, anyway. Now he didn't want to be—er—personal or anything like that, and of course he wouldn't think of saying that Mr. Speranza wasn't a nice enough man for—well, for—for . . . You see, everybody wasn't as particular as he and Mrs. Snow were. But—

Here Senor Speranza interrupted. He politely desired to know if the person speaking was endeavoring to convey the idea that he, Miguel Carlos Speranza, was not of sufficient poseetion, goodness, standing, what it is? to be considered as suitor for that person's daughter's hand. Did Meester Snow comprehend to whom he addressed himself?

The interview terminated not long after. The captain's parting remark was in the nature of an ultimatum. It was to the effect that if Speranza, or any other condemned undesirable like him, dared to so much as look in the direction of Jane Olivia Snow, his daughter, he personally would see that the return for that look was a charge of buckshot. Speranza, white-faced and furiously gesticulative, commanded the astonished bellboy to put that "Bah! pig-idiot!" out into the hall and air the room immediately afterward.

Having, as he considered, satisfactorily attended to the presumptuous lover, Captain Zelotes returned to the school and to what he believed would be the comparatively easy task, the bringing of his daughter to reason. Jane had always been an obedient girl, she was devoted to her parents. Of course, although she might feel rather disappointed at first, she would soon get over it. The idea that she might flatly refuse to get over it, that she might have a will of her own, and a determination equal to that of the father from whom she inherited it, did not occur to the captain at all.

But his enlightenment was prompt and complete. Jane did not rage or become hysterical, she did not even weep in his presence. But, quietly, with a set of her square little chin, she informed Captain Zelotes that she loved Speranza, that she meant to marry him and that she should marry him, some day or other. The captain raged, commanded, pleaded, begged. What was the matter with her? What had come over her? Didn't she love her father and mother any more that she should set out to act this way? Yes, she declared that she loved them as much as ever, but that she loved her lover more than all the world, and no one—not even her parents—should separate them.

Captain Zelotes gave it up at last. That is, he gave up the appeal to reason and the pleadings. But he did not give up the idea of having his own way in the matter; being Zelotes Snow, he certainly did not give that up. Instead he took his daughter home with him to South Harniss, where a tearful and heart-broken Olive added her persuasions to his. But, when she found Jane obdurate, Mrs. Snow might have surrendered. Not her husband, however. Instead he conceived a brilliant idea. He was about to start on a voyage to Rio Janeiro; he would take his wife and daughter with him. Under their immediate observation and far removed from the influence of "that Portygee," Jane would be in no danger and might forget.

Jane made no remonstrance. She went to Rio and returned. She was always calm, outwardly pleasant and quiet, never mentioned her lover unless in answer to a question; but she never once varied from her determination not to give him up. The Snows remained at home for a month. Then Zelotes, Jane accompanying him, sailed from Boston to Savannah. Olive did not go with them; she hated the sea and by this time both she and her husband were somewhat reassured. So far as they could learn by watchful observation of their daughter, the latter had not communicated with Speranza nor received communications from him. If she had not forgotten him it seemed likely that he had forgotten her. The thought made the captain furiously angry, but it comforted him, too.

During the voyage to Savannah this sense of comfort became stronger. Jane seemed in better spirits. She was always obedient, but now she began to seem almost cheerful, to speak, and even laugh occasionally just as she used to. Captain Zelotes patted himself on the back, figuratively. His scheme had been a good one.

And in Savannah, one afternoon, Jane managed to elude her father's observation, to leave the schooner and to disappear completely. And that night came a letter. She and Miguel Carlos Speranza had been in correspondence all the time, how or through whose connivance is a mystery never disclosed. He had come to Savannah, in accordance with mutual arrangement; they had met, were married, and had gone away together.

"I love you, Father," Jane wrote in the letter. "I love you and Mother so very, VERY much. Oh, PLEASE believe that! But I love him, too. And I could not give him up. You will see why when you know him, really know him. If it were not for you I should be SO happy. I know you can't forgive me now, but some day I am sure you will forgive us both."

Captain Zelotes was far, far from forgiveness as he read that letter. His first mate, who was beside him when he opened and read it, was actually frightened when he saw the look on the skipper's face. "He went white," said the mate; "not pale, but white, same as a dead man, or—or the underside of a flatfish, or somethin'. 'For the Lord sakes, Cap'n,' says I, 'what's the matter?' He never answered me, stood starin' at the letter. Then he looked up, not at me, but as if somebody else was standin' there on t'other side of the cabin table. 'Forgive him!' he says, kind of slow and under his breath. 'I won't forgive his black soul in hell.' When I heard him say it I give you my word my hair riz under my cap. If ever there was killin' in a man's voice and in his looks 'twas in Cap'n Lote's that night. When I asked him again what was the matter he didn't answer any more than he had the first time. A few minutes afterwards he went into his stateroom and shut the door. I didn't see him again until the next mornin'."

Captain Zelotes made no attempt to follow the runaway couple. He did take pains to ascertain that they were legally married, but that was all. He left his schooner in charge of the mate at Savannah and journeyed north to South Harniss and his wife. A week he remained at home with her, then returned to the Olive S. and took up his command and its duties as if nothing had happened. But what had happened changed his whole life. He became more taciturn, a trifle less charitable, a little harder and more worldly. Before the catastrophe he had been interested in business success and the making of money chiefly because of his plans for his daughter's future. Now he worked even harder because it helped him to forget. He became sole owner of the Olive S., then of other schooners. People spoke of him as one destined to become a wealthy man.

Jane lived only a few years after her marriage. She died at the birth of her second child, who died with her. Her first, a boy, was born a year after the elopement. She wrote her mother to tell that news and Olive answered the letter. She begged permission of her husband to invite Jane and the baby to visit the old home. At first Zelotes said no, flatly; the girl had made her bed, let her lie in it. But a year later he had so far relented as to give reluctant consent for Jane and the child to come, provided her condemned husband did not accompany them. "If that low-lived Portygee sets foot on my premises, so help me God, I'll kill him!" declared the captain. In his vernacular all foreigners were "Portygees."

But Jane was as proud and stubborn as he. Where her husband was not welcome she would not go. And a little later she had gone on the longest of all journeys. Speranza did not notify her parents except to send a clipped newspaper account of her death and burial, which arrived a week after the latter had taken place. The news prostrated Olive, who was ill for a month. Captain Zelotes bore it, as he had borne the other great shock, with outward calm and quiet. Yet a year afterward he suddenly announced his determination of giving up the sea and his prosperous and growing shipping business and of spending the rest of his days on the Cape.

Olive was delighted, of course. Riches—that is, more than a comfortable competency—had no temptations for her. The old house, home of three generations of Snows, was painted, repaired and, to some extent, modernized. For another year Captain Zelotes "loafed," as he called it, although others might have considered his activities about the place anything but that. At the end of that year he surprised every one by buying from the heirs of the estate the business equipment of the late Eben Raymond, hardware dealer and lumber merchant of South Harniss, said equipment comprising an office, a store and lumber yards near the railway station. "Got to have somethin' to keep me from gettin' barnacled," declared Captain Lote. "There's enough old hulks rottin' at their moorin's down here as 'tis. I don't know anything about lumber and half as much about hardware, but I cal'late I can learn." As an aid in the learning process he retained as bookkeeper Laban Keeler, who had acted in that capacity for the former proprietor.

The years slipped away, a dozen of them, as smoothly and lazily as South Harniss years have always slipped. Captain Zelotes was past sixty now, but as vigorous as when forty, stubborn as ever, fond of using quarter-deck methods on shore and especially in town-meeting, and very often in trouble in consequence. He was a member of the Board of Selectmen and was in the habit of characterizing those whose opinions differed from his as "narrow-minded." They retorted by accusing him of being "pig-headed." There was some truth on both sides. His detest of foreigners had not abated in the least.

And then, in this December of the year 1910, fell as from a clear sky the legacy of a grandson. From Senor Miguel Carlos Speranza the Snows had had no direct word, had received nothing save the newspaper clipping already mentioned. Olive had never seen him; her husband had seen him only on the occasion of the memorable interview in the hotel room. They never spoke of him, never mentioned him to each other. Occasionally, in the Boston newspapers, his likeness in costume had appeared amid the music notes or theatrical jottings. But these had not been as numerous of late. Of his son, their own daughter's child, they knew nothing; he might be alive or he might be dead. Sometimes Olive found herself speculating concerning him, wondering if he was alive, and if he resembled Jane. But she put the speculation from her thoughts; she could not bear to bring back memories of the old hopes and their bitter ending. Sometimes Captain Lote at his desk in the office of "Z. Snow & Co., Lumber and Builders' Hardware," caught himself dreaming of his idolized daughter and thinking how different the future might have been for him had she married a "white man," the kind of man he had meant for her to marry. There might be grandchildren growing up now, fine boys and girls, to visit the old home at South Harniss. "Ah hum! Well! . . . Labe, how long has this bill of Abner Parker's been hangin' on? For thunder sakes, why don't he pay up? He must think we're runnin' a meetin'-house Christmas tree."

The letter from the lawyer had come first. It was written in New York, was addressed to "Captain Lotus Snow," and began by taking for granted the fact that the recipient knew all about matters of which he knew nothing. Speranza was dead, so much was plain, and the inference was that he had been fatally injured in an automobile accident, "particulars of which you have of course read in the papers." Neither Captain Lote nor his wife had read anything of the kind in the papers. The captain had been very busy of late and had read little except political news, and Mrs. Snow never read of murders and accidents, their details at least. She looked up from the letter, which her husband had hastened home from the office to bring her, with a startled face.

"Oh, Zelotes," she cried, "he's dead!"

The captain nodded.

"Seems so," he said. "That part's plain enough, but go on. The rest of it is what I can't get a hand-hold on. See what you make of the rest of it, Olive."

The rest of it was to the effect that the writer, being Mr. Speranza's business adviser, "that is to say, as much or more so than any one else," had been called in at the time of the accident, had conferred with the injured man, and had learned his last wishes. "He expressed himself coherently concerning his son," went on the letter, "and it is in regard to that son that I am asking an interview with you. I should have written sooner, but have been engaged with matters pertaining to Mr. Speranza's estate and personal debts. The latter seem to be large—"

"I'LL bet you!" observed Captain Zelotes, sententiously, interrupting his wife's reading by pointing to this sentence with a big forefinger.

"'And the estate's affairs much tangled,'" went on Olive, reading aloud. "'It seems best that I should see you concerning the boy at once. I don't know whether or not you are aware that he is at school in — —, New York. I am inclined to think that the estate itself will scarcely warrant the expense of his remaining there. Could you make it convenient to come to New York and see me at once? Or, if not, I shall be in Boston on Friday of next week and can you meet me there? It seems almost impossible for me to come to you just now, and, of course, you will understand that I am acting as a sort of temporary executor merely because Mr. Speranza was formerly my friend and not because I have any pecuniary interest in the settlement of his affairs.

"'Very truly yours,

"'MARCUS W. WEISSMANN.'"

"Weissman! Another Portygee!" snorted Captain Lote.

"But—but what does it MEAN?" begged Mrs. Snow. "Why—why should he want to see you, Zelotes? And the boy—why—why, that's HER boy. It's Janie's boy he must mean, Zelotes."

Her husband nodded.

"Hers and that blasted furriner's," he muttered. "I suppose so."

"Oh, DON'T speak that way, Zelotes! Don't! He's dead."

Captain Lote's lips tightened. "If he'd died twenty years ago 'twould have been better for all hands," he growled.

"Janie's boy!" repeated Olive slowly. "Why—why, he must be a big boy now. Almost grown up."

Her husband did not speak. He was pacing the floor, his hands in his pockets.

"And this man wants to see you about him," said Olive. Then, after a moment, she added timidly: "Are you goin', Zelotes?"

"Goin'? Where?"

"To New York? To see this lawyer man?"

"I? Not by a jugful! What in blazes should I go to see him for?"

"Well—well, he wants you to, you know. He wants to talk with you about the—the boy."

"Humph!"

"It's her boy, Zelotes."

"Humph! Young Portygee!"

"Don't, Zelotes! Please! . . . I know you can't forgive that—that man. We can't either of us forgive him; but—"

The captain stopped in his stride. "Forgive him!" he repeated. "Mother, don't talk like a fool. Didn't he take away the one thing that I was workin' for, that I was plannin' for, that I was LIVIN' for? I—"

She interrupted, putting a hand on his sleeve.

"Not the only thing, dear," she said. "You had me, you know."

His expression changed. He looked down at her and smiled.

"That's right, old lady," he admitted. "I had you, and thank the Almighty for it. Yes, I had you . . . But," his anger returning, "when I think how that damned scamp stole our girl from us and then neglected her and killed her—"

"ZELOTES! How you talk! He DIDN'T kill her. How can you!"

"Oh, I don't mean he murdered her, of course. But I'll bet all I've got that he made her miserable. Look here, Mother, you and she used to write back and forth once in a while. In any one of those letters did she ever say she was happy?"

Mrs. Snow's answer was somewhat equivocal. "She never said she was unhappy," she replied. Her husband sniffed and resumed his pacing up and down.

After a little Olive spoke again.

"New York IS a good ways," she said. "Maybe 'twould be better for you to meet this lawyer man in Boston. Don't you think so?"

"Bah!"

Another interval. Then: "Zelotes?"

"Yes," impatiently. "What is it?"

"It's her boy, after all, isn't it? Our grandson, yours and mine. Don't you think—don't you think it's your duty to go, Zelotes?"

Captain Lote stamped his foot.

"For thunderation sakes, Olive, let up!" he commanded. "You ought to know by this time that there's one thing I hate worse than doin' my duty, that's bein' preached to about it. Let up! Don't you say another word."

She did not, having learned much by years of experience. He said the next word on the subject himself. At noon, when he came home for dinner, he said, as they rose from the table: "Where's my suitcase, up attic?"

"Why, yes, I guess likely 'tis. Why?"

Instead of answering he turned to the housekeeper, Mrs. Ellis.

"Rachel," he said, "go up and get that case and fetch it down to the bedroom, will you? Hurry up! Train leaves at half-past two and it's 'most one now."

Both women stared at him. Mrs. Ellis spoke first.

"Why, Cap'n Lote," she cried; "be you goin' away?"

Her employer's answer was crisp and very much to the point. "I am if I can get that case time enough to pack it and make the train," he observed. "If you stand here askin' questions I probably shall stay to home."

The housekeeper made a hasty exit by way of the back stairs. Mrs. Snow still gazed wonderingly at her husband.

"Zelotes," she faltered, "are you—are you—"

"I'm goin' to New York on to-night's boat. I've telegraphed that—that Weiss—Weiss—what-do-you-call-it—that Portygee lawyer—that I'll be to his office to-morrow mornin'."

"But, Zelotes, we haven't scarcely talked about it, you and I, at all. You might have waited till he came to Boston. Why do you go so SOON?"

The captain's heavy brows drew together.

"You went to the dentist's last Friday," he said. "Why didn't you wait till next week?"

"Why—why, what a question! My tooth ached and I wanted to have it fixed quick as possible."

"Um-m, yes. Well, this tooth aches and I want it fixed or hauled out, one or t'other. I want the thing off my mind. . . . Don't TALK to me?" he added, irritably. "I know I'm a fool. And," with a peremptory wave of the hand, "don't you DARE say anything about DUTY!"

He was back again two days later. His wife did not question him, but waited for him to speak. Those years of experience already mentioned had taught her diplomacy. He looked at her and pulled his beard. "Well," he observed, when they were alone together, "I saw him."

"The—the boy?" eagerly.

"No, no! Course not! The boy's at school somewhere up in New York State; how could I see him! I saw that lawyer and I found out about—about the other scamp. He was killed in an auto accident, drunk at the time, I cal'late. Nigh's I can gather he's been drinkin' pretty heavy for the last six or seven years. Always lived high, same as his kind generally does, and spent money like water, I judge—but goin' down hill fast lately. His voice was givin' out on him and he realized it, I presume likely. Now he's dead and left nothin' but trunks full of stage clothes and photographs and," contemptuously, "letters from fool women, and debts—Lord, yes! debts enough."

"But the boy, Zelotes. Janie's boy?"

"He's been at this school place for pretty nigh ten years, so the lawyer feller said. That lawyer was a pretty decent chap, too, for a furriner. Seems he used to know this—Speranza rascal—when Speranza was younger and more decent—if he ever was really decent, which I doubt. But this lawyer man was his friend then and about the only one he really had when he was hurt. There was plenty of make-believe friends hangin' on, like pilot-fish to a shark, for what they could get by spongin' on him, but real friends were scarce."

"And the boy—"

"For the Lord sakes, Mother, don't keep sayin' 'The boy,' 'the boy,' over and over again like a talkin' machine! Let me finish about the father first. This Weis—er—thingamajig—the lawyer, had quite a talk with Speranza afore he died, or while he was dyin'; he only lived a few hours after the accident and was out of his head part of that. But he said enough to let Weiss—er—er—Oh, why CAN'T I remember that Portygee's name?—to let him know that he'd like to have him settle up what was left of his affairs, and to send word to us about—about the boy. There! I hope you feel easier, Mother; I've got 'round to 'the boy' at last."

"But why did he want word sent to us, Zelotes? He never wrote a line to us in his life."

"You bet he didn't!" bitterly; "he knew better. Why did he want word sent now? The answer to that's easy enough. 'Cause he wanted to get somethin' out of us, that's the reason. From what that lawyer could gather, and from what he's found out since, there ain't money enough for the boy to stay another six weeks at that school, or anywhere else, unless the young feller earns it himself. And, leavin' us out of the count, there isn't a relation this side of the salt pond. There's probably a million or so over there in Portygee-land," with a derisive sniff; "those foreigners breed like flies. But THEY don't count."

"But did he want word sent to us about the—"

"Sshh! I'm tellin' you, Olive, I'm tellin' you. He wanted word sent because he was in hopes that we—you and I, Mother—would take that son of his in at our house here and give him a home. The cheek of it! After what he'd done to you and me, blast him! The solid brass nerve of it!"

He stormed up and down the room. His wife did not seem nearly so much disturbed as he at the thought of the Speranza presumption. She looked anxious—yes, but she looked eager, too, and her gaze was fixed upon her husband's face.

"Oh!" she said, softly. "Oh! . . . And—and what did you say, Zelotes?"

"What did I say? What do you suppose I said? I said no, and I said it good and loud, too."

Olive made no comment. She turned away her head, and the captain, who now in his turn was watching her, saw a suspicious gleam, as of moisture, on her cheek. He stopped his pacing and laid a hand on her shoulder.

"There, there, Mother," he said, gently. "Don't cry. He's comin'."

"Comin'?" She turned pale. "Comin'?" she repeated. "Who?"

"That boy! . . . Sshh! shh!" impatiently. "Now don't go askin' me questions or tellin' me what I just said I said. I SAID the right thing, but— Well, hang it all, what else could I DO? I wrote the boy—Albert—a letter and I wrote the boss of the school another one. I sent a check along for expenses and—Well, he'll be here 'most any day now, I shouldn't wonder. And WHAT in the devil are we goin' to do with him?"

His wife did not reply to this outburst. She was trembling with excitement.

"Is—is his name Albert?" she faltered.

"Um-hm. Seems so."

"Why, that's your middle name! Do you—do you s'pose Janie could have named him for—for you?"

"I don't know."

"Of course," with some hesitation, "it may be she didn't. If she'd named him Zelotes—"

"Good heavens, woman! Isn't one name like that enough in the family? Thank the Lord we're spared two of 'em! But there! he's comin'. And when he gets here—then what?"

Olive put her arm about her big husband.

"I hope—yes, I'm sure you did right, Zelotes, and that all's goin' to turn out to be for the best."

"Are you? Well, *I* ain't sure, not by a thousand fathom."

"He's Janie's boy."

"Yes. And he's that play-actor's boy, too. One Speranza pretty nigh ruined your life and mine, Olive. What'll this one do? . . . Well, God knows, I suppose likely, but He won't tell. All we can do is wait and see. I tell you honest I ain't very hopeful."

CHAPTER III

A brisk rap on the door; then a man's voice.

"Hello, there! Wake up."

Albert rolled over, opened one eye, then the other and raised himself on his elbow.

"Eh? Wh-what?" he stammered.

"Seven o'clock! Time to turn out."

The voice was his grandfather's. "Oh—oh, all right!" he answered.

"Understand me, do you?"

"Yes—yes, sir. I'll be right down."

The stairs creaked as Captain Zelotes descended them. Albert yawned cavernously, stretched and slid one foot out of bed. He drew it back instantly, however, for the sensation was that of having thrust it into a bucket of cold water. The room had been cold the previous evening; plainly it was colder still now. The temptation was to turn back and go to sleep again, but he fought against it. Somehow he had a feeling that to disregard his grandfather's summons would be poor diplomacy.

He set his teeth and, tossing back the bed clothes, jumped to the floor. Then he jumped again, for the floor was like ice. The window was wide open and he closed it, but there was no warm radiator to cuddle against while dressing. He missed his compulsory morning shower, a miss which did not distress him greatly. He shook himself into his clothes, soused his head and neck in a basin of ice water poured from a pitcher, and, before brushing his hair, looked out of the window.

It was a sharp winter morning. The wind had gone down, but before subsiding it had blown every trace of mist or haze from the air, and from his window-sill to the horizon every detail was clean cut and distinct. He was looking out, it seemed, from the back of the house. The roof of the kitchen extension was below him and, to the right, the high roof of the barn. Over the kitchen roof and to the left he saw little rolling hills, valleys, cranberry swamps, a pond. A road wound in and out and, scattered along it, were houses, mostly white with green blinds, but occasionally varied by the gray of unpainted, weathered shingles. A long, low-spreading building a half mile off looked as if it might be a summer hotel, now closed and shuttered. Beyond it was a cluster of gray shanties and a gleam of water, evidently a wharf and a miniature harbor. And, beyond that, the deep, brilliant blue of the sea. Brown and blue were the prevailing colors, but, here and there, clumps and groves of pines gave splashes of green.

There was an exhilaration in the crisp air. He felt an unwonted liveliness and a desire to be active which would have surprised some of his teachers at the school he had just left. The depression of spirits of which he had been conscious the previous night had disappeared along with his premonitions of unpleasantness. He felt optimistic this morning. After giving his curls a rake with the comb, he opened the door and descended the steep stairs to the lower floor.

His grandmother was setting the breakfast table. He was a little surprised to see her doing it. What was the use of having servants if one did the work oneself? But perhaps the housekeeper was ill.

"Good morning," he said.

Mrs. Snow, who had not heard him enter, turned and saw him. When he crossed the room, she kissed him on the cheek.

"Good morning, Albert," she said. "I hope you slept well."

Albert replied that he had slept very well indeed. He was a trifle disappointed that she made no comment on his promptness in answering his grandfather's summons. He felt such promptness deserved commendation. At school they rang two bells at ten minute intervals, thus giving a fellow a second chance. It had been a point of senior etiquette to accept nothing but that second chance. Here, apparently, he was expected to jump at the first. There was a matter of course about his grandmother's attitude which was disturbing.

She went on setting the table, talking as she did so.

"I'm real glad you did sleep," she said. "Some folks can hardly ever sleep the first night in a strange room. Zelotes—I mean your grandpa—'s gone out to see to the horse and feed the hens and the pig. He'll be in pretty soon. Then we'll have breakfast. I suppose you're awful hungry."

As a matter of fact he was not very hungry. Breakfast was always a more or less perfunctory meal with him. But he was surprised to see the variety of eatables upon that table. There were cookies there, and doughnuts, and even half an apple pie. Pie for breakfast! It had been a newspaper joke at which he had laughed many times. But it seemed not to be a joke here, rather a solemn reality.

The kitchen door opened and Mrs. Ellis put in her head. To Albert's astonishment the upper part of the head, beginning just above the brows, was swathed in a huge bandage. The lower part was a picture of hopeless misery.

"Has Cap'n Lote come in yet?" inquired the housekeeper, faintly.

"Not yet, Rachel," replied Mrs. Snow. "He'll be here in a minute, though. Albert's down, so you can begin takin' up the things."

The head disappeared. A sigh of complete wretchedness drifted in as the door closed. Albert looked at his grandmother in alarm.

"Is she sick?" he faltered.

"Who? Rachel? No, she ain't exactly sick . . . Dear me! Where did I put that clean napkin?"

The boy stared at the kitchen door. If his grandmother had said the housekeeper was not exactly dead he might have understood. But to say she was not exactly sick—

"But—but what makes her look so?" he stammered. "And—and what's she got that on her head for? And she groaned! Why, she MUST be sick!"

Mrs. Snow, having found the clean napkin, laid it beside her husband's plate.

"No," she said calmly. "It's one of her sympathetic attacks; that's what she calls 'em, sympathetic attacks. She has 'em every time Laban Keeler starts in on one of his periodics. It's nerves, I suppose. Cap'n Zelotes—your grandfather—says it's everlastin' foolishness. Whatever 'tis, it's a nuisance. And she's so sensible other times, too."

Albert was more puzzled than ever. Why in the world Mrs. Ellis should tie up her head and groan because the little Keeler person had gone on a spree was beyond his comprehension.

His grandmother enlightened him a trifle.

"You see," she went on, "she and Laban have been engaged to be married ever since they were young folks. It's Laban's weakness for liquor that's kept 'em apart so long. She won't marry him while he drinks and he keeps swearin' off and then breaking down. He's a good man, too; an awful good man and capable as all get-out when he's sober. Lately that is, for the last seven or eight years, beginnin' with the time when that lecturer on mesmerism and telegraphy—no, telepathy—thought-transfers and such— was at the town hall—Rachel has been havin' these sympathetic attacks of hers. She declares that alcohol-takin' is a disease and that Laban suffers when he's tipsy and that she and he are so bound up together that she suffers just the same as he does. I must say I never noticed him sufferin' very much, not at the beginnin,' anyhow—acts more as he was havin' a good time—but she seems to. I don't wonder you smile," she added. "'Tis funny, in a way, and it's queer that such a practical, common-sense woman as Rachel Ellis is, should have such a notion. It's hard on us, though. Don't say anything to her about it, and don't laugh at her, whatever you do."

Albert wanted to laugh very much. "But, Mrs. Snow—" he began.

"Mercy sakes alive! You ain't goin' to call me 'Mrs. Snow,' I hope."

"No, of course not. But, Grandmother why do you and Captain—you and Grandfather keep her and Keeler if they are so much trouble? Why don't you let them go and get someone else?"

"Let 'em go? Get someone else! Why, we COULDN'T get anybody else, anyone who would be like them. They're almost a part of our family; that is, Rachel is, she's been here since goodness knows when. And, when he's sober Laban almost runs the lumber business. Besides, they're nice folks—almost always."

Plainly the ways of South Harniss were not the ways of the world he had known. Certainly these people were "Rubes" and queer Rubes, too. Then he remembered that two of them were his grandparents and that his immediate future was, so to speak, in their hands. The thought was not entirely comforting or delightful. He was still pondering upon it when his grandfather came in from the barn.

The captain said good morning in the same way he had said good night, that is, he and Albert shook hands and the boy was again conscious of the gaze which took him in from head to foot and of the quiet twinkle in the gray eyes.

"Sleep well, son?" inquired Captain Zelotes.

"Yes . . . Yes, sir."

"That's good. I judged you was makin' a pretty good try at it when I thumped on your door this mornin'. Somethin' new for you to be turned out at seven, eh?"

"No, sir."

"Eh? It wasn't?"

"No, sir. The rising bell rang at seven up at school. We were supposed to be down at breakfast at a quarter past."

The Portygee | 41

"Humph! You were, eh? Supposed to be? Does that mean that you were there?"

"Yes, sir."

There was a surprised look in the gray eyes now, a fact which Albert noticed with inward delight. He had taken one "rise" out of his grandfather, at any rate. He waited, hoping for another opportunity, but it did not come. Instead they sat down to breakfast.

Breakfast, in spite of the morning sunshine at the windows, was somewhat gloomy. The homesickness, although not as acute as on the previous night, was still in evidence. Albert felt lost, out of his element, lonely. And, to add a touch of real miserableness, the housekeeper served and ate like a near relative of the deceased at a funeral feast. She moved slowly, she sighed heavily, and the bandage upon her forehead loomed large and portentous. When spoken to she seldom replied before the third attempt. Captain Zelotes lost patience.

"Have another egg?" he roared, brandishing the spoon containing it at arm's length and almost under her nose. "Egg! Egg! EGG! If you can't hear it, smell it. Only answer, for heaven sakes!"

The effect of this outburst was obviously not what he had hoped. Mrs. Ellis stared first at the egg quivering before her face, then at the captain. Then she rose and marched majestically to the kitchen. The door closed, but a heartrending sniff drifted in through the crack. Olive laid down her knife and fork.

"There!" she exclaimed, despairingly. "Now see what you've done. Oh, Zelotes, how many times have I told you you've got to treat her tactful when she's this way?"

Captain Lote put the egg back in the bowl.

"DAMN!" he observed, with intense enthusiasm.

His wife shook her head.

"Swearin' don't help it a mite, either," she declared. "Besides I don't know what Albert here must think of you." Albert, who, between astonishment and a wild desire to laugh, was in a critical condition, appeared rather embarrassed. His grandfather looked at him and smiled grimly.

"I cal'late one damn won't scare him to death," he observed. "Maybe he's heard somethin' like it afore. Or do they say, 'Oh, sugar!' up at that school you come from?" he added.

Albert, not knowing how to reply, looked more embarrassed than ever. Olive seemed on the point of weeping.

"Oh, Zelotes, how CAN you!" she wailed. "And to-day, of all days! His very first mornin'!"

Captain Lote relented.

"There, there, Mother!" he said. "I'm sorry. Forget it. Sorry if I shocked you, Albert. There's times when salt-water language is the only thing that seems to help me out . . . Well, Mother, what next? What'll we do now?"

"You know just as well as I do, Zelotes. There's only one thing you can do. That's go out and beg her pardon this minute. There's a dozen places she could get right here in South Harniss without turnin' her hand over. And if she should leave I don't know WHAT I'd do."

"Leave! She ain't goin' to leave any more'n than the ship's cat's goin' to jump overboard. She's been here so long she wouldn't know how to leave if she wanted to."

"That don't make any difference. The pitcher that goes to the well—er—er—"

She had evidently forgotten the rest of the proverb. Her husband helped her out.

"Flocks together or gathers no moss, or somethin', eh? All right, Mother, don't fret. There ain't really any occasion to, considerin' we've been through somethin' like this at least once every six months for ten years."

"Zelotes, won't you PLEASE go and ask her pardon?"

The captain pushed back his chair. "I'll be hanged if it ain't a healthy note," he grumbled, "when the skipper has to go and apologize to the cook because the cook's made a fool of herself! I'd like to know what kind of rum Labe drinks. I never saw any but his kind that would go to somebody else's head. Two people gettin' tight and only one of 'em drinkin' is somethin'—"

He disappeared into the kitchen, still muttering. Mrs. Snow smiled feebly at her grandson.

"I guess you think we're funny folks, Albert," she said. "But Rachel is one hired help in a thousand and she has to be treated just so."

Five minutes later Cap'n 'Lote returned. He shrugged his shoulders and sat down at his place.

"All right, Mother, all right," he observed. "I've been heavin' ile on the troubled waters and the sea's smoothin' down. She'll be kind and condescendin' enough to eat with us in a minute or so."

She was. She came into the dining-room with the air of a saint going to martyrdom and the remainder of the meal was eaten by the quartet almost in silence. When it was over the captain said:

"Well, Al, feel like walkin', do you?"

"Why, why, yes, sir, I guess so."

"Humph! You don't seem very wild at the prospect. Walkin' ain't much in your line, maybe. More used to autoin', perhaps?"

Mrs. Snow put in a word. "Don't talk so, Zelotes," she said. "He'll think you're makin' fun of him."

"Who? Me? Not a bit of it. Well, Al, do you want to walk down to the lumber yard with me?"

The boy hesitated. The quiet note of sarcasm in his grandfather's voice was making him furiously angry once more, just as it had done on the previous night.

"Do you want me to?" he asked, shortly.

"Why, yes, I cal'late I do."

Albert, without another word, walked to the hat-rack in the hall and began putting on his coat. Captain Lote watched him for a moment and then put on his own.

"We'll be back to dinner, Mother," he said. "Heave ahead, Al, if you're ready."

There was little conversation between the pair during the half mile walk to the office and yards of "Z. Snow and Co., Lumber and Builders' Hardware." Only once did the captain offer a remark. That was just as they came out by the big posts at the entrance to the driveway. Then he said:

"Al, I don't want you to get the idea from what happened at the table just now—that foolishness about Rachel Ellis—that your grandmother ain't a sensible woman. She is, and there's no better one on earth. Don't let that fact slip your mind."

Albert, somewhat startled by the abruptness of the observation, looked up in surprise. He found the gray eyes looking down at him.

"I noticed you lookin' at her," went on his grandfather, "as if you was kind of wonderin' whether to laugh at her or pity her. You needn't do either. She's kind-hearted and that makes her put up with Rachel's silliness. Then, besides, Rachel herself is common sense and practical nine-tenths of the time. It's always a good idea, son, to sail one v'yage along with a person before you decide whether to class 'em as A. B. or just roustabout."

The blood rushed to the boy's face. He felt guilty and the feeling made him angrier than ever.

"I don't see why," he burst out, indignantly, "you should say I was laughing at—at Mrs. Snow—"

"At your grandmother."

"Well—yes—at my grandmother. I don't see why you should say that. I wasn't."

"Wasn't you? Good! I'm glad of it. I wouldn't, anyhow. She's liable to be about the best friend you'll have in this world."

To Albert's mind flashed the addition: "Better than you, that means," but he kept it to himself.

The lumber yards were on a spur track not very far from the railway station where he had spent that miserable half hour the previous evening. The darkness then had prevented his seeing them. Not that he would have been greatly interested if he had seen them, nor was he more interested now, although his grandfather took him on a personally conducted tour between the piles of spruce and pine and hemlock and pointed out which was which and added further details. "Those are two by fours," he said. Or, "Those are larger joist, different sizes." "This is good, clear stock, as good a lot of white pine as we've got hold of for a long spell." He gave particulars concerning the "handiest way to drive a team" to one or the other of the piles. Albert found it rather boring. He longed to speak concerning enormous lumber yards he had seen in New York or Chicago or elsewhere. He felt almost a pitying condescension toward this provincial grandparent who seemed to think his little piles of "two by fours" so important.

It was much the same, perhaps a little worse, when they entered the hardware shop and the office. The rows and rows of little drawers and boxes, each with samples of its contents—screws, or bolts, or hooks, or knobs—affixed to its front, were even more boring than the lumber piles. There was a countryfied, middle-aged person in overalls sweeping out the shop and Captain Zelotes introduced him.

"Albert," he said, "this is Mr. Issachar Price, who works around the place here. Issy, let me make you acquainted with my grandson, Albert."

Mr. Price, looking over his spectacles, extended a horny hand and observed: "Yus, yus. Pleased to meet you, Albert. I've heard tell of you."

Albert's private appraisal of "Issy" was that the latter was another funny Rube. Whatever Issy's estimate of his employer's grandson might have been, he, also, kept it to himself.

Captain Zelotes looked about the shop and glanced into the office.

"Humph!" he grunted. "No sign or symptoms of Laban this mornin', I presume likely?"

Issachar went on with his sweeping.

"Nary one," was his laconic reply.

"Humph! Heard anything about him?"

Mr. Price moistened his broom in a bucket of water. "I see Tim Kelley on my way down street," he said. "Tim said he run afoul of Laban along about ten last night. Said he cal'lated Labe was on his way. He was singin' 'Hyannis on the Cape' and so Tim figgered he'd got a pretty fair start already."

The captain shook his head. "Tut, tut, tut!" he muttered. "Well, that means I'll have to do office work for the next week or so. Humph! I declare it's too bad just now when I was countin' on him to—" He did not finish the sentence, but instead turned to his grandson and said: "Al, why don't you look around the hardware store here while I open the mail and the safe. If there's anything you see you don't understand Issy'll tell you about it."

He went into the office. Albert sauntered listlessly to the window and looked out. So far as not understanding anything in the shop was concerned he was quite willing to remain in ignorance. It did not interest him in the least. A moment later he felt a touch on his elbow. He turned, to find Mr. Price standing beside him.

"I'm all ready to tell you about it now," volunteered the unsmiling Issy. "Sweepin's all finished up."

Albert was amused. "I guess I can get along," he said.

"Don't worry."

"*I* ain't worried none. I don't believe in worryin'; worryin' don't do folks no good, the way I look at it. But long's Cap'n Lote wants me to tell you about the hardware I'd ruther do it now, than any time. Henry Cahoon's team'll be here for a load of lath in about ten minutes or so, and then I'll have to leave you. This here's the shelf where we keep the butts—hinges, you understand. Brass along here, and iron here. Got quite a stock, ain't we."

He took the visitor's arm in his mighty paw and led him from shelves to drawers and from drawers to boxes, talking all the time, so the boy thought, "like a catalogue." Albert tried gently to break away several times and yawned often, but yawns and hints were quite lost on his guide, who was intent only upon the business—and victim—in hand. At the window looking across toward the main road Albert paused longest. There was a girl in sight—she looked, at that distance, as if she might be a rather pretty girl—and the young man was languidly interested. He had recently made the discovery that pretty girls may be quite interesting; and, moreover, one or two of them whom he had met at the school dances—when the young ladies from the Misses Bradshaws' seminary had come over, duly guarded and chaperoned, to one-step and fox-trot with the young gentlemen of the school—one or two of these young ladies had intimated a certain interest in him. So the feminine possibility across the road attracted his notice—only slightly, of course; the sophisticated metropolitan notice is not easily aroused—but still, slightly.

"Come on, come on," urged Issachar Price. "I ain't begun to show ye the whole of it yet . . . Eh? Oh, Lord, there comes Cahoon's team now! Well, I got to go. Show you the rest some other time. So long . . . Eh? Cap'n Lote's callin' you, ain't he?"

Albert went into the office in response to his grandfather's call to find the latter seated at an old-fashioned roll-top desk, piled with papers.

"I've got to go down to the bank, Al," he said. "Some business about a note that Laban ought to be here to see to, but ain't. I'll be back pretty soon. You just stay here and wait for me. You might be lookin' over the books, if you want to. I took 'em out of the safe and they're on Labe's desk there," pointing to the high standing desk by the window. "They're worth lookin' at, if only to see how neat they're kept. A set of books like that is an example to any young man. You might be lookin' 'em over."

He hurried out. Albert smiled condescendingly and, instead of looking over Mr. Keeler's books, walked over to the window and looked out of that. The girl was not in sight now, but she might be soon. At any rate watching for her was as exciting as any amusement he could think of about that dull hole. Ah hum! he wondered how the fellows were at school.

The girl did not reappear. Signs of animation along the main road were limited. One or two men went by, then a group of children obviously on their way to school. Albert yawned again, took the silver cigarette case from his pocket and looked longingly at its contents. He wondered what his grandfather's ideas might be on the tobacco question. But his grandfather was not there then . . . and he might not return for some time . . . and . . . He took a cigarette from the case, tapped, with careful carelessness, its end upon the case—he would not have dreamed of smoking without first going through the tapping process—lighted the cigarette and blew a large and satisfying cloud. Between puffs he sang:

"To you, beautiful lady,
I raise my eyes.
My heart, beautiful lady,
To your heart cries:
Come, come, beautiful lady,
To Par-a-dise,
As the sweet, sweet—'"

Some one behind him said: "Excuse me." The appeal to the beautiful lady broke off in the middle, and he whirled about to find the girl whom he had seen across the road and for whose reappearance he had been watching at the window, standing in the office doorway. He looked at her and she looked at him. He was embarrassed. She did not seem to be.

"Excuse me," she said: "Is Mr. Keeler here?"

She was a pretty girl, so his hasty estimate made when he had first sighted her was correct. Her hair was dark, so were her eyes, and her cheeks were becomingly colored by the chill of the winter air. She was a country girl, her hat and coat proved that; not that they were in bad taste or unbecoming, but they were simple and their style perhaps nearer to that which the young ladies of the Misses Bradshaws' seminary had worn the previous winter. All this Albert noticed in detail later on. Just then the particular point which attracted his embarrassed attention was the look in the dark eyes. They seemed to have almost the same disturbing quality which he had noticed in his grandfather's gray ones. Her mouth was very proper and grave, but her eyes looked as if she were laughing at him.

Now to be laughed at by an attractive young lady is disturbing and unpleasant. It is particularly so when the laughter is from the provinces and the laughee—so to speak—a dignified and sophisticated city man. Albert summoned the said dignity and sophistication to his rescue, knocked the ashes from his cigarette and said, haughtily:

"I beg your pardon?"

"Is Mr. Keeler here?" repeated the girl.

"No, he is out."

"Will he be back soon, do you think?"

Recollections of Mr. Price's recent remark concerning the missing bookkeeper's "good start" came to Albert's mind and he smiled, slightly. "I should say not," he observed, with delicate irony.

"Is Issy—I mean Mr. Price, busy?"

"He's out in the yard there somewhere, I believe. Would you like to have me call him?"

"Why, yes—if you please—sir."

The "sir" was flattering, if it was sincere. He glanced at her. The expression of the mouth was as grave as ever, but he was still uncertain about those eyes. However, he was disposed to give her the benefit of the doubt, so, stepping to the side door of the office—that leading to the yards— he opened it and shouted: "Price! . . . Hey, Price!"

There was no answer, although he could hear Issachar's voice and another above the rattle of lath bundles.

"Price!" he shouted, again. "Pri-i-ce!"

The rattling ceased. Then, in the middle distance, above a pile of "two by fours," appeared Issachar's head, the features agitated and the forehead bedewed with the moisture of honest toil.

"Huh?" yelled Issy. "What's the matter? Be you hollerin' to me?"

"Yes. There's some one here wants to see you."

"Hey?"

"I say there's some one here who wants to see you."

"What for?"

"I don't know."

"Well, find out, can't ye? I'm busy."

Was that a laugh which Albert heard behind him? He turned around, but the young lady's face wore the same grave, even demure, expression.

"What do you want to see him for?" he asked.

"I wanted to buy something."

"She wants to buy something," repeated Albert, shouting.

"Hey?"

"She wants to—BUY—something." It was humiliating to have to scream in this way.

"Buy? Buy what?"

"What do you want to buy?"

"A hook, that's all. A hook for our kitchen door. Would you mind asking him to hurry? I haven't much time."

"She wants a hook."

The Portygee | 49

"Eh? We don't keep books. What kind of a book?"

"Not book—HOOK. H-O-O-K! Oh, great Scott! Hook! HOOK! Hook for a door! And she wants you to hurry."

"Eh? Well, I can't hurry now for nobody. I got to load these laths and that's all there is to it. Can't you wait on him?" Evidently the customer's sex had not yet been made clear to the Price understanding. "You can get a hook for him, can't ye? You know where they be, I showed ye. Ain't forgot so soon, 'tain't likely."

The head disappeared behind the "two by fours." Its face was red, but no redder than Mr. Speranza's at that moment.

"Fool rube!" he snorted, disgustedly.

"Excuse me, but you've dropped your cigarette," observed the young lady.

Albert savagely slammed down the window and turned away. The dropped cigarette stump lay where it had fallen, smudging and smelling.

His caller looked at it and then at him.

"I'd pick it up, if I were you," she said. "Cap'n Snow HATES cigarettes."

Albert, his dignity and indignation forgotten, returned her look with one of anxiety.

"Does he, honest?" he asked.

"Yes. He hates them worse than anything."

The cigarette stump was hastily picked up by its owner.

"Where'll I put it?" he asked, hurriedly.

"Why don't you—Oh, don't put it in your pocket! It will set you on fire. Put it in the stove, quick."

Into the stove it went, all but its fragrance, which lingered.

"Do you think you COULD find me that hook?" asked the girl.

"I'll try. *I* don't know anything about the confounded things."

"Oh!" innocently. "Don't you?"

"No, of course I don't. Why should I?"

"Aren't you working here?"

"Here? Work HERE? ME? Well, I—should—say—NOT!"

"Oh, excuse me. I thought you must be a new bookkeeper, or—or a new partner, or something."

Albert regarded her intently and suspiciously for some seconds before making another remark. She was as demurely grave as ever, but his suspicions were again aroused. However, she WAS pretty, there could be no doubt about that.

"Maybe I can find the hook for you," he said. "I can try, anyway."

"Oh, thank you ever so much," gratefully. "It's VERY kind of you to take so much trouble."

"Oh," airily, "that's all right. Come on; perhaps we can find it together."

They were still looking when Mr. Price came panting in.

"Whew!" he observed, with emphasis. "If anybody tells you heavin' bundles of laths aboard a truck-wagon ain't hard work you tell him for me he's a liar, will ye. Whew! And I had to do the heft of everything, 'cause Cahoon sent that one-armed nephew of his to drive the team. A healthy lot of good a one-armed man is to help heave lumber! I says to him, says I: 'What in time did—' Eh? Why, hello, Helen! Good mornin'. Land sakes! you're out airly, ain't ye?"

The young lady nodded. "Good morning, Issachar," she said. "Yes, I am pretty early and I'm in a dreadful hurry. The wind blew our kitchen door back against the house last night and broke the hook. I promised Father I would run over here and get him a new one and bring it back to him before I went to school. And it's quarter to nine now."

"Land sakes, so 'tis! Ain't—er—er—what's-his-name—Albert here, found it for you yet? He ain't no kind of a hand to find things, is he? We'll have to larn him better'n that. Yes indeed!"

Albert laughed, sarcastically. He was about to make a satisfyingly crushing reproof to this piece of impertinence when Mr. Price began to sniff the air.

"What in tunket?" he demanded. "Sn'f! Sn'f! Who's been smokin' in here? And cigarettes, too, by crimus! Sn'f! Sn'f! Yes, sir, cigarettes, by crimustee! Who's been smokin' cigarettes in here? If Cap'n Lote knew anybody'd smoked a cigarette in here I don't know's he wouldn't kill 'em. Who done it?"

Albert shivered. The girl with the dark blue eyes flashed a quick glance at him. "I think perhaps someone went by the window when it was open just now," she suggested. "Perhaps they were smoking and the smoke blew in."

"Eh? Well, maybe so. Must have been a mighty rank cigarette to smell up the whole premises like this just goin' past a window. Whew! Gosh!

no wonder they say them things are rank pison. I'd sooner smoke skunk-cabbage myself; 'twouldn't smell no worse and 'twould be a dum sight safer. Whew! . . . Well, Helen, there's about the kind of hook I cal'late you need. Fifteen cents 'll let you out on that. Cheap enough for half the money, eh? Give my respects to your pa, will ye. Tell him that sermon he preached last Sunday was fine, but I'd like it better if he'd laid it on to the Univer'lists a little harder. Folks that don't believe in hell don't deserve no consideration, 'cordin' to my notion. So long, Helen . . . Oh say," he added, as an afterthought, "I guess you and Albert ain't been introduced, have ye? Albert, this is Helen Kendall, she's our Orthodox minister's daughter. Helen, this young feller is Albert—er—er—Consarn it, I've asked Cap'n Lote that name a dozen times if I have once! What is it, anyway?"

"Speranza," replied the owner of the name.

"That's it, Sperandy. This is Albert Sperandy, Cap'n Lote's grandson."

Albert and Miss Kendall shook hands.

"Thanks," said the former, gratefully and significantly.

The young lady smiled.

"Oh, you're welcome," she said. "I knew who you were all the time—or I guessed who you must be. Cap'n Snow told me you were coming."

She went out. Issachar, staring after her, chuckled admiringly. "Smartest girl in THIS town," he observed, with emphasis. "Head of her class up to high school and only sixteen and three-quarters at that."

Captain Zelotes came bustling in a few minutes later. He went to his desk, paying little attention to his grandson. The latter loitered idly up and down the office and hardware shop, watching Issachar wait on customers or rush shouting into the yard to attend to the wants of others there. Plainly this was Issachar's busy day.

"Crimus!" he exclaimed, returning from one such excursion and mopping his forehead. "This doin' two men's work ain't no fun. Every time Labe goes on a time seem's if trade was brisker'n it's been for a month. Seems as if all creation and part of East Harniss had been hangin' back waitin' till he had a shade on 'fore they come to trade. Makes a feller feel like votin' the Prohibition ticket. I WOULD vote it, by crimustee, if I thought 'twouldn't do any good. 'Twouldn't though; Labe would take to drinkin' bay rum or Florida water or somethin', same as Hoppy Rogers done when he was alive. Jim Young says he went into Hoppy's barber-shop once and there was Hoppy with a bottle of a new kind of hair-tonic in his hand. 'Drummer that was here left it for a sample,' says Hoppy. 'Wanted me to try it and, if

I liked it, he cal'lated maybe I'd buy some. I don't think I shall, though,' he says; 'don't taste right to me.' Yes, sir, Jim Young swears that's true. Wan't enough snake-killer in that hair tonic to suit Hoppy. I—Yes, Cap'n Lote, what is it? Want me, do ye?"

But the captain did not, as it happened, want Mr. Price at that time. It was Albert whose name he had called. The boy went into the office and his grandfather rose and shut the door.

"Sit down, Al," he said, motioning toward a chair. When his grandson had seated himself Captain Zelotes tilted back his own desk chair upon its springs and looked at him.

"Well, son," he said, after a moment, "what do you think of it?"

"Think of it? I don't know exactly what—"

"Of the place here. Shop, yards, the whole business. Z. Snow and Company—what do you think of it?"

Privately Albert was inclined to classify the entire outfit as one-horse and countrified, but he deemed it wiser not to express this opinion. So he compromised and replied that it "seemed to be all right."

His grandfather nodded. "Thanks," he observed, dryly. "Glad you find it that way. Well, then, changin' the subject for a minute or two, what do you think about yourself?"

"About myself? About me? I don't understand?"

"No, I don't suppose you do. That's what I got you over here this mornin' for, so as we could understand—you and me. Al, have you given any thought to what you're goin' to do from this on? How you're goin' to live?"

Albert looked at him uncomprehendingly.

"How I'm going to live?" he repeated. "Why—why, I thought—I supposed I was going to live with you—with you and Grandmother."

"Um-hm, I see."

"I just kind of took that for granted, I guess. You sent for me to come here. You took me away from school, you know."

"Yes, so I did. You know why I took you from school?"

"No, I—I guess I DON'T, exactly. I thought—I supposed it was because you didn't want me to go there any more."

"'Twasn't that. I don't know whether I would have wanted you to go there or not if things had been different. From what I hear it was a pretty extravagant place, and lookin' at it from the outside without knowin' too much about it, I should say it was liable to put a lot of foolish and expensive notions into a boy's head. I may be wrong, of course; I have been wrong at least a few times in my life."

It was evident that he considered the chances of his being wrong in this instance very remote. His tone again aroused in the youth the feeling of obstinacy, of rebellion, of desire to take the other side.

"It is one of the best schools in this country," he declared. "My father said so."

Captain Zelotes picked up a pencil on his desk and tapped his chin lightly with the blunt end. "Um," he mused. "Well, I presume likely he knew all about it."

"He knew as much as—most people," with a slight but significant hesitation before the "most."

"Um-hm. Naturally, havin' been schooled there himself, I suppose."

"He wasn't schooled there. My father was a Spaniard."

"So I've heard. . . . Well, we're kind of off the subject, ain't we? Let's leave your father's nationality out of it for a while. And we'll leave the school, too, because no matter if it was the best one on earth you couldn't go there. I shouldn't feel 'twas right to spend as much money as that at any school, and you—well, son, you ain't got it to spend. Did you have any idea what your father left you, in the way of tangible assets?"

"No. I knew he had plenty of money always. He was one of the most famous singers in this country."

"Maybe so."

"It WAS so," hotly. "And he was paid enough in one week to buy this whole town—or almost. Why, my father—"

"Sshh! Sssh!"

"No, I'm not going to hush. I'm proud of my father. He was a—a great man. And—and I'm not going to stand here and have you—"

Between indignation and emotion he choked and could not finish the sentence. The tears came to his eyes.

"I'm not going to have you or anyone else talk about him that way," he concluded, fiercely.

His grandfather regarded him with a steady, but not at all unkindly, gaze.

"I ain't runnin' down your father, Albert," he said.

"Yes, you are. You hated him. Anybody could see you hated him."

The captain slowly rapped the desk with the pencil. He did not answer at once.

"Well," he said, after a moment, "I don't know as I ought to deny that. I don't know as I can deny it and be honest. Years ago he took away from me what amounted to three-quarters of everything that made my life worth while. Some day you'll know more about it than you do now, and maybe you'll understand my p'int of view better. No, I didn't like your father—Eh? What was you sayin'?"

Albert, who had muttered something, was rather confused. However, he did not attempt to equivocate. "I said I guessed that didn't make much difference to Father," he answered, sullenly.

"I presume likely it didn't. But we won't go into that question now. What I'm tryin' to get at in this talk we're having is you and your future. Now you can't go back to school because you can't afford it. All your father left when he died was—this is the honest truth I'm tellin' you now, and if I'm puttin' it pretty blunt it's because I always think it's best to get a bad mess out of the way in a hurry—all your father left was debts. He didn't leave money enough to bury him, hardly."

The boy stared at him aghast. His grandfather, leaning a little toward him, would have put a hand on his knee, but the knee was jerked out of the way.

"There, that's over, Al," went on Captain Zelotes. "You know the worst now and you can say, 'What of it?' I mean just that: What of it? Bein' left without a cent, but with your health and a fair chance to make good—that, at seventeen or eighteen ain't a bad lookout, by any manner of means. It's the outlook *I* had at fifteen—exceptin' the chance—and I ain't asked many favors of anybody since. At your age, or a month or two older, do you know where I was? I was first mate of a three-masted schooner. At twenty I was skipper; and at twenty-five, by the Almighty, I owned a share in her. Al, all you need now is a chance to go to work. And I'm goin' to give you that chance."

Albert gasped. "Do you mean—do you mean I've got to be a—a sailor?" he stammered.

Captain Zelotes put back his head and laughed, laughed aloud.

"A sailor!" he repeated. "Ho, ho! No wonder you looked scared. No, I wan't cal'latin' to make a sailor out of you, son. For one reason, sailorin' ain't what it used to be; and, for another, I have my doubts whether a young feller of your bringin' up would make much of a go handlin' a bunch of fo'mast hands the first day out. No, I wasn't figgerin' to send you to sea . . . What do you suppose I brought you down to this place for this mornin'?"

And then Albert understood. He knew why he had been conducted through the lumber yards, about the hardware shop, why his grandfather and Mr. Price had taken so much pains to exhibit and explain. His heart sank.

"I brought you down here," continued the captain, "because it's a first-rate idea to look a vessel over afore you ship aboard her. It's kind of late to back out after you have shipped. Ever since I made up my mind to send for you and have you live along with your grandmother and me I've been plannin' what to do with you. I knew, if you was a decent, ambitious young chap, you'd want to do somethin' towards makin' a start in life. We can use—that is, this business can use that kind of a chap right now. He could larn to keep books and know lumber and hardware and how to sell and how to buy. He can larn the whole thing. There's a chance here, son. It's your chance; I'm givin' it to you. How big a chance it turns out to be 'll depend on you, yourself."

He stopped. Albert was silent. His thoughts were confused, but out of their dismayed confusion two or three fixed ideas reared themselves like crags from a whirlpool. He was to live in South Hamiss always—always; he was to keep books—Heavens, how he hated mathematics, detail work of any kind!—for drunken old Keeler; he was to "heave lumber" with Issy Price. He—Oh, it was dreadful! It was horrible. He couldn't! He wouldn't! He—

Captain Zelotes had been watching him, his heavy brows drawing closer together as the boy delayed answering.

"Well?" he asked, for another minute. "Did you hear what I said?"

"Yes."

"Understood, did you?"

"Yes—sir."

"Well?"

Albert was clutching at straws. "I—I don't know how to keep books," he faltered.

"I didn't suppose you did. Don't imagine they teach anything as practical as bookkeepin' up at that school of yours. But you can larn, can't you?"

"I—I guess so."

"I guess so, too. Good Lord, I HOPE so! Humph! You don't seem to be jumpin' for joy over the prospect. There's a half dozen smart young fellers here in South Harniss that would, I tell you that."

Albert devoutly wished they had jumped—and landed—before his arrival. His grandfather's tone grew more brusque.

"Don't you want to work?" he demanded.

"Why, yes, I—I suppose I do. I—I hadn't thought much about it."

"Humph! Then I think it's time you begun. Hadn't you had ANY notion of what you wanted to do when you got out of that school of yours?"

"I was going to college."

"Humph! . . . Yes, I presume likely. Well, after you got out of college, what was you plannin' to do then?"

"I wasn't sure. I thought I might do something with my music. I can play a little. I can't sing—that is, not well enough. If I could," wistfully, "I should have liked to be in opera, as father was, of course."

Captain Zelotes' only comment was a sniff or snort, or combination of both. Albert went on.

"I had thought of writing—writing books and poems, you know. I've written quite a good deal for the school magazine. And I think I should like to be an actor, perhaps. I—"

"Good God!" His grandfather's fist came down upon the desk before him. Slowly he shook his head.

"A—a poetry writer and an actor!" he repeated. "Whew! . . . Well, there! Perhaps maybe we hadn't better talk any more just now. You can have the rest of the day to run around town and sort of get acquainted, if you want to. Then to-morrow mornin' you and I'll come over here together and we'll begin to break you in. I shouldn't wonder," he added, dryly, "if you found it kind of dull at first—compared to that school and poetry makin' and such—but it'll be respectable and it'll pay for board and clothes and somethin' to eat once in a while, which may not seem so important to you now as 'twill later on. And some day I cal'late—anyhow we'll hope—you'll be mighty glad you did it."

Poor Albert looked and felt anything but glad just then. Captain Zelotes, his hands in his pockets, stood regarding him. He, too, did not look particularly happy.

"You'll remember," he observed, "or perhaps you don't know, that when your father asked us to look out for you—"

Albert interrupted. "Did—did father ask you to take care of me?" he cried, in surprise.

"Um-hm. He asked somebody who was with him to ask us to do just that."

The boy drew a long breath. "Well, then," he said, hopelessly, "I'll—I'll try."

"Thanks. Now you run around town and see the sights. Dinner's at half past twelve prompt, so be on hand for that."

After his grandson had gone, the captain, hands still in his pockets, stood for some time looking out of the window. At length he spoke aloud.

"A play actor or a poetry writer!" he exclaimed. "Tut, tut, tut! No use talkin', blood will tell!"

Issachar, who was putting coal on the office fire, turned his head.

"Eh?" he queried.

"Nothin'," said Captain Lote.

He would have been surprised if he could have seen his grandson just at that moment. Albert, on the beach whither he had strayed in his desire to be alone, safely hidden from observation behind a sand dune, was lying with his head upon his arms and sobbing bitterly.

A disinterested person might have decided that the interview which had just taken place and which Captain Zelotes hopefully told his wife that morning would probably result in "a clear, comf'table understandin' between the boy and me"—such a disinterested person might have decided that it had resulted in exactly the opposite. In calculating the results to be obtained from that interview the captain had not taken into consideration two elements, one his own and the other his grandson's. These elements were prejudice and temperament.

CHAPTER IV

The next morning, with much the same feeling that a convict must experience when he enters upon a life imprisonment, Albert entered the employ of "Z. Snow and Co., Lumber and Builders' Hardware." The day, he would have sworn it, was at least a year long. The interval between breakfast and dinner was quite six months, yet the dinner hour itself was the shortest sixty minutes he had ever known. Mr. Keeler had not yet returned to his labors, so there was no instruction in bookkeeping; but his grandfather gave him letters to file and long dreary columns of invoice figures to add. Twice Captain Zelotes went out and then, just as Albert settled back for a rest and breathing spell, Issachar Price appeared, warned apparently by some sort of devilish intuition, and invented "checking up stock" and similar menial and tiresome tasks to keep him uncomfortable till the captain returned. The customers who came in asked questions concerning him and he was introduced to at least a dozen citizens of South Harniss, who observed "Sho!" and "I want to know!" when told his identity and, in some instances, addressed him as "Bub," which was of itself a crime deserving capital punishment.

That night, as he lay in bed in the back bedroom, he fell asleep facing the dreary prospect of another monotonous imprisonment the following day, and the next day, and the day after that, and after that—and after that—and so on—and on—and on—forever and ever, as long as life should last. This, then, was to be the end of all his dreams, this drudgery in a country town among these commonplace country people. This was the end of his dreams of some day writing deathless odes and sonnets or thrilling romances; of treading the boards as the hero of romantic drama while star-eyed daughters of multi-millionaires gazed from the boxes in spellbound rapture. This . . . The thought of the star-eyed ones reminded him of the girl who had come into the office the afternoon of his first visit to that torture chamber. He had thought of her many times since their meeting and always with humiliation and resentment. It was his own foolish tongue which had brought the humiliation upon him. When she had suggested that he might be employed by Z. Snow and Co. he had replied: "Me? Work HERE! Well, I should say NOT!" And all the time she, knowing who he was, must have known he was doomed to work there. He resented that superior knowledge of hers. He had made a fool of himself but she was to blame for it. Well, by George, he would NOT work there! He would run away, he would show her, and his grandfather and all the rest what was what. Night after night he fell asleep vowing to run away, to do all sorts of desperate deeds, and morning after morning he went back to that office.

On the fourth morning the prodigal came home, the stray lamb returned to the fold—Mr. Keeler returned to his desk and his duties. There was a premonition of his return at the Snow breakfast table. For three days Mrs. Ellis had swathed her head in white and her soul in black. For three days her favorite accompaniment to conversation had been a groan or a sigh. Now, on this fourth morning, she appeared without the bandage on her brow or the crape upon her spirit. She was not hilarious but she did not groan once, and twice during the meal she actually smiled. Captain Lote commented upon the change, she being absent from table momentarily.

"Whew!" he observed, in an undertone, addressing his wife. "If it ain't a comfort to see the wrinkles on Rachel's face curvin' up instead of down. I'm scared to death that she'll go out some time in a cold spell when she's havin' one of them sympathetics of hers, and her face'll freeze that way. Well, Albert," turning to his grandson, "the colors'll be h'isted to the truck now instead of half-mast and life'll be somethin' besides one everlastin' 'last look at the remains.' Now we can take off the mournin' till the next funeral."

"Yes," said Olive, "and Laban'll be back, too. I'm sure you must have missed him awfully, Zelotes."

"Missed him! I should say so. For one thing, I miss havin' him between me and Issy. When Labe's there Is talks to him and Labe keeps on thinkin' of somethin' else and so it don't worry him any. I can't do that, and my eardrums get to wearin' thin and that makes me nervous. Maybe you've noticed that Issy's flow of conversation ain't what you'd call a trickle," he added, turning to Albert.

Albert had noticed it. "But," he asked, "what makes Rachel—Mrs. Ellis—so cheerful this morning? Does she know that Mr. Keeler will be back at work? How does she know? She hasn't seen him, has she?"

"No," replied the captain. "She ain't seen him. Nobody sees him, far's that goes. He generally clears out somewheres and locks himself up in a room, I judge, till his vacation's over. I suppose that's one way to have fun, but it ain't what I'd call hilarious."

"Don't, Zelotes," said Mrs. Snow. "I do wish you wouldn't call it fun."

"I don't, but Laban seems to. If he don't do it for fun I don't know what he does it for. Maybe it's from a sense of duty. It ain't to oblige me, I know that."

Albert repeated his question. "But how does she know he will be back to-day?" he asked.

His grandmother shook her head. "That's the mysterious part about it," she whispered. "It makes a person think there may be somethin' in the sympathetic notion she talks so much about. She don't see him at all and yet we can always tell when he's comin' back to work by her spirits. If he ain't back to-day he will be to-morrow, you'll see. She never misses by more than a day. *I* think it's real sort of mysterious, but Zelotes laughs at me."

Captain Lote's lip twitched. "Yes, Mother," he said, "it's about as mysterious as the clock's strikin' twelve when it's noon. *I* know it's morally sartin that Labe'll be back aboard to-day or to-morrow because his sprees don't ever last more than five days. I can't swear to how she knows, but that's how *I* know—and I'm darned sure there's no 'sympathy' about my part." Then, as if realizing that he had talked more than usual, he called, brusquely: "Come on, Al, come on. Time we were on the job, boy."

Sure enough, as they passed the window of the office, there, seated on the stool behind the tall desk, Albert saw the diminutive figure of the man who had been his driver on the night of his arrival. He was curious to see how the delinquent would apologize for or explain his absence. But Mr. Keeler did neither, nor did Captain Snow ask a question. Instead the pair greeted each other as if they had parted in that office at the close of business on the previous day.

"Mornin', Cap'n Lote," said Laban, quietly.

"Mornin', Labe," replied the captain, just as calmly.

He went on and opened his own desk, leaving his grandson standing by the door, not knowing whether to speak or offer to shake hands. The situation was a little difficult, particularly as Mr. Keeler gave no sign of recognition, but, after a glance at his employer's companion, went on making entries in the ledger.

Captain Zelotes looked up a moment later. His gray eyes inspected the pair and the expression on Albert's face caused them to twinkle slightly. "Labe," he said, "this is my grandson, Albert, the one I told you was comin' to live with us."

Laban turned on the stool, regarded Albert over his spectacles, and extended a hand.

"Pleased to meet you," he said. "Yes, yes . . . Yes, yes, yes. . . Pleased to meet you. Cap'n Lote said you was comin'—er—er—Alfred. Howdy do."

They shook hands. Mr. Keeler's hand trembled a little, but that was the only symptom of his recent "vacation" which the youth could notice. Certain vivid remembrances of his father's bad humor on mornings following convivial evenings recurred to him. Was it possible that this odd, precise, dried-up little man had been on a spree for four days? It did not seem possible. He looked more as if he might be expected to rap on the desk and ask the school to come to order.

"Albert's goin' to take hold here with us in the office," went on Captain Lote. "You'll remember I spoke to you about that when we talked about his comin'. Al, Labe—Mr. Keeler here—will start you in larnin' to bookkeep. He'll be your first mate from now on. Don't forget you're a fo'mast hand yet awhile and the way for a fo'mast hand to get ahead is to obey orders. And don't," he added, with a quiet chuckle, "do any play-actin' or poetry-makin' when it's your watch on deck. Laban nor I ain't very strong for play-actin', are we, Labe?"

Laban, to whom the reference was anything but clear, replied rather vaguely that he didn't know as he was, very. Albert's temper flared up again. His grandfather was sneering at him once more; he was always sneering at him. All right, let him sneer—now. Some day he would be shown. He scowled and turned away. And Captain Zelotes, noticing the scowl, was reminded of a scowl he had seen upon the face of a Spanish opera singer some twenty years before. He did not like to be reminded of that man.

He went out soon afterward and then Laban, turning to Albert, asked a few questions.

"How do you think you're goin' to like South Harniss, Ansel?" he asked.

Albert was tempted to reply that he, Keeler, had asked him that very question before, but he thought it best not to do so.

"I don't know yet," he answered, carelessly. "Well enough, I guess."

"You'll like it fust-rate bimeby. Everybody does when they get used to it. Takes some time to get used to a place, don't you know it does, Ansel?"

"My name is Albert."

"Eh? Yes, yes, so 'tis. Yes, yes, yes. I don't know why I called you Ansel, 'less 'twas on account of my knowin' an Ansel Olsen once . . . Hum . . . Yes, yes. Well, you'll like South Harniss when you get used to it."

The boy did not answer. He was of the opinion that he should die long before the getting used process was completed. Mr. Keeler continued.

"Come on yesterday's train, did you?" he asked.

Albert looked at him. Was the fellow joking? He did not look as if he was.

"Why no," he replied. "I came last Monday night. Don't you remember?"

"Eh? Oh, yes . . . Yes, yes, yes . . . Last Monday night you come, eh? On the night train, eh?" He hesitated a moment and then asked. "Cap'n Lote fetch you down from the depot?"

Albert stared at him open-mouthed.

"Why, no!" he retorted. "You drove me down yourself."

For the first time a slight shade of embarrassment crossed the bookkeeper's features. He drew a long breath.

"Yes," he mused. "Yes, yes, yes. I kind of thought I—yes, yes,—I—I thought likely I did . . . Yes, yes, course I did, course I did. Well, now maybe we'd better be startin' you in to work—er—Augustus. Know anything about double-entry, do you?"

Albert did not, nor had he the slightest desire to learn. But before the first hour was over he foresaw that he was destined to learn, if he remained in that office, whether he wanted to or not. Laban Keeler might be, and evidently was, peculiar in his ways, but as a bookkeeper he was thoroughness personified. And as a teacher of his profession he was just as thorough. All that forenoon Albert practiced the first principles of "double entry" and, after the blessed hour for dinner, came back to practice the remainder of the working day.

And so for many days. Little by little he learned to invoice and journalize and "post in the ledger" and all the rest of the detail of bookkeeping. Not that his instructor permitted him to do a great deal of actual work upon the books of Z. Snow and Co. Those books were too spotless and precious for that. Looking over them Albert was surprised and obliged to admit a grudging admiration at the manner in which, for the most part, they had been kept. Page after page of the neatest of minute figures, not a blot, not a blur, not an erasure. So for months; then, in the minor books, like the day-book or journal, would suddenly break out an eruption of smudges and scrawls in the rugged handwriting of Captain Zelotes. When he first happened upon one of these Albert unthinkingly spoke to Mr. Keeler about it. He asked the latter what it meant.

Laban slowly stroked his nose with his thumb and finger, a habit he had.

"I cal'late I was away for a spell then," he said, gravely. "Yes, yes . . . Yes, yes, yes. I was away for a little spell."

He went soberly back to his desk. His new assistant, catching a glimpse of his face, felt a pang of real pity for the little man. Of course the reason for the hiatus in the books was plain enough. He knew about those "little spells." Oddly enough Laban seemed to feel sorry for them. He remembered how funny the bookkeeper had appeared at their first meeting, when one "spell" was just developing, and the contrast between the singing, chirruping clown and the precise, grave little person at the desk struck even his youthful mind as peculiar. He had read "Doctor Jekyll and Mr. Hyde," and now here was an example of something similar. He was beginning to like Laban Keeler, although he was perfectly sure that he should never like bookkeeping.

He did not slave at the books all the time, of course. For stretches, sometimes lasting whole days, his slavery was of another sort. Then he was working in the lumber yard with Issachar, or waiting on customers in the hardware shop. The cold of winter set in in earnest now and handling "two by fours" and other timber out where the raw winds swept piercingly through one's overcoat and garments and flesh to the very bone was a trying experience. His hands were chapped and cracked, even though his grandmother had knit him a pair of enormous red mittens. He appreciated the warmth of the mittens, but he hated the color. Why in the name of all that was inartistic did she choose red; not a deep, rich crimson, but a screeching vermilion, like a fireman's shirt?

Issachar, when he had the opportunity, was a hard boss. It suited Mr. Price to display his superior knowledge and to find fault with his helper's lack of skill. Albert's hot temper was at the boiling point many times, but he fought it down. Occasionally he retorted in kind, but his usual and most effective weapon was a more or less delicate sarcasm. Issachar did not understand sarcasm and under rapid fire he was inclined to lose his head.

"Consarn it!" he snapped, irritably, on one occasion. "Consarn it, Al, why don't you h'ist up on t'other end of that j'ist? What do you cal'late you're out here along of me for; to look harnsome?"

Albert shook his head. "No, Is," he answered, gravely. "No, that wouldn't be any use. With you around nobody else has a look-in at the 'handsome' game. Issy, what do you do to your face?"

"Do to it? What do you mean by do to it?"

"What do you do to it to make it look the way it does? Don't tell me it grew that way naturally."

"Grew! Course it grew! What kind of talk's that?"

"Issy, with a face like yours how do you keep the birds away?"

"Eh? Keep the birds away! Now look here, just—"

"Excuse me. Did I say 'birds,' Issy? I didn't mean birds like—like crows. Of course a face like yours would keep the crows away all right enough. I meant girls. How do you keep the girls away? I should think they would be making love all the time."

"Aw, you shut up! Just 'cause you're Cap'n Lote's grandson I presume likely you think you can talk any kind of talk, don't ye?"

"Not any kind, Is. I can't talk like you. Will you teach me?"

"Shut up! Now, by Crimus, you—you furriner—you Speranzy—"

Mr. Keeler appeared at the office window. His shrill voice rose pipingly in the wintry air as he demanded to know what was the trouble out there.

Mr. Price, still foaming, strode toward the window; Albert laughingly followed him.

"What's the matter?" repeated Laban. "There's enough noise for a sewin' circle. Be still, Is, can't you, for a minute. Al, what's the trouble?"

"Issy's been talking about his face," explained Albert, soberly.

"I ain't neither. I was h'istin' up my end of a j'ist, same as I'm paid to do, and, 'stead of helpin' he stands there and heaves out talk about—about—"

"Well, about what?"

"Aw, about—about me and—and girls—and all sorts of dum foolishness. I tell ye, I've got somethin' else to do beside listen to that kind of cheap talk."

"Um. Yes, yes. I see. Well, Al, what have you got to say?"

"Nothing. I'm sure I don't know what it is all about. I was working as hard as I could and all at once he began pitching into me."

"Pitchin' into you? How?"

"Oh, I don't know. Something about my looks he didn't like, I guess. Wanted to know if I thought I was as handsome as he was, or something like that."

"Eh? I never neither! All I said was—"

Mr. Keeler raised his hand. "Seems to be a case for an umpire," he observed. "Um. Seem's if 'twas, seems so, seems so. Well, Captain Lote's just comin' across the road and, if you say the word, I'll call him in to referee. What do you say?"

They said nothing relevant to the subject in hand. Issachar made the only remark. "Crimus-TEE!" he ejaculated. "Come on, Al, come on."

The pair hurried away to resume lumber piling. Laban smiled slightly and closed the window. It may be gathered from this incident that when the captain was in charge of the deck there was little idle persiflage among the "fo'mast hands." They, like others in South Harniss, did not presume to trifle with Captain Lote Snow.

So the business education of Alberto Miguel Carlos Speranza progressed. At the end of the first six weeks in South Harniss he had learned a little about bookkeeping, a little about selling hardware, a little about measuring and marking lumber. And it must be admitted that that little had been acquired, not because of vigorous application on the part of the pupil, but because, being naturally quick and intelligent, he could not help learning something. He liked the work just as little as he had in the beginning of his apprenticeship. And, although he was forgetting his thoughts of running away, of attempting fortune on his own hook, he was just as rebellious as ever against a future to be spent in that office and at that work.

Outside the office and the hateful bookkeeping he was beginning to find several real interests. At the old house which had for generations been called "the Snow place," he was beginning to feel almost at home. He and his grandmother were becoming close friends. She was not looking for trouble, she never sat for long intervals gazing at him as if she were guessing, guessing, guessing concerning him. Captain Zelotes did that, but Olive did not. She had taken the boy, her "Janie's boy," to her heart from the moment she saw him and she mothered him and loved him in a way which—so long as it was not done in public—comforted his lonely soul. They had not yet reached the stage where he confided in her to any great extent, but that was certain to come later. It was his grandmother's love and the affection he was already beginning to feel for her which, during these first lonesome, miserable weeks, kept him from, perhaps, turning the running away fantasy into a reality.

Another inmate of the Snow household with whom Albert was becoming better acquainted with was Mrs. Rachel Ellis. Their real acquaintanceship began one Sunday forenoon when Captain Zelotes and Olive had gone to church. Ordinarily he would have accompanied them, to sit in the straight-backed old pew on a cushion which felt lumpy and smelt ancient and musty, and pretend to listen while old Mr. Kendall preached a sermon which was ancient and musty likewise.

But this Sunday morning he awoke with a headache and his grandmother had pleaded for him, declaring that he ought to "lay to bed" a while and get over it. He got over it with surprising quickness after the church bell ceased ringing, and came downstairs to read Ivanhoe in the sitting room. He had read it several times before, but he wanted to read something and the choice of volumes in the Snow bookcase was limited. He was stretched out on the sofa with the book in his hand when the housekeeper entered, armed with a dust-cloth. She went to church only "every other" Sunday. This was one of the others without an every, and she was at home.

"What are you readin', Albert?" she asked, after a few' minutes vigorous wielding of the dust-cloth. "It must be awful interestin', you stick at it so close."

The Black Knight was just then hammering with his battle-axe at the gate of Front de Buef's castle, not minding the stones and beams cast down upon him from above "no more than if they were thistle-down or feathers." Albert absently admitted that the story was interesting. The housekeeper repeated her request to be told its name.

"Ivanhoe," replied the boy; adding, as the name did not seem to convey any definite idea to his interrogator's mind: "It's by Walter Scott, you know."

Mrs. Ellis made no remark immediately. When she did it was to the effect that she used to know a colored man named Scott who worked at the hotel once. "He swept out and carried trunks and such things," she explained. "He seemed to be a real nice sort of colored man, far as ever I heard."

Albert was more interested in the Black Knight of Ivanhoe than the black man of the hotel, so he went on reading. Rachel sat down in a chair by the window and looked out, twisting and untwisting the dust-cloth in her lap.

"I presume likely lots and lots of folks have read that book, ain't they?" she asked, after another interval.

"What? Oh, yes, almost everybody. It's a classic, I suppose."

"What's that?"

"What's what?"

"What you said the book was. A class-somethin' or other?"

"Oh, a classic. Why, it's—it's something everybody knows about, or—or ought to know about. One of the big things, you know. Like—like Shakespeare or—or Robinson Crusoe or Paradise Lost or—lots of them. It's a book everybody reads and always will."

"I see. Humph! Well, I never read it.... I presume likely you think that's pretty funny, don't you?"

Albert tore himself away from the fight at the gate.

"Why, I don't know," he replied.

"Yes, you do. You think it's awful funny. Well, you wouldn't if you knew more about how busy I've been all my life. I ain't had time to read the way I'd ought to. I read a book once though that I'll never forget. Did you ever read a book called Foul Play?"

"No.... Why, hold on, though; I think I have. By Charles Reade, wasn't it?"

"Yes, that's who wrote it, a man named Charles Reade. Laban told me that part of it; he reads a lot, Laban does. I never noticed who wrote it, myself. I was too interested in it to notice little extry things like that. But ain't that a WONDERFUL book? Ain't that the best book you ever read in all your LIFE?"

She dropped the dust-cloth and was too excited and enthusiastic to pick it up. Albert did his best to recall something definite concerning Foul Play. The book had been in the school library and he, who read almost everything, had read it along with the others.

"Let me see," he said musingly. "About a shipwreck—something about a shipwreck in it, wasn't there?"

"I should say there was! My stars above! Not the common kind of shipwreck, neither, the kind they have down to Setuckit P'int on the shoals. No sir-ee! This one was sunk on purpose. That Joe Wylie bored holes right down through her with a gimlet, the wicked thing! And that set 'em afloat right out on the sea in a boat, and there wan't anything to eat till Robert Penfold—oh, HE was the smart one; he'd find anything, that man!—he found the barnacles on the bottom of the boat, just the same as he found out how to diffuse intelligence tied onto a duck's leg over land knows how many legs—leagues, I mean—of ocean. But that come later. Don't you remember THAT?"

Albert laughed. The story was beginning to come back to him.

"Oh, sure!" he exclaimed. "I remember now. He—the Penfold fellow—and the girl landed on this island and had all sorts of adventures, and fell in love and all that sort of stuff, and then her dad came and took her back to England and she—she did something or other there to—to get the Penfold guy out of trouble."

"Did somethin'! I should say she did! Why, she found out all about who forged the letter—the note, I mean—that's what she done. 'Twas Arthur Wardlaw, that's who 'twas. And he was tryin' to get Helen all the time for himself, the skinner! Don't talk to me about that Arthur Wardlaw! I never could bear HIM."

She spoke as if she had known the detested Wardlaw intimately from childhood. Young Speranza was hugely amused. Ivanhoe was quite forgotten.

"Foul Play was great stuff," he observed. "When did you read it?"

"Eh? When? Oh, ever and ever so long ago. When I was about twenty, I guess, and laid up with the measles. That's the only time I ever was real what you might call down sick in my life, and I commenced with measles. That's the way a good many folks commence, I know, but they don't generally wait till they're out of their 'teens afore they start. I was workin' for Mrs. Philander Bassett at the time, and she says to me: 'Rachel,' she says, 'you're on the mendin' hand now, wouldn't you like a book to read?' I says, 'Why, maybe I would.' And she fetched up three of 'em. I can see 'em now, all three, plain as day. One was Barriers Burned Away. She said that was somethin' about a big fire. Well, I'm awful nervous about fires, have been from a child, so I didn't read that. And another had the queerest kind of a name, if you'd call it a name at all; 'twas She."

Albert nodded.

"Yes," he said. "I've read that."

"Have you? Well, I begun to, but my stars, THAT wasn't any book to give to a person with nerve symptoms. I got as far as where those Indians or whatever they was started to put red-hot kettles on folks's heads, and that was enough for ME. 'Give me somethin' civilized,' says I, 'or not at all.' So I commenced Foul Play, and I tell you I kept right on to the end.

"I don't suppose," she went on, "that there ever was a much better book than that wrote, was there?"

Albert temporized. "It is a good one," he admitted.

"Don't seem to me there could be much better. Laban says it's good, though he won't go so far as to say it's the very best. He's read lots and lots of books, Laban has. Reads an awful lot in his spare time. He's what you'd call an educated person, which is what I ain't. And I guess you'll say that last is plain enough without bein' told," she added.

Her companion, not exactly knowing how to answer, was silent for a moment. Rachel, who had picked up and was again twisting the dust-cloth, returned to the subject she so delighted in.

"But that Foul Play book," she continued, "I've read till I've pretty nigh wore the covers off. When Mrs. Bassett saw how much I liked it she gave it to me for a present. I read a little bit in it every little while. I kind of fit the folks in that book to folks in real life, sort of compare 'em, you know. Do you ever do that?"

Albert, repressing a chuckle, said, "Sure!" again. She nodded.

"Now there's General Rolleson in that book," she said. "Do you know who he makes me think of? Cap'n Lote, your grandpa, that's who."

General Rolleson, as Albert remembered him, was an extremely dignified, cultured and precise old gentleman. Just what resemblance there might be between him and Captain Zelotes Snow, ex-skipper of the Olive S., he could not imagine. He could not repress a grin, and the housekeeper noticed it.

"Seems funny to you, I presume likely," she said. "Well, now you think about it. This General Rolleson man was kind of proud and sot in his ways just as your grandpa is, Albert. He had a daughter he thought all the world of; so did Cap'n Lote. Along come a person that wanted to marry the daughter. In the book 'twas Robert Penfold, who had been a convict. In your grandpa's case, 'twas your pa, who had been a play-actor. So you see—"

Albert sat up on the sofa. "Hold on!" he interrupted indignantly. "Do you mean to compare my father with a—with a CONVICT? I want you to understand—"

Mrs. Ellis held up the dust-cloth. "Now, now, now," she protested. "Don't go puttin' words in my mouth that I didn't say. I don't doubt your pa was a nice man, in his way, though I never met him. But 'twan't Cap'n Lote's way any more than Robert Penfold's was General Rolleson's."

"My father was famous," declared the youth hotly. "He was one of the most famous singers in this country. Everybody knows that—that is, everybody but Grandfather and the gang down here," he added, in disgust.

"I don't say you're wrong. Laban tells me that some of those singin' folks get awful high wages, more than the cap'n of a steamboat, he says, though that seems like stretchin' it to me. But, as I say, Cap'n Lote was proud, and nobody but the best would satisfy him for Janie, your mother. Well, in that way, you see, he reminds me of General Rolleson in the book."

"Look here, Mrs. Ellis. Tell me about this business of Dad's marrying my mother. I never knew much of anything about it."

"You didn't? Did your pa never tell you?"

"No."

"Humph! That's funny. Still, I don't know's as 'twas, after all, considerin' you was only a boy. Probably he'd have told you some day. Well, I don't suppose there's any secret about it. 'Twas town talk down here when it happened."

She told him the story of the runaway marriage. Albert listened with interest and the almost incredulous amazement with which the young always receive tales of their parents' love affairs. Love, for people of his age or a trifle older, was a natural and understandable thing, but for his father, as he remembered him, to have behaved in this way was incomprehensible.

"So," said Rachel, in conclusion, "that's how it happened. That's why Cap'n Lote couldn't ever forgive your father."

He tossed his head. "Well, he ought to have forgiven him," he declared. "He was dead lucky to get such a man for a son-in-law, if you ask me."

"He didn't think so. And he wouldn't ever mention your pa's name."

"Oh, I don't doubt that. Anybody can see how he hated Father. And he hates me the same way," he added moodily.

Mrs. Ellis was much disturbed. "Oh, no, he don't," she cried. "You mustn't think that, Albert. He don't hate you, I'm sure of it. He's just kind of doubtful about you, that's all. He remembers how your pa acted—or how he thinks he acted—and so he can't help bein' the least mite afraid the same thing may crop out in you. If you just stick to your job over there at the lumber yards and keep on tryin' to please him, he'll get all over that suspicion, see if he don't. Cap'n Lote Snow is stubborn sometimes and hard to turn, but he's square as a brick. There's some that don't like him, and a good many that don't agree with him—but everybody respects him."

Albert did not answer. The housekeeper rose from her chair.

"There!" she exclaimed. "I don't know when I've set down for so long. Goodness knows I've got work enough to do without settin' around talkin'. I can't think what possessed me to do it this time, unless 'twas seein' you readin' that book." She paused a moment and then said: "Albert, I—I don't want you and your grandpa to have any quarrels. You see—well, you see, I used to know your mother real well, and—and I thought an awful sight of her. I wish—I do wish when you and the cap'n have any trouble or anything, or when you think you're liable to have any, you'd come and talk it over with me. I'm like the feller that Laban tells about in his dog-fight yarn. This feller was watchin' the fight and when they asked him to stop it afore one or t'other of the dogs was killed, he just shook his head. 'No-o,' he says, kind of slow and moderate, 'I guess I shan't interfere. One of 'em's been stealin' my chickens and the other one bit me. I'm a friend to both parties,' he says. Course I don't mean it exactly that way," she added, with a smile, "but you know what I do mean, I guess. WILL you talk things over with me sometimes, Albert?"

His answer was not very enthusiastic, but he said he guessed so, and Rachel seemed satisfied with that. She went on with her dusting, and he with his reading, but the conversation was the first of many between the pair. The housekeeper appeared to consider his having read her beloved Foul Play a sort of password admitting him to her lodge and that thereafter they were, in consequence, to be confidants and comrades. She never hesitated to ask him the most personal questions concerning his work, his plans, the friends or acquaintances he was making in the village. Some of those questions he answered honestly and fully, some he dodged, some he did not answer at all. Mrs. Ellis never resented his not answering. "I presume likely that ain't any of my business, is it?" she would say, and ask about something else.

On the other hand, she was perfectly outspoken concerning her own affairs. He was nearly overcome with hilarious joy when, one day, she admitted that, in her mind, Robert Penfold, the hero of Foul Play, lived again in the person of Laban Keeler.

"Why, Mrs. Ellis," he cried, as soon as he could trust himself to speak at all, "I don't see THAT. Penfold was a six-footer, wasn't he? And—and athletic, you know, and—and a minister, and young—younger, I mean—and—"

Rachel interrupted. "Yes, yes, I know," she said. "And Laban is little, and not very young, and, whatever else he is, he ain't a minister. I know all that. I know the outside of him don't look like Robert Penfold at all. But," somewhat apologetically, "you see I've been acquainted with him so many years I've got into the habit of seein' his INSIDE. Now that sounds kind of ridiculous, I know," she added. "Sounds as if I—I—well, as if I was in the habit of takin' him apart, like a watch or somethin'. What I mean is that I know him all through. I've known him for a long, long while. He ain't much to look at, bein' so little and sort of dried up, but he's got a big, fine heart and big brains. He can do 'most anything he sets his hand to. When I used to know him, when I was a girl, folks was always prophesyin' that Laban Keeler would turn out to be a whole lot more'n the average. He would, too, only for one thing, and you know what that is. It's what has kept me from marryin' him all this time. I swore I'd never marry a man that drinks, and I never will. Why, if it wasn't for liquor Labe would have been runnin' his own business and gettin' rich long ago. He all but runs Cap'n Lote's place as 'tis. The cap'n and a good many other folks don't realize that, but it's so."

It was plain that she worshiped the little bookkeeper and, except during the periods of "vacation" and "sympathetics," was tremendously proud of him. Albert soon discovered that Mr. Keeler's feeling for her was equally strong. In his case, though, there was also a strong strain of gratitude.

"She's a fine woman, Al," he confided to his assistant on one occasion. "A fine woman. . . . Yes, yes, yes. They don't make 'em any finer. Ah hum! And not so long ago I read about a passel of darn fools arguin' that the angels in heaven was all he-ones. . . . Umph! . . . Sho, sho! If men was as good as women, Ansel—Alfred—Albert, I mean—we could start an opposition heaven down here most any time. 'Most any time—yes, yes."

It was considerable for him to say. Except when on a vacation, Laban was not loquacious.

Each Sunday afternoon, when the weather was pleasant, he came, dressed in his best black cutaway, shiny at elbows and the under part of the sleeves, striped trousers and a pearl gray soft hat with a black band, a hat which looked as much out of place above his round, withered little face as a red roof might have looked on a family vault, and he and the housekeeper went for a walk.

Rachel, in her Sunday black, bulked large beside him. As Captain Zelotes said, the pair looked like "a tug takin' a liner out to sea."

CHAPTER V

Outside of the gates of the Snow place Albert was making many acquaintances and a few friends. After church on Sundays his grandmother had a distressful habit of suddenly seizing his arm or his coat-tail as he was hurrying toward the vestibule and the sunshine of outdoors, and saying: "Oh, Albert, just a minute! Here's somebody you haven't met yet, I guess. Elsie"—or Nellie or Mabel or Henry or Charlie or George, whichever it happened to be—"this is my grandson, Albert Speranza." And the young person to whom he was thus introduced would, if a male, extend a hesitating hand, give his own an embarrassed shake, smile uncertainly and say, "Yes—er—yes. Pleased to meet you." Or, if of the other sex, would blush a little and venture the observation that it was a lovely morning, and wasn't the sermon splendid.

These Sabbath introductions led to week-day, or rather week-evening, meetings. The principal excitement in South Harniss was "going for the mail." At noon and after supper fully one-half of the village population journeyed to the post office. Albert's labors for Z. Snow and Co. prevented his attending the noon gatherings—his grandfather usually got the morning mail—but he early formed the habit of sauntering "down street" in the evening if the weather was not too cold or disagreeable. There he was certain to find groups of South Harniss youth of both sexes, talking, giggling, skylarking and flirting. Sometimes he joined one or the other of these groups; quite as often he did not, but kept aloof and by himself, for it may as well be acknowledged now, if it is not already plain, that the son of Miguel Carlos Speranza had inherited a share of his father's temperament and self-esteem. The whim of the moment might lead him to favor these young people with his society, but he was far from considering himself under obligation to do so. He had not the least idea that he was in any way a snob, he would have hotly resented being called one, but he accepted his estimate of his own worth as something absolute and certain, to be taken for granted.

Now this attitude of mind had its dangers. Coupled with its possessor's extraordinary good looks, it was fascinating to a large percentage of the village girls. The Speranza eyes and the Speranza curls and nose and chin were, when joined with the easy condescension of the Speranza manner, a combination fatal to the susceptible. The South Harniss "flappers," most of them, enthused over the new bookkeeper in the lumber office. They ogled and giggled and gushed in his presence, and he was tolerant or bored, just as he happened to be feeling at the moment. But he never displayed a marked interest in any one of them, for the very good reason that he had no such interest. To him they were merely girls, nice enough in their way, perhaps, but that way not his. Most of the town young fellows of his age he found had a "girl" and almost every girl had a "fellow"; there was calf love in abundance, but he was a different brand of veal.

However, a great man must amuse himself, and so he accepted invitations to church socials and suppers and to an occasional dance or party. His style of dancing was not that of South Harniss in the winter. It was common enough at the hotel or the "tea house" in July and August when the summer people were there, but not at the town hall at the Red Men's Annual Ball in February. A fellow who could foxtrot as he could swept all before him. Sam Thatcher, of last year's class in the high school, but now clerking in the drug store, who had hitherto reigned as the best "two-stepper" in town, suddenly became conscious of his feet. Then, too, the contents of the three trunks which had been sent on from school were now in evidence. No Boston or Brockton "Advanced Styles" held a candle to those suits which the tailor of the late Miguel Carlos had turned out for his patron's only son. No other eighteen-year-older among the town's year-around residents possessed a suit of evening clothes. Albert wore his "Tux" at the Red Men's Ball and hearts palpitated beneath new muslin gowns and bitter envy stirred beneath the Brockton "Advanced Styles."

In consequence, by spring the social status of Albert Speranza among those of his own age in the village had become something like this: He was in high favor with most of the girls and in corresponding disfavor with most of the young fellows. The girls, although they agreed that he was "stand-offish and kind of queer," voted him "just lovely, all the same." Their envious beaux referred to him sneeringly among themselves as a "stuck-up dude." Some one of them remembered having been told that Captain Zelotes, years before, had been accustomed to speak of his hated son-in-law as "the Portygee." Behind his back they formed the habit of referring to their new rival in the same way. The first time Albert heard himself called a "Portygee" was after prayer meeting on Friday evening, when, obeying a whim, he had walked home with Gertie Kendrick, quite forgetful of the fact that Sam Thatcher, who aspired to be Gertie's "steady," was himself waiting on the church steps for that privilege.

Even then nothing might have come of it had he and Sam not met in the path as he was sauntering back across lots to the main road and home. It was a brilliant moonlight night and the pair came together, literally, at the bend where the path turns sharply around the corner of Elijah Doane's cranberry shanty. Sam, plowing along, head down and hands in his pockets, swung around that corner and bumped violently into Albert, who, a cigarette between his lips—out here in the fields, away from civilization and Captain Zelotes, was a satisfyingly comfortable place to smoke a cigarette—was dreaming dreams of a future far away from South Harniss. Sam had been thinking of Gertie. Albert had not. She had been a mere incident of the evening; he had walked home with her because he happened to be in the mood for companionship and she was rather pretty and always talkative. His dreams during the stroll back alone in the moonlight had been of lofty things, of poetry and fame and high emprise; giggling Gerties had no place in them. It was distinctly different with Sam Thatcher.

They crashed together, gasped and recoiled.

"Oh, I'm sorry!" exclaimed Albert.

"Can't you see where you're goin', you darned Portygee half-breed?" demanded Sam.

Albert, who had stepped past him, turned and came back.

"What did you say?" he asked.

"I said you was a darned half-breed, and you are. You're a no-good Portygee, like your father."

It was all he had time to say. For the next few minutes he was too busy to talk. The Speranzas, father and son, possessed temperament; also they possessed temper. Sam's face, usually placid and good-natured, for Sam was by no means a bad fellow in his way, was fiery red. Albert's, on the contrary, went perfectly white. He seemed to settle back on his heels and from there almost to fly at his insulter. Five minutes or so later they were both dusty and dirty and dishevelled and bruised, but Sam was pretty thoroughly licked. For one thing, he had been taken by surprise by his adversary's quickness; for another, Albert's compulsory training in athletics at school gave him an advantage. He was by no means an unscarred victor, but victor he was. Sam was defeated, and very much astonished. He leaned against the cranberry house and held on to his nose. It had been a large nose in the beginning, it was larger now.

Albert stood before him, his face—where it was not a pleasing combination of black and blue—still white.

"If you—if you speak of my father or me again like that," he panted, "I'll—I'll kill you!"

Then he strode off, a bit wobbly on his legs, but with dignity.

Oddly enough, no one except the two most interested ever knew of this encounter. Albert, of course, did not tell. He was rather ashamed of it. For the son of Miguel Carlos Speranza to conquer dragons was a worthy and heroic business, but there seemed to be mighty little heroism in licking Sam Thatcher behind 'Lije Doane's cranberry shack. And Sam did not tell. Gertie next day confided that she didn't care two cents for that stuck-up Al Speranza, anyway; she had let him see her home only because Sam had danced so many times with Elsie Wixon at the ball that night. So Sam said nothing concerning the fight, explaining the condition of his nose by saying that he had run into something in the dark. And he did not appear to hold a grudge against his conqueror; on the contrary when others spoke of the latter as a "sissy," Sam defended him. "He may be a dude," said Sam; "I don't say he ain't. But he ain't no sissy."

When pressed to tell why he was so certain, his answer was: "Because he don't act like one." It was not a convincing answer, the general opinion being that that was exactly how Al Speranza did act.

There was one young person in the village toward whom Albert found himself making exceptions in his attitude of serenely impersonal tolerance. That person was Helen Kendall, the girl who had come into his grandfather's office the first morning of his stay in South Harniss. He was forced to make these exceptions by the young lady herself. When he met her the second time—which was after church on his first Sunday—his manner was even more loftily reserved than usual. He had distinct recollections of their first conversation. His own part in it had not been brilliant, and in it he had made the absurd statement—absurd in the light of what came after—that he was certainly NOT employed by Z. Snow and Co.

So he was cool and superior when his grandmother brought them together after the meeting was over. If Helen noticed the superiority, she was certainly not over-awed by it, for she was so simple and natural and pleasant that he was obliged to unbend and be natural too. In fact, at their third meeting he himself spoke of the interview in the lumber office and again expressed his thanks for warning him of his grandfather's detestation of cigarettes.

"Gee!" he exclaimed, "I'm certainly glad that you put me on to the old boy's feelings. I think he'd have murdered me if he had come back and found me puffing a Pall Mall in there."

She smiled. "He does hate them, doesn't he?" she said.

"Hate them! I should say he did. Hating cigarettes is about the only point where he and Issy get along without an argument. If a traveler for a hardware house comes into the office smoking a cig, Issy opens all the windows to let the smell out, and Grandfather opens the door to throw the salesman out. Well, not exactly to throw him out, of course, but he never buys a single cent's worth of a cigarette smoker."

Helen glanced at him. "You must be awfully glad you're not a traveling salesman," she said demurely.

Albert did not know exactly what to make of that remark. He, in his turn, looked at her, but she was grave and quite unconcerned.

"Why?" he asked, after a moment.

"Why—what?"

"Why ought I to be glad I'm not a traveling salesman?"

"Oh, I don't know. It just seemed to me that you ought, that's all."

"But why?"

"Well, if you were you wouldn't make a great hit with your grandfather, would you?"

"Eh? . . . Oh, you mean because I smoke. Say, YOU'RE not silly enough to be down on cigarettes the way grandfather is, are you?"

"No-o, I'm not down on them, especially. I'm not very well acquainted with them."

"Neither is he. He never smoked one in his life. It's just country prejudice, that's all."

"Well, I live in the country, too, you know."

"Yes, but you're different."

"How do you know I am?"

"Oh, because any one can see you are." The manner in which this remark was made, a manner implying a wide knowledge of humanity and a hint of personal interest and discriminating appreciation, had been found quite effective by the precocious young gentleman uttering it. With variations to suit the case and the individual it had been pleasantly received by several of the Misses Bradshaw's pupils. He followed it with another equally tried and trustworthy.

"Say," he added, "would YOU rather I didn't smoke?"

The obvious reply should have been, "Oh, would you stop if I asked you to?" But Helen Kendall was a most disconcerting girl. Instead of purring a pleased recognition of the implied flattery, she laughed merrily. The Speranza dignity was hurt.

"What is there to laugh at?" he demanded. "Are you laughing at me?"

The answer was as truthful as truth itself.

"Why, of course I am," she replied; and then completed his discomfiture by adding, "Why should I care whether you smoke or not? You had better ask your grandfather that question, I should think."

Now Alberto Miguel Carlos Speranza had not been accustomed to this sort of treatment from young persons of the other sex, and he walked away in a huff. But the unusual is always attractive, and the next time he and Miss Kendall met he was as gracious and cordial as ever. But it was not long before he learned that the graciousness was, in her case, a mistake. Whenever he grew lofty, she took him down, laughed at him with complete frankness, and refused to treat him as anything but a boy. So they gradually grew friendly, and when they met at parties or church socials he spent most of the time in her company, or, rather, he would have so spent it had she permitted. But she was provokingly impartial and was quite as likely to refuse a dance with him to sit out one with Sam Thatcher or Ben Hammond or any other village youth of her acquaintance. However, although she piqued and irritated him, he was obliged to admit to his inner consciousness that she was the most interesting person he had yet discovered in South Harniss, also that even in the eyes of such connoisseurs as his fellow members of the senior class at school she would have been judged a "good looker," in spite of her country clothes.

He met her father, of course. The Reverend Mr. Kendall was a dreamy little old gentleman with white hair and the stooped shoulders of a student. Everybody liked him, and it was for that reason principally that he was still the occupant of the Congregational pulpit, for to quote Captain Zelotes, his sermons were inclined to be like the sandy road down to Setuckit Point, "ten mile long and dry all the way." He was a widower and his daughter was his companion and managing housekeeper. There was a half-grown girl, one of the numerous Price family, a cousin of Issachar's, who helped out with the sweeping, dish-washing and cooking, but Helen was the real head of the household.

"And she's a capable one, too," declared Mrs. Snow, when at supper one evening Helen's name had come into the conversation. "I declare when I was there yesterday to see the minister about readin' poetry to us at sewin'-circle next Monday that parlor was as neat as wax. And 'twas all Helen's work that kept it so, that was plain enough. You could see her way of settin' a vase or puttin' on a table cloth wherever you looked. Nobody else has just that way. And she does it after school or before school or 'most any odd time. And whatever 'tis is done right."

The housekeeper put in a word. "There's no doubt about that," she said, "and there ain't any more doubt that she don't get much help from her pa or that Maria B." There were so many Prices within the township limits that individuals were usually distinguished by their middle initial. "As for Mr. Kendall," went on Rachel, "he moves with his head in the clouds and his feet cruisin' with nobody at the wheel two-thirds of the time. Emma Smith says to me yesterday, says she, 'Mr. Kendall is a saint on earth, ain't he,' says she. 'Yes,' says I, 'and he'll be one in heaven any minute if he goes stumblin' acrost the road in front of Doctor Holliday's automobile the way I see him yesterday.' The doctor put on the brakes with a slam and a yell. The minister stopped right there in the middle of the road with the front wheels of that auto not MORE'N two foot from his old baggy trousers' knees, and says he, 'Eh? Did you want me, Doctor?' The doctor fetched a long breath. 'Why, no, Mr. Kendall,' he says, 'I didn't, but I come darn nigh gettin' you.' I don't know what WOULD become of him if he didn't have Helen to look out for him."

As they came to know each other better their conversation dealt with matters more personal. They sometimes spoke of plans for the future. Albert's plans and ambitions were lofty, but rather vague. Helen's were practical and definite. She was to graduate from high school that spring. Then she was hoping to teach in the primary school there in the village; the selectmen had promised her the opportunity.

"But, of course," she said, "I don't mean to stay here always. When I can, after I have saved some money and if Father doesn't need me too badly, I shall go away somewhere, to Bridgewater, or perhaps to Radcliffe, and study. I want to specialize in my teaching, you know."

Albert regarded her with amused superiority.

"I don't see why on earth you are so anxious to be a school-marm," he said. "That's the last job I'd want."

Her answer was given promptly, but without the least trace of temper. That was one of the most provoking things about this girl, she would not lose her temper. He usually lost his trying to make her. She spoke now, pleasantly, and deliberately, but as if she were stating an undesirable fact.

"I think it would be the last one you would get," she said.

"Why? Great Scott! I guess I could teach school if I wanted to. But you bet I wouldn't want to! . . . NOW what are you laughing at?"

"I'm not laughing."

"Yes, you are. I can always tell when you're laughing; you get that look in your eyes, that sort of—of—Oh, I can't tell you what kind of look it is, but it makes me mad. It's the same kind of look my grandfather has, and I could punch him for it sometimes. Why should you and he think I'm not going to amount to anything?"

"I don't think so. And I'm sure he doesn't either. And I wasn't laughing at you. Or, if I was, it—it was only because—"

"Well, because what?"

"Oh, because you are so AWFULLY sure you know—well, know more than most people."

"Meaning I'm stuck on myself, I suppose. Well, now I tell you I'm not going to hang around in this one-horse town all my life to please grandfather or any one else."

When he mentioned his determination to win literary glory she was always greatly interested. Dreams of histrionic achievement were more coldly received. The daughter of a New England country clergyman, even in these days of broadening horizons, could scarcely be expected to look with favor upon an actor's career.

June came and with it the first of the summer visitors. For the next three months Albert was happy with a new set of acquaintances. They were HIS kind, these young folks from the city, and his spare moments were for the most part spent in their society. He was popular with them, too. Some of them thought it queer that he should be living all the year in the village and keeping books for a concern like Z. Snow and Co., but juvenile society is tolerant and a youth who could sing passably, dance wonderfully and, above all, was as beautifully picturesque as Albert Speranza, was welcomed, especially by the girls. So the Saturdays and Sundays and evenings of that summer were pleasant for him. He saw little of Helen or Gertie Kendrick while the hotel or the cottages remained open.

Then came the fall and another long, dreary winter. Albert plodded on at his desk or in the yard, following Mr. Keeler's suggestions, obeying his grandfather's orders, tormenting Issy, doing his daily stint because he had to, not because he liked it. For amusement he read a good deal, went to the usual number of sociables and entertainments, and once took part in amateur theatricals, a play given by the church society in the town hall. There was where he shone. As the dashing young hero he was resplendent. Gertie Kendrick gazed upon him from the third settee center with shining eyes. When he returned home after it was over his grandmother and Mrs. Ellis overwhelmed him with praises.

"I declare you was perfectly splendid, Albert!" exclaimed Olive. "I was so proud of you I didn't know what to do."

Rachel looked upon him as one might look upon a god from Olympus.

"All I could think of was Robert Penfold," she said. "I says so to Laban: 'Laban,' says I, ain't he Robert Penfold and nobody else?' There you was, tellin' that Hannibal Ellis that you was innocent and some day the world would know you was, just the way Robert Penfold done in the book. I never did like that Hannie Ellis!"

Mrs. Snow smiled. "Mercy, Rachel," she said, "I hope you're not blamin' Hannie because of what he did in that play. That was his part, he had to do it."

But Rachel was not convinced. "He didn't have to be so everlastin' mean and spiteful about it, anyhow," she declared. "But there, that family of Ellises never did amount to nothin' much. But, as I said to Laban, Albert, you was Robert Penfold all over."

"What did Labe say to that?" asked Albert, laughing.

"He never had a chance to say nothin'. Afore he could answer, that Maria B. Price—she was settin' right back of me and eatin' molasses candy out of a rattly paper bag till I thought I SHOULD die—she leaned forward and she whispered: 'He looks more to me like that Stevie D. that used to work for Cap'n Crowell over to the Center. Stevie D. had curly hair like that and HE was part Portygee, you remember; though there was a little nigger blood in him, too,' she says. I could have shook her! And then she went to rattlin' that bag again."

Even Mr. Keeler congratulated him at the office next morning. "You done well, Al," he said. "Yes—yes—yes. You done fust-rate, fust-rate."

His grandfather was the only one who refused to enthuse.

"Well," inquired Captain Zelotes, sitting down at his desk and glancing at his grandson over his spectacles, "do you cal'late to be able to get down to earth this mornin' far enough to figger up the payroll? You can put what you made from play-actin' on a separate sheet. It's about as much as the average person makes at that job," he added.

Albert's face flushed. There were times when he hated his grandfather. Mr. Keeler, a moment later, put a hand on his shoulder.

"You mustn't mind the old man, Al," he whispered. "I expect that seein' you last night brought your dad's job back to him strong. He can't bear play-actin', you know, on your dad's account. Yes—yes. That was it. Yes—yes—yes."

It may have been a truthful explanation, but as an apology it was a limited success.

"My father was a gentleman, at any rate," snapped Albert. Laban opened his mouth to reply, but closed it again and walked back to his books.

In May, which was an unusually balmy month, the Congregational Sunday School gave an automobile excursion and box-luncheon party at High Point Light down at Trumet. As Rachel Ellis said, it was pretty early for picnickin', but if the Almighty's season was ahead of time there didn't seem to be any real good reason why one of his Sunday schools shouldn't be. And, which was the principal excuse for the hurry, the hotel busses could be secured, which would not be the case after the season opened.

Albert went to the picnic. He was not very keen on going, but his grandfather had offered him a holiday for the purpose, and it was one of his principles never to refuse a chance to get away from that office. Besides, a number of the young people of his age were going, and Gertie Kendrick had been particularly insistent.

"You just MUST come, Al," she said. "It won't be any fun at all if you don't come."

It is possible that Gertie found it almost as little fun when he did come. He happened to be in one of his moods that day; "Portygee streaks," his grandfather termed these moods, and told Olive that they were "that play-actor breakin' out in him." He talked but little during the ride down in the bus, refused to sing when called upon, and, after dinner, when the dancing in the pavilion was going on, stepped quietly out of the side door and went tramping along the edge of the bluff, looking out over the sea or down to the beach, where, one hundred and fifty feet below, the big waves were curling over to crash into a creamy mass of froth and edge the strand with lacy ripples.

The high clay bluffs of Trumet are unique. No other part of the Cape shows anything just like them. High Point Light crowns their highest and steepest point and is the flashing beacon the rays of which spell "America" to the incoming liner Boston bound.

Along the path skirting the edge of the bluff Albert strolled, his hands in his pockets and his thoughts almost anywhere except on the picnic and the picnickers of the South Harniss Congregational Church. His particular mood on this day was one of discontent and rebellion against the fate which had sentenced him to the assistant bookkeeper's position in the office of Z. Snow and Co. At no time had he reconciled himself to the idea of that position as a permanent one; some day, somehow he was going to break away and do—marvelous things. But occasionally, and usually after a disagreeable happening in the office, he awoke from his youthful day dreams of glorious futures to a realization of the dismal to-day.

The happening which had brought about realization in this instance was humorous in the eyes of two-thirds of South Harniss's population. They were chuckling over it yet. The majority of the remaining third were shocked. Albert, who was primarily responsible for the whole affair, was neither amused nor shocked; he was angry and humiliated.

The Reverend Seabury Calvin, of Providence, R. I., had arrived in town and opened his summer cottage unusually early in the season. What was quite as important, Mrs. Seabury Calvin had arrived with him. The Reverend Calvin, whose stay was in this case merely temporary, was planning to build an addition to his cottage porch. Mrs. Calvin, who was the head of the summer "Welfare Workers," whatever they were, had called a meeting at the Calvin house to make Welfare plans for the season.

The lumber for the new porch was ordered of Z. Snow and Co. The Reverend Calvin ordered it himself in person. Albert received the order.

"I wish this delivered to-morrow without fail," said Mr. Calvin. Albert promised.

But promises are not always easy to keep. One of Z. Snow and Co.'s teams was busy hauling lumber for the new schoolhouse at Bayport. The other Issachar had commandeered for deliveries at Harniss Center and refused to give up his claim. And Laban Keeler, as it happened, was absent on one of his "vacations." Captain Zelotes was attending a directors' meeting at Osham and from there was going to Boston for a day's stay.

"The ship's in your hands, Al," he had said to his grandson. "Let me see how you handle her."

So, in spite of Albert's promise, the Calvin lumber was not delivered on time. The Reverend gentleman called to ask why. His manner was anything but receptive so far as excuses were concerned.

"Young man," he said loftily, "I am accustomed to do business with business people. Did you or did you not promise to deliver my order yesterday?"

"Why, yes sir, I promised, but we couldn't do it. We—"

"I don't care to know why you didn't do it. The fact that you did not is sufficient. Will that order of mine be delivered to-day?"

"If it is a possible thing, Mr. Calvin, it—"

"Pardon me. Will it be delivered?"

The Speranza temper was rising. "Yes," said the owner of that temper, succinctly.

"Does yes mean yes, in this case; or does it mean what it meant before?"

"I have told you why—"

"Never mind. Young man, if that lumber is not delivered to-day I shall cancel the order. Do you understand?"

Albert swallowed hard. "I tell you, Mr. Calvin, that it shall be delivered," he said. "And it will be."

But delivering it was not so easy. The team simply could NOT be taken off the schoolhouse job, fulfillment of a contract was involved there. And the other horse had gone lame and Issachar swore by all that was solemn that the animal must not be used.

"Let old Calvin wait till to-morrow," said Issy. "You can use the big team then. And Cap'n Lote'll be home, besides."

But Albert was not going to let "old Calvin" wait. That lumber was going to be delivered, if he had to carry it himself, stick by stick. He asked Mr. Price if an extra team might not be hired.

"Ain't none," said Issy. "Besides, where'd your granddad's profits be if you spent money hirin' extry teams to haul that little mite of stuff? I've been in this business a good long spell, and I tell you—"

He did not get a chance to tell it, for Albert walked off and left him. At half-past twelve that afternoon he engaged "Vessie" Young—christened Sylvester Young and a brother to the driver of the depot wagon—to haul the Calvin lumber in his rickety, fragrant old wagon. Simpson Mullen—commonly called "Simp"—was to help in the delivery.

Against violent protests from Issy, who declared that Ves Young's rattle-trap wan't fit to do nothin' but haul fish heads to the fertilizer factory, the Calvin beams and boards were piled high on the wagon and with Ves on the driver's seat and Simp perched, like a disreputable carrion crow on top of the load, the equipage started.

"There!" exclaimed Albert, with satisfaction. "He can't say it wasn't delivered this time according to promise."

"Godfreys!" snorted Issy, gazing after the departing wagon. "He won't be able to say nothin' when he sees that git-up—and smells it. Ves carts everything in that cart from dead cows to gurry barrels. Whew! I'd hate to have to set on that porch when 'twas built of that lumber. And, unless I'm mistook, Ves and Simp had been havin' a little somethin' strong to take, too."

Mr. Price, as it happened, was not "mistook." Mr. Young had, as the South Harniss saying used to be, "had a jug come down" on the train from Boston that very morning. The jug was under the seat of his wagon and its contents had already been sampled by him and by Simp. The journey to the Calvin cottage was enlivened by frequent stops for refreshment.

Consequently it happened that, just as Mrs. Calvin's gathering of Welfare Workers had reached the cake and chocolate stage in their proceedings and just as the Reverend Mr. Calvin had risen by invitation to say a few words of encouragement, the westerly wind blowing in at the open windows bore to the noses and ears of the assembled faithful a perfume and a sound neither of which was sweet.

Above the rattle and squeak of the Young wagon turning in at the Calvin gate arose the voices of Vessie and Simp uplifted in song.

"'Here's to the good old whiskey, drink 'er daown,'" sang Mr. Young.

> *"'Here's to the good old whiskey,*
>
> *Drink 'er daown!*
>
> *Here's to the good old whiskey,*
>
> *It makes you feel so frisky,*
>
> *Drink 'er—'*

Git up there, blank blank ye! What the blankety blank you stoppin' here for? Git up!"

The horse was not the only creature that got up. Mrs. Calvin rose from her chair and gazed in horror at the window. Her husband, being already on his feet, could not rise but he broke off short the opening sentence of his "few words" and stared and listened. Each Welfare Worker stared and listened also.

"Git up, you blankety blank blank," repeated Ves Young, with cheerful enthusiasm. Mr. Mullen, from the top of the load of lumber, caroled dreamily on:

> *"'Here's to the good old rum,*
> *Drink 'er daown!*
> *Here's to the good old rum,*
> *Drink 'er daown!*
> *Here's to the good old rum,*
> *Ain't you glad that you've got some?*
> *Drink 'er daown! Drink 'er daown!*
> *Drink 'er daown!'"*

And floating, as it were, upon the waves of melody came the odor of the Young wagon, an odor combining deceased fish and late lamented cow and goodness knows what beside.

The dissipated vehicle stopped beneath the parlor windows of the Calvin cottage. Mr. Young called to his assistant.

"Here we be, Simp!" he yelled. "A-a-ll ashore that's goin' ashore! Wake up there, you unmentionably described old rum barrel and help unload this everlastingly condemned lumber."

Mr. Calvin rushed to the window. "What does this mean?" he demanded, in frothing indignation.

Vessie waved at him reassuringly. "'Sall right, Mr. Calvin," he shouted. "Here's your lumber from Ze-lotes Snow and Co., South Harniss, Mass., U. S. A. 'Sall right. Let 'er go, Simp! Let 'er blankety-blank go!"

Mr. Mullen responded with alacrity and a whoop. A half dozen boards crashed to the ground beneath the parlor windows. Mrs. Calvin rushed to her husband's side.

"This is DREADFUL, Seabury!" she cried. "Send those creatures and — and that horrible wagon away at once."

The Reverend Calvin tried to obey orders. He commanded Mr. Young to go away from there that very moment. Vessie was surprised.

"Ain't this your lumber?" he demanded.

"It doesn't make any difference whether it is or not, I—"

"Didn't you tell Z. Snow and Co. that this lumber'd got to be delivered to-day or you'd cancel the order?"

"Never mind. That is my business, sir. You—"

"Hold on! Ho-o-ld on! *I* got a business, too. My business is deliverin' what I'm paid to deliver. Al Speranzy he says to me: 'Ves,' he says, 'if you don't deliver that lumber to old man Calvin to-day you don't get no money, see. Will you deliver it?' Says I, 'You bet your crashety-blank life I'll (hic) d'liver it! What I say I'll do, I'll do!' And I'm deliverin' it, ain't I? Hey? Ain't I? Well, then, what the—" And so forth and at length, while Mrs. Calvin collapsed half fainting in an easy-chair, and horrified Welfare Workers covered their ears—and longed to cover their noses.

The lumber was delivered that day. Its delivery was, from the viewpoint of Messrs. Young and Mullen, a success. The spring meeting of the Welfare Workers was not a success.

The following day Mr. Calvin called at the office of Z. Snow and Co. He had things to say and said them. Captain Zelotes, who had returned from Boston, listened. Then he called his grandson.

"Tell him what you've just told me, Mr. Calvin," he said.

The reverend gentleman told it, with added details.

"And in my opinion, if you'll excuse me, Captain Snow," he said, in conclusion, "this young man knew what he was doing when he sent those drunken scoundrels to my house. He did it purposely, I am convinced."

Captain Zelotes looked at him.

"Why?" he asked.

"Why, because—because of—of what I said to him—er—er—when I called here yesterday morning. He—I presume he took offense and—and this outrage is the result. I am convinced that—"

"Wait a minute. What did you say for him to take offense at?"

"I demanded that order should be delivered as promised. I am accustomed to do business with business men and—"

"Hold on just a minute more, Mr. Calvin. We don't seem to be gettin' at the clam in this shell as fast as we'd ought to. Al, what have you got to say about all this business?"

Albert was white, almost as white as when he fought Sam Thatcher, but as he stood up to Sam so also did he face the irate clergyman. He told of the latter's visit to the office, of the threat to cancel the order unless delivery was promised that day, of how his promise to deliver was exacted, of his effort to keep that promise.

"I HAD to deliver it, Grandfather," he said hotly. "He had all but called me a liar and—and by George, I wasn't going to—"

His grandfather held up a warning hand.

"Sshh! Ssh!" he said. "Go on with your yarn, boy."

Albert told of the lame horse, of his effort to hire another team, and finally how in desperation he had engaged Ves Young as a last resort. The captain's face was serious but there was the twinkle under his heavy brows. He pulled at his beard.

"Humph!" he grunted. "Did you know Ves and Simp had been drinkin' when you hired 'em?"

"Of course I didn't. After they had gone Issy said he suspected that they had been drinking a little, but *I* didn't know it. All I wanted was to prove to HIM," with a motion toward Mr. Calvin, "that I kept my word."

Captain Zelotes pulled at his beard. "All right, Al," he said, after a moment; "you can go."

Albert went out of the private office. After he had gone the captain turned to his irate customer.

"I'm sorry this happened, Mr. Calvin," he said, "and if Keeler or I had been here it probably wouldn't. But," he added, "as far as I can see, the boy did what he thought was the best thing to do. And," the twinkle reappeared in the gray eyes, "you sartinly did get your lumber when 'twas promised."

Mr. Calvin stiffened. He had his good points, but he suffered from what Laban Keeler once called "ingrowin' importance," and this ailment often affected his judgment. Also he had to face Mrs. Calvin upon his return home.

"Do I understand," he demanded, "that you are excusing that young man for putting that outrage upon me?"

"We-ll, as I say, I'm sorry it happened. But, honest, Mr. Calvin, I don't know's the boy's to blame so very much, after all. He delivered your lumber, and that's somethin'."

"Is that all you have to say, Captain Snow? Is that—that impudent young clerk of yours to go unpunished?"

"Why, yes, I guess likely he is."

"Then I shall NEVER buy another dollar's worth of your house again, sir."

Captain Zelotes bowed. "I'm sorry to lose your trade, Mr. Calvin," he said. "Good mornin'."

Albert, at his desk in the outer office, was waiting rebelliously to be called before his grandfather and upbraided. And when so called he was in a mood to speak his mind. He would say a few things, no matter what happened in consequence. But he had no chance to say them. Captain Zelotes did not mention the Calvin affair to him, either that day or afterward. Albert waited and waited, expecting trouble, but the trouble, so far as his grandfather was concerned, did not materialize. He could not understand it.

But if in that office there was silence concerning the unusual delivery of the lumber for the Calvin porch, outside there was talk enough and to spare. Each Welfare Worker talked when she reached home and the story spread. Small boys shouted after Albert when he walked down the main street, demanding to know how Ves Young's cart was smellin' these days. When he entered the post office some one in the crowd was almost sure to hum, "Here's to the good old whiskey, drink her down." On the train on the way to the picnic, girls and young fellows had slyly nagged him about it. The affair and its consequence were the principal causes of his mood that day; this particular "Portygee streak" was due to it.

The path along the edge of the high bluff entered a grove of scraggy pitch pines about a mile from the lighthouse and the picnic ground. Albert stalked gloomily through the shadows of the little grove and emerged on the other side. There he saw another person ahead of him on the path. This other person was a girl. He recognized her even at this distance. She was Helen Kendall.

She and he had not been quite as friendly of late. Not that there was any unfriendliness between them, but she was teaching in the primary school and, as her father had not been well, spent most of her evenings at home. During the early part of the winter he had called occasionally but, somehow, it had seemed to him that she was not quite as cordial, or as interested in his society and conversation as she used to be. It was but a slight indifference on her part, perhaps, but Albert Speranza was not accustomed to indifference on the part of his feminine acquaintances. So he did not call again. He had seen her at the picnic ground and they had spoken, but not at any length.

And he did not care to speak with her now. He had left the pavilion because of his desire to be alone, and that desire still persisted. However, she was some little distance ahead of him and he waited in the edge of the grove until she should go over the crest of the little hill at the next point.

But she did not go over the crest. Instead, when she reached it, she walked to the very edge of the bluff and stood there looking off at the ocean. The sea breeze ruffled her hair and blew her skirts about her and she made a pretty picture. But to Albert it seemed that she was standing much too near the edge. She could not see it, of course, but from where he stood he could see that the bank at that point was much undercut by the winter rains and winds, and although the sod looked firm enough from above, in reality there was little to support it. Her standing there made him a trifle uneasy and he had a mind to shout and warn her. He hesitated, however, and as he watched she stepped back of her own accord. He turned, re-entered the grove and started to walk back to the pavilion.

He had scarcely done so when he heard a short scream followed by a thump and a rumbling, rattling sound. He turned like a flash, his heart pounding violently.

The bluff edge was untenanted. A semi-circular section of the sod where Helen had stood was missing. From the torn opening where it had been rose a yellow cloud of dust.

CHAPTER VI

A goodly number of the South Harniss "natives," those who had not seen him play tennis, would have been willing to swear that running was, for Albert Speranza, an impossibility. His usual gait was a rather languid saunter. They would have changed their minds had they seen him now.

He ran along that path as he had run in school at the last track meet, where he had been second in the hundred-yard dash. He reached the spot where the sod had broken and, dropping on his knees, looked fearfully over. The dust was still rising, the sand and pebbles were still rattling in a diminishing shower down to the beach so far below. But he did not see what he had so feared to see.

What he did see, however, was neither pleasant nor altogether reassuring. The bluff below the sod at its top dropped sheer and undercut for perhaps ten feet. Then the sand and clay sloped outward and the slope extended down for another fifty feet, its surface broken by occasional clinging chunks of beach grass. Then it broke sharply again, a straight drop of eighty feet to the mounds and dunes bordering the beach.

Helen had of course fallen straight to the upper edge of the slope, where she had struck feet first, and from there had slid and rolled to the very edge of the long drop to the beach. Her skirt had caught in the branches of an enterprising bayberry bush which had managed to find roothold there, and to this bush and a clump of beach grass she was clinging, her hands outstretched and her body extended along the edge of the clay precipice.

Albert gasped.

"Helen!" he called breathlessly.

She turned her head and looked up at him. Her face was white, but she did not scream.

"Helen!" cried Albert, again. "Helen, do you hear me?"

"Yes."

"Are you badly hurt?"

"No. No, I don't think so."

"Can you hold on just as you are for a few minutes?"

"Yes, I—I think so."

"You've got to, you know. Here! You're not going to faint, are you?"

"No, I—I don't think I am."

"You can't! You mustn't! Here! Don't you do it! Stop!"

There was just a trace of his grandfather in the way he shouted the order. Whether or not the vigor of the command produced the result is a question, but at any rate she did not faint.

"Now you stay right where you are," he ordered again. "And hang on as tight as you can. I'm coming down."

Come down he did, swinging over the brink with his face to the bank, dropping on his toes to the upper edge of the slope and digging boots and fingers into the clay to prevent sliding further.

"Hang on!" he cautioned, over his shoulder. "I'll be there in a second. There! Now wait until I get my feet braced. Now give me your hand—your left hand. Hold on with your right."

Slowly and cautiously, clinging to his hand, he pulled her away from the edge of the precipice and helped her to scramble up to where he clung. There she lay and panted. He looked at her apprehensively.

"Don't go and faint now, or any foolishness like that," he ordered sharply.

"No, no, I won't. I'll try not to. But how are we ever going to climb up—up there?"

Above them and at least four feet out of reach, even if they stood up, and that would be a frightfully risky proceeding, the sod projected over their heads like the eaves of a house.

Helen glanced up at it and shuddered.

"Oh, how CAN we?" she gasped.

"We can't. And we won't try."

"Shall we call for help?"

"Not much use. Nobody to hear us. Besides, we can always do that if we have to. I think I see a way out of the mess. If we can't get up, perhaps we can get down."

"Get DOWN?"

"Yes, it isn't all as steep as it is here. I believe we might sort of zig-zag down if we were careful. You hold on here just as you are; I'm going to see what it looks like around this next point."

The "point" was merely a projection of the bluff about twenty feet away. He crawfished along the face of the slope, until he could see beyond it. Helen kept urging him to be careful—oh, be careful!

"Of course I'll be careful," he said curtly. "I don't want to break my neck. Yes—yes, by George, it IS easier around there! We could get down a good way. Here, here; don't start until you take my hand. And be sure your feet are braced before you move. Come on, now."

"I—I don't believe I can."

"Of course you can. You've GOT to. Come on. Don't look down. Look at the sand right in front of you."

Getting around that point was a decidedly ticklish operation, but they managed it, he leading the way, making sure of his foothold before moving and then setting her foot in the print his own had made. On the other side of the projection the slope was less abrupt and extended much nearer to the ground below. They zigzagged down until nearly to the edge of the steep drop. Then Albert looked about for a new path to safety. He found it still farther on.

"It takes us down farther," he said, "and there are bushes to hold on to after we get there. Come on, Helen! Brace up now, be a sport!"

She was trying her best to obey orders, but being a sport was no slight undertaking under the circumstances. When they reached the clump of bushes her guide ordered her to rest.

"Just stop and catch your breath," he said. "The rest is going to be easier, I think. And we haven't so very far to go."

He was too optimistic. It was anything but easy; in fact, the last thirty feet was almost a tumble, owing to the clay giving way beneath their feet. But there was soft sand to tumble into and they reached the beach safe, though in a dishevelled, scratched and thoroughly smeared condition. Then Helen sat down and covered her face with her hands. Her rescuer gazed triumphantly up at the distant rim of broken sod and grinned.

"There, by George!" he exclaimed. "We did it, didn't we? Say, that was fun!"

She removed her hands and looked at him.

"WHAT did you say it was?" she faltered.

"I said it was fun. It was great! Like something out of a book, eh?"

She began to laugh hysterically. He turned to her in indignant surprise. "What are you laughing at?" he demanded.

"Oh—oh, don't, please! Just let me laugh. If I don't laugh I shall cry, and I don't want to do that. Just don't talk to me for a few minutes, that's all."

When the few minutes were over she rose to her feet.

"Now we must get back to the pavilion, I suppose," she said. "My, but we are sights, though! Do let's see if we can't make ourselves a little more presentable."

She did her best to wipe off the thickest of the clay smears with her handkerchief, but the experiment was rather a failure. As they started to walk back along the beach she suddenly turned to him and said:

"I haven't told you how—how much obliged I am for—for what you did. If you hadn't come, I don't know what would have happened to me."

"Oh, that's all right," he answered lightly. He was reveling in the dramatic qualities of the situation. She did not speak again for some time and he, too, walked on in silence enjoying his day dream. Suddenly he became aware that she was looking at him steadily and with an odd expression on her face.

"What is it?" he asked. "Why do you look at me that way?"

Her answer was, as usual, direct and frank.

"I was thinking about you," she said. "I was thinking that I must have been mistaken, partly mistaken, at least."

"Mistaken? About me, do you mean?"

"Yes; I had made up my mind that you were—well, one sort of fellow, and now I see that you are an entirely different sort. That is, you've shown that you can be different."

"What on earth do you mean by that?"

"Why, I mean—I mean—Oh, I'm sure I had better not say it. You won't like it, and will think I had better mind my own affairs—which I should do, of course."

"Go on; say it."

She looked at him again, evidently deliberating whether or not to speak her thought. Then she said:

"Well, I will say it. Not that it is really my business, but because in a way it is begging your pardon, and I ought to do that. You see, I had begun to believe that you were—that you were—well, that you were not very—very active, you know."

"Active? Say, look here, Helen! What—"

"Oh, I don't wonder you don't understand. I mean that you were rather—rather fond of not doing much—of—of—"

"Eh? Not doing much? That I was lazy, do you mean?"

"Why, not exactly lazy, perhaps, but—but—Oh, how CAN I say just what I mean! I mean that you were always saying that you didn't like the work in your grandfather's office."

"Which I don't."

"And that some day you were going to do something else."

"Which I am."

"Write or act or do something—"

"Yes, and that's true, too."

"But you don't, you know. You don't do anything. You've been talking that way ever since I knew you, calling this a one-horse town and saying how you hated it, and that you weren't going to waste your life here, and all that, but you keep staying here and doing just the same things. The last long talk we had together you told me you knew you could write poems and plays and all sorts of things, you just felt that you could. You were going to begin right away. You said that some months ago, and you haven't done any writing at all. Now, have you?"

"No-o. No, but that doesn't mean I shan't by and by."

"But you didn't begin as you said you would. That was last spring, more than a year ago, and I don't believe you have tried to write a single poem. Have you?"

He was beginning to be ruffled. It was quite unusual for any one, most of all for a girl, to talk to him in this way.

"I don't know that I have," he said loftily. "And, anyway, I don't see that it is—is—"

"My business whether you have or not. I know it isn't. I'm sorry I spoke. But, you see, I—Oh, well, never mind. And I do want you to know how much I appreciate your helping me as you did just now. I don't know how to thank you for that."

But thanks were not exactly what he wanted at that moment.

"Go ahead and say the rest," he ordered, after a short pause. "You've said so much that you had better finish it, seems to me. I'm lazy, you think. What else am I?"

"You're brave, awfully brave, and you are so strong and quick—yes, and—and—masterful; I think that is the right word. You ordered me about as if I were a little girl. I didn't want to keep still, as you told me to; I wanted to scream. And I wanted to faint, too, but you wouldn't let me. I had never seen you that way before. I didn't know you could be like that. That is what surprises me so. That is why I said you were so different."

Here was balm for wounded pride. Albert's chin lifted. "Oh, that was nothing," he said. "Whatever had to be done must be done right off, I could see that. You couldn't hang on where you were very long."

She shuddered. "No," she replied, "I could not. But *I* couldn't think WHAT to do, and you could. Yes, and did it, and made me do it."

The chin lifted still more and the Speranza chest began to expand. Helen's next remark was in the natures of a reducer for the said expansion.

"If you could be so prompt and strong and—and energetic then," she said, "I can't help wondering why you aren't like that all the time. I had begun to think you were just—just—"

"Lazy, eh?" he suggested.

"Why—why, no-o, but careless and indifferent and with not much ambition, certainly. You had talked so much about writing and yet you never tried to write anything, that—that—"

"That you thought I was all bluff. Thanks! Any more compliments?"

She turned on him impulsively. "Oh, don't!" she exclaimed. "Please don't! I know what I am saying sounds perfectly horrid, and especially now when you have just saved me from being badly hurt, if not killed. But don't you see that—that I am saying it because I am interested in you and sure you COULD do so much if you only would? If you would only try."

This speech was a compound of sweet and bitter. Albert characteristically selected the sweet.

"Helen," he asked, in his most confidential tone, "would you like to have me try and write something? Say, would you?"

"Of course I would. Oh, will you?"

"Well, if YOU asked me I might. For your sake, you know."

She stopped and stamped her foot impatiently.

"Oh, DON'T be silly!" she exclaimed. "I don't want you to do it for my sake. I want you to do it for your own sake. Yes, and for your grandfather's sake."

"My grandfather's sake! Great Scott, why do you drag him in? HE doesn't want me to write poetry."

"He wants you to do something, to succeed. I know that."

"He wants me to stay here and help Labe Keeler and Issy Price. He wants me to spend all my life in that office of his; that's what HE wants. Now hold on, Helen! I'm not saying anything against the old fellow. He doesn't like me, I know, but—"

"You DON'T know. He does like you. Or he wants to like you very much indeed. He would like to have you carry on the Snow Company's business after he has gone, but if you can't—or won't—do that, I know he would be very happy to see you succeed at anything—anything."

Albert laughed scornfully. "Even at writing poetry?" he asked.

"Why, yes, at writing; although of course he doesn't know a thing about it and can't understand how any one can possibly earn a living that way. He has read or heard about poets and authors starving in garrets and he thinks they're all like that. But if you could only show him and prove to him that you could succeed by writing, he would be prouder of you than any one else would be. I know it."

He regarded her curiously. "You seem to know a lot about my grandfather," he observed.

"I do know something about him. He and I have been friends ever since I was a little girl, and I like him very much indeed. If he were my grandfather I should be proud of him. And I think you ought to be."

She flashed the last sentence at him in a sudden heat of enthusiasm. He was surprised at her manner.

"Gee! You ARE strong for the old chap, aren't you?" he said. "Well, admitting that he is all right, just why should I be proud of him? I AM proud of my father, of course; he was somebody in the world."

"You mean he was somebody just because he was celebrated and lots of people knew about him. Celebrated people aren't the only ones who do worth while things. If I were you, I should be proud of Captain Zelotes because he is what he has made himself. Nobody helped him; he did it all. He was a sea captain and a good one. He has been a business man and a good one, even if the business isn't so very big. Everybody here in South Harniss—yes, and all up and down the Cape—knows of him and respects him. My father says in all the years he has preached in his church he has never heard a single person as much as hint that Captain Snow wasn't absolutely honest, absolutely brave, and the same to everybody, rich or poor. And all his life he has worked and worked hard. What HE has belongs to him; he has earned it. That's why I should be proud of him if he were my grandfather."

Her enthusiasm had continued all through this long speech. Albert whistled.

"Whew!" he exclaimed. "Regular cheer for Zelotes, fellows! One—two—! Grandfather's got one person to stand up for him, I'll say that. But why this sudden outbreak about him, anyhow? It was me you were talking about in the beginning—though I didn't notice any loud calls for cheers in that direction," he added.

She ignored the last part of the speech. "I think you yourself made me think of him," she replied. "Sometimes you remind me of him. Not often, but once in a while. Just now, when we were climbing down that awful place you seemed almost exactly like him. The way you knew just what to do all the time, and your not hesitating a minute, and the way you took command of the situation and," with a sudden laugh, "bossed me around; every bit of that was like him, and not like you at all. Oh, I don't mean that," she added hurriedly. "I mean it wasn't like you as you usually are. It was different."

"Humph! Well, I must say—See here, Helen Kendall, what is it you expect me to do; sail in and write two or three sonnets and a 'Come Into the Garden, Maud,' some time next week? You're terribly keen about Grandfather, but he has rather got the edge on me so far as age goes. He's in the sixties, and I'm just about nineteen."

"When he was nineteen he was first mate of a ship."

"Yes, so I've heard him say. Maybe first-mating is a little bit easier than writing poetry."

"And maybe it isn't. At any rate, he didn't know whether it was easy or not until he tried. Oh, THAT'S what I would like to see you do—TRY to do something. You could do it, too, almost anything you tried, I do believe. I am confident you could. But—Oh, well, as you said at the beginning, it isn't my business at all, and I've said ever and ever so much more than I meant to. Please forgive me, if you can. I think my tumble and all the rest must have made me silly. I'm sorry, Albert. There are the steps up to the pavilion. See them!"

He was tramping on beside her, his hands in his pockets. He did not look at the long flight of steps which had suddenly come into view around the curve of the bluff. When he did look up and speak it was in a different tone, some such tone as she had heard him use during her rescue.

"All right," he said, with decision, "I'll show you whether I can try or not. I know you think I won't, but I will. I'm going up to my room to-night and I'm going to try to write something or other. It may be the rottenest poem that ever was ground out, but I'll grind it if it kills me."

She was pleased, that was plain, but she shook her head.

"Not to-night, Albert," she said. "To-night, after the picnic, is Father's reception at the church. Of course you'll come to that."

"Of course I won't. Look here, you've called me lazy and indifferent and a hundred other pet names this afternoon. Well, this evening I'll make you take some of 'em back. Reception be hanged! I'm going to write to-night."

That evening both Mrs. Snow and Rachel Ellis were much disturbed because Albert, pleading a headache, begged off from attendance at the reception to the Reverend Mr. Kendall. Either, or both ladies would have been only too willing to remain at home and nurse the sufferer through his attack, but he refused to permit the sacrifice on their part. After they had gone his headache disappeared and, supplied with an abundance of paper, pens and ink, he sat down at the table in his room to invoke the Muse. The invocation lasted until three A. M. At that hour, with a genuine headache, but a sense of triumph which conquered pain, Albert climbed into bed. Upon the table lay a poem, a six stanza poem, having these words at its head:

TO MY LADY'S SPRING HAT

By A. M. Speranza.

The following forenoon he posted that poem to the editor of The Cape Cod Item. And three weeks later it appeared in the pages of that journal. Of course there was no pecuniary recompense for its author, and the fact was indisputable that the Item was generally only too glad to publish contributions which helped to fill its columns. But, nevertheless, Albert Speranza had written a poem and that poem had been published.

CHAPTER VII

It was Rachel who first discovered "To My Lady's Spring Hat" in the Item three weeks later. She came rushing into the sitting room brandishing the paper.

"My soul! My soul! My soul!" she cried.

Olive, sitting sewing by the window, was, naturally, somewhat startled. "Mercy on us, Rachel!" she exclaimed. "What IS it?"

"Look!" cried the housekeeper, pointing to the contribution in the "Poets' Corner" as Queen Isabella may have pointed at the evidence of her proteges discovery of a new world. "LOOK!"

Mrs. Snow looked, read the verses to herself, and then aloud.

"Why, I declare, they're real sort of pretty, ain't they?" she exclaimed, in astonished admiration.

"Pretty! They're perfectly elegant! And right here in the paper for all hands to see. Ain't you PROUD of him, Mrs. Snow?"

Olive had been growing more and more proud of her handsome grandson ever since his arrival. She was prouder still now and said so. Rachel nodded, triumphantly.

"He'll be a Robert Penfold afore he dies, or I miss MY guess!" she declared.

She showed it to feminine acquaintances all over town, and Olive, when callers came, took pains to see that a copy of the Item, folded with the "Poets' Corner" uppermost, lay on the center table. Customers, dropping in at the office, occasionally mentioned the poem to its author.

"See you had a piece in the Item, Al," was their usual way of referring to it. "Pretty cute piece 'twas, too, seemed to me. Say, that girl of yours must have SOME spring bunnit. Ho, ho!"

Issachar deigned to express approval, approval qualified with discerning criticism of course, but approval nevertheless.

"Pretty good piece, Al," he observed. "Pretty good. Glad to see you done so well. Course you made one little mistake, but 'twan't a very big one.

That part where you said—What was it, now? Where'd I put that piece of poetry? Oh, yes, here 'tis! Where you said—er—er—

> 'It floats upon her golden curls
> As froth upon the wave.'

Now of course nothin'—a hat or nothin' else—is goin' to float on top of a person's head. Froth floatin', that's all right, you understand; but even if you took froth right out of the water and slapped it up onto anybody's hair 'twouldn't FLOAT up there. If you'd said,

> 'It SETS up onto her golden curls,
> Same as froth sets on top of a wave.'

that would have been all right and true. But there, don't feel bad about it. It's only a little mistake, same as anybody's liable to make. Nine persons out of ten wouldn't have noticed it. I'm extry partic'lar, I presume likely. I'm findin' mistakes like that all the time."

Laban's comment was less critical, perhaps, but more reserved.

"It's pretty good, Al," he said. "Yes—er—yes, sir, it's pretty good. It ain't all new, there's some of it that's been written before, but I rather guess that might have been said about Shakespeare's poetry when he fust commenced. It's pretty good, Al. Yes—yes, yes. It is so."

Albert was inclined to resent the qualified strain in the bookkeeper's praise. He was tempted to be sarcastic.

"Well," he observed, "of course you've read so much real poetry that you ought to know."

Laban nodded, slowly. "I've read a good deal," he said quietly. "Readin' is one of the few things I ain't made a failure of in this life. Um-hm. One of the few. Yes yes—yes."

He dipped his pen in the inkwell and carefully made an entry in the ledger. His assistant felt a sudden pang of compunction.

"I beg your pardon, Mr. Keeler," he said. "That was pretty fresh of me. I'm sorry."

Laban looked up in mild surprise. "Sorry?" he repeated. "What for? . . . Oh, that's all right, Al, that's all right. Lord knows I'm the last one on earth who'd ought to criticize anybody. All I had in mind in sayin' what I did was to—well, to kind of keep you from bein' too well satisfied and not try harder on the next one. It don't pay to be too well satisfied. . . . Years ago, I can remember, *I* was pretty well satisfied—with myself and my work. Sounds like a joke, I know, but 'twas so.... Well, I've had a nice long chance to get over it. Um-hm. Yes—yes. So I have, so I have."

Only Captain Zelotes at first said nothing about the poem. He read it, his wife saw to that, but his comment even to her was a non-committal grunt.

"But don't you think it's real sort of pretty, Zelotes?" she asked.

The captain grunted again. "Why, I guess likely 'tis if you say so, Mother. I don't know much about such things."

"But everybody says it is."

"Want to know! Well, then 'twon't make much difference whether I say it or not."

"But ain't you goin' to say a word to Albert about it, Zelotes?"

"Humph! I don't know's I know what to say."

"Why, say you like it."

"Ye-es, and if I do he'll keep on writin' more. That's exactly what I don't want him to do. Come now, Mother, be sensible. This piece of his may be good or it may not, *I* wouldn't undertake to say. But this I do know: I don't want the boy to spend his time writin' poetry slush for that 'Poets' Corner.' Letitia Makepeace did that—she had a piece in there about every week—and she died in the Taunton asylum."

"But, Zelotes, it wasn't her poetry got her into the asylum."

"Wan't it? Well, she was in the poorhouse afore that. I don't know whether 'twas her poetryin' that got her in there, but I know darned well it didn't get her out."

"But ain't you goin' to say one word? 'Twould encourage him so."

"Good Lord! We don't want to encourage him, do we? If he was takin' to thievin' you wouldn't encourage him in that, would you?"

"Thievin'! Zelotes Snow, you don't mean to say you compare a poet to a THIEF!"

The captain grinned. "No-o, Mother," he observed drily. "Sometimes a thief can manage to earn a livin' at his job. But there, there, don't feel bad. I'll say somethin' to Al, long's you think I ought to."

The something was not much, and yet Captain Zelotes really meant it to be kindly and to sound like praise. But praising a thing of which you have precious little understanding and with which you have absolutely no sympathy is a hard job.

"See you had a piece in the Item this week, Al," observed the captain.

"Why—yes, sir," said Albert.

"Um-hm. I read it. I don't know much about such things, but they tell me it is pretty good."

"Thank you, sir."

"Eh? Oh, you're welcome."

That was all. Perhaps considering its source it was a good deal, but Albert was not of the age where such considerations are likely to be made.

Helen's praise was warm and enthusiastic. "I knew you could do it if you only would," she declared. "And oh, I'm SO glad you did! Now you must keep on trying."

That bit of advice was quite superfluous. Young Speranza having sampled the sublime intoxication of seeing himself in print, was not ready to sober off yet a while. He continued to bombard the Item with verses. They were invariably accepted, but when he sent to a New York magazine a poem which he considered a gem, the promptness with which it was returned staggered his conceit and was in that respect a good thing for him.

However, he kept on trying. Helen would not have permitted him to give up even if he had wished. She was quite as much interested in his literary aspirations as he was himself and her encouragement was a great help to him. After months of repeated trial and repeated rejection he opened an envelope bearing the name of a fairly well-known periodical to find therein a kindly note stating that his poem, "Sea Spaces" had been accepted. And a week later came a check for ten dollars. That was a day of days. Incidentally it was the day of a trial balance in the office and the assistant bookkeeper's additions and multiplications contained no less than four ghastly errors.

The next afternoon there was an interview in the back office. Captain Zelotes and his grandson were the participants. The subject discussed was "Business versus Poetry," and there was a marked difference of opinion. Albert had proclaimed his triumph at home, of course, had exhibited his check, had been the recipient of hugs and praises from his grandmother and had listened to paeans and hallelujahs from Mrs. Ellis. When he hurried around to the parsonage after supper, Helen had been excited and delighted at the good news. Albert had been patted on the back quite as much as was good for a young man whose bump of self-esteem was not inclined toward under-development. When he entered the private office of Z. Snow and Co. in answer to his grandfather's summons, he did so light-heartedly, triumphantly, with self-approval written large upon him.

But though he came like a conquering hero, he was not received like one. Captain Zelotes sat at his desk, the copy of the Boston morning paper which he had been reading sticking out of the waste basket into which it had been savagely jammed a half hour before. The news had not been to the captain's liking. These were the September days of 1914; the German Kaiser was marching forward "mit Gott" through Belgium, and it began to look as if he could not be stopped short of Paris. Consequently, Captain Zelotes, his sympathies from the first with England and the Allies, was not happy in his newspaper reading.

Albert entered, head erect and eyes shining. If Gertie Kendrick could have seen him then she would have fallen down and worshiped. His grandfather looked at him in silence for a moment, tapping his desk with the stump of a pencil. Albert, too, was silent; he was already thinking of another poem with which to dazzle the world, and his head was among the rosy clouds.

"Sit down, Al," said Captain Zelotes shortly.

Albert reluctantly descended to earth and took the battered armchair standing beside the desk. The captain tapped with his pencil upon the figure-covered sheet of paper before him. Then he said:

"Al, you've been here three years come next December, ain't you?"

"Why—yes, sir, I believe I have."

"Um-hm, you have. And for the heft of that time you've been in this office."

"Yes, sir."

"Yes. And Labe Keeler and I have been doin' our best to make a business man out of you. You understand we have, don't you?"

Albert looked puzzled and a little uneasy. Into his roseate dreams was just beginning to filter the idea that his grandfather's tone and manner were peculiar.

"Why, yes, sir, of course I understand it," he replied.

"Well, I asked you because I wasn't quite sure whether you did or not. Can you guess what this is I've got on my desk here?"

He tapped the figure-covered sheet of paper once more. Before Albert could speak the captain answered his own question.

"I'll tell you what it is," he went on. "It's one of the latest samples of your smartness as a business man. I presume likely you know that Laban worked here in this office until three o'clock this mornin', didn't you?"

Albert did not know it. Mr. Keeler had told him nothing of the sort.

"Why, no," he replied. "Did he? What for?"

"Ye-es, he did. And what for? Why, just to find out what was the matter with his trial balance, that's all. When one of Labe's trial balances starts out for snug harbor and ends up on a reef with six foot of water in her hold, naturally Labe wants to get her afloat and pumped dry as quick as possible. He ain't used to it, for one thing, and it makes him nervous."

Albert's uneasiness grew. When his grandfather's speech became sarcastic and nautical, the young man had usually found that there was trouble coming for somebody.

"I—I'm sorry Laban had to stay so late," he stammered. "I should have been glad to stay and help him, but he didn't ask me."

"No-o. Well, it may possibly be that he cal'lated he was carryin' about all your help that the craft would stand, as 'twas. Any more might sink her. See here, young feller—" Captain Zelotes dropped his quiet sarcasm and spoke sharp and brisk: "See here," he said, "do you realize that this sheet of paper I've got here is what stands for a day's work done by you yesterday? And on this sheet there was no less than four silly mistakes that a child ten years old hadn't ought to make, that an able-bodied idiot hadn't ought to make. But YOU made 'em, and they kept Labe Keeler here till three o'clock this mornin'. Now what have you got to say for yourself?"

As a matter of fact, Albert had very little to say, except that he was sorry, and that his grandfather evidently did not consider worth the saying. He waved the protestation aside.

"Sorry!" he repeated impatiently. "Of course you're sorry, though even at that I ain't sure you're sorry enough. Labe was sorry, too, I don't doubt, when his bedtime went by and he kept runnin' afoul of one of your mistakes after another. I'm sorry, darned sorry, to find out that you can make such blunders after three years on board here under such teachin' as you've had. But bein' sorry don't help any to speak of. Any fool can be sorry for his foolishness, but if that's all, it don't help a whole lot. Is bein' sorry the best excuse you've got to offer? What made you make the mistakes in the first place?"

Albert's face was darkly red under the lash of his grandfather's tongue. Captain Zelotes and he had had disagreements and verbal encounters before, but never since they had been together had the captain spoken like this. And the young fellow was no longer seventeen, he was twenty. The flush began to fade from his cheeks and the pallor which meant the rise of the Speranza temper took its place.

"What made you make such fool blunders?" repeated the captain. "You knew better, didn't you?"

"Yes," sullenly, "I suppose I did."

"You know mighty well you did. And as nigh as I can larn from what I got out of Laban—which wasn't much; I had to pump it out of him word by word—this ain't the first set of mistakes you've made. You make 'em right along. If it wasn't for him helpin' you out and coverin' up your mistakes, this firm would be in hot water with its customers two-thirds of the time and the books would be fust-rate as a puzzle, somethin' to use for a guessin' match, but plaguey little good as straight accounts of a goin' concern. Now what makes you act this way? Eh? What makes you?"

"Oh, I don't know. See here, Grandfather—"

"Hold on a minute. You don't know, eh? Well, I know. It ain't because you ain't smart enough to keep a set of books and keep 'em well. I don't expect you to be a Labe Keeler; there ain't many bookkeepers like him on this earth. But I do know you're smart enough to keep my books and keep 'em as they'd ought to be, if you want to keep 'em. The trouble with you is that you don't want to. You've got too much of your good-for-nothin—" Captain Lote pulled up short, cleared his throat, and went on: "You've got too much 'poet' in you," he declared, "that's what's the matter."

Albert leaned forward. "That wasn't what you were going to say," he said quickly. "You were going to say that I had too much of my father in me."

It was the captain's turn to redden. "Eh?" he stammered. "Why, I—I—How do you know what I was goin' to say?"

"Because I do. You say it all the time. Or, if you don't say it, you look it. There is hardly a day that I don't catch you looking at me as if you were expecting me to commit murder or do some outrageous thing or other. And I know, too, that it is all because I'm my father's son. Well, that's all right; feel that way about me if you want to, I can't help it."

"Here, here, Al! Hold on! Don't—"

"I won't hold on. And I tell you this: I hate this work here. You say I don't want to keep books. Well, I don't. I'm sorry I made the errors yesterday and put Keeler to so much trouble, but I'll probably make more. No," with a sudden outburst of determination, "I won't make any more. I won't, because I'm not going to keep books any more. I'm through."

Captain Zelotes leaned back in his chair.

"You're what?" he asked slowly.

"I'm through. I'll never work in this office another day. I'm through."

The captain's brows drew together as he stared steadily at his grandson. He slowly tugged at his beard.

"Humph!" he grunted, after a moment. "So you're through, eh? Goin' to quit and go somewheres else, you mean?"

"Yes."

"Um-hm. I see. Where are you goin' to go?"

"I don't know. But I'm not going to make a fool of myself at this job any longer. I can't keep books, and I won't keep them. I hate business. I'm no good at it. And I won't stay here."

"I see. I see. Well, if you won't keep on in business, what will you do for a livin'? Write poetry?"

"Perhaps."

"Um-m. Be kind of slim livin', won't it? You've been writin' poetry for about a year and a half, as I recollect, and so far you've made ten dollars."

"That's all right. If I don't make it I may starve, as you are always saying that writers do. But, starve or not, I shan't ask YOU to take care of me."

"I've taken care of you for three years or so."

"Yes. But you did it because—because—Well, I don't know why you did, exactly, but you won't have to do it any longer. I'm through."

The captain still stared steadily, and what he saw in the dark eyes which flashed defiance back at him seemed to trouble him a little. His tugs at his beard became more strenuous.

"Humph!" he muttered. "Humph! . . . Well, Al, of course I can't make you stay by main force. Perhaps I could—you ain't of age yet—but I shan't. And you want to quit the ship altogether, do you?"

"If you mean this office—yes, I do."

"I see, I see. Want to quit South Harniss and your grandmother—and Rachel—and Labe—and Helen—and all the rest of 'em?"

"Not particularly. But I shall have to, of course."

"Yes. . . . Um-hm. . . . Yes. Have you thought how your grandmother's liable to feel when she hears you are goin' to clear out and leave her?"

Albert had not thought in that way, but he did now. His tone was a trifle less combative as he answered.

"She'll be sorry at first, I suppose," he said, "but she'll get over it."

"Um-hm. Maybe she will. You can get over 'most anything in time—'MOST anything. Well, and how about me? How do you think I'll feel?"

Albert's chin lifted. "You!" he exclaimed. "Why, you'll be mighty glad of it."

Captain Zelotes picked up the pencil stump and twirled it in his fingers. "Shall I?" he asked. "You think I will, do you?"

"Of course you will. You don't like me, and never did."

"So I've heard you say. Well, boy, don't you cal'late I like you at least as much as you like me?"

"No. What do you mean? I like you well enough. That is, I should if you gave me half a chance. But you don't do it. You hate me because my father—"

The captain interrupted. His big palm struck the desk.

"DON'T say that again!" he commanded. "Look here, if I hated you do you suppose I'd be talkin' to you like this? If I hated you do you cal'late I'd argue when you gave me notice? Not by a jugful! No man ever came to me and said he was goin' to quit and had me beg him to stay. If we was at sea he stayed until we made port; then he WENT, and he didn't hang around waitin' for a boat to take him ashore neither. I don't hate you, son. I'd ask nothin' better than a chance to like you, but you won't give it to me."

Albert's eyes and mouth opened.

"*I* won't give YOU a chance?" he repeated.

"Sartin. DO you give me one? I ask you to keep these books of mine. You could keep 'em A Number One. You're smart enough to do it. But you won't. You let 'em go to thunder and waste your time makin' up fool poetry and such stuff."

"But I like writing, and I don't like keeping books."

"Keepin' books is a part of l'arnin' the business, and business is the way you're goin' to get your livin' by and by."

"No, it isn't. I am going to be a writer."

"Now DON'T say that silly thing again! I don't want to hear it."

"I shall say it because it is true."

"Look here, boy: When I tell you or anybody else in this office to do or not to do a thing, I expect 'em to obey orders. And I tell you not to talk any more of that foolishness about bein' a writer. D'you understand?"

"Yes, of course I understand."

"All right, then, that much is settled. . . . Here! Where are you goin'?"

Albert had turned and was on his way out of the office. He stopped and answered over his shoulder, "I'm going home," he said.

"Goin' HOME? Why, you came from home not more than an hour and a half ago! What are you goin' there again now for?"

"To pack up my things."

"To pack up your things! To pack up—Humph! So you really mean it! You're really goin' to quit me like this? And your grandma, too!"

The young man felt a sudden pang of compunction, a twinge of conscience.

"Grandfather," he said, "I'm sorry. I—"

But the change in his attitude and tone came too late. Captain Lote's temper was boiling now, contradiction was its worst provocative.

"Goin' to quit!" he sneered. "Goin' to quit because you don't like to work. All right, quit then! Go ahead! I've done all I can to make a man of you. Go to the devil in your own way."

"Grandfather, I—"

"Go ahead! *I* can't stop you. It's in your breed, I cal'late."

That was sufficient. Albert strode out of the private office, head erect. Captain Zelotes rose and slammed the door after his departing grandson.

At ten that evening Albert was in his room, sitting in a chair by the window, gloomily looking out. The packing, most of it, had been done. He had not, as he told his grandfather he intended doing, left the office immediately and come straight home to pack. As he emerged from the inner office after the stormy interview with the captain he found Laban Keeler hard at work upon the books. The sight of the little man, so patiently and cheerfully pegging away, brought another twinge of conscience to the assistant bookkeeper. Laban had been such a brick in all their relationships. It must have been a sore trial to his particular, business-like soul, those errors in the trial balance. Yet he had not found fault nor complained. Captain Zelotes himself had said that every item concerning his grandson's mistakes and blunders had been dragged from Mr. Keeler much against the latter's will. Somehow Albert could not bear to go off and leave him at once. He would stay and finish his day's work, for Labe Keeler's sake.

So stay he did and when Captain Zelotes later came out of his private office and found him there neither of them spoke. At home, during supper, nothing was said concerning the quarrel of the afternoon. Yet Albert was as determined to leave as ever, and the Captain, judging by the expression of his face, was just as determined to do nothing more to prevent him. After supper the young man went to his room and began the packing. His grandfather went out, an unusual proceeding for him, saying that he guessed he would go down street for a spell.

Now Albert, as he sat there by the window, was gloomy enough. The wind, howling and wailing about the gables of the old house, was not an aid to cheerfulness and he needed every aid. He had sworn to go away, he was going away—but where should he go? He had a little money put by, not much but a little, which he had been saving for quite another purpose. This would take him a little way, would pay his bills for a short time, but after that—Well, after that he could earn more. With the optimism of youth and the serene self-confidence which was natural to him he was sure of succeeding sooner or later. It was not the dread of failure and privation which troubled him. The weight which was pressing upon his spirit was not the fear of what might happen to him.

There was a rap upon the door. Then a voice, the housekeeper's voice, whispered through the crack.

"It's me, Al," whispered Mrs. Ellis. "You ain't in bed yet, are you? I'd like to talk with you a minute or two, if I might."

He was not anxious to talk to her or anyone else just then, but he told her to come in. She entered on tiptoe, with the mysterious air of a conspirator, and shut the door carefully after her.

"May I set down just a minute?" she asked. "I can generally talk better settin'."

He pulled forward the ancient rocker with the rush seat. The cross-stitch "tidy" on the back was his mother's handiwork, she had made it when she was fifteen. Rachel sat down in the rocker.

"Al" she began, still in the same mysterious whisper, "I know all about it."

He looked at her. "All about what?" he asked.

"About the trouble you and Cap'n Lote had this afternoon. I know you're plannin' to leave us all and go away somewheres and that he told you to go, and all that. I know what you've been doin' up here to-night. Fur's that goes," she added, with a little catch in her breath and a wave of her hand toward the open trunk and suitcase upon the floor, "I wouldn't need to know, I could SEE."

Albert was surprised and confused. He had supposed the whole affair to be, so far, a secret between himself and his grandfather.

"You know?" he stammered. "You—How did you know?"

"Laban told me. Labe came hurryin' over here just after supper and told me the whole thing. He's awful upset about it, Laban is. He thinks almost as much of you as he does of Cap'n Lote or—or me," with an apologetic little smile.

Albert was astonished and troubled. "How did Labe know about it?" he demanded.

"He heard it all. He couldn't help hearin'."

"But he couldn't have heard. The door to the private office was shut."

"Yes, but the window at the top—the transom one, you know—was wide open. You and your grandpa never thought of that, I guess, and Laban couldn't hop up off his stool and shut it without givin' it away that he'd been hearin'. So he had to just set and listen and I know how he hated doin' that. Laban Keeler ain't the listenin' kind. One thing about it all is a mercy," she added, fervently. "It's the Lord's own mercy that that Issy Price wasn't where HE could hear it, too. If Issy heard it you might as well paint it up on the town-hall fence; all creation and his wife wouldn't larn it any sooner."

Albert drew a long breath. "Well," he said, after a moment, "I'm sorry Labe heard, but I don't suppose it makes much difference. Everyone will know all about it in a day or two . . . I'm going."

Rachel leaned forward.

"No, you ain't, Al," she said.

"I'm not? Indeed I am! Why, what do you mean?"

"I mean just what I say. You ain't goin'. You're goin' to stay right here. At least I hope you are, and I THINK you are. . . . Oh, I know," she added, quickly, "what you are goin' to say. You're goin' to tell me that your grandpa is down on you on account of your father, and that you don't like bookkeepin', and that you want to write poetry and—and such. You'll say all that, and maybe it's all true, but whether 'tis or not ain't the point at all just now. The real point is that you're Janie Snow's son and your grandpa's Cap'n Lote Snow and your grandma's Olive Snow and there ain't goin' to be another smash-up in this family if I can help it. I've been through one and one's enough. Albert, didn't you promise me that Sunday forenoon three years ago when I came into the settin'-room and we got talkin' about books and Robert Penfold and everything—didn't you promise me then that when things between you and your grandpa got kind of—of snarled up and full of knots you'd come to me with 'em and we'd see if we couldn't straighten 'em out together? Didn't you promise me that, Albert?"

Albert remembered the conversation to which she referred. As he remembered it, however, he had not made any definite promise.

"You asked me to talk them over with you, Rachel," he admitted. "I think that's about as far as it went."

"Well, maybe so, but now I ask you again. Will you talk this over with me, Albert? Will you tell me every bit all about it, for my sake? And for your grandma's sake. . . . Yes, more'n that, for your mother's sake, Albert; she was pretty nigh like my own sister, Jane Snow was. Different as night from day of course, she was pretty and educated and all that and I was just the same then as I am now, but we did think a lot of each other, Albert. Tell me the whole story, won't you, please. Just what Cap'n Lote said and what you said and what you plan to do—and all? Please, Albert."

There were tears in her eyes. He had always liked her, but it was a liking with a trace of condescension in it. She was peculiar, her "sympathetic attacks" were funny, and she and Laban together were an odd pair. Now he saw her in a new light and he felt a sudden rush of real affection for her. And with this feeling, and inspired also by his loneliness, came the impulse to comply with her request, to tell her all his troubles.

He began slowly at first, but as he went on the words came quicker. She listened eagerly, nodding occasionally, but saying nothing. When he had finished she nodded again.

"I see," she said. "'Twas almost what Laban said and about what he and I expected. Well, Albert, I ain't goin' to be the one to blame you, not very much anyhow. I don't see as you are to blame; you can't help the way you're made. But your grandfather can't help bein' made his way, either. He can't see with your spectacles and you can't see with his."

He stirred rebelliously. "Then we had better go our own ways, I should say," he muttered.

"No, you hadn't. That's just what you mustn't do, not now, anyhow. As I said before, there's been enough of all hands goin' their own ways in this family and look what came of it."

"But what do you expect me to do? I will not give up every plan I've made and my chance in the world just because he is too stubborn and cranky to understand them. I will NOT do it."

"I don't want you to. But I don't want you to upset the whole kettle just because the steam has scalded your fingers. I don't want you to go off and leave your grandma to break her heart a second time and your grandpa to give up all his plans and hopes that he's been makin' about you."

"Plans about me? He making plans about me? What sort of plans?"

"All sorts. Oh, he don't say much about 'em, of course; that ain't his way. But from things he's let drop I know he has hoped to take you in with him as a partner one of these days, and to leave you the business after he's gone."

"Nonsense, Rachel!"

"No, it ain't nonsense. It's the one big dream of Cap'n Lote's life. That Z. Snow and Co. business is his pet child, as you might say. He built it up, he and Labe together, and when he figgered to take you aboard with him 'twas SOME chance for you, 'cordin' to his lookout. Now you can't hardly blame him for bein' disappointed when you chuck that chance away and take to writin' poetry pieces, can you?"

"But—but—why, confound it, Rachel, you don't understand!"

"Yes, I do, but your grandpa don't. And you don't understand him. . . . Oh, Albert, DON'T be as stubborn as he is, as your mother was—the Lord and she forgive me for sayin' it. She was partly right about marryin' your pa and Cap'n Lote was partly right, too. If they had met half way and put the two 'partlys' together the whole thing might have been right in the end. As 'twas, 'twas all wrong. Don't, don't, DON'T, Albert, be as stubborn as that. For their sakes, Al,—yes, and for my sake, for I'm one of your family, too, or seems as if I was—don't."

She hastily wiped her eyes with her apron. He, too was greatly moved.

"Don't cry, Rachel," he muttered, hurriedly. "Please don't. . . . I didn't know you felt this way. I didn't know anybody did. I don't want to make trouble in the family—any more trouble. Grandmother has been awfully good to me; so, too, has Grandfather, I suppose, in his way. But—oh, what am I going to do? I can't stay in that office all my life. I'm not good at business. I don't like it. I can't give up—"

"No, no, course you mustn't. I don't want you to give up."

"Then what do you want me to do?"

"I want you to go to your grandpa and talk to him once more. Not givin' up your plans altogether but not forcin' him to give up his either, not right away. Tell him you realize he wants you to go on with Z. Snow and Company and that you will—for a while—"

"But—"

"For a while, I said; three or four years, say. You won't be so dreadful old then, not exactly what you'd call a Methusalem. Tell him you'll do that and on his side he must let you write as much as you please, provided you don't let the writin' interfere with the Z. Snow and Co. work. Then, at the end of the three or four years, if you still feel the same as you do now, you can tackle your poetry for keeps and he and you'll still be friends. Tell him that, Albert, and see what he says. . . . Will you?"

Albert took some moments to consider. At length he said: "If I did I doubt if he would listen."

"Oh, yes he would. He'd more than listen, I'm pretty sartin. I think he'd agree."

"You do?"

"Yes, I do. You see," with a smile, "while I've been talkin' to you there's been somebody else talkin' to him. . . . There, there! don't you ask any questions. I promised not to tell anybody and if I ain't exactly broke that promise, I've sprained its ankle, I'm afraid. Good night, Albert, and thank you ever and ever so much for listenin' so long without once tellin' me to mind my own business."

"Good night, Rachel. . . . And thank you for taking so much interest in my affairs. You're an awfully good friend, I can see that."

"Don't—don't talk that way. And you WILL have that talk with your grandpa?"

"Yes, I will."

"Oh, I'm SO glad! There! Good night. I come pretty nigh kissin' you then and for a woman that's been engaged to be married for upwards of eighteen years that's a nice way to act, ain't it! Good night, good night."

She hurried out of the room. Albert sat down again in his chair by the window. He had promised to go to his grandfather and talk to him. As he sat there, thinking of the coming interview, he realized more and more that the keeping of that promise was likely to be no easy matter. He must begin the talk, he must break the ice—and how should he break it? Timid and roundabout approaches would be of little use; unless his grandfather's state of mind had changed remarkably since their parting in the Z. Snow and Co. office they and their motive would be misunderstood. No, the only way to break the ice was to break it, to plunge immediately into the deepest part of the subject. It promised to be a chilly plunge. He shivered at the prospect.

A half hour later he heard the door of the hall open and shut and knew that Captain Zelotes had returned. Rising, he descended the stairs. He descended slowly. Just as he reached the foot of the narrow flight Captain Zelotes entered the hall from the dining-room and turned toward him. Both were surprised at the meeting. Albert spoke first.

"Good evening, Grandfather," he stammered. "I—I was just coming down to see you. Were you going to bed?"

Captain Lote shook his head. "No-o," he said, slowly, "not exactly."

"Do you mind waiting a minute? I have a few things—I have something to say to you and—and I guess I shall sleep better if I say it to-night. I—I won't keep you long."

The captain regarded him intently for an instant, then he turned and led the way to the dining-room.

"Go ahead," he ordered, laconically. Albert squared his shoulders, preparatory to the plunge.

"Grandfather," he began, "first of all I want to tell you I am sorry for— for some of the things I said this afternoon."

He had rehearsed this opening speech over and over again, but in spite of the rehearsals it was dreadfully hard to make. If his grandfather had helped him even a little it might have been easier, but the captain merely stood there, expressionless, saying nothing, waiting for him to continue.

Albert swallowed, clenched his fists, and took a new start.

"Of course," he began, "I am sorry for the mistakes I made in my bookkeeping, but that I have told you before. Now—now I want to say I am sorry for being so—well, so pig-headed about the rest of it. I realize that you have been mighty kind to me and that I owe you about everything that I've got in this world."

He paused again. It had seemed to him that Captain Zelotes was about to speak. However, he did not, so the young man stumbled on.

"And—and I realize, too," he said, "that you have, I guess, been trying to give me a real start in business, the start you think I ought to have."

The captain nodded slowly. "That was my idea in startin' you," he said.

"Yes—and fact that I haven't done more with the chance is because I'm made that way, I guess. But I do want to—yes, and I MEAN to try to succeed at writing poetry or stories or plays or something. I like that and I mean to give it a trial. And so—and so, you see, I've been thinking our talk over and I've concluded that perhaps you may be right, maybe I'm not old enough to know what I really am fitted for, and yet perhaps *I* may be partly right, too. I—I've been thinking that perhaps some sort of—of—"

"Of what?"

"Well, of half-way arrangement—some sort of—of compromise, you know, might be arranged. I might agree to stay in the office and do my very best with bookkeeping and business for—well, say, three years or so. During that time I should be trying to write of course, but I would only do that sort of writing evenings or on Saturdays and holidays. It shouldn't interfere with your work nor be done in the time you pay me for. And at the end of the three or four years—"

He paused again. This time the pause was longer than ever. Captain Lote broke the silence. His big right hand had wandered upward and was tugging at his beard.

"Well? . . . And then?" he asked.

"Why, then—if—if—Well, then we could see. If business seemed to be where I was most likely to succeed we'd call it settled and I would stay with Z. Snow and Co. If poetry-making or—or—literature seemed more likely to be the job I was fitted for, that would be the job I'd take. You—you see, don't you, Grandfather?"

The captain's beard-pulling continued. He was no longer looking his grandson straight in the eye. His gaze was fixed upon the braided mat at his feet and he answered without looking up.

"Ye-es," he drawled, "I cal'late I see. Well, was that all you had to say?"

"No-o, not quite. I—I wanted to say that which ever way it turned out, I—I hoped we—you and I, you know—would agree to be—to be good-natured about it and—and friends just the same. I—I—Well, there! That's all, I guess. I haven't put it very well, I'm afraid, but—but what do you think about it, Grandfather?"

And now Captain Zelotes did look up. The old twinkle was in his eye. His first remark was a question and that question was rather surprising.

"Al," he asked, "Al, who's been talkin' to you?"

The blood rushed to his grandson's face. "Talking to me?" he stammered. "Why—why, what do you mean?"

"I mean just that. You didn't think out this scheme all by yourself. Somebody's been talkin' to you and puttin' you up to it. Haven't they?"

"Why—why, Grandfather, I—"

"Haven't they?"

"Why—Well, yes, someone has been talking to me, but the whole idea isn't theirs. I WAS sorry for speaking to you as I did and sorry to think of leaving you and grandmother. I—I was sitting up there in my room and feeling blue and mean enough and—and—"

"And then Rachel came aboard and gave you your sailin' orders; eh?"

Albert gasped. "For heaven's sake how did you know that?" he demanded. "She—Why, she must have told you, after all! But she said—"

"Hold on, boy, hold on!" Captain Lote chuckled quietly. "No," he said, "Rachel didn't tell me; I guessed she was the one. And it didn't take a Solomon in all his glory to guess it, neither. Labe Keeler's been talkin' to ME, and when you come down here and began proposin' the same scheme that I was just about headin' up to your room with to propose to you, then—well, then the average whole-witted person wouldn't need more'n one guess. It couldn't be Labe, 'cause he'd been whisperin' in MY ear, so it must have been the other partner in the firm. That's all the miracle there is to it."

Albert's brain struggled with the situation. "I see," he said, after a moment. "She hinted that someone had been talking to you along the same line. Yes, and she was so sure you would agree. I might have known it was Laban."

"Um-hm, so you might. . . . Well, there have been times when if a man had talked to me as Labe did to-night I'd have knocked him down, or told him to go to—um—well, the tropics—told him to mind his own business, at least. But Labe is Labe, and besides MY conscience was plaguin' me a little mite, maybe . . . maybe."

The young man shook his head. "They must have talked it over, those two, and agreed that one should talk to you and the other to me. By George, I wonder they had the nerve. It wasn't their business, really."

"Not a darn bit."

"Yet—yet I—I'm awfully glad she said it to me. I—I needed it, I guess."

"Maybe you did, son. . . . And—humph—well, maybe I needed it, too. . . . Yes, I know that's consider'ble for me to say," he added dryly.

Albert was still thinking of Laban and Rachel.

"They're queer people," he mused. "When I first met them I thought they were about the funniest pair I ever saw. But—but now I can't help liking them and—and—Say, Grandfather, they must think a lot of your—of our family."

"Cal'late they do, son. . . . Well, boy, we've had our sermon, you and me, what shall we do? Willin' to sign for the five years trial cruise if I will, are you?"

Albert couldn't help smiling. "It was three years Rachel proposed, not five," he said.

"Was, eh? Suppose we split the difference and make it four? Willin' to try that?"

"Yes, sir."

"Agreement bein' that you shall stick close to Z. Snow and Co. durin' work hours and write as much poetry as you darned please other times, neither side to interfere with those arrangements? That right?"

"Yes, sir."

"Good! Shall we shake hands on it?"

They shook, solemnly. Captain Lote was the first to speak after ratification of the contract.

"There, now I cal'late I'll go aloft and turn in," he observed. Then he added, with a little hesitation, "Say, Al, maybe we'd better not trouble your grandma about all this fool business—the row this afternoon and all. 'Twould only worry her and—" he paused, looked embarrassed, cleared his throat, and said, "to tell you the truth, I'm kind of ashamed of my part—-er—er—that is, some of it."

His grandson was very much astonished. It was not often that Captain Zelotes Snow admitted having been in the wrong. He blurted out the question he had been dying to ask.

"Grandfather," he queried, "had you—did you really mean what you said about starting to come to my room and—and propose this scheme of ours—I mean of Rachel's and Labe's—to me?"

"Eh? . . . Ye-es—yes. I was on my way up there when I met you just now."

"Well, Grandfather, I—I—"

"That's all right, boy, that's all right. Don't let's talk any more about it."

"We won't. And—and—But, Grandfather, I just want you to know that I guess I understand things a little better than I did, and—and when my father—"

The captain's heavy hand descended upon his shoulder.

"Heave short, Al!" he commanded. "I've been doin' consider'ble thinkin' since Labe finished his—er—discourse and pronounced the benediction, and I've come to a pretty definite conclusion on one matter. I've concluded that you and I had better cut out all the bygones from this new arrangement of ours. We won't have fathers or—or—elopements—or past-and-done-with disapp'intments in it. This new deal—this four year trial v'yage of ours—will be just for Albert Speranza and Zelotes Snow, and no others need apply. . . . Eh? . . . Well, good night, Al."

CHAPTER VIII

So the game under the "new deal" began. At first it was much easier than the old. And, as a matter of fact, it was never as hard as before. The heart to heart talk between Captain Zelotes and his grandson had given each a glimpse of the other's inner self, a look from the other's point of view, and thereafter it was easier to make allowances. But the necessity for the making of those allowances was still there and would continue to be there. At first Albert made almost no mistakes in his bookkeeping, was almost painfully careful. Then the carefulness relaxed, as it was bound to do, and some mistakes occurred. Captain Lote found little fault, but at times he could not help showing some disappointment. Then his grandson would set his teeth and buckle down to painstaking effort again. He was resolved to live up to the very letter of the agreement.

In his spare time he continued to write and occasionally he sold something. Whenever he did so there was great rejoicing among the feminine members of the Snow household; his grandmother and Rachel Ellis were enraptured. It was amusing to see Captain Zelotes attempt to join the chorus. He evidently felt that he ought to praise, or at least that praise was expected from him, but it was also evident that he did not approve of what he was praising.

"Your grandma says you got rid of another one of your poetry pieces, Al," he would say. "Pay you for it, did they?"

"Not yet, but they will, I suppose."

"I see, I see. How much, think likely?"

"Oh, I don't know. Ten dollars, perhaps."

"Um-hm . . . I see. . . . Well, that's pretty good, considerin', I suppose. . . . We did first-rate on that Hyannis school-house contract, didn't we. Nigh's I can figger it we cleared over fourteen hundred and eighty dollars on that."

He invariably followed any reference to the profit from the sale of verses by the casual mention of a much larger sum derived from the sale of lumber or hardware. This was so noticeable that Laban Keeler was impelled to speak of it.

"The old man don't want you to forget that you can get more for hard pine than you can for soft sonnets, sellin' 'em both by the foot," observed Labe, peering over his spectacles. "More money in shingles than there is in jingles, he cal'lates.... Um.... Yes, yes.... Consider'ble more, consider'ble."

Albert smiled, but it astonished him to find that Mr. Keeler knew what a sonnet was. The little bookkeeper occasionally surprised him by breaking out unexpectedly in that way.

From the indiscriminate praise at home, or the reluctant praise of his grandfather, he found relief when he discussed his verses with Helen Kendall. Her praise was not indiscriminate, in fact sometimes she did not praise at all, but expressed disapproval. They had some disagreements, marked disagreements, but it did not affect their friendship. Albert was a trifle surprised to find that it did not.

So as the months passed he ground away at the books of Z. Snow and Company during office hours and at the poetry mill between times. The seeing of his name in print was no longer a novelty and he poetized not quite as steadily. Occasionally he attempted prose, but the two or three short stories of his composition failed to sell. Helen, however, urged him to try again and keep trying. "I know you can write a good story and some day you are going to," she said.

His first real literary success, that which temporarily lifted him into the outer circle of the limelight of fame, was a poem written the day following that upon which came the news of the sinking of the Lusitania. Captain Zelotes came back from the post-office that morning, a crumpled newspaper in his hand, and upon his face the look which mutinous foremast hands had seen there just before the mutiny ended. Laban Keeler was the first to notice the look. "For the land sakes, Cap'n, what's gone wrong?" he asked. The captain flung the paper upon the desk. "Read that," he grunted. Labe slowly spread open the paper; the big black headlines shrieked the crime aloud.

"Good God Almighty!" exclaimed the little bookkeeper. Captain Zelotes snorted. "He didn't have anything to do with it," he declared. "The bunch that pulled that off was handled from the other end of the line. And I wish to thunder I was young enough to help send 'em back there," he added, savagely.

That evening Albert wrote his poem. The next day he sent it to a Boston paper. It was published the following morning, spread across two columns on the front page, and before the month was over had been copied widely over the country. Within the fortnight its author received his first request, a bona fida request for verse from a magazine. Even Captain Lote's praise of the Lusitania poem was whole-hearted and ungrudging.

That summer was a busy one in South Harniss. There was the usual amount of summer gaiety, but in addition there were the gatherings of the various committees for war relief work. Helen belonged to many of these committees. There were dances and theatrical performances for the financial benefit of the various causes and here Albert shone. But he did not shine alone. Helen Kendall was very popular at the social gatherings, popular not only with the permanent residents but with the summer youth as well. Albert noticed this, but he did not notice it so particularly until Issy Price called his attention to it.

"Say, Al," observed Issy, one afternoon in late August of that year, "how do YOU like that Raymond young feller?"

Albert looked up absently from the page of the daybook.

"Eh? What?" he asked.

"I say how do YOU like that Eddie Raymond, the Down-at-the-Neck one?"

"Down at the neck? There's nothing the matter with his neck that I know of."

"Who said there was? He LIVES down to the Neck, don't he? I mean that young Raymond, son of the New York bank man, the ones that's had the Cahoon house all summer. How do you like him?"

Albert's attention was still divided between the day-book and Mr. Price. "Oh, I guess he's all right," he answered, carelessly. "I don't know him very well. Don't bother me, Issy, I'm busy."

Issachar chuckled. "He's busy, too," he observed. "He, he, he! He's busy trottin' after Helen Kendall. Don't seem to have time for much else these days. Noticed that, ain't you, Al? He, he!"

Albert had not noticed it. His attention left the day-book altogether. Issachar chuckled again.

"Noticed it, ain't you, Al?" he repeated. "If you ain't you're the only one. Everybody's cal'latin' you'll be cut out if you ain't careful. Folks used to figger you was Helen's steady comp'ny, but it don't look as much so as it did. He, he! That's why I asked you how you liked the Raymond one. Eh? How do you, Al? Helen, SHE seems to like him fust-rate. He, he, he!"

Albert was conscious of a peculiar feeling, partly of irritation at Issachar, partly something else. Mr. Price crowed delightedly.

"Hi!" he chortled. "Why, Al, your face is gettin' all redded up. Haw, haw! Blushin', ain't you, Al? Haw, haw, haw! Blushin', by crimustee!"

Albert laid down his pen. He had learned by experience that, in Issy's case, the maxim of the best defensive being a strong offensive was absolutely true. He looked with concern about the office.

"There's a window open somewhere, isn't there, Is?" he inquired. "There's a dreadful draught anyhow."

"Eh? Draught? I don't feel no draught. Course the window's open; it's generally open in summer time, ain't it. Haw, haw!"

"There it is again! Where—Oh, *I* see! It's your mouth that's open, Issy. That explains the draught, of course. Yes, yes, of course."

"Eh? My mouth! Never you mind my mouth. What you've got to think about is that Eddie Raymond. Yes sir-ee! Haw, haw!"

"Issy, what makes you make that noise?"

"What noise?"

"That awful cawing. If you're trying to make me believe you're a crow you're wasting your time."

"Say, look here, Al Speranzy, be you crazy?"

"No-o, I'M not. But in your case—well, I'll leave it to any fair-minded person—"

And so on until Mr. Price stamped disgustedly out of the office. It was easy enough, and required nothing brilliant in the way of strategy or repartee, to turn Issachar's attack into retreat. But all the rest of that afternoon Albert was conscious of that peculiar feeling of uneasiness. After supper that night he did not go down town at once but sat in his room thinking deeply. The subjects of his thoughts were Edwin Raymond, the young chap from New York, Yale, and "The Neck"—and Helen Kendall. He succeeded only in thinking himself into an even more uneasy and unpleasant state of mind. Then he walked moodily down to the post-office. He was a little late for the mail and the laughing and chatting groups were already coming back after its distribution. One such group he met was made up of half a dozen young people on their way to the drug store for ices and sodas. Helen was among them and with her was young Raymond. They called to him to join them, but he pretended not to hear.

Now, in all the years of their acquaintance it had not once occurred to Albert Speranza that his interest in Helen Kendall was anything more than that of a friend and comrade. He liked her, had enjoyed her society—when he happened to be in the mood to wish society—and it pleased him to feel that she was interested in his literary efforts and his career. She was the only girl in South Harniss who would have "talked turkey" to him as she had on the day of their adventure at High Point Light and he rather admired her for it. But in all his dreams of romantic attachments and sentimental adventure, and he had such dreams of course, she had never played a part. The heroines of these dreams were beautiful and mysterious strangers, not daughters of Cape Cod clergymen.

But now, thanks to Issy's mischievous hints, his feelings were in a puzzled and uncomfortable state. He was astonished to find that he did not relish the idea of Helen's being particularly interested in Ed Raymond. He, himself, had not seen her as frequently of late, she having been busy with her war work and he with his own interests. But that, according to his view, was no reason why she should permit Raymond to become friendly to the point of causing people to talk. He was not ready to admit that he himself cared, in a sentimental way, for Helen, but he resented any other fellow's daring to do so. And she should not have permitted it, either. As a matter of fact, Alberto Miguel Carlos Speranza, hitherto reigning undisputed king of hearts in South Harniss, was for the first time in his imperial life feeling the pangs of jealousy.

He stalked gloomily on to the post-office. Gertie Kendrick, on the arm of Sam Thatcher, passed him and he did not even notice her. Gertie whispered to Sam that he, Albert, was a big stuck-up nothing, but she looked back over Sam's shoulder, nevertheless. Albert climbed the post-office steps and walked over to the rack of letter boxes. The Snow box contained little of interest to him, and he was turning away when he heard his name spoken.

"Good evening, Mr. Speranza," said a feminine voice.

Albert turned again, to find Jane Kelsey and another young lady, a stranger, standing beside him. Miss Kelsey was one of South Harniss's summer residents. The Kelsey "cottage," which was larger by considerable than the Snow house, was situated on the Bay Road, the most exclusive section of the village. Once, and not so many years before, the Bay Road was contemptuously referred to as "Poverty Lane" and dwellers along its winding, weed-grown track vied with one another in shiftless shabbiness. But now all shabbiness had disappeared and many-gabled "cottages" proudly stood where the shanties of the Poverty Laners once humbly leaned.

Albert had known Jane Kelsey for some time. They had met at one of the hotel tea-dances during his second summer in South Harniss. He and she were not intimate friends exactly, her mother saw to that, but they were well acquainted. She was short and piquant, had a nose which freckled in the Cape Cod sunshine, and she talked and laughed easily.

"Good evening, Mr. Speranza," she said, again. "You looked so very forlorn I couldn't resist speaking. Do tell us why you are so sad; we're dying to know."

Albert, taken by surprise, stammered that he didn't know that he was sad. Miss Kelsey laughed merrily and declared that everyone who saw him knew it at once. "Oh, excuse me, Madeline," she added. "I forgot that you and Mr. Speranza had not met. Of course as you're going to live in South Harniss you must know him without waiting another minute. Everybody knows everybody down here. He is Albert Speranza—and we sometimes call him Albert because here everybody calls everyone else by their first names. There, now you know each other and it's all very proper and formal."

The young lady who was her companion smiled. The smile was distinctly worth looking at, as was the young lady herself, for that matter.

"I doubt if Mr. Speranza knows me very well, Jane," she observed.

"Doesn't know you! Why, you silly thing, haven't I just introduced you?"

"Well, I don't know much about South Harniss introductions, but isn't it customary to mention names? You haven't told him mine."

Miss Kelsey laughed in high delight. "Oh, how perfectly ridiculous!" she exclaimed. "Albert—Mr. Speranza, I mean—this is my friend Miss Madeline Fosdick. She is from New York and she has decided to spend her summers in South Harniss—which *I* consider very good judgment. Her father is going to build a cottage for her to spend them in down on the Bay Road on the hill at the corner above the Inlet. But of course you've heard of THAT!"

Of course he had. The purchase of the Inlet Hill land by Fletcher Fosdick, the New York banker, and the price paid Solomon Dadgett for that land, had been the principal topics of conversation around South Harniss supper tables for the past ten days. Captain Lote Snow had summed up local opinion of the transaction when he said: "We-ll, Sol Dadgett's been talkin' in prayer-meetin' ever since I can remember about the comin' of Paradise on earth. Judgin' by the price he got for the Inlet Hill sand heap he must have cal'lated Paradise had got here and he was sellin' the golden streets by the runnin' foot." Or, as Laban Keeler put it: "They say King Soloman was a wise man, but I guess likely 'twas a good thing for him that Sol Dadgett wasn't alive in his time. King Sol would have needed all his wisdom to keep Dadgett from talkin' him into buying the Jerusalem salt-ma'sh to build the temple on. . . . Um. . . . Yes—yes—yes."

So Albert, as he shook hands with Miss Fosdick, regarded her with unusual interest. And, judging by the way in which she looked at him, she too was interested. After some minutes of the usual conventional summertime chat the young gentleman suggested that they adjourn to the drug store for refreshments. The invitation was accepted, the vivacious Miss Kelsey acting as spokesman—or spokeswoman—in the matter.

"I think you must be a mind-reader, Mr. Speranza," she declared. "I am dying for a sundae and I have just discovered that I haven't my purse or a penny with me. I should have been reduced to the humiliation of borrowing from Madeline here, or asking that deaf old Burgess man to trust me until to-morrow. And he is so frightfully deaf," she added in explanation, "that when I asked him the last time he made me repeat it until I thought I should die of shame, or exhaustion, one or the other. Every time I shouted he would say 'Hey?' and I was obliged to shout again. Of course, the place was crowded, and—Oh, well, I don't like to even think about it. Bless you, bless you, Albert Speranza! And do please let's hurry!"

When they entered the drug store—it also sold, according to its sign, "Cigars, soda, ice-cream, patent medicines, candy, knick-knacks, chewing gum, souvenirs and notions"—the sextette of which Helen Kendall made one was just leaving. She nodded pleasantly to Albert and he nodded in return, but Ed Raymond's careless bow he did not choose to see. He had hitherto rather liked that young gentleman; now he felt a sudden but violent detestation for him.

Sundaes pleasant to the palate and disastrous to all but youthful digestions were ordered. Albert's had a slight flavor of gall and wormwood, but he endeavored to counterbalance this by the sweetness derived from the society of Jane Kelsey and her friend. His conversation was particularly brilliant and sparkling that evening. Jane laughed much and chatted more. Miss Fosdick was quieter, but she, too, appeared to be enjoying herself. Jane demanded to know how the poems were developing. She begged him to have an inspiration now—"Do, PLEASE, so that Madeline and I can see you." It seemed to be her idea that having an inspiration was similar to having a fit. Miss Fosdick laughed at this, but she declared that she adored poetry and specified certain poems which were objects of her especial adoration. The conversation thereafter became what Miss Kelsey described as "high brow," and took the form of a dialogue between Miss Fosdick and Albert. It was interrupted by the arrival of the Kelsey limousine, which rolled majestically up to the drug store steps. Jane spied it first.

"Oh, mercy me, here's mother!" she exclaimed. "And your mother, too, Madeline. We are tracked to our lair.... No, no, Mr. Speranza, you mustn't go out. No, really, we had rather you wouldn't. Thanks, ever so much, for the sundaes. Come, Madeline."

Miss Fosdick held out her hand.

"Thank you, Mr. Speranza," she said. "I have enjoyed our poetry talk SO much. It must be wonderful to write as you do. Good night."

She looked admiringly into his eyes as she said it. In spite of the gall and wormwood Albert found it not at all unpleasant to be looked at in that way by a girl like Madeline Fosdick. His reflections on that point were interrupted by a voice from the car.

"Come, Madeline, come," it said, fussily. "What ARE you waiting for?"

Albert caught a glimpse of a majestic figure which, seated beside Mrs. Kelsey on the rear seat of the limousine, towered above that short, plump lady as a dreadnaught towers above a coal barge. He surmised this figure to be that of the maternal Fosdick. Madeline climbed in beside her parent and the limousine rolled away.

Albert's going-to-bed reflections that evening were divided in flavor, like a fruit sundae, a combination of sweet and sour. The sour was furnished by thoughts of Edwin Raymond and Helen Kendall, the former's presumption in daring to seek her society as he did, and Helen's amazing silliness in permitting such a thing. The sweet, of course, was furnished by a voice which repeated to his memory the words, "It must be wonderful to write as you do." Also the tone of that voice and the look in the eyes.

Could he have been privileged to hear the closing bits of a conversation which was taking place at that moment his reflections might have been still further saccharined. Miss Jane Kelsey was saying: "And NOW what do you think of our Cape Cod poet? Didn't I promise you to show you something you couldn't find on Fifth Avenue?" And to this Miss Madeline Fosdick made reply: "I think he is the handsomest creature I ever saw. And so clever! Why, he is wonderful, Jane! How in the world does he happen to be living here—all the time?"

It is perhaps, on the whole, a good thing that Albert Speranza could not hear this. It is certainly a good thing that Captain Zelotes Snow did not hear it.

And although the balance of sweet and sour in Albert's mind that night was almost even, the sour predominated next day and continued to predominate. Issachar Price had sowed the seed of jealousy in the mind of the assistant bookkeeper of Z. Snow and Company, and that seed took root and grew as it is only too likely to do under such circumstances. That evening Albert walked again to the post-office. Helen was not there, neither was Miss Kelsey or Miss Fosdick. He waited for a time and then determined to call at the Kendall home, something he had not done for some time. As he came up to the front walk, between the arbor-vitae hedges, he saw that the parlor windows were alight. The window shade was but partially drawn and beneath it he could see into the room. Helen was seated at the piano and Edwin Raymond was standing beside her, ready to turn the page of her music.

Albert whirled on his heel and walked out of the yard and down the street toward his own home. His attitude of mind was a curious one. He had a mind to wait until Raymond left and then go into the Kendall parlor and demand of Helen to know what she meant by letting that fellow make such a fool of himself. What right had he—Raymond—to call upon her, and turn her music and—and set the whole town talking? Why—Oh, he could think of many things to ask and say. The trouble was that the saying of them would, he felt sure, be distinctly bad diplomacy on his part. No one—not even he—could talk to Helen Kendall in that fashion; not unless he wished it to be their final conversation.

So he went home, to fret and toss angrily and miserably half the night. He had never before considered himself in the slightest degree in love with Helen, but he had taken for granted the thought that she liked him better than anyone else. Now he was beginning to fear that perhaps she did not, and, with his temperament, wounded vanity and poetic imagination supplied the rest. Within a fortnight he considered himself desperately in love with her.

During this fortnight he called at the parsonage, the Kendall home, several times. On the first of these occasions the Reverend Mr. Kendall, having just completed a sermon dealing with the war and, being full of his subject, read the said sermon to his daughter and to Albert. The reading itself lasted for three-quarters of an hour and Mr. Kendall's post-argument and general dissertation on German perfidy another hour after that. By that time it was late and Albert went home. The second call was even worse, for Ed Raymond called also and the two young men glowered at each other until ten o'clock. They might have continued to glower indefinitely, for neither meant to leave before the other, but Helen announced that she had some home-study papers to look over and she knew they would excuse her under the circumstances. On that hint they departed simultaneously, separating at the gate and walking with deliberate dignity in opposite directions.

At his third attempt, however, Albert was successful to the extent that Helen was alone when he called and there was no school work to interrupt.

But in no other respect was the interview satisfactory. All that week he had been boiling with the indignation of the landed proprietor who discovers a trespasser on his estate, and before this call was fifteen minutes old his feelings had boiled over.

"What IS the matter with you, Al?" asked Helen. "Do tell me and let's see if I can't help you out of your trouble."

Her visitor flushed. "Trouble?" he repeated, stiffly. "I don't know what you mean."

"Oh yes, do. You must. What IS the matter?"

"There is nothing the matter with me."

"Nonsense! Of course there is. You have scarcely spoken a word of your own accord since you came, and you have been scowling like a thundercloud all the time. Now what is it? Have I done something you don't like?"

"There is nothing the matter, I tell you."

"Please don't be so silly. Of course there is. I thought there must be something wrong the last time you were here, that evening, when Ed called, too. It seemed to me that you were rather queer then. Now you are queerer still. What is it?"

This straightforward attack, although absolutely characteristic of Helen, was disconcerting. Albert met it by an attack of his own.

"Helen," he demanded, "what does that Raymond fellow mean by coming to see you as he does?"

Now whether or not Helen was entirely in the dark as to the cause of her visitor's "queerness" is a question not to be answered here. She was far from being a stupid young person and it is at least probable that she may have guessed a little of the truth. But, being feminine, she did not permit Albert to guess that she had guessed. If her astonishment at the question was not entirely sincere, it certainly appeared to be so.

"What does he mean?" she repeated. "What does he mean by coming to see me? Why, what do YOU mean? I should think that was the question. Why shouldn't he come to see me, pray?"

Now Albert has a dozen reasons in his mind, each of which was to him sufficiently convincing. But expressing those reasons to Helen Kendall he found singularly difficult. He grew confused and stammered.

"Well—well, because he has no business to come here so much," was the best he could do. Helen, strange to say, was not satisfied.

"Has no business to?" she repeated. "Why, of course he has. I asked him to come."

"You did? Good heavens, you don't LIKE him, do you?"

"Of course I like him. I think he is a very nice fellow. Don't you?"

"No, I don't."

"Why not?"

"Well—well, because I don't, that's all. He has no business to monopolize you all the time. Why, he is here about every night in the week, or you're out with him, down town, or—or somewhere. Everybody is talking about it and—"

"Wait a minute, please. You say everybody is talking about Ed Raymond and me. What do you mean by that? What are they saying?"

"They're saying. . . . Oh, they're saying you and he are—are—"

"Are what?"

"Are—are—Oh, they're saying all sorts of things. Look here, Helen, I—"

"Wait! I want to know more about this. What have you heard said about me?"

"Oh, a lot of things. . . . That is—er—well, nothing in particular, perhaps, but—"

"Wait! Who have you heard saying it?"

"Oh, never mind! Helen—"

"But I do mind. Who have you heard saying this 'lot of things' about me?"

"Nobody, I tell you. . . . Oh, well, if you must know, Issy Price said—well, he said you and this Raymond fellow were what he called 'keeping company' and—and that the whole town was talking about it."

She slowly shook her head.

"Issy Price!" she repeated. "And you listened to what Issy Price said. Issy Price, of all people!"

"Well—well, he said everyone else said the same thing."

"Did he say more than that?"

"No, but that was enough, wasn't it. Besides, the rest was plain. I could see it myself. He is calling here about every night in the week, and—and being around everywhere with you and—and—Oh, anyone can see!"

Helen's usually placid temper was beginning to ruffle.

"Very well," she said, "then they may see. Why shouldn't he call here if he wishes—and I wish? Why shouldn't I be 'around with him,' as you say? Why not?"

"Well, because I don't like it. It isn't the right thing for you to do. You ought to be more careful of—of what people say."

He realized, almost as soon as this last sentence was blurted out, the absolute tactlessness of it. The quiet gleam of humor he had so often noticed in Helen's eyes was succeeded now by a look he had never before seen there.

"Oh, I'm sorry," he added, hastily. "I beg your pardon, Helen. I didn't mean to say that. Forgive me, will you?"

She did not answer immediately. Then she said, "I don't know whether I shall or not. I think I shall have to think it over. And perhaps you had better go now."

"But I'M sorry, Helen. It was a fool thing to say. I don't know why I was such an idiot. Do forgive me; come!"

She slowly shook her head. "I can't—yet," she said. "And this you must understand: If Ed Raymond, or anyone else, calls on me and I choose to permit it, or if I choose to go out with him anywhere at any time, that is my affair and not 'everyone else's'—which includes Issachar Price. And my FRIENDS—my real friends—will not listen to mean, ridiculous gossip. Good night."

So that was the end of that attempt at asserting the Divine Right by the South Harniss king of hearts. Albert was more miserable than ever, angrier than ever—not only at Raymond and Helen, but at himself—and his newly-discovered jealousy burned with a brighter and greener flame. The idea of throwing everything overboard, going to Canada and enlisting in the Canadian Army—an idea which had had a strong and alluring appeal ever since the war broke out—came back with redoubled force. But there was the agreement with his grandfather. He had given his word; how could he break it? Besides, to go away and leave his rival with a clear field did not appeal to him, either.

On a Wednesday evening in the middle of September the final social event of the South Harniss summer season was to take place. The Society for the Relief of the French Wounded was to give a dance in the ballroom of the hotel, the proceeds from the sale of tickets to be devoted to the purpose defined by the name of this organization. Every last member of the summer colony was to attend, of course, and all those of the permanent residents who aspired to social distinction and cared to pay the high price of admission.

Albert was going, naturally. That is, he had at first planned to go, then—after the disastrous call at the parsonage—decided that he would go under no circumstances, and at the last changed his mind once more to the affirmative. Miss Madeline Fosdick, Jane Kelsey's friend, was responsible for the final change. She it was who had sold him his ticket and urged him to be present. He and she had met several times since the first meeting at the post-office. Usually when they met they talked concerning poetry and kindred lofty topics. Albert liked Miss Fosdick. It is hard not to like a pretty, attractive young lady who takes such a flattering interest in one's aspirations and literary efforts. The "high brow chit-chats"—quoting Miss Kelsey again—were pleasant in many ways; for instance, they were in the nature of a tonic for weakened self-esteem, and the Speranza self-esteem was suffering just at this time, from shock.

Albert had, when he first heard that the dance was to take place, intended inviting Helen to accompany him. He had taken her acceptance for granted, he having acted as her escort to so many dances and social affairs. So he neglected inviting her and then came Issy's mischief-making remarks and the trouble which followed. So, as inviting her was out of the question, he resolved not to attend, himself. But Miss Fosdick urged so prettily that he bought his ticket and promised to be among those present.

"Provided, of course," he ventured, being in a reckless mood, "that you save me at least four dances." She raised her brows in mock dismay.

"Oh, my goodness!" she exclaimed. "I'm afraid I couldn't do that. Four is much too many. One I will promise, but no more."

However, as he persisted, she yielded another. He was to have two dances and, possibly an "extra."

"And you are a lucky young man," declared Jane Kelsey, who had also promised two. "If you knew how many fellows have begged for just one. But, of course," she added, "THEY were not poets, second editions of Tennyson and Keats and all that. It is Keats who was the poet, isn't it, Madeline?" she added, turning to her friend. "Oh, I'm so glad I got it right the first time. I'm always mixing him up with Watts, the man who invented the hymns and wrote the steam-engine—or something."

The Wednesday evening in the middle of September was a beautiful one and the hotel was crowded. The Item, in its account the following week, enumerating those present, spoke of "Our new residents, Mrs. Fletcher Story Fosdick and Miss Madeline Fosdick, who are to occupy the magnificent residence now about being built on the Inlet Hill by their husband and father, respectively, Fletcher Story Fosdick, Esquire, the well-known New York banker." The phrasing of this news note caused much joy in South Harniss, and the Item gained several new and hopeful subscribers.

But when the gushing reporter responsible for this added that "Miss Fosdick was a dream of loveliness on this occasion" he was stating only the truth. She was very beautiful indeed and a certain young man who stepped up to claim his first dance realized the fact. The said young man was outwardly cool, but red-hot within, the internal rise in temperature being caused by the sight of Helen Kendall crossing the floor arm in arm with Edwin Raymond. Albert's face was white with anger, except for two red spots on his cheeks, and his black eyes flashed. Consequently he, too, was considered quite worth the looking at and feminine glances followed him.

"Who is that handsome, foreign-looking fellow your friend is dancing with?" whispered one young lady, a guest at the hotel, to Miss Kelsey. Jane told her.

"But he isn't a foreigner," she added. "He lives here in South Harniss all the year. He is a poet, I believe, and Madeline, who knows about such things—inherits it from her mother, I suppose—says his poetry is beautiful."

Her companion watched the subject of their conversation as, with Miss Fosdick, he moved lightly and surely through the crowd on the floor.

"He LOOKS like a poet," she said, slowly. "He is wonderfully handsome, so distinguished, and SUCH a dancer! But why should a poet live here—all the year? Is that all he does for a living—write poetry?"

Jane pretended not to hear her and, a masculine friend coming to claim his dance, seized the opportunity to escape. However, another "sitter out" supplied the information.

"He is a sort of assistant bookkeeper at the lumber yard by the railroad station," said this person. "His grandfather owns the place, I believe. One would never guess it to look at him now. . . . Humph! I wonder if Mrs. Fosdick knows. They say she is—well, not democratically inclined, to say the least."

Albert had his two promised dances with Madeline Fosdick, but the "extra" he did not obtain. Mrs. Fosdick, the ever watchful, had seen and made inquiries. Then she called her daughter to her and issued an ultimatum.

"I am SO sorry," said the young lady, in refusing the plea for the "extra." "I should like to, but I—but Mother has asked me to dance with a friend of ours from home. I—I AM sorry, really."

She looked as if she meant it. Albert was sorry, too. This had been a strange evening, another combination of sweet and sour. He glanced across the floor and saw Helen and the inevitable Raymond emerge together from the room where the refreshments were served. Raging jealousy seized him at the sight. Helen had not been near him, had scarcely spoken to him since his arrival. He forgot that he had not been near nor spoken to her.

He danced twice or thrice more with acquaintances, "summer" or permanent, and then decided to go home. Madeline Fosdick he saw at the other end of the room surrounded by a group of young masculinity. Helen he could not see at the moment. He moved in the direction of the coatroom. Just as he reached the door he was surprised to see Ed Raymond stride by him, head down and looking anything but joyful. He watched and was still more astonished to see the young man get his coat and hat from the attendant and walk out of the hotel. He saw him stride away along the drive and down the moonlit road. He was, apparently, going home—going home alone.

He got his own coat and hat and, before putting them on, stepped back for a final look at the ballroom. As he stood by the cloakroom door someone touched his arm. Turning he saw Helen.

"Why—why, Helen!" he exclaimed, in surprise.

"Are you going home?" she asked, in a low tone.

"Yes, I—"

"And you are going alone?"

"Yes."

"Would you mind—would it trouble you too much to walk with me as far as our house?"

"Why—why of course not. I shall be delighted. But I thought you—I thought Ed Raymond—"

"No, I'm alone. Wait here; I will be ready in just a minute."

She hurried away. He gazed after her in bewilderment. She and he had scarcely exchanged a word during the evening, and now, when the evening was almost over, she came and asked him to be her escort. What in the wide world—?

The minute she had specified had hardly elapsed when she reappeared, ready for out of doors. She took his arm and they walked down the steps of the hotel, past the group of lights at the head of the drive and along the road, with the moon shining down upon it and the damp, salt breeze from the ocean blowing across it. They walked for the first few minutes in silence. There were a dozen questions he would have liked to ask, but his jealous resentment had not entirely vanished and his pride forbade. It was she who spoke first.

"Albert," she said, "you must think this very odd."

He knew what she meant, but he did not choose to admit it.

"What?" he asked.

"Why, my asking you to walk home with me, after—after our trouble. It is strange, I suppose, particularly as you had not spoken before this whole evening."

"*I*—spoken to YOU? Why, you bowed to me when I came into the room and that was the only sign of recognition you gave me until just now. Not a dance—not one."

"Did you expect me to look you up and beg you to dance with me?"

"Did you expect me to trot at that fellow's heels and wait my chance to get a word with you, to take what he left? I should say not! By George, Helen, I—"

She interrupted him. "Hush, hush!" she pleaded. "This is all so silly, so childish. And we mustn't quarrel any more. I have made up my mind to that. We mustn't."

"Humph! All right, *I* had no thought of quarreling in the beginning. But there are some things a self-respecting chap can't stand. I have SOME pride, I hope."

She caught her breath quickly. "Do you think," she asked, "that it was no sacrifice to my pride to beg you to walk home with me? After—after the things you said the other evening? Oh, Albert, how could you say them!"

"Well—" he hesitated, and then added, "I told you I was sorry."

"Yes, but you weren't really sorry. You must have believed the things that hateful Issachar Price said or you wouldn't have repeated them. . . . Oh, but never mind that now, I didn't mean to speak of it at all. I asked you to walk home with me because I wanted to make up our quarrel. Yes, that was it. I didn't want to go away and feel that you and I were not as good friends as ever. So, you see, I put all MY pride to one side—and asked."

One phrase in one sentence of this speech caught and held the young man's attention. He forgot the others.

"You are going away?" he repeated. "What do you mean? Where are you going?"

"I am going to Cambridge to study. I am going to take some courses at Radcliffe. You know I told you I hoped to some day. Well, it has been arranged. I am to live with my cousin, father's half sister in Somerville. Father is well enough to leave now and I have engaged a capable woman, Mrs. Peters, to help Maria with the housework. I am going Friday morning, the day after to-morrow."

He stopped short to stare at her.

"You are going away?" he asked, again. "You are going to do that and — and — Why didn't you tell me before?"

It was a characteristic return to his attitude of outraged royalty. She had made all these plans, had arranged to do this thing, and he had not been informed. At another time Helen might have laughed at him; she generally did when he became what she called the "Grand Bashaw." She did not laugh now, however, but answered quietly.

"I didn't know I was going to do it until a little more than a week ago," she said. "And I have not seen you since then."

"No, you've been too busy seeing someone else."

She lost patience for the instant. "Oh, don't, don't, don't!" she cried. "I know who you mean, of course. You mean Ed Raymond. Don't you know why he has been at the house so much of late? Why he and I have been so much together? Don't you really know?"

"What? . . . No, I don't—except that you and he wanted to be together."

"And it didn't occur to you that there might be some other reason? You forgot, I suppose, that he and I were appointed on the Ticket Committee for this very dance?"

He had forgotten it entirely. Now he remembered perfectly the meeting of the French Relief Society at which the appointment had been made. In fact Helen herself had told him of it at the time. For the moment he was staggered, but he rallied promptly.

"Committee meetings may do as an excuse for some things," he said, "but they don't explain the rest—his calls here every other evening and— and so on. Honest now, Helen, you know he hasn't been running after you in this way just because he is on that committee with you; now don't you?"

They were almost at the parsonage. The light from Mr. Kendall's study window shone through the leaves of the lilac bush behind the white fence. Helen started to speak, but hesitated. He repeated his question.

"Now don't you?" he urged.

"Why, why, yes, I suppose I do," she said, slowly. "I do know—now. But I didn't even think of such a thing until—until you came that evening and told me what Issy Price said."

"You mean you didn't guess at all?"

"Well—well, perhaps I—I thought he liked to come—liked to—Oh, what is the use of being silly! I did think he liked to call, but only as a friend. He was jolly and lots of fun and we were both fond of music. I enjoyed his company. I never dreamed that there was anything more than that until you came and were so—disagreeable. And even then I didn't believe—until to-night."

Again she hesitated. "To-night?" he repeated. "What happened to-night?"

"Oh nothing. I can't tell you. Oh, why can't friends be friends and not. . . . That is why I spoke to you, Albert, why I wanted to have this talk with you. I was going away so soon and I couldn't bear to go with any unfriendliness between us. There mustn't be. Don't you see?"

He heard but a part of this. The memory of Raymond's face as he had seen it when the young man strode out of the cloakroom and out of the hotel came back to him and with it a great heart-throbbing sense of relief, of triumph. He seized her hand.

"Helen," he cried, "did he—did you tell him—Oh, by George, Helen, you're the most wonderful girl in the world! I'm—I—Oh, Helen, you know I—I—"

It was not his habit to be at a loss for words, but he was just then. He tried to retain her hand, to put his arm about her.

"Oh, Helen!" he cried. "You're wonderful! You're splendid! I'm crazy about you! I really am! I—"

She pushed him gently away. "Don't! Please don't!" she said. "Oh, don't!"

"But I must. Don't you see I. . . . Why, you're crying!"

Her face had, for a moment, been upturned. The moon at that moment had slipped behind a cloud, but the lamplight from the window had shown him the tears in her eyes. He was amazed. He could have shouted, have laughed aloud from joy or triumphant exultation just then, but to weep! What occasion was there for tears, except on Ed Raymond's part?

"You're crying!" he repeated. "Why, Helen—!"

"Don't!" she said, again. "Oh, don't! Please don't talk that way."

"But don't you want me to, Helen? I—I want you to know how I feel. You don't understand. I—"

"Hush! . . . Don't, Al, don't, please. Don't talk in that way. I don't want you to."

"But why not?"

"Oh, because I don't. It's—it is foolish. You're only a boy, you know."

"A boy! I'm more than a year older than you are."

"Are you? Why yes, I suppose you are, really. But that doesn't make any difference. I guess girls are older than boys when they are our age, lots older."

"Oh, bother all that! We aren't kids, either of us. I want you to listen. You don't understand what I'm trying to say."

"Yes, I do. But I'm sure you don't. You are glad because you have found you have no reason to be jealous of Ed Raymond and that makes you say— foolish things. But I'm not going to have our friendship spoiled in that way. I want us to be real friends, always. So you mustn't be silly."

"I'm not silly. Helen, if you won't listen to anything else, will you listen to this? Will you promise me that while you are away you won't have other fellows calling on you or—or anything like that? And I'll promise you that I'll have nothing to say to another girl—in any way that counts, I mean. Shall we promise each other that, Helen? Come!"

She paused for some moment before answering, but her reply, when it came, was firm.

"No," she said, "I don't think we should promise anything, except to remain friends. You might promise and then be sorry, later."

"*I* might? How about you?"

"Perhaps we both might. So we won't take the risk. You may come and see me to-morrow evening and say good-by, if you like. But you mustn't stay long. It is my last night with father for some time and I mustn't cheat him out of it. Good night, Albert. I'm so glad our misunderstanding is over, aren't you?"

"Of course I am. But, Helen—"

"I must go in now. Good night."

The reflections of Alberto Speranza during his walk back to the Snow place were varied but wonderful. He thought of Raymond's humiliation and gloried in it. He thought of Helen and rhapsodized. And if, occasionally, he thought also of the dance and of Madeline Fosdick, forgive him. He was barely twenty-one and the moon was shining.

CHAPTER IX

The good-by call the following evening was, to him at least, not very satisfactory. Helen was tired, having been busy all day with the final preparations for leaving, and old Mr. Kendall insisted on being present during the entire visit and in telling long and involved stories of the trip abroad he had made when a young man and the unfavorable opinion which he had then formed of Prussians as traveling companions. Albert's opinion of Prussians was at least as unfavorable as his own, but his complete and even eager agreement with each of the old gentleman's statements did not have the effect of choking the latter off, but rather seemed to act as encouragement for more. When ten o'clock came and it was time to go Albert felt as if he had been listening to a lecture on the Hohenzollerns. "Great Scott, Helen," he whispered, as she came to the door with him, "I don't feel as if I had talked with you a minute. Why, I scarcely—"

But just here Mr. Kendall came hurrying from the sitting-room to tell of one incident which he had hitherto forgotten, and so even this brief interval of privacy was denied. But Albert made one more attempt.

"I'm going to run over to the station to-morrow morning to see you off," he called from the gate. "Good night."

The morning train left at nine o'clock, and at a quarter to nine Albert, who had kept his eye on the clock ever since eight, his hour of arriving at the office, called to Mr. Price.

"I say," he said, in a low tone and one as casual as he could assume, "I am going to run out for a few minutes. I'll be right back."

Issachar's response was as usual anything but low.

"Eh?" he shouted. "Goin' out? Where you goin'?"

"Oh, I'm just going out—er—on an errand."

"What kind of an errand? I was cal'latin' to run out myself for a little spell. Can't I do your errand for you?"

"No, no... There, there, don't bother me any more. I'm in a hurry."

"Hurry! So'm I in a hurry. I was cal'latin' to run acrost to the deepo and see Helen Kendall start for Boston. She's goin' this morning; did you know it?"

Before the somewhat flustered assistant bookkeeper could reply Captain Zelotes called from the inner office:

"Wouldn't wonder if that was where Al was bound, too," he observed. "And I was thinkin' of the same thing. Suppose we all go together. Labe'll keep shop, won't you, Labe?"

Mr. Keeler looked over his spectacles. "Eh?" he observed. "Oh, yes, yes . . . yes, yes, yes. And say good-by to Helen for me, some of you, if you happen to think of it. Not that 'twill make much difference to her," he added, "whether she gets my good-bys or not, but it might make some to me. . . . Um, yes, yes."

Mr. Price was eager to oblige.

"I'll tell her you sent 'em, Labe," he said, patronizingly. "Set your mind to rest; I'll tell her."

Laban's lip twitched. "Much obliged, Is," he chirruped. "That's a great relief! My mind's rested some already."

So, instead of going alone to the railway station, Albert made one of a delegation of three. And at the station was Mr. Kendall, and two of the school committee, and one or two members of the church sewing circle, and the president and secretary of the Society for the Relief of the French Wounded. So far from being an intimate confidential farewell, Helen's departure was in the nature of a public ceremony with speech-making. Mr. Price made most of the speeches, in fact the lower portion of his countenance was in violent motion most of the ten minutes.

"Take care of yourself, Helen," he urged loudly. "Don't you worry about your pa, we'll look out for him. And don't let none of them Boston fellers carry you off. We'll watch and see that Eddie Raymond and Al here don't get into mischief while you're gone. I . . . Crimustee! Jim Young, what in time's the matter with you? Can't ye see nothin'?"

This last outburst was directed at the driver of the depot-wagon, who, wheeling a trunk on a baggage truck, had bumped violently into the rear of Mr. Price's legs, just at the knee joint, causing their owner to bend backward unexpectedly, and with enthusiasm.

"Can't you see nothin' when it's right in front of ye?" demanded Issachar, righteously indignant.

Jim Young winked over his shoulder at Albert. "Sorry, Is," he said, as he continued toward the baggage car. "I didn't notice you WAS in front of me."

"Well, then, you'd better. . . . Eh? See here, what do you mean by that?"

Even after Mr. Price had thus been pushed out of the foreground, so to speak, Albert was denied the opportunity of taking his place by Helen's side. Her father had a few last messages to deliver, then Captain Zelotes shook her hand and talked for a moment, and, after that, the ladies of the sewing circle and the war work society felt it their duty to, severally and jointly, kiss her good-by. This last was a trying operation to watch.

Then the engine bell rang and the train began to move. Albert, running beside the platform of the last car, held up his hand for a farewell clasp.

"Good-by," he said, and added in a whisper, "You'll write, won't you?"

"Of course. And so must you. Good-by."

The last car and the handkerchief waving figure on its platform disappeared around the curve. The little group by the station broke up. Albert and his grandfather walked over to the office together.

"There goes a good girl, Al," was Captain Lote's only comment. "A mighty good capable girl."

Albert nodded. A moment later he lifted his hat to a group in a passing automobile.

"Who were those folks?" asked the Captain.

"The Fosdicks," was the reply. "The people who are going to build down by the Inlet."

It was Madeline and her mother. The latter had been serenely indifferent, but the young lady had smiled and bowed behind the maternal shoulders.

"Oh; that so?" observed Captain Zelotes, looking after the flying car with interest. "That's who 'tis, eh? Nice lookin', the young one, ain't she?"

Albert did not answer. With the noise of the train which was carrying Helen out of his life still ringing in his ears it seemed wicked even to mention another girl's name, to say nothing of commenting upon her good looks. For the rest of that day he was a gloomy spirit, a dark shadow in the office of Z. Snow and Co.

Before the end of another fortnight the season at South Harniss was definitely over. The hotel closed on the Saturday following the dance, and by October first the last of the cottages was locked and shuttered. The Kelseys went on the twentieth and the Fosdicks went with them. Albert met Madeline and Jane at the post-office in the evening of the nineteenth and there more farewells were said.

"Don't forget us down here in the sand, will you?" he suggested to Miss Fosdick. It was Jane Kelsey who answered.

"Oh, she won't forget," returned that young lady. "Why she has your photograph to remember you by."

Madeline colored becomingly and was, as Jane described it, "awfully fussed."

"Nonsense!" she exclaimed, with much indignation, "I haven't any such thing. You know I haven't, Jane."

"Yes, you have, my dear. You have a photograph of him standing in front of the drug store and looking dreamily in at—at the strawberry sundaes. It is a most romantic pose, really."

Albert laughed. He remembered the photograph. It was one of a series of snapshots taken with Miss Kelsey's camera one Saturday afternoon when a party of young people had met in front of the sundae dispensary. Jane had insisted on "snapping" everyone.

"That reminds me that I have never seen the rest of those photographs," he said.

"Haven't you?" exclaimed Jane. "Well, you ought to see them. I have Madeline's with me. It is a dream, if I do say it as I took it."

She produced the snapshot, which showed her friend standing beside the silver-leaf tree before the druggist's window and smiling at the camera. It was a good likeness and, consequently, a very pretty picture.

"Isn't it a dream, just as I said?" demanded the artist. "Honest now, isn't it?"

Albert of course declared it to be beyond praise.

"May I have this one?" he asked, on the impulse of the moment.

"Don't ask me, stupid," commanded Jane, mischievously. "It isn't my funeral—or my portrait, either."

"May I?" he repeated, turning to Madeline. She hesitated.

"Why—why yes, you may, if you care for it," she said. "That particular one is Jane's, anyway, and if she chooses to give it away I don't see how I can prevent her. But why you should want the old thing I can't conceive. I look as stiff and wooden as a sign-post."

Jane held up a protesting finger.

"Fibs, fibs, fibs," she observed. "Can't conceive why he should want it! As if you weren't perfectly aware that he will wear it next his heart and— Oh, don't put it in THAT pocket! I said next your heart, and that isn't on your RIGHT side."

Albert took the photograph home and stuck it between the frame and glass of his bureau. Then came a sudden remembrance of his parting with Helen and with it a twinge of conscience. He had begged her to have nothing to do with any other fellow. True she had refused to promise and consequently he also was unbound, but that made no difference—should not make any. So he put the photograph at the back of the drawer where he kept his collars and ties, with a resolve never to look at it. He did not look at it—very often.

Then came another long winter. He ground away at the bookkeeping—he was more proficient at it, but he hated it as heartily as ever—and wrote a good deal of verse and some prose. For the first time he sold a prose article, a short story, to a minor magazine. He wrote long letters to Helen and she replied. She was studying hard, she liked her work, and she had been offered the opportunity to tutor in a girls' summer camp in Vermont during July and August and meant to accept provided her father's health continued good. Albert protested violently against her being absent from South Harniss for so long. "You will scarcely be home at all," he wrote. "I shall hardly see you. What am I going to do? As it is now I miss you—" and so on for four closely written pages. Having gotten into the spirit of composition he, so to speak, gloried in his loneliness, so much so that Helen was moved to remonstrate. "Your letter made me almost miserable," she wrote, "until I had read it over twice. Then I began to suspect that you were enjoying your wretchedness, or enjoying writing about it. I truly don't believe anyone—you especially—could be quite as lonesome as all that. Honestly now, Albert, weren't you exaggerating a little? I rather think you were?"

He had been, of course, but it irritated him to think that she recognized the fact. She had an uncanny faculty of seeing through his every pretense. In his next letter he said nothing whatever about being lonesome.

At home, and at the office, the war was what people talked about most of the time. Since the Lusitania's sinking Captain Zelotes had been a battle charger chafing at the bit. He wanted to fight and to fight at once.

"We've got to do it, Mother," he declared, over and over again. "Sooner or later we've got to fight that Kaiser gang. What are we waitin' for; will somebody tell me that?"

Olive, as usual, was mild and unruffled.

"Probably the President knows as much about it as you and me, Zelotes," she suggested. "I presume likely he has his own reasons."

"Humph! When Seth Bassett got up in the night and took a drink out of the bottle of Paris Green by mistake 'Bial Cahoon asked him what in time he kept Paris Green in his bedroom for, anyhow. All that Seth would say was that he had his own reasons. The rest of the town was left to guess what those reasons was. That's what the President's doin'—keepin' us guessin'. By the everlastin', if I was younger I'd ship aboard a British lime-juicer and go and fight, myself!"

It was Rachel Ellis who caused the Captain to be a bit more restrained in his remarks.

"You hadn't ought to talk that way, Cap'n Lote," she said. "Not when Albert's around, you hadn't."

"Eh? Why not?"

"Because the first thing you know he'll be startin' for Canada to enlist. He's been crazy to do it for 'most a year."

"He has? How do you know he has?"

"Because he's told me so, more'n once."

Her employer looked at her.

"Humph!" he grunted. "He seems to tell you a good many things he doesn't tell the rest of us."

The housekeeper nodded. "Yes," she said gravely, "I shouldn't wonder if he did." A moment later she added, "Cap'n Lote, you will be careful, won't you? You wouldn't want Al to go off and leave Z. Snow and Company when him and you are gettin' on so much better. You ARE gettin' on better, ain't you?"

The captain pulled at his beard.

"Yes," he admitted, "seems as if we was. He ain't any wonder at bookkeepin', but he's better'n he used to be; and he does seem to try hard, I'll say that for him."

Rachael beamed gratification. "He'll be a Robert Penfold yet," she declared; "see if he isn't. So you musn't encourage him into enlistin' in the Canadian army. You wouldn't want him to do that any more'n the rest of us would."

The captain gazed intently into the bowl of the pipe which he had been cleaning. He made no answer.

"You wouldn't want him to do that, would you?" repeated the housekeeper.

Captain Lote blew through the pipe stem. Then he said, "No, I wouldn't ... but I'm darn glad he's got the spunk to WANT to do it. We may get that Portygee streak out of him, poetry and all, give us time; eh, Rachael?"

It was the first time in months that he had used the word "Portygee" in connection with his grandson. Mrs. Ellis smiled to herself.

In April the arbutus buds began to appear above the leaf mold between the scrub oaks in the woods, and the walls of Fletcher Fosdick's new summer home began to rise above the young pines on the hill by the Inlet in the Bay Road. The Item kept its readers informed, by weekly installments, of the progress made by the builders.

The lumber for Mr. Fletcher Fosdick's new cottage is beginning to be hauled to his property on Inlet Hill in this town. Our enterprising firm of South Harniss dealers, Z. Snow & Co., are furnishing said lumber. Mr. Nehemiah Nickerson is to do the mason work. Mr. Fosdick shows good judgment as well as a commendable spirit in engaging local talent in this way. We venture to say he will never regret it.

A week later:

Mr. Fletcher Fosdick's new residence is beginning building, the foundation being pretty near laid.

And the following week:

The Fosdick mansion is growing fast. South Harniss may well be proud of its new ornament.

The rise in three successive numbers from "cottage" to "mansion" is perhaps sufficient to indicate that the Fosdick summer home was to be, as Issachar Price described it, "Some considerable house! Yes sir, by crimus, some considerable!"

In June, Helen came home for a week. At the end of the week she left to take up her new duties at the summer camp for girls in Vermont. Albert and she were together a good deal during that week. Anticipating her arrival, the young man's ardent imagination had again fanned what he delighted to think of as his love for her into flame. During the last months of the winter he had not played the languishing swain as conscientiously as during the autumn. Like the sailor in the song "is 'eart was true to Poll" always, but he had broken away from his self-imposed hermitage in his room at the Snow place several times to attend sociables, entertainments and, even, dances. Now, when she returned he was eagerly awaiting her and would have haunted the parsonage before and after working hours of every day as well as the evening, if she had permitted, and when with her assumed a proprietary air which was so obvious that even Mr. Price felt called upon to comment on it.

"Say, Al," drawled Issachar, "cal'late you've cut out Eddie Raymond along with Helen, ain't ye? Don't see him hangin' around any since she got back, and the way you was actin' when I see you struttin' into the parsonage yard last night afore mail time made me think you must have a first mortgage on Helen and her pa and the house and the meetin'-house and two-thirds of the graveyard. I never see such an important-lookin' critter in MY life. Haw, haw! Eh? How 'bout it?"

Albert did not mind the Price sarcasm; instead he felt rather grateful to have the proletariat recognize that he had triumphed again. The fly in his ointment, so to speak, was the fact that Helen herself did not in the least recognize that triumph. She laughed at him.

"Don't look at me like that, please, please, don't," she begged.

"Why not?" with a repetition of the look.

"Because it is silly."

"Silly! Well, I like that! Aren't you and I engaged? Or just the same as engaged?"

"No, of course we are not."

"But we promised each other—"

"No, we did not. And you know we didn't."

"Helen, why do you treat me that way? Don't you know that—that I just worship the ground you tread on? Don't you know you're the only girl in this world I could ever care for? Don't you know that?"

They were walking home from church Sunday morning and had reached the corner below the parsonage. There, screened by the thicket of young silver-leafs, she stopped momentarily and looked into his face. Then she walked on.

"Don't you know how much I care?" he repeated.

She shook her head. "You think you do now, perhaps," she said, "but you will change your mind."

"What do you mean by that? How do you know I will?"

"Because I know you. There, there, Albert, we won't quarrel, will we? And we won't be silly. You're an awfully nice boy, but you are just a boy, you know."

He was losing his temper.

"This is ridiculous!" he declared. "I'm tired of being grandmothered by you. I'm older than you are, and I know what I'm doing. Come, Helen, listen to me."

But she would not listen, and although she was always kind and frank and friendly, she invariably refused to permit him to become sentimental. It irritated him, and after she had gone the irritation still remained. He wrote her as before, although not quite so often, and the letters were possibly not quite so long. His pride was hurt and the Speranza pride was a tender and important part of the Speranza being. If Helen noted any change in his letters she did not refer to it nor permit it to influence her own, which were, as always, lengthy, cheerful, and full of interest in him and his work and thoughts.

During the previous fall, while under the new influence aroused in him by his discovery that Helen Kendall was "the most wonderful girl in the world," said discovery of course having been previously made for him by the unfortunate Raymond, he had developed a habit of wandering off into the woods or by the seashore to be alone and to seek inspiration. When a young poet is in love, or fancies himself in love, inspiration is usually to be found wherever sought, but even at that age and to one in that condition solitude is a marked aid in the search. There were two or three spots which had become Albert Speranza's favorites. One was a high, wind-swept knoll, overlooking the bay, about a half mile from the hotel, another was a secluded nook in the pine grove beside Carver's Pond, a pretty little sheet of water on the Bayport boundary. On pleasant Saturday afternoons or Sundays, when the poetic fit was on him, Albert, with a half dozen pencils in his pocket, and a rhyming dictionary and a scribbling pad in another, was wont to stroll towards one or the other of these two retreats. There he would sprawl amid the beachgrass or upon the pine-needles and dream and think and, perhaps, ultimately write.

One fair Saturday in late June he was at the first of these respective points. Lying prone on the beach grass at the top of the knoll and peering idly out between its stems at the water shimmering in the summer sun, he was endeavoring to find a subject for a poem which should deal with love and war as requested by the editor of the Columbian Magazine. "Give us something with a girl and a soldier in it," the editor had written. Albert's mind was lazily drifting in search of the pleasing combination.

The sun was warm, the breeze was light, the horizon was veiled with a liquid haze. Albert's mind was veiled with a similar haze and the idea he wanted would not come. He was losing his desire to find it and was, in fact, dropping into a doze when aroused by a blood-curdling outburst of barks and yelps and growls behind him, at his very heels. He came out of his nap with a jump and, scrambling to a sitting position and turning, he saw a small Boston bull-terrier standing within a yard of his ankles and, apparently, trying to turn his brindled outside in, or his inside out, with spiteful ferocity. Plainly the dog had come upon him unexpectedly and was expressing alarm, suspicion and disapproval.

Albert jerked his ankles out of the way and said "Hello, boy," in as cheerfully cordial a tone as he could muster at such short notice. The dog took a step forward, evidently with the idea of always keeping the ankles within jumping distance, showed a double row of healthy teeth and growled and barked with renewed violence.

"Nice dog," observed Albert. The nice dog made a snap at the nearest ankle and, balked of his prey by a frenzied kick of the foot attached to the ankle, shrieked, snarled and gurgled like a canine lunatic.

"Go home, you ugly brute," commanded the young man, losing patience, and looking about for a stone or stick. On the top of that knoll the largest stone was the size of a buckshot and the nearest stick was, to be Irish, a straw.

"Nice doggie! Nice old boy! Come and be patted! . . . Clear out with you! Go home, you beast!"

Flatteries and threats were alike in their result. The dog continued to snarl and growl, darting toward the ankles occasionally. Evidently he was mustering courage for the attack. Albert in desperation scooped up a handful of sand. If worst came to worst he might blind the creature temporarily. What would happen after that was not clear. Unless he might by a lucky cast fill the dog's interior so full of sand that—like the famous "Jumping Frog"—it would be too heavy to navigate, he saw no way of escape from a painful bite, probably more than one. What Captain Zelotes had formerly called his "Portygee temper" flared up.

"Oh, damn you, clear out!" he shouted, springing to his feet.

From a little way below him; in fact, from behind the next dune, between himself and the beach, a feminine voice called his name.

"Oh, Mr. Speranza!" it said. "Is it you? I'm so glad!"

Albert turned, but the moment he did so the dog made a dash at his legs, so he was obliged to turn back again and kick violently.

"Oh, I am so glad it is you," said the voice again. "I was sure it was a dreadful tramp. Googoo loathes tramps."

As an article of diet that meant, probably. Googoo—if that was the dog's name—was passionately fond of poets, that was self-evident, and intended to make a meal of this one, forthwith. He flew at the Speranza ankles. Albert performed a most undignified war dance, and dashed his handful of sand into Googoo's open countenance. For a minute or so there was a lively shindy on top of that knoll. At the end of the minute the dog, held tightly in a pair of feminine arms, was emitting growls and coughs and sand, while Madeline Fosdick and Albert Speranza were kneeling in more sand and looking at each other.

"Oh, did he bite you?" begged Miss Fosdick.

"No . . . no, I guess not," was the reply. "I—I scarcely know yet. . . . Why, when did you come? I didn't know you were in town."

"We came yesterday. Motored from home, you know. I—be still, Goo, you bad thing! It was such a lovely day that I couldn't resist going for a walk along the beach. I took Googoo because he does love it so, and—Goo, be still, I tell you! I am sure he thinks you are a tramp, out here all alone in the—in the wilderness. And what were you doing here?"

Albert drew a long breath. "I was half asleep, I guess," he said, "when he broke loose at my heels. I woke up quick enough then, as you may imagine. And so you are here for the summer? Your new house isn't finished, is it?"

"No, not quite. Mother and Goo and I are at the hotel for a month. But you haven't answered my question. What were you doing off here all alone? Have you been for a walk, too?"

"Not exactly. I—well, I come here pretty often. It is one of my favorite hiding places. You see, I . . . don't laugh if I tell you, will you?"

"Of course not. Go on; this is very mysterious and interesting."

"Well, I come here sometimes on pleasant days, to be alone—and write."

"Write? Write poetry, do you mean?"

"Yes."

"Oh, how wonderful! Were you writing when I—when Goo interrupted you?"

"No; I had made two or three attempts, but nothing that I did satisfied me. I had just about decided to tear them up and to give up trying for this afternoon."

"Oh, I hope you won't tear them up. I'm sure they shouldn't be. Perhaps you were not in a proper mood to judge, yourself."

"Perhaps not. Perhaps they might look a little less hopeless to some one else. But that person would have to be really interested, and there are few people in South Harniss who know or care anything about poetry."

"I suppose that is true. I—I don't suppose you would care to show them to me, would you?"

"Why," eagerly, "would you really care to see them?"

"Indeed I should! Not that my judgment or advice is worth anything, of course. But I am very, very fond of poetry, and to see how a real poet wrote would be wonderful. And if I could help you, even the least little bit, it would be such an honor."

This sort of thing was balm to the Speranza spirit. Albert's temperamental ego expanded under it like a rosebud under a summer sun. Yet there was a faint shadow of doubt—she might be making fun of him. He looked at her intently and she seemed to read his thoughts, for she said:

"Oh, I mean it! Please believe I do. I haven't spoken that way when Jane was with me, for she wouldn't understand and would laugh, but I mean it, Mr. Speranza. It would be an honor—a great honor."

So the still protesting and rebellious Googoo was compelled to go a few feet away and lie down, while his mistress and the young man whom he had attempted to devour bent their heads together over a scribbling-pad and talked and exclaimed during the whole of that hour and a full three-quarters of the next. Then the distant town clock in the steeple of the Congregational church boomed five times and Miss Fosdick rose to her feet.

"Oh," she said, "it can't really be five o'clock, can it? But it is! What WILL mother fancy has become of me? I must go this minute. Thank you, Mr. Speranza. I have enjoyed this so much. It has been a wonderful experience."

Her cheeks were flushed and her eyes were shining. She had grown handsomer than ever during the winter months. Albert's eyes were shining also as he impulsively seized her hand.

"Thank you, Miss Fosdick," he said. "You have helped me more than I can tell you. I was about to give up in despair before you came, and now— now I KNOW I shall write the best thing I have ever done. And you will be responsible for it."

She caught her breath. "Oh, not really!" she exclaimed. "You don't mean it, really?"

"Indeed I do! If I might have your help and sympathy once in awhile, I believe—I believe I could do almost anything. Will you help me again some day? I shall be here almost every pleasant Saturday and Sunday afternoon. Will you come again?"

She hesitated. "I—I'll see; perhaps," she answered hurriedly. "But I must go now. Come, Goo."

She hastened away, down the knoll and along the beach toward the hotel. Googoo followed her, turning occasionally to cast diabolical glances at the Speranza ankles. Albert gazed until the graceful figure in the trim sport costume disappeared behind the corner of the point of the beach. Just at the point she paused to wave to him. He waved in return. Then he tramped homeward. There was deep sand beneath his feet and, later, pine-needles and grass. They were all alike to him, for he was traveling on air.

That evening at supper his radiant appearance caused comment.

"What makes you look so happy, Albert?" asked his grandmother. "Seems to me I never saw you look so sort of—well, glorified, as you might say. What is the reason?"

The glorified one reddened and was confused. He stammered that he did not know, he was not aware of any particular reason.

Mrs. Ellis beamed upon him. "I presume likely his bookkeepin' at the office has been goin' pretty well lately," she suggested.

Captain Zelote's gray eyes twinkled. "Cal'late he's been makin' up more poetry about girls," was his offering. "Another one of those pieces about teeth like pearls and hair all curls, or somethin' like that. Say, Al, why don't you poetry-makin' fellers try a new one once in a while? Say, 'Her hair's like rope and her face has lost hope.' Eh? Why not, for a change?"

The protests on the part of Olive and the housekeeper against the captain's innovation in poetry-making had the effect of distracting attention from Albert's "glorified" appearance. The young man himself was thankful for the respite.

That night before he retired he took Madeline Fosdick's photograph from the back of the drawer among the ties and collars and looked at it for five minutes at least. She was a handsome girl, certainly. Not that that made any difference to him. And she was an intelligent girl; she understood his poetry and appreciated it. Yes, and she understood him, too, almost as well as Helen. . . . Helen! He hastily returned the Fosdick photograph to the drawer; but this time he did not put it quite so near the back.

On the following Saturday he was early at the knoll, a brand-new scribbling-pad in his pocket and in his mind divine gems which were later, and with Miss Fosdick's assistance, to be strung into a glittering necklace of lyric song and draped, with the stringer's compliments, about the throat of a grateful muse. But no gems were strung that day. Madeline did not put in an appearance, and by and by it began to rain, and Albert walked home, damp, dejected, and disgusted. When, a day or two later, he met Miss Fosdick at the post office and asked why she had not come he learned that her mother had insisted upon a motor trip to Wapatomac that afternoon.

"Besides," she said, "you surely mustn't expect me EVERY Saturday."

"No," he admitted grudgingly, "I suppose not. But you will come sometimes, won't you? I have a perfectly lovely idea for a ballad and I want to ask your advice about it."

"Oh, do you really? You're not making fun? You mean that my advice is really worth something? I can't believe it."

He convinced her that it was, and the next Saturday afternoon they spent together at the inspiration point among the dunes, at work upon the ballad. It was not finished on that occasion, nor on the next, for it was an unusually long ballad, but progress was made, glorious progress.

And so, during that Summer, as the Fosdick residence upon the Bay Road grew and grew, so did the acquaintanceship, the friendship, the poetic partnership between the Fosdick daughter and the grandson of Captain Zelotes Snow grow and grow. They met almost every Saturday, they met at the post office on week evenings, occasionally they saw each other for a moment after church on Sunday mornings. Mrs. Fletcher Fosdick could not imagine why her only child cared to attend that stuffy little country church and hear that prosy Kendall minister drone on and on. "I hope, my dear, that I am as punctilious in my religious duties as the average woman, but one Kendall sermon was sufficient for me, thank you. What you see in THAT church to please you, *I* can't guess."

If she had attended as often as Madeline did she might have guessed and saved herself much. But she was busy organizing, in connection with Mrs. Seabury Calvin, a Literary Society among the summer people of South

Harniss. The Society was to begin work with the discussion of the poetry of Rabindranath Tagore. Mrs. Fosdick said she doted on Tagore; Mrs. Calvin expressed herself as being positively insane about him. A warm friendship had sprung up between the two ladies, as each was particularly fond of shining as a literary light and neither under any circumstances permitted a new lion to roar unheard in her neighborhood, provided, of course, that the said roarings had been previously endorsed and well advertised by the critics and the press.

So Mrs. Fosdick was too busy to accompany Madeline to church on Sunday or to walk on Saturday, and the young lady was left to wander pretty much at her own sweet will. That sweet will led her footsteps to trails frequented by Albert Speranza and they walked and talked and poetized together. As for Mr. Fletcher Fosdick, he was busy at his office in New York and came to South Harniss only for infrequent week-ends.

The walks and talks and poetizings were innocent enough. Neither of the partners in poesy had the least idea of anything more than being just that. They liked each other, they had come to call each other by their Christian names, and on Albert's bureau Madeline's photograph now stood openly and without apology. Albert had convinced himself there was nothing to apologize for. She was his friend, that was all. He liked to write and she liked to help him—er—well, just as Helen used to when she was at home. He did not think of Helen quite as often as formerly, nor were his letters to her as frequent or as long.

So the summer passed and late August came, the last Saturday afternoon of that month. Albert and Madeline were together, walking together along the beach from the knoll where they had met so often. It was six o'clock and the beach was deserted. There was little wind, the tiny waves were lapping and plashing along the shore, and the rosy light of the sinking sun lay warm upon the water and the sand. They were thinking and speaking of the summer which was so near its end.

"It has been a wonderful summer, hasn't it?" said Albert.

"Yes, wonderful," agreed Madeline.

"Yes, I—I—by George, I never believed a summer could be so wonderful."

"Nor I."

Silence. Then Albert, looking at her, saw her eyes looking into his and saw in them—

He kissed her.

That morning Albert Speranza had arisen as usual, a casual, careless, perfectly human young fellow. He went to bed that night a superman, an archangel, a demi-god, with his head in the clouds and the earth a cloth of gold beneath his feet. Life was a pathway through Paradise arched with rainbows.

He and Madeline Fosdick loved each other madly, devotedly. They were engaged to be married. They had plighted troth. They were to be each other's, and no one else's, for ever—and ever—and ever.

CHAPTER X

The remainder of that summer was a paradisical meandering over the cloth of gold beneath the rainbows. Albert and his Madeline met often, very often. Few poems were written at these meetings. Why trouble to put penciled lines on paper when the entire universe was a poem especially composed for your benefit? The lovers sat upon the knoll amid the sand dunes and gazed at the bay and talked of themselves separately, individually, and, more especially, collectively. They strolled through the same woody lanes and discussed the same satisfactory subjects. They met at the post office or at the drug store and gazed into each other's eyes. And, what was the most astonishing thing about it all, their secret remained undiscovered. Undiscovered, that is to say, by those by whom discovery would have meant calamity. The gossips among the townspeople winked and chuckled and cal'lated Fletcher Fosdick had better look out or his girl would be took into the firm of Z. Snow and Co. Issachar Price uttered sarcastic and sly innuendoes. Jane Kelsey and her set ragged the pair occasionally. But even these never really suspected that the affair was serious. And neither Mrs. Fletcher Fosdick nor Captain and Mrs. Zelotes Snow gave it a minute's attention.

It was serious enough with the principals, however. To them it was the only serious matter in the world. Not that they faced or discussed the future with earnest and complete attention. Some day or other—that was of course the mutually accepted idea—some day or other they were to marry. In the meantime here was the blissful present with its roses and rainbows and here, for each, was the other. What would be likely to happen when the Fosdick parents learned of the engagement of their only child to the assistant bookkeeper of the South Harniss lumber and hardware company was unpleasant to contemplate, so why contemplate it? Upon one point they were agreed—never, never, NEVER would they give each other up. No power on earth—which included parents and grandparents—should or could separate them.

Albert's conscience troubled him slightly at first when he thought of Helen Kendall. It had been in reality such a short time—although of course it seemed ages and ages—since he had fancied himself in love with her.

Only the previous fall—yes, even that very spring, he had asked her to pledge herself to him. Fortunately—oh, how very fortunately!—she had refused, and he had been left free. Now he knew that his fancied love for her had been merely a passing whim, a delusion of the moment. This—THIS which he was now experiencing was the grand passion of his life. He wrote a poem with the title, "The Greater Love"—and sold it, too, to a sensational periodical which circulated largely among sentimental shopgirls. It is but truthful to state that the editor of the magazine to which he first submitted it sent it back with the brief note—"This is a trifle too syrupy for our use. Fear the pages might stick. Why not send us another war verse?" Albert treated the note and the editor with the contempt they deserved. He pitied the latter; poor soul, doubtless HE had never known the greater love.

He and Madeline had agreed that they would tell no one—no one at all—of their betrothal. It should be their own precious secret for the present. So, under the circumstances, he could not write Helen the news. But ought he to write her at all? That question bothered him not a little. He no longer loved her—in fact, he was now certain that he never had loved her—but he liked her, and he wanted her to keep on liking him. And she wrote to him with regularity. What ought he to do about writing her?

He debated the question with himself and, at last, and with some trepidation, asked Madeline's opinion of his duty in the matter. Her opinion was decisive and promptly given. Of course he must not write Helen again. "How would you like it if I corresponded with another fellow?" she asked. Candor forced him to admit that he should not like it at all. "But I want to behave decently," he said. "She is merely a friend of mine"—oh, how short is memory!—"but we have been friends for a long time and I wouldn't want to hurt her feelings." "No, instead you prefer to hurt mine." "Now, dearest, be reasonable." It was their nearest approach to a quarrel and was a very, very sad affair. The making-up was sweet, of course, but the question of further correspondence with Helen Kendall remained just where it was at the beginning. And, meanwhile, the correspondence lapsed.

September came far, far too soon—came and ended. And with it ended also the stay of the Fosdicks in South Harniss. Albert and Madeline said good-by at their rendezvous by the beach. It was a sad, a tearful, but a very precious farewell. They would write each other every day, they would think of each other every minute of every day, they would live through the winter somehow and look forward to the next spring and their next meeting.

"You will write—oh, ever and ever so many poems, won't you, dear?" begged Madeline. "You know how I love them. And whenever I see one of your poems in print I shall be so proud of you—of MY poet."

Albert promised to write ever and ever so many. He felt that there would be no difficulty in writing reams of poems—inspired, glorious poems. The difficulty would be in restraining himself from writing too many of them. With Madeline Fosdick as an inspiration, poetizing became as natural as breathing.

Then, which was unusual for them, they spoke of the future, the dim, vague, but so happy future, when Albert was to be the nation's poet laureate and Madeline, as Mrs. Laureate, would share his glory and wear, so to speak, his second-best laurels. The disagreeable problems connected with the future they ignored, or casually dismissed with, "Never mind, dear, it will be all right by and by." Oh, it was a wonderful afternoon, a rosy, cloudy, happy, sorrowful, bitter-sweet afternoon.

And the next morning Albert, peeping beneath Z. Snow and Co.'s office window shade, saw his heart's desire step aboard the train, saw that train puff out of the station, saw for just an instant a small hand waved behind the dingy glass of the car window. His own hand waved in reply. Then the raucous voice of Mr. Price broke the silence.

"Who was you flappin' your flipper at?" inquired Issachar. "Girl, I'll bet you! Never saw such a critter as you be to chase after the girls. Which one is it this time?"

Albert made no reply. Between embarrassment and sorrow he was incapable of speech. Issachar, however, was not in that condition; at all times when awake, and sometimes when asleep, Mr. Price could, and usually did, speak.

"Which one is it this time, Al?" demanded Issy. "Eh? Crimus, see him get red! Haw, haw! Labe," to Mr. Keeler, who came into the office from the inner room, "which girl do you cal'late Al here is wavin' by-bye to this mornin'? Who's goin' away on the cars this mornin', Labe?"

Laban, his hands full of the morning mail, absently replied that he didn't know.

"Yes, you do, too," persisted Issy. "You ain't listenin', that's all. Who's leavin' town on the train just now?"

"Eh? Oh, I don't know. The Small folks are goin' to Boston, I believe. And George Bartlett's goin' to Ostable on court business, he told me. Oh, yes, I believe Cap'n Lote said that Fosdick woman and her daughter were goin' back to New York. Back to New York—yes—yes—yes."

Mr. Price crowed triumphantly. "Ah, ha!" he crowed. "Ah, ha! That's the answer. That's the one he's shakin' day-days to, that Fosdick girl. I've seen you 'round with her at the post office and the ice cream s'loon. I'm onto you, Al. Haw, haw! What's her name? Adeline? Dandelion? Madeline?—that's it! Say, how do you think Helen Kendall's goin' to like your throwin' kisses to the Madeline one, eh?"

The assistant bookkeeper was still silent. The crimson, however, was leaving his face and the said face was paling rapidly. This was an ominous sign had Mr. Price but known it. He did not know it and cackled merrily on,

"Guess I'll have to tell Helen when she comes back home," he announced. "Cal'late I'll put a flea in her ear. 'Helen,' I'll say, 'don't feel too bad now, don't cry and get your handkerchief all soakin', or nothin' like that. I just feel it's my duty to tell ye that your little Albert is sparkin' up to somebody else. He's waitin' on a party by the name of Padeline—no, Madeline—Woodtick—no, Fosdick—and . . .' Here! let go of me! What are you doin'?"

That last question was in the nature of a gurgle. Albert, his face now very white indeed, had strode across the office, seized the speaker by the front of his flannel shirt and backed him against the wall.

"Stop," commanded Albert, between his teeth. "That's enough of that. Don't you say any more!"

"Eh? Ugh! Ur-gg! Leggo of my shirt."

Albert let go, but he did not step back. He remained where he was, exactly in front of Mr. Price.

"Don't you say any more about—about what you were saying," he repeated.

"Eh? Not say any more? Why not? Who's goin' to stop me, I'd like to know?"

"I am."

"I want to know! What'll you do?"

"I don't know. If you weren't so old, I would—but I'll stop you, anyhow."

Albert felt a hand on his arm and heard Mr. Keeler's voice at his ear.

"Careful, Al, careful," it said. "Don't hit him."

"Of course I shan't hit him," indignantly. "What do you think I am? But he must promise not to mention—er—Miss Fosdick's name again."

"Better promise, Is," suggested Laban. Issachar's mouth opened, but no promise came forth.

"Promise be darned!" he yelled furiously. "Mention her name! I'll mention any name I set out to, and no Italyun Portygee is goin' to stop me, neither."

Albert glanced about the office. By the wall stood two brimming pails of water, brought in by Mr. Price for floor-washing purposes. He lifted one of the pails.

"If you don't promise I'll duck you," he declared. "Let go of me, Keeler, I mean it."

"Careful, Al, careful," said Mr. Keeler. "Better promise, Is."

"Promise nawthin'! Fosdick! What in time do I care for Fosdicks, Madelines or Padelines or Dandelions or—"

His sentence stopped just there. The remainder of it was washed back and down his throat by the deluge from the bucket. Overcome by shock and surprise, Mr. Price leaned back against the wall and slid slowly down that wall until he reclined in a sitting posture, upon the floor.

"Crimustee," he gasped, as soon as he could articulate, "I'm—awk—I'm drownded."

Albert put down the empty bucket and picked up the full one.

"Promise," he said again.

Laban Keeler rubbed his chin.

"I'd promise if I was you, Is," he said. "You're some subject to rheumatism, you know."

Issachar, sitting in a spreading puddle, looked damply upward at the remaining bucket. "By crimustee—" he began. Albert drew the bucket backward; the water dripped from its lower brim.

"I—I—darn ye, I promise!" shouted Issachar. Albert put down the bucket and walked back to his desk. Laban watched him curiously, smiling just a little. Then he turned to Mr. Price, who was scrambling to his feet.

"Better get your mop and swab up here, Is," he said. "Cap'n Lote'll be in 'most any minute."

When Captain Zelotes did return to the office, Issachar was industriously sweeping out, Albert was hard at work at the books, and Laban was still rubbing his chin and smiling at nothing in particular.

The next day Albert and Issachar made it up. Albert apologized.

"I'm sorry, Issy," he said. "I shouldn't have done it, but you made me mad. I have a—rather mean temper, I'm afraid. Forgive me, will you?"

He held out his hand, and Issachar, after a momentary hesitation, took it.

"I forgive you this time, Al," he said solemnly, "but don't never do nothin' like it again, will ye? When I went home for dinner yesterday noon I give you my word my clothes was kind of dampish even then. If it hadn't been nice warm sunshine and I was out doors and dried off considerable I'd a had to change everything, underclothes and all, and 'tain't but the middle of the week yet."

His ducking had an effect which Albert noticed with considerable satisfaction—he was never quite as flippantly personal in his comments concerning the assistant bookkeeper. He treated the latter, if not with respect, at least with something distantly akin to it.

After Madeline's departure the world was very lonely indeed. Albert wrote long, long letters and received replies which varied in length but never in devotion. Miss Fosdick was obliged to be cautious in her correspondence with her lover. "You will forgive me if this is not much more than a note, won't you, dear?" she wrote. "Mother seems to be very curious of late about my letters and to whom I write and I had to just steal the opportunity this morning." An older and more apprehensive person might have found Mrs. Fosdick's sudden interest in her daughter's correspondence suspicious and a trifle alarming, but Albert never dreamed of being alarmed.

He wrote many poems, all dealing with love and lovers, and sold some of them. He wrote no more letters to Helen. She, too, had ceased to write him, doubtless because of the lack of reply to her last two or three letters. His conscience still troubled him about Helen; he could not help feeling that his treatment of her had not been exactly honorable. Yet what else under the circumstances could he do? From Mr. Kendall he learned that she was coming home to spend Thanksgiving. He would see her then. She would ask him questions? What should his answer be? He faced the situation in anticipation many, many times, usually after he had gone to bed at night, and lay awake through long torturing hours in consequence.

But when at last Helen and he did meet, the day before Thanksgiving, their meeting was not at all the dreadful ordeal he had feared. Her greeting was as frank and cordial as it had always been, and there was no reproach in her tone or manner. She did not even ask him why he had stopped writing. It was he, himself, who referred to that subject, and he did so as they walked together down the main road. Just why he referred to it he could not probably have told. He was aware only that he felt mean and contemptible and that he must offer some explanation. His not having any to offer made the task rather difficult.

But she saved him the trouble. She interrupted one of his blundering, stumbling sentences in the middle.

"Never mind, Albert," she said quietly. "You needn't explain. I think I understand."

He stopped and stared at her. "You understand?" he repeated. "Why—why, no, you don't. You can't."

"Yes, I can, or I think I can. You have changed your mind, that is all."

"Changed my mind?"

"Yes. Don't you remember I told you you would change your mind about—well, about me? You were so sure you cared so very, very much for me, you know. And I said you mustn't promise anything because I thought you would change your mind. And you have. That is it, isn't it? You have found some one else."

He gazed at her as if she were a witch who had performed a miracle.

"Why—why—well, by George!" he exclaimed. "Helen—how—how did you know? Who told you?"

"No one told me. But I think I can even guess who it is you have found. It is Madeline Fosdick, isn't it?"

His amazement now was so open-mouthed as well as open-eyed that she could not help smiling.

"Don't! Don't stare at me like that," she whispered. "Every one is looking at you. There is old Captain Pease on the other side of the street; I'm sure he thinks you have had a stroke or something. Here! Walk down our road a little way toward home with me. We can talk as we walk. I'm sure," she added, with just the least bit of change in her tone, "that your Madeline won't object to our being together to that extent."

She led the way down the side street toward the parsonage and he followed her. He was still speechless from surprise.

"Well," she went on, after a moment, "aren't you going to say anything?"

"But—but, Helen," he faltered, "how did you know?"

She smiled again. "Then it IS Madeline," she said. "I thought it must be."

"You—you thought—What made you think so?"

For an instant she seemed on the point of losing her patience.

Then she turned and laid her hand on his arm.

"Oh, Al," she said, "please don't think I am altogether an idiot. I surmised when your letters began to grow shorter and—well, different—that there was something or some one who was changing them, and I suspected it was some one. When you stopped writing altogether, I KNEW there must be. Then father wrote in his letters about you and about meeting you, and so often Madeline Fosdick was wherever he met you. So I guessed—and, you see, I guessed right."

He seized her hand.

"Oh, Helen," he cried, "if you only knew how mean I have felt and how ashamed I am of the way I have treated you! But, you see, I—I COULDN'T write you and tell you because we had agreed to keep it a secret. I couldn't tell ANY ONE."

"Oh, it is as serious as that! Are you two really and truly engaged?"

"Yes. There! I've told it, and I swore I would never tell."

"No, no, you didn't tell. I guessed. Now tell me all about her. She is very lovely. Is she as sweet as she looks?"

He rhapsodized for five minutes. Then all at once he realized what he was saying and to whom he was saying it. He stopped, stammering, in the very middle of a glowing eulogium.

"Go on," said Helen reassuringly. But he could not go on, under the circumstances. Instead he turned very red. As usual, she divined his thought, noticed his confusion, and took pity on it.

"She must be awfully nice," she said. "I don't wonder you fell in love with her. I wish I might know her better."

"I wish you might. By and by you must. And she must know you. Helen, I—I feel so ashamed of—of—"

"Hush, or I shall begin to think you are ashamed because you liked me—or thought you did."

"But I do like you. Next to Madeline there is no one I like so much. But, but, you see, it is different."

"Of course it is. And it ought to be. Does her mother—do her people know of the engagement?"

He hesitated momentarily. "No-o," he admitted, "they don't yet. She and I have decided to keep it a secret from any one for the present. I want to get on a little further with my writing, you know. She is like you in that, Helen—she's awfully fond of poetry and literature."

"Especially yours, I'm sure. Tell me about your writing. How are you getting on?"

So he told her and, until they stood together at the parsonage gate, Madeline's name was not again mentioned. Then Helen put out her hand.

"Good morning, Albert," she said. "I'm glad we have had this talk, ever so glad."

"By George, so am I! You're a corking friend, Helen. The chap who does marry you will be awfully lucky."

She smiled slightly. "Perhaps there won't be any such chap," she said. "I shall always be a schoolmarm, I imagine."

"Indeed you won't," indignantly. "I have too high an opinion of men for that."

She smiled again, seemed about to speak, and then to change her mind. An instant later she said,

"I must go in now. But I shall hope to see you again before I go back to the city. And, after your secret is out and the engagement is announced, I want to write Madeline, may I?"

"Of course you may. And she'll like you as much as I do."

"Will she? . . . Well, perhaps; we'll hope so."

"Certainly she will. And you won't let my treating you as—as I have make any difference in our friendship?"

"No. We shall always be friends, I hope. Good-by."

She went into the house. He waited a moment, hoping she might turn again before entering, but she did not. He walked home, pondering deeply, his thoughts a curious jumble of relief and dissatisfaction. He was glad Helen had seen her duty and given him over to Madeline, but he felt a trifle piqued to think she had done it with such apparent willingness. If she had wept or scolded it would have been unpleasant but much more gratifying to his self-importance.

He could not help realizing, however, that her attitude toward him was exceptionally fine. He knew well that he, if in her place, would not have behaved as she had done. No spite, no sarcasm, no taunts, no unpleasant reminders of things said only a few months before. And with all her forgiveness and forbearance and understanding there had been always that sense of greater age and wisdom; she had treated him as she might have treated a boy, younger brother, perhaps.

"She IS older than I am," he thought, "even if she really isn't. It's funny, but it's a fact."

December came and Christmas, and then January and the new year, the year 1917. In January, Z. Snow and Co. took its yearly account of stock, and Captain Lote and Laban and Albert and Issachar were truly busy during the days of stock-taking week and tired when evening came. Laban worked the hardest of the quartette, but Issy made the most fuss about it. Labe, who had chosen the holiday season to go on one of his periodical vacations, as rather white and shaky and even more silent than usual. Mr. Price, however, talked with his customary fluency and continuity, so there was no lack of conversation. Captain Zelotes was moved to comment.

"Issy," he suggested gravely, looking up from a long column of figures, "did you ever play 'Door'?"

Issachar stared at him.

"Play 'Door'?" he repeated. "What's that?"

"It's a game. Didn't you ever play it?"

"No, don't know's I ever did."

"Then you'd better begin right this minute. The first thing to do is to shut up and the next is to stay that way. You play 'Door' until I tell you to do somethin' else; d'you hear?"

At home the week between Christmas and the New Year was rather dismal. Mr. Keeler's holiday vacation had brought on one of his fiancee's "sympathetic attacks," and she tied up her head and hung crape upon her soul, as usual. During these attacks the Snow household walked on tiptoe, as if the housekeeper were an invalid in reality. Even consoling speeches from Albert, who with Laban when the latter was sober, enjoyed in her mind the distinction of being the reincarnation of "Robert Penfold," brought no relief to the suffering Rachel. Nothing but the news brought by the milkman, that "Labe was taperin' off," and would probably return to his desk in a few days, eased her pain.

One forenoon about the middle of the month Captain Zelotes himself stopped in at the post office for the morning mail. When he returned to the lumber company's building he entered quietly and walked to his own desk with a preoccupied air. For the half hour before dinner time he sat there, smoking his pipe, and speaking to no one unless spoken to. The office force noticed his preoccupation and commented upon it.

"What ails the old man, Al?" whispered Issachar, peering in around the corner of the door at the silent figure tilted back in the revolving chair, its feet upon the corner of the desk. "Ain't said so much as 'Boo' for up'ards of twenty minutes, has he? I was in there just now fillin' up his ink-stand and, by crimus, I let a great big gob of ink come down ker-souse right in the middle of the nice, clean blottin' paper in front of him. I held my breath, cal'latin' to catch what Stephen Peter used to say he caught when he went fishin' Sundays. Stevey said he generally caught cold when he went and always caught the Old Harry when he got back. I cal'lated to catch the Old Harry part sure, 'cause Captain Lote is always neat and fussy 'bout his desk. But no, the old man never said a word. I don't believe he knew the ink was spilled at all. What's on his mind, Al; do you know?"

Albert did not know, so he asked Laban. Laban shook his head.

"Give it up, Al," he whispered. "Somethin's happened to bother him, that's sartin'. When Cap'n Lote gets his feet propped up and his head tilted back that way I can 'most generally cal'late he's doin' some real thinkin'. Real thinkin'—yes, sir-ee—um-hm—yes—yes. When he h'ists his boots up to the masthead that way it's safe to figger his brains have got steam up. Um-hm—yes indeed."

"But what is he thinking about? And why is he so quiet?"

"I give up both riddles, Al. He's the only one's got the answers and when he gets ready enough maybe he'll tell 'em. Until then it'll pay us fo'mast hands to make believe we're busy, even if we ain't. Hear that, do you, Is?"

"Hear what?" demanded Issachar, who was gazing out of the window, his hands in his pockets.

"I say it will pay us—you and Al and me—to make believe we're workin' even if we ain't."

"'Workin'!" indignantly. "By crimus, I AM workin'! I don't have to make believe."

"That so? Well, then, I'd pick up that coal-hod and make believe play for a spell. The fire's 'most out. Almost—um-hm—pretty nigh—yes—yes."

Albert and his grandfather walked home to dinner together, as was their custom, but still the captain remained silent. During dinner he spoke not more than a dozen words and Albert several times caught Mrs. Snow regarding her husband intently and with a rather anxious look. She did not question him, however, but Rachel was not so reticent.

"Mercy on us, Cap'n Lote," she demanded, "what IS the matter? You're as dumb as a mouthful of mush. I don't believe you've said ay, yes or no since we sat down to table. Are you sick?"

Her employer's calm was unruffled.

"No-o," he answered, with deliberation.

"That's a comfort. What's the matter, then; don't you WANT to talk?"

"No-o."

"Oh," with a toss of the head, "well, I'm glad I know. I was beginnin' to be afraid you'd forgotten how."

The captain helped himself to another fried "tinker" mackerel.

"No danger of that around here, Rachel," he said serenely. "So long as my hearin's good I couldn't forget—not in this house."

Olive detained her grandson as he was following Captain Zelotes from the dining room.

"What's wrong with him, Albert?" she whispered. "Do you know?"

"No, I don't, Grandmother. Do you think there is anything wrong?"

"I know there's somethin' troublin' him. I've lived with him too many years not to know the signs. Oh, Albert—you haven't done anything to displease him, have you?"

"No, indeed, Grandmother. Whatever it is, it isn't that."

When they reached the office, the captain spoke to Mr. Keeler.

"Had your dinner, Labe?" he asked.

"Yes—yes, indeed. Don't take me long to eat—not at my boardin' house. A feller'd have to have paralysis to make eatin' one of Lindy Dadgett's meals take more'n a half hour. Um-hm—yes."

Despite his preoccupation, Captain Zelotes could not help smiling.

"To make it take an hour he'd have to be ossified, wouldn't he, like the feller in the circus sideshow?" he observed.

Laban nodded. "That—or dead," he replied. "Yes—just about—just so, Cap'n."

"Where's Issachar?"

"He's eatin' yet, I cal'late. He don't board at Lindy's."

"When he gets back set him to pilin' that new carload of spruce under Number Three shed. Keep him at it."

"Yes, sir. Um-hm. All right."

Captain Zelotes turned to his grandson. "Come in here, Al," he said. "I want to see you for a few minutes."

Albert followed him into the inner office. He wondered what in the world his grandfather wished to see him about, in this very private fashion.

"Sit down, Al," said the captain, taking his own chair and pointing to another. "Oh, wait a minute, though! Maybe you'd better shut that hatch first."

The "hatch" was the transom over the door between the offices. Albert, remembering how a previous interview between them had been overheard because of that open transom, glanced at his grandfather. The twinkle in the latter's eye showed that he too, remembered. Albert closed the "hatch." When he came back to his seat the twinkle had disappeared; Captain Zelotes looked serious enough.

"Well, Grandfather?" queried the young man, after waiting a moment. The captain adjusted his spectacles, reached into the inside pocket of his coat and produced an envelope. It was a square envelope with either a trademark or a crest upon the back. Captain Lote did not open the envelope, but instead tapped his desk with it and regarded his grandson in a meditative way.

"Al," he said slowly, "has it seemed to you that your cruise aboard this craft of ours here had been a little smoother the last year or two than it used to be afore that?"

Albert, by this time well accustomed to his grandfather's nautical phraseology, understood that the "cruise" referred to was his voyage as assistant bookkeeper with Z. Snow and Co. He nodded.

"I have tried to make it so," he answered. "I mean I have tried to make it smoother for you."

"Um-hm, I think you have tried. I don't mind tellin' you that it has pleased me consid'ble to watch you try. I don't mean by that," he added, with a slight curve of the lip, "that you'd win first prize as a lightnin'-calculator even yet, but you're a whole lot better one than you used to be. I've been considerable encouraged about you; I don't mind tellin' you that either. . . . And," he added, after another interval during which he was, apparently, debating just how much of an admission it was safe to make, "so far as I can see, this poetry foolishness of yours hasn't interfered with your work any to speak of."

Albert smiled. "Thanks, Grandfather," he said.

"You're welcome. So much for that. But there's another side to our relations together, yours and mine, that I haven't spoken of to you afore. And I have kept still on purpose. I've figgered that so long as you kept straight and didn't go off the course, didn't drink or gamble, or go wild or the like of that, what you did was pretty much your own business. I've noticed you're considerable of a feller with the girls, but I kept an eye on the kind of girls and I will say that so far as I can see, you've picked the decent kind. I say so far as I can see. Of course I ain't fool enough to believe I see all you do, or know all you do. I've been young myself, and when I get to thinkin' how much I know about you I try to set down and remember how much my dad didn't know about me when I was your age. That—er—helps some toward givin' me my correct position on the chart."

He paused. Albert's brain was vainly striving to guess what all this meant. What was he driving at? The captain crossed his legs and continued.

"I did think for a spell," he said, "that you and Helen Kendall were gettin' to understand each other pretty well. Well, Helen's a good girl and your grandma and I like her. Course we didn't cal'late anything very serious was liable to come of the understandin', not for some time, anyhow, for with your salary and—well, sort of unsettled prospects, I gave you credit for not figgerin' on pickin' a wife right away. . . . Haven't got much laid by to support a wife on, have you, Al?"

Albert's expression had changed during the latter portion of the speech. Now he was gazing intently at his grandfather and at the letter in the latter's hands. He was beginning to guess, to dread, to be fearful.

"Haven't got much to support a wife on, Al, have you?" repeated Captain Zelotes.

"No, sir, not now."

"Um. . . . But you hope to have by and by, eh? Well, I hope you will. But UNTIL you have it would seem to older folks like me kind of risky navigatin' to—to . . . Oh, there was a letter in the mail for you this mornin, Al."

He put down the envelope he had hitherto held in his hand and, reaching into his pocket, produced another. Even before he had taken it from his grandfather's hand Albert recognized the handwriting. It was from Madeline.

Captain Zelotes, regarding him keenly, leaned back again in his chair. "Read it if you want to, Al," he said. "Maybe you'd better. I can wait."

Albert hesitated a moment and then tore open the envelope. The note within was short, evidently written in great haste and agitation and was spotted with tear stains. He read it, his cheeks paling and his hand shaking as he did so. Something dreadful had happened. Mother—Mrs. Fosdick, of course—had discovered everything. She had found all his—Albert's—letters and read them. She was furious. There had been the most terrible scene. Madeline was in her own room and was smuggling him this letter by Mary, her maid, who will do anything for me, and has promised to mail it. Oh, dearest, they say I must give you up. They say—Oh, they say dreadful things about you! Mother declares she will take me to Japan or some frightful place and keep me there until I forget you. I don't care if they take me to the ends of the earth, I shall NEVER forget you. I will never—never—NEVER give you up. And you mustn't give me up, will you, darling? They say I must never write you again. But you see I have—and I shall. Oh, what SHALL we do? I was SO happy and now I am so miserable. Write me the minute you get this, but oh, I KNOW they won't let me see your letters and then I shall die. But write, write just the same, every day. Oh what SHALL we do?

Yours, always and always, no matter what everyone does or says, lovingly and devotedly,

MADELINE.

When the reading was finished Albert sat silently staring at the floor, seeing it through a wet mist. Captain Zelotes watched him, his heavy brows drawn together and the smoke wreaths from his pipe curling slowly upward toward the office ceiling. At length he said:

"Well, Al, I had a letter, too. I presume likely it came from the same port even if not from the same member of the family. It's about you, and I think you'd better read it, maybe. I'll read it to you, if you'd rather."

Albert shook his head and held out his hand for the second letter. His grandfather gave it to him, saying as he did so: "I'd like to have you understand, Al, that I don't necessarily believe all that she says about you in this thing."

"Thanks, Grandfather," mechanically.

"All right, boy."

The second letter was, as he had surmised, from Mrs. Fosdick. It had evidently been written at top speed and at a mental temperature well above the boiling point. Mrs. Fosdick addressed Captain Zelotes Snow because she had been given to understand that he was the nearest relative, or guardian, or whatever it was, of the person concerning whom the letter was written and therefore, it was presumed, might be expected to have some measure of control over that person's actions. The person was, of course, one Albert Speranza, and Mrs. Fosdick proceeded to set forth her version of his conduct in sentences which might almost have blistered the paper. Taking advantage of her trust in her daughter's good sense and ability to take care of herself—which trust it appeared had been in a measure misplaced—he, the Speranza person, had sneakingly, underhandedly and in a despicably clandestine fashion—the lady's temper had rather gotten away from her here—succeeded in meeting her daughter in various places and by various disgraceful means and had furthermore succeeded in ensnaring her youthful affections, et cetera, et cetera.

"The poor child actually believes herself in love with him," wrote the poor child's mother. "She protests ridiculously that she is engaged to him and will marry him in spite of her father or myself or the protests of sensible people. I write to you, therefore, assuming you likewise to be a sensible person, and requesting that you use your influence with the—to put the most charitable interpretation of his conduct—misguided and foolish young man and show him the preposterous folly of his pretended engagement to my daughter. Of course the whole affair, CORRESPONDENCE INCLUDED, must cease and terminate AT ONCE."

And so on for two more pages. The color had returned to Albert's cheeks long before he finished reading. When he had finished he rose to his feet and, throwing the letter upon his grandfather's desk, turned away.

"Well, Al?" queried Captain Zelotes.

Albert's face, when he turned back to answer, was whiter than ever, but his eyes flashed fire.

"Do you believe that?" he demanded.

"What?"

"That—that stuff about my being a—a sneak and—and ensnaring her—and all the rest? Do you?"

The captain took his pipe from his mouth.

"Steady, son, steady," he said. "Didn't I tell you before you begun to read at all that I didn't necessarily believe it because that woman wrote it."

"You—you or no one else had better believe it. It's a lie."

"All right, I'm glad to hear you say so. But there's a little mite of truth here and there amongst the lies, I presume likely. For instance, you and this Fosdick girl have been—er—keepin' company?"

"Her name is Madeline—and we are engaged to be married."

"Oh! Hum—I see—I see. And, bein' as the old lady—her mother, Mrs. Fosdick, I mean—hasn't suspected anything, or, at any rate, hasn't found out anything until now, yesterday, or whenever it was, I judge you have been meetin'—er—Madeline at places where there wasn't—well, too large a crowd. Eh?"

Albert hesitated and was, momentarily, a trifle embarrassed. But he recovered at once.

"I met her first at the drug store last summer," he said defiantly. "Then I met her after that at the post office and at the hotel dance last fall, and so on. This year I met her—well, I met her first down by the beach, where I went to write. She liked poetry and—and she helped me with mine. After that she came—well, she came to help me again. And after that—after that—"

"After that it just moved along kind of natural, eh? Um-hm, I see."

"Look here, Grandfather, I want you to understand that she is—is—by George, she is the cleanest, finest, best girl in the world. Don't you get the idea that—that she isn't. She came to meet me just because she was interested in my verse and wanted to help. It wasn't until the very last that we—that we found out we cared for each other."

"All right, boy, all right. Go on, tell me the whole yarn, if you feel like it. I don't want to pry too much into your affairs, but, after all, I AM interested in those affairs, Al. Tell me as much as you can."

"I'll tell you the whole. There's nothing I can't tell, nothing I'm not proud to tell. By George, I ought to be proud! Why, Grandfather, she's wonderful!"

"Sartin, son, sartin. They always are. I mean she is, of course. Heave ahead."

So Albert told his love story. When he had finished Captain Zelote's pipe was empty, and he put it down.

"Albert," he said slowly, "I judge you mean this thing seriously. You mean to marry her some day."

"Yes, indeed I do. And I won't give her up, either. Her mother—why, what right has her mother got to say—to treat her in this way? Or to call me what she calls me in that letter? Why, by George—"

"Easy, son. As I understand it, this Madeline of yours is the only child the Fosdicks have got and when our only child is in danger of bein' carried off by somebody else—why, well, their mothers and fathers are liable to be just a little upset, especially if it comes on 'em sudden. . . . Nobody knows that better than I do," he added slowly.

Albert recognized the allusion, but he was not in the mood to be affected by it. He was not, just then, ready to make allowances for any one, particularly the parental Fosdicks.

"They have no business to be upset—not like that, anyhow," he declared. "What does that woman know about me? What right has she to say that I ensnared Madeline's affection and all that rot? Madeline and I fell in love with each other, just as other people have, I suppose."

"You suppose right," observed Captain Zelotes, dryly. "Other people have—a good many of 'em since Adam's time."

"Well, then! And what right has she to give orders that I stop writing or seeing Madeline,—all that idiotic stuff about ceasing and terminating at once? She—she—" His agitation was making him incoherent—"She talks like Lord Somebody-or-other in an old-fashioned novel or play or something. Those old fools were always rejecting undesirable suitors and ordering their daughters to do this and that, breaking their hearts, and so on. But that sort of thing doesn't go nowadays. Young people have their own ideas."

"Um-hm, Al; so I've noticed."

"Yes, indeed they have. Now, if Madeline wants to marry me and I want to marry her, who will stop us?"

The captain pulled at his beard.

"Why, nobody, Al, as I know of," he said; "provided you both keep on wantin' to marry each other long enough."

"Keep on wanting long enough? What do you mean by that?"

"Why, nothin' much, perhaps; only gettin' married isn't all just goin' to the parson. After the ceremony the rent begins and the grocers' bills and the butchers' and the bakers' and a thousand or so more. Somebody's got to pay 'em, and the money's got to come from somewhere. Your wages here, Al, poetry counted in, ain't so very big yet. Better wait a spell before you settle down to married life, hadn't you?"

"Well—well, I—I didn't say we were to be married right away, Grandfather. She and I aren't unreasonable. I'm doing better and better with my writings. Some day I'll make enough, and more. Why not?"

There was enough of the Speranza egotism in this confident assurance to bring the twinkle to the captain's eye. He twisted his beard between his finger and thumb and regarded his grandson mildly.

"Have you any idea how much 'enough' is liable to be, Al?" he inquired. "I don't know the facts about 'em, of course, but from what I have heard I judge the Fosdicks have got plenty of cash. I've heard it estimated around town from one million to fifty millions. Allowin' it's only one million, it seems likely that your—er—what's-her-name—Madeline has been used to havin' as much as fifty cents to spend whenever she wanted it. Do you cal'late to be able to earn enough makin' up poetry to keep her the way her folks have been doin'?"

"No, of course not—not at first."

"Oh, but later on—when the market price of poetry has gone up—you can, eh?"

"Look here, Grandfather, if you're making fun of me I tell you I won't stand it. This is serious; I mean it. Madeline and I are going to be married some time and no one can stop us."

"All right, son, all right. But it did seem to me that in the light of this letter from—er—your mother-in-law that's goin' to be, we ought to face the situation moderately square, anyhow. First comes marriage. Well, that's easy; any fool can get married, lots of 'em do. But then, as I said, comes supportin' yourself and wife—bills, bills, and more bills. You'll say that you and she will economize and fight it out together. Fine, first-rate, but later on there may be more of you, a child, children perhaps—"

"Grandfather!"

"It's possible, son. Such things do happen, and they cost money. More mouths to feed. Now I take it for granted that you aren't marryin' the Fosdick girl for her money—"

The interruption was prompt and made with fiery indignation.

"I never thought of her money," declared Albert. "I don't even know that she has any. If she has, I don't want it. I wouldn't take it. She is all I want."

Captain Zelotes' lip twitched.

"Judgin' from the tone of her ma's last letter to me," he observed, "she is all you would be liable to get. It don't read as if many—er—weddin' presents from the bride's folks would come along with her. But, there, there, Al don't get mad. I know this is a long ways from bein' a joke to you and, in a way, it's no joke for me. Course I had realized that some day you'd be figgerin', maybe, on gettin' married, but I did hope the figgerin' wouldn't begin for some years yet. And when you did, I rather hoped—well, I—I hoped. . . . However, we won't stop to bother with that now. Let's stick to this letter of Mrs. Fosdick's here. I must answer that, I suppose, whether I want to or not, to-day. Well, Al, you tell me, I understand that there has been nothin' underhand in your acquaintance with her daughter. Other than keepin' the engagement a secret, that is?"

"Yes, I do."

"And you mean to stick by your guns and. . . . Well, what is it? Come in!"

There had been a knock upon the office door. In answer to his employer's summons, Mr. Keeler appeared. He held a card in his hand.

"Sorry to disturb you, Cap'n Lote," he said. "Yes, I be, yes, sir. But I judged maybe 'twas somethin' important about the lumber for his house and he seemed anxious to see you, so I took the risk and knocked. Um-hm—yes, yes, yes."

Captain Zelotes looked at the card. Then he adjusted his spectacles and looked again.

"Humph!" he grunted. "Humph! . . . We-ell, Labe, I guess likely you might show him in here. Wait just a minute before you do it, though. I'll open the door when I want him to come."

"All right, Cap'n Lote. Yes, yes," observed Mr. Keeler and departed. The captain looked thoughtfully at the card.

"Al," he said, after a moment's reflection, "we'll have to cut this talk of ours short for a little spell. You go back to your desk and wait there until I call you. Hold on," as his grandson moved toward the door of the outer office. "Don't go that way. Go out through the side door into the yard and come in the front way. There's—er—there's a man waitin' to see me, and—er—perhaps he'd better not see you first."

Albert stared at him uncomprehendingly.

"Better not see ME?" he repeated. "Why shouldn't he see me?"

Captain Zelotes handed the card to Albert.

"Better let me talk with him first, Al," he said. "You can have your chance later on."

The card bore the name of Mr. Fletcher Story Fosdick.

CHAPTER XI

Albert read the name on the card. He was too astonished to speak. Her father! He was here! He—

His grandfather spoke again, and his tone was brisk and businesslike.

"Go on, Al," he ordered. "Out through this side door and around to the front. Lively, son, lively!"

But the young man's wits were returning. He scowled at the card.

"No," he said stoutly, "I'm not going to run away. I'm not afraid of him. I haven't done anything to be ashamed of."

The captain nodded. "If you had, I should ASK you to run away," he said. "As it is, I just ask you to step out and wait a little while, that's all."

"But, Grandfather, I WANT to see him."

"All right, I want you to—but not until he and I have talked first. Come, boy, come! I've lived a little longer than you have, and maybe I know about half as much about some things. This is one of 'em. You clear out and stand by. I'll call you when I want you."

Albert went, but reluctantly. After he had gone his grandfather walked to the door of the outer office and opened it.

"Step aboard, Mr. Fosdick," he said. "Come in, sir."

Mr. Fletcher Fosdick was a large man, portly, and with a head which was rapidly losing its thatch. His smoot-shaven face was ruddy and his blue eye mild. He entered the private office of Z. Snow and Co. and shook the hand which Captain Zelotes proffered.

"How do you do, Captain Snow?" he asked pleasantly. "You and I have had some business dealings, but we have never met before, I believe."

The captain waved toward a chair. "That's a fact, Mr. Fosdick," he said. "I don't believe we ever have, but it's better late than by and by, as the feller said. Sit down, sit down, Mr. Fosdick. Throw off your coat, won't you? It's sort of warm in here compared to out door."

The visitor admitted the difference in temperature between the interior and exterior of the building, and removed his overcoat. Also he sat down. Captain Zelotes opened a drawer of his desk and produced a box of cigars.

"Have a smoke, won't you?" he inquired.

Mr. Fosdick glanced at the label on the box.

"Why—why, I was rather hoping you would smoke one of mine," he said. "I have a pocket full."

"When I come callin' on you at your place in New York I will smoke yours. Now it kind of looks to me as if you'd ought to smoke mine. Seems reasonable when you think it over, don't it?"

Fosdick smiled. "Perhaps you're right," he said. He took one of the gaudily banded perfectos from his host's box and accepted a light from the match the captain held. Both men blew a cloud of smoke and through those clouds each looked at the other. The preliminaries were over, but neither seemed particularly anxious to begin the real conversation. It was the visitor who, at last, began it.

"Captain Snow," he said, "I presume your clerk told you I wished to see you on a matter of business."

"Who? Oh, Labe, you mean? Yes, he told me."

"I told him to tell you that. It may surprise you, however, to learn that the business I wished to see you about—that I came on from New York to see you about—has nothing whatever to do with the house I'm building down here."

Captain Zelotes removed his cigar from his lips and looked meditatively at its burning end. "No-o," he said slowly, "that don't surprise me very much. I cal'lated 'twasn't about the house you wished to see me."

"Oh, I see! . . . Humph!" The Fosdick mild blue eye lost, for the moment, just a trifle of its mildness and became almost keen, as its owner flashed a glance at the big figure seated at the desk. "I see," said Mr. Fosdick. "And have you—er—guessed what I did come to see you about?"

"No-o. I wouldn't call it guessin', exactly."

"Wouldn't you? What would you call it?"

"We-ll, I don't know but I'd risk callin' it knowin'. Yes, I think likely I would."

"Oh, I see. . . . Humph! Have you had a letter—on the subject?"

"Ye-es."

"I see. From Mrs. Fosdick, of course. She said she was going to write—I'm not sure she didn't say she had written; but I had the impression it was to—well, to another member of your family, Captain Snow."

"No, 'twas to me. Come this mornin's mail."

"I see. My mistake. Well, I'm obliged to her in a way. If the news has been broken to you, I shan't have to break it and we can get down to brass tacks just so much sooner. The surprise being over—I take it, it WAS a surprise, Captain?"

"You take it right. Just as much of a surprise to me as you."

"Of course. Well, the surprise being over for both of us, we can talk of the affair—calmly and coolly. What do you think about it, Captain?"

"Oh, I don't know as I know exactly what to think. What do YOU think about it, Mr. Fosdick?"

"I think—I imagine I think very much as you do."

"I shouldn't be surprised. And—er—what's your notion of what I think?"

Captain Zelotes' gray eye twinkled as he asked the question, and the Fosdick blue eye twinkled in return. Both men laughed.

"We aren't getting very far this way, Captain," observed the visitor. "There's no use dodging, I suppose. I, for one, am not very well pleased. Mrs. Fosdick, for another, isn't pleased at all; she is absolutely and entirely opposed to the whole affair. She won't hear of it, that's all, and she said so much that I thought perhaps I had better come down here at once, see you, and—and the young fellow with the queer name—"

"My grandson."

"Why yes. He is your grandson, isn't he? I beg your pardon."

"That's all right. I shan't fight with you because you don't like his name. Go ahead. You decided to come and see him—and me—?"

"Yes, I did. I decided to come because it has been my experience that a frank, straight talk is better, in cases like this, than a hundred letters. And that the time to talk was now, before matters between the young foo—the young people went any further. Don't you agree with me?"

Captain Zelotes nodded.

"That now is a good time to talk? Yes, I do," he said.

"Good! Then suppose we talk."

"All right."

There was another interval of silence. Then Fosdick broke it with a chuckle. "And I'm the one to do the talking, eh?" he said.

Captain Lote's eye twinkled. "We-ll, you came all the way from New York on purpose, you know," he observed. Then he added: "But there, Mr. Fosdick, I don't want you to think I ain't polite or won't talk, myself. I'll do my share when the time comes. But it does seem to me that you ought to do yours first as it's your family so far that's done the objectin'.... Your cigar's gone out. Have another light, won't you?"

The visitor shook his head. "No, thank you, not now," he said hastily, placing the defunct cigar carefully on the captain's desk. "I won't smoke for the minute. So you want me to begin the talking, do you? It seems to me I have begun it. I told you that I do not like the idea of my daughter's being engaged to—to say nothing of marrying—your grandson. My wife likes it even less than I do. That is enough of a statement to begin with, isn't it?"

"Why, no, not exactly, if you'll excuse my sayin' so. Your daughter herself—how does she feel about it?"

"Oh, she is enthusiastic, naturally. She appears to be suffering from temporary insanity on the subject."

"She don't seem to think it's quite as—er—preposterous, and ridiculous and outrageous—and Lord knows what all—as your wife does, eh?"

"No. I say, Snow, I hope you're not too deeply offended by what my wife wrote you. I judge you are quoting from her letter and apparently she piled it on red-hot. You'll have to excuse her; she was almost wild all day yesterday. I'll ask your pardon on her behalf."

"Sho, sho! No need, Mr. Fosdick, no need at all. I know what women are, even the easy-goin' kind, when they've got steam up. I've got a wife—and I had a daughter. But, gettin' back on the course again, you think your daughter's crazy because she wants to marry my grandson. Is that it?"

"Why, no, I wouldn't say that, exactly. Of course, I wouldn't say that."

"But, you see, you did say it. However, we'll leave that to one side for a spell. What objection—what real objection is there to those two marryin'—my grandson and your daughter—provided that they care for each other as they'd ought to?"

Mr. Fosdick's expression changed slightly. His tone, as he replied to the question, was colder and his manner less cordial.

"I don't know that it is worth while answering that in detail," he said, after an instant's pause. "Frankly, Captain Snow, I had rather hoped you would see, for yourself, the reasons why such a marriage wouldn't be desirable. If you don't see them, if you are backing up your grandson in his business, why—well, there is no use in our discussing the matter any further, is there? We should only lose our tempers and not gain much. So we had better end it now, I think."

He rose to his feet. Captain Zelotes, leaning forward, held up a protesting hand.

"Now—now, Mr. Fosdick," he said earnestly, "I don't want you to misunderstand me. And I'm sorry if what I said has made you mad."

Fosdick smiled. "Oh, I'm not mad," he answered cheerfully. "I make it a rule in all my business dealings not to get mad, or, more especially, not to let the other fellow know that I'm getting that way. My temper hasn't a ruffle in it just now, and I am leaving merely because I want it to remain smooth. I judge that you and I aren't going to agree. All right, then we'll differ, but we'll differ without a fight, that's all. Good afternoon, Captain."

But Captain Lote's hand still remained uplifted.

"Mr. Fosdick," he said, "just a minute now—just a minute. You never have met Albert, my grandson, have you? Never even seen him, maybe?"

"No, but I intend to meet him and talk with him before I leave South Harniss. He was one of the two people I came here to meet."

"And I was the other, eh? Um-hm. . . . I see. You think you've found out where I stand and now you'll size him up. Honest, Mr. Fosdick, I . . . Humph! Mind if I tell you a little story? 'Twon't take long. When I was a little shaver, me and my granddad, the first Cap'n Lote Snow—there's been two since—were great chums. When he was home from sea he and I stuck together like hot pitch and oakum. One day we were sittin' out in the front yard of his house—it's mine, now—watchin' a hoptoad catch flies. You've seen a toad catch flies, haven't you, Mr. Fosdick? Mr. Toad sits there, lookin' half asleep and as pious and demure as a pickpocket at camp-meetin', until a fly comes along and gets too near. Then, Zip! out shoots about six inches of toad tongue and that fly's been asked in to dinner. Well, granddad and I sat lookin' at our particular toad when along came a bumble-bee and lighted on a honeysuckle blossom right in front of the critter. The toad didn't take time to think it over, all he saw was a square meal, and his tongue flashed out and nailed that bumble-bee and snapped it into the pantry. In about a half second, though, there was a change. The pantry had been emptied, the bumble-bee was on his way again, and Mr. Toad was on his, hoppin' lively and huntin' for—well, for ice water or somethin' coolin', I guess likely. Granddad tapped me on the shoulder. 'Sonny,' says he, 'there's a lesson for you. That hoptoad didn't wait to make sure that bumble-bee was good to eat; he took it for granted, and was sorry afterward. It don't pay to jump at conclusions, son,' he says. 'Some conclusions are like that bumble-bee's, they have stings in 'em.'"

Captain Lote, having finished his story, felt in his pocket for a match. Fosdick, for an instant, appeared puzzled. Then he laughed.

"I see," he said. "You think I made too quick a jump when I concluded you were backing your grandson in this affair. All right, I'm glad to hear it. What do you want me to do, sit down again and listen?"

He resumed his seat as he asked the question. Captain Zelotes nodded.

"If you don't mind," he answered. "You see, you misunderstood me, Mr. Fosdick. I didn't mean any more than what I said when I asked you what real objection there was, in your opinion to Albert's marryin' your—er—Madeline, that's her name, I believe. Seems to me the way for us to get to an understandin'—you and I—is to find out just how the situation looks to each of us. When we've found out that, we'll know how nigh we come to agreein' or disagreein' and can act accordin'. Sounds reasonable, don't it?"

Fosdick nodded in his turn. "Perfectly," he admitted. "Well, ask your questions, and I'll answer them. After that perhaps I'll ask some myself. Go ahead."

"I have gone ahead. I've asked one already."

"Yes, but it is such a general question. There may be so many objections."

"I see. All right, then I'll ask some: What do the lawyers call 'em?—Atlantic? Pacific? I've got it—I'll ask some specific questions. Here's one. Do you object to Al personally? To his character?"

"Not at all. We know nothing about his character. Very likely he may be a young saint."

"Well, he ain't, so we'll let that slide. He's a good boy, though, so far as I've ever been able to find out. Is it his looks? You've never seen him, but your wife has. Don't she like his looks?"

"She hasn't mentioned his looks to me."

"Is it his money? He hasn't got any of his own."

"We-ell, of course that does count a little bit. Madeline is our only child, and naturally we should prefer to have her pick out a husband with a dollar or so in reserve."

"Um-hm. Al's twenty-one, Mr. Fosdick. When I was twenty-one I had some put by, but not much. I presume likely 'twas different with you, maybe. Probably you were pretty well fixed."

Fosdick laughed aloud. "You make a good cross-examiner, Snow," he observed. "As a matter of fact, when I was twenty-one I was assistant bookkeeper in a New Haven broker's office. I didn't have a cent except my salary, and I had that only for the first five days in the week."

"However, you got married?"

"Yes, I did. More fool I! If I had known anything, I should have waited five years at least. I didn't have any one to tell me so. My father and mother were both dead."

"Think you'd have listened to 'em if they had been alive and had told you? However, however, that's all to one side. Well, Albert's havin' no money to speak of is an objection—and a good honest one from your point of view. His prospects here in this business of mine are fair, and he is doin' better at it than he was, so he may make a comf'table livin'—a comf'table South Harniss livin', that is—by and by."

"Oh, he is with you, then? Oh, yes, I remember my wife said he worked in your office. But she said more about his being some sort of a—a poet, wasn't it?"

For the first time since the interview began the captain looked ill at ease and embarrassed.

"Thunderation!" he exclaimed testily, "you mustn't pay attention to that. He does make up poetry' pieces—er—on the side, as you might say, but I keep hopin' all the time he'll grow out of it, give him time. It 'ain't his regular job, you mustn't think 'tis."

The visitor laughed again. "I'm glad of that," he said, "both for your sake and mine. I judge that you and I, Snow, are in complete agreement as far as our opinion of poetry and that sort of stuff is concerned. Of course I'm not condemning all poetry, you understand. Longfellow and Tennyson and the regular poets are all right. You understand what I'm getting at?"

"Sartin. I used to know 'Down went the R'yal George with all her crew complete,' and a lot more. Used to say 'em over to myself when I first went to sea and stood watch alone nights. But they were different, you know; they—they—"

"Sure! My wife—why, I give you my word that my own wife and her set go perfectly daffy over chaps who write stuff that rhymes and that the papers are printing columns about. Snow, if this grandson of yours was a genuine press-touted, women's club poet instead of a would-be—well, I don't know what might happen. In that case she might be as strong FOR this engagement as she is now against it."

The Portygee | 183

He paused, seeming a bit ashamed of his own heat. Captain Zelotes, however, regarded him with more approval than he had yet shown.

"It's been my observation that women are likely to get off the course chasin' false signals like that," he observed. "When a man begins lettin' his hair and his mouth run wild together seems as if the combination had an attraction for a good many women folks. Al keeps his hair cut, though, I'll say that for him," he added. "It curls some, but it ain't long. I wouldn't have him in the office if 'twas."

"Well, Mr. Fosdick," he continued, "what other objections are they? Manners? Family and relations? Education? Any objections along that line?"

"No-o, no; I—well, I don't know; you see, I don't know much about the young fellow."

"Perhaps I can help you out. As to manners—well, you can judge them for yourself when you see him. He seems to be in about every kind of social doin's there is down here, and he's as much or more popular with the summer folks than with the year-'rounders. Education? Well, that's fair to middlin', as I see it. He spent nine or ten years in a mighty expensive boardin' school up in New York State."

"Did he? What school?"

The captain gave the name of the school. Fosdick looked surprised.

"Humph! That IS a good school," he said.

"Is it? Depends on what you call good, I cal'late. Al learned a good deal of this and that, a little bit of foreign language, some that they call dead and some that ought to be dead—and buried, 'cordin' to my notion. When he came to me he couldn't add up a column of ten figgers without makin' a mistake, and as for business—well, what he knew about business was about equal to what Noah knew about a gas engine."

He paused to chuckle, and Fosdick chuckled with him.

"As to family," went on Captain Lote, "he's a Snow on his mother's side, and there's been seven generations of Snow's in this part of the Cape since the first one landed here. So far as I know, they've all managed to keep out of jail, which may have been more good luck than deservin' in some cases."

"His father?" queried Fosdick.

The captain's heavy brows drew together. "His father was a Portygee—or Spaniard, I believe is right—and he was a play-actor, one of those—what do you call 'em?—opera singers."

Fosdick seemed surprised and interested. "Oh, indeed," he exclaimed, "an opera singer? . . . Why, he wasn't Speranza, the baritone, was he?"

"Maybe; I believe he was. He married my daughter and—well, we won't talk about him, if you don't mind."

"But Speranza was a—"

"IF you don't mind, Mr. Fosdick."

Captain Lote lapsed into silence, drumming the desk with his big fingers. His visitor waited for a few moments. At length he said:

"Well, Captain Snow, I have answered your questions and you have answered mine. Do you think we are any nearer an agreement now?"

Captain Zelotes seemed to awake with a start. "Eh?" he queried. "Agreement? Oh, I don't know. Did you find any—er—what you might call vital objections in the boy's record?"

"No-o. No, all that is all right. His family and his education and all the rest are good enough, I'm sure. But, nevertheless—"

"You still object to the young folks gettin' married."

"Yes, I do. Hang it all, Snow, this isn't a thing one can reason out, exactly. Madeline is our only child; she is our pet, our baby. Naturally her mother and I have planned for her, hoped for her, figured that some day, when we had to give her up, it would be to—to—"

"To somebody that wasn't Albert Speranza of South Harniss, Mass. . . . Eh?"

"Yes. Not that your grandson isn't all right. I have no doubt he is a tip-top young fellow. But, you see—"

Captain Lote suddenly leaned forward. "Course I see, Mr. Fosdick," he interrupted. "Course I see. You object, and the objection ain't a mite weaker on account of your not bein' able to say exactly what 'tis."

"That's the idea. Thank you, Captain."

"You're welcome. I can understand. I know just how you feel, because I've been feelin' the same way myself."

"Oh, you have? Good! Then you can sympathize with Mrs. Fosdick and with me. You see—you understand why we had rather our daughter did not marry your grandson."

"Sartin. You see, I've had just the same sort of general kind of objection to Al's marryin' your daughter."

Mr. Fletcher Fosdick leaned slowly backward in his chair. His appearance was suggestive of one who has received an unexpected thump between the eyes.

"Oh, you have!" he said again, but not with the same expression.

"Um-hm," said Captain Zelotes gravely. "I'm like you in one way; I've never met your Madeline any more than you have met Al. I've seen her once or twice, and she is real pretty and nice-lookin'. But I don't know her at all. Now I don't doubt for a minute but that she's a real nice girl and it might be that she'd make Al a fairly good wife."

"Er—well,—thanks."

"Oh, that's all right, I mean it. It might be she would. And I ain't got a thing against you or your folks."

"Humph,—er—thanks again."

"That's all right; you don't need to thank me. But it's this way with me—I live in South Harniss all the year round. I want to live here till I die, and—after I die I'd like first-rate to have Al take up the Z. Snow and Co. business and the Snow house and land and keep them goin' till HE dies. Mind, I ain't at all sure that he'll do it, or be capable of doin' it, but that's what I'd like. Now you're in New York most of the year, and so's your wife and daughter. New York is all right—I ain't sayin' a word against it—but New York and South Harniss are different."

The Fosdick lip twitched. "Somewhat different," he admitted.

"Um-hm. That sounds like a joke, I know; but I don't mean it so, not now. What I mean is that I know South Harniss and South Harniss folks. I don't know New York—not so very well, though I've been there plenty of times—and I don't know New York ways. But I do know South Harniss ways, and they suit me. Would they suit your daughter—not just for summer, but as a reg'lar thing right straight along year in and out? I doubt it, Mr. Fosdick, I doubt it consid'able. Course I don't know your daughter—"

"I do—and I share your doubts."

"Um-hm. But whether she liked it or not she'd have to come here if she married my grandson. Either that or he'd have to go to New York. And if he went to New York, how would he earn his livin'? Get a new bookkeepin' job and start all over again, or live on poetry?"

Mr. Fosdick opened his mouth as if to speak, seemed to change his mind and closed it again, without speaking. Captain Zelotes, looking keenly at him, seemed to guess his thoughts.

"Of course," he said deliberately, but with a firmness which permitted no misunderstanding of his meaning, "of course you mustn't get it into your head for one minute that the boy is figgerin' on your daughter's bein' a rich girl. He hasn't given that a thought. You take my word for that, Mr. Fosdick. He doesn't know how much money she or you have got and he doesn't care. He doesn't care a continental darn."

His visitor smiled slightly. "Nevertheless," he began. The captain interrupted him.

"No, there ain't any nevertheless," he said. "Albert has been with me enough years now so that I know a little about him. And I know that all he wants is your daughter. As to how much she's worth in money or how they're goin' to live after he's got her—I know that he hasn't given it one thought. I don't imagine she has, either. For one reason," he added, with a smile, "he is too poor a business man to think of marriage as a business, bill-payin' contract, and for another,—for another—why, good Lord, Fosdick!" he exclaimed, leaning forward, "don't you know what this thing means to those two young folks? It means just moonshine and mush and lookin' into each other's eyes, that's about all. THEY haven't thought any practical thoughts about it. Why, think what their ages are! Think of yourself at that age! Can't you remember. . . . Humph! Well, I'm talkin' fifty revolutions to the second. I beg your pardon."

"That's all right, Snow. And I believe you have the situation sized up as it is. Still—"

"Excuse me, Mr. Fosdick, but don't you think it's about time you had a look at the boy himself? I'm goin' to ask him to come in here and meet you."

Fosdick looked troubled. "Think it is good policy?" he asked doubtfully. "I want to see him and speak with him, but I do hate a scene."

"There won't be any scene. You just meet him face to face and talk enough with him to get a little idea of what your first impression is. Don't contradict or commit yourself or anything. And I'll send him out at the end of two or three minutes."

Without waiting for a reply, he rose, opened the door to the outer office and called, "Al, come in here!" When Albert had obeyed the order he closed the door behind him and turning to the gentleman in the visitor's chair, said: "Mr. Fosdick, this is my grandson, Albert Speranza. Al, shake hands with Mr. Fosdick from New York."

While awaiting the summons to meet the father of his adored, Albert had been rehearsing and re-rehearsing the speeches he intended making when that meeting took place. Sitting at his desk, pen in hand and pretending to be busy with the bookkeeping of Z. Snow and Company, he had seen, not the ruled page of the day book, but the parental countenance of the Honorable Fletcher Fosdick. And, to his mind's eye, that countenance was as rugged and stern as the rock-bound coast upon which the Pilgrims landed, and about as unyielding and impregnable as the door of the office safe. So, when his grandfather called him, he descended from the tall desk stool and crossed the threshold of the inner room, a trifle pale, a little shaky at the knees, but with the set chin and erect head of one who, facing almost hopeless odds, intends fighting to the last gasp.

To his astonishment the Fosdick countenance was not as his imagination had pictured it. The blue eyes met his, not with a glare or a glower, but with a look of interest and inquiry. The Fosdick hand shook his with politeness, and the Fosdick manner was, if not genial, at least quiet and matter of fact. He was taken aback. What did it mean? Was it possible that Madeline's father was inclined to regard her engagement to him with favor? A great throb of joy accompanied the thought. Then he remembered the letter he had just read, the letter from Madeline's mother, and the hope subsided.

"Albert," said Captain Zelotes, "Mr. Fosdick has come on here to talk with us; that is, with me and you, about your affairs. He and I have talked up to the point where it seemed to me you ought to come in for a spell. I've told him that the news that you and his daughter were—er—favorably disposed toward each other was as sudden and as big a surprise to me as 'twas to him. Even your grandma don't know it yet. Now I presume likely he'd like to ask you a few questions. Heave ahead, Mr. Fosdick."

He relit his cigar stump and leaned back in his chair. Mr. Fosdick leaned forward in his. Albert stood very straight, his shoulders braced for the encounter. The quizzical twinkle shone in Captain Lote's eye as he regarded his grandson. Fosdick also smiled momentarily as he caught the expression of the youth's face.

"Well, Speranza," he began, in so cheerful a tone that Albert's astonishment grew even greater, "your grandfather has been kind enough to get us through the preliminaries, so we'll come at once to the essentials. You and my daughter consider yourselves engaged to marry?"

"Yes, sir. We ARE engaged."

"I see. How long have you—um—been that way, so to speak?"

"Since last August."

"Why haven't you said anything about it to us—to Mrs. Fosdick or me or your people here? You must excuse these personal questions. As I have just said to Captain Snow, Madeline is our only child, and her happiness and welfare mean about all there is in life to her mother and me. So, naturally, the man she is going to marry is an important consideration. You and I have never met before, so the quickest way of reaching an understanding between us is by the question route. You get my meaning?"

"Yes, sir, I guess I do."

"Good! Then we'll go ahead. Why have you two kept it a secret so long?"

"Because—well, because we knew we couldn't marry yet a while, so we thought we had better not announce it for the present."

"Oh! . . . And the idea that perhaps Mrs. Fosdick and I might be slightly interested didn't occur to you?"

"Why, yes, sir, it did. But,—but we thought it best not to tell you until later."

"Perhaps the suspicion that we might not be overjoyed by the news had a little weight with you, eh? Possibly that helped to delay the—er—announcement?"

"No, sir, I—I don't think it did."

"Oh, don't you! Perhaps you thought we WOULD be overjoyed?"

"No, sir. We didn't think so very much about it. Well, that's not quite true. Madeline felt that her mother—and you, too, sir, I suppose, although she didn't speak as often of you in that way—she felt that her mother would disapprove at first, and so we had better wait."

"Until when?"

"Until—until by and by. Until I had gone ahead further, you know."

"I'm not sure that I do know. Gone ahead how? Until you had a better position, more salary?"

"No, not exactly. Until my writings were better known. Until I was a little more successful."

"Successful? Until you wrote more poetry, do you mean?"

"Yes, sir. Poetry and other things, stories and plays, perhaps."

"Do you mean—Did you figure that you and Madeline were to live on what you made by writing poetry and the other stuff?"

"Yes, sir, of course."

Fosdick looked across at Captain Zelotes. The Captain's face was worth looking at.

"Here, here, hold on!" he exclaimed, jumping into the conversation. "Al, what are you talkin' about? You're bookkeeper for me, ain't you; for this concern right here where you are? What do you mean by talkin' as if your job was makin' up poetry pieces? That's only what you do on the side, and you know it. Eh, ain't that so?"

Albert hesitated. He had, momentarily, forgotten his grandfather and the latter's prejudices. After all, what was the use of stirring up additional trouble.

"Yes, Grandfather," he said.

"Course it's so. It's in this office that you draw your wages."

"Yes, Grandfather."

"All right. Excuse me for nosin' in, Mr. Fosdick, but I knew the boy wasn't puttin' the thing as plain as it ought to be, and I didn't want you to get the wrong notion. Heave ahead."

Fosdick smiled slightly. "All right, Captain," he said. "I get it, I think. Well, then," turning again to Albert, "your plan for supporting my daughter was to wait until your position here, plus the poetry, should bring in sufficient revenue. It didn't occur to you that—well, that there might be a possibility of getting money—elsewhere?"

Albert plainly did not understand, but it was just as plain that his grandfather did. Captain Zelotes spoke sharply.

"Mr. Fosdick," he said, "I just answered that question for you."

"Yes, I know. But if you were in my place you might like to have him answer it. I don't mean to be offensive, but business is business, and, after all, this is a business talk. So—"

The Captain interrupted. "So we'll talk it in a business way, eh?" he snapped. "All right. Al, what Mr. Fosdick means is had you cal'lated that, if you married his daughter, maybe her dad's money might help you and her to keep goin'? To put it even plainer: had you planned some on her bein' a rich girl?"

Fosdick looked annoyed. "Oh, I say, Snow!" he cried. "That's too strong, altogether."

"Not a mite. It's what you've had in the back of your head all along. I'm just helpin' it to come out of the front. Well, Al?"

The red spots were burning in the Speranza cheeks. He choked as he answered.

"No," he cried fiercely. "Of course I haven't planned on any such thing. I don't know how rich she is. I don't care. I wish she was as poor as—as I am. I want HER, that's all. And she wants me. We don't either of us care about money. I wouldn't take a cent of your money, Mr. Fosdick. But I—I want Madeline and—and—I shall have her."

"In spite of her parents, eh?"

"Yes.... I'm sorry to speak so, Mr. Fosdick, but it is true. We—we love each other. We—we've agreed to wait for each other, no matter—no matter if it is years and years. And as for the money and all that, if you disinherit her, or—or whatever it is they do—we don't care. I—I hope you will. I—she—"

Captain Zelotes' voice broke in upon the impassioned outburst.

"Steady, Al; steady, son," he cautioned quietly. "I cal'late you've said enough. I don't think any more's necessary. You'd better go back to your desk now."

"But, Grandfather, I want him to understand—"

"I guess likely he does. I should say you'd made it real plain. Go now, Al."

Albert turned, but, with a shaking hand upon the doorknob, turned back again.

"I'm—I—I'm sorry, Mr. Fosdick," he faltered. "I—I didn't mean to say anything to hurt your feelings. But—but, you see, Madeline—she and I—we—"

He could not go on. Fosdick's nod and answer were not unkindly. "All right, Speranza," he said, "I'm not offended. Hope I wasn't too blunt, myself. Good-day."

When the door had closed behind the young man he turned to Captain Lote.

"Sorry if I offended you, Snow," he observed. "I threw in that hint about marrying just to see what effect it would have, that's all."

"Um-hm. So I judged. Well, you saw, didn't you?"

"I did. Say, Captain, except as a prospective son-in-law, and then only because I don't see him in that light—I rather like that grandson of yours. He's a fine, upstanding young chap."

The captain made no reply. He merely pulled at his beard. However, he did not look displeased.

"He's a handsome specimen, isn't he?" went on Fosdick. "No wonder Madeline fell for his looks. Those and the poetry together are a combination hard to resist—at her age. And he's a gentleman. He handled himself mighty well while I was stringing him just now."

The beard tugging continued. "Um-hm," observed Captain Zelotes dryly; "he does pretty well for a—South Harniss gentleman. But we're kind of wastin' time, ain't we, Mr. Fosdick? In spite of his looks and his manners and all the rest, now that you've seen him you still object to that engagement, I take it."

"Why, yes, I do. The boy is all right, I'm sure, but—"

"Sartin, I understand. I feel the same way about your girl. She's all right, I'm sure, but—"

"We're agreed on everything, includin' the 'but.' And the 'but' is that New York is one place and South Harniss is another."

"Exactly."

"So we don't want 'em to marry. Fine. First rate! Only now we come to the most important 'but' of all. What are we going to do about it? Suppose we say no and they say yes and keep on sayin' it? Suppose they decide to get married no matter what we say. How are we goin' to stop it?"

His visitor regarded him for a moment and then broke into a hearty laugh.

"Snow," he declared, "you're all right. You surely have the faculty of putting your finger on the weak spots. Of course we can't stop it. If these two young idiots have a mind to marry and keep that mind, they WILL marry and we can't prevent it any more than we could prevent the tide coming in to-morrow morning. *I* realized that this was a sort of fool's errand, my coming down here. I know that this isn't the age when parents can forbid marriages and get away with it, as they used to on the stage in the old plays. Boys and girls nowadays have a way of going their own gait in such matters. But my wife doesn't see it in exactly that way, and she was so insistent on my coming down here to stop the thing if I could that—well, I came."

"I'm glad you did, Mr. Fosdick, real glad. And, although I agree with you that the very worst thing to do, if we want to stop this team from pullin' together, is to haul back on the bits and holler 'Whoa,' still I'm kind of hopeful that, maybe . . . humph! I declare, it looks as if I'd have to tell you another story. I'm gettin' as bad as Cap'n Hannibal Doane used to be, and they used to call him 'The Rope Walk' 'cause he spun so many yarns."

Fosdick laughed again. "You may go as far as you like with your stories, Captain," he said. "I can grow fat on them."

"Thanks. Well, this ain't a story exactly; it just kind of makes the point I'm tryin' to get at. Calvin Bangs had a white mare one time and the critter had a habit of runnin' away. Once his wife, Hannah J., was in the buggy all by herself, over to the Ostable Fair, Calvin havin' got out to buy some peanuts or somethin'. The mare got scared of the noise and crowd and bolted. As luck would have it, she went right through the fence and out onto the trottin' track. And around that track she went, hell bent for election. All hands was runnin' alongside hollerin' 'Stop her! Stop her! 'but not Calvin—no SIR! He waited till the mare was abreast of him, the mare on two legs and the buggy on two wheels and Hannah 'most anywheres between the dasher and the next world, and then he sung out: 'Give her her head, Hannah! Give her her head. She'll stop when she runs down.'"

He laughed and his visitor laughed with him.

"I gather," observed the New Yorker, "that you believe it the better policy to give our young people their heads."

"In reason—yes, I do. It's my judgment that an affair like this will hurry more and more if you try too hard to stop it. If you don't try at all so any one would notice it, it may run down and stop of itself, the way Calvin's mare did."

Fosdick nodded reflectively. "I'm inclined to agree with you," he said. "But does that mean that they're to correspond, write love letters, and all that?"

"Why, in reason, maybe. If we say no to that, they'll write anyhow, won't they?"

"Of course.... How would it do to get them to promise to write nothing that their parents might not see? Of course I don't mean for your grandson to show you his letters before he sends them to Madeline. He's too old for that, and he would refuse. But suppose you asked him to agree to write nothing that Madeline would not be willing to show her mother—or me. Do you think he would?"

"Maybe. I'll ask him.... Yes, I guess likely he'd do that."

"My reason for suggesting it is, frankly, not so much on account of the young people as to pacify my wife. I am not afraid—not very much afraid of this love affair. They are young, both of them. Give them time, and—as you say, Snow, the thing may run down, peter out."

"I'm in hopes 'twill. It's calf love, as I see it, and I believe 'twill pay to give the calves rope enough."

"So do I. No, I'm not much troubled about the young people. But Mrs. Fosdick—well, my trouble will be with her. She'll want to have your boy shot or jailed or hanged or something."

"I presume likely. I guess you'll have to handle her the way another feller who used to live here in South Harniss said he handled his wife. 'We don't never have any trouble at all,' says he. 'Whenever she says yes or no, I say the same thing. Later on, when it comes to doin', I do what I feel like.' . . . Eh? You're not goin', are you, Mr. Fosdick?"

His visitor had risen and was reaching for his coat. Captain Zelotes also rose.

"Don't hurry, don't hurry," he begged.

"Sorry, but I must. I want to be back in New York tomorrow morning."

"But you can't, can you? To do that you'll have to get up to Boston or Fall River, and the afternoon train's gone. You'd better stay and have supper along with my wife and me, stay at our house over night, and take the early train after breakfast to-morrow."

"I wish I could; I'd like nothing better. But I can't."

"Sure?" Then, with a smile, he added: "Al needn't eat with us, you know, if his bein' there makes either of you feel nervous."

Fosdick laughed again. "I think I should be willing to risk the nervousness," he replied. "But I must go, really. I've hired a chap at the garage here to drive me to Boston in his car and I'll take the midnight train over."

"Humph! Well, if you must, you must. Hope you have a comf'table trip, Mr. Fosdick. Better wrap up warm; it's pretty nigh a five-hour run to Boston and there's some cool wind over the Ostable marshes this time of year. Good-by, sir. Glad to have had this talk with you."

His visitor held out his hand. "So am I, Snow," he said heartily. "Mighty glad."

"I hope I wasn't too short and brisk at the beginnin'. You see, I'd just read your wife's letter, and—er—well, of course, I didn't know—just—you see, you and I had never met, and so—"

"Certainly, certainly. I quite understand. And, fool's errand or not, I'm very glad I came here. If you'll pardon my saying so, it was worth the trip to get acquainted with you. I hope, whatever comes of the other thing, that our acquaintanceship will continue."

"Same here, same here. Go right out the side door, Mr. Fosdick, saves goin' through the office. Good day, sir."

He watched the bulky figure of the New York banker tramping across the yard between the piles of lumber. A moment later he entered the outer office. Albert and Keeler were at their desks. Captain Zelotes approached the little bookkeeper.

"Labe," he queried, "there isn't anything particular you want me to talk about just now, is there?"

Lahan looked up in surprise from his figuring.

"Why—why, no, Cap'n Lote, don't know's there is," he said. "Don't know's there is, not now, no, no, no."

His employer nodded. "Good!" he exclaimed. "Then I'm goin' back inside there and sit down and rest my chin for an hour, anyhow. I've talked so much to-day that my jaws squeak. Don't disturb me for anything short of a fire or a mutiny."

CHAPTER XII

He was not disturbed and that evening, after supper was over, he was ready to talk again. He and Albert sat together in the sitting room—Mrs. Snow and Rachel were in the kitchen washing dishes—and Captain Zelotes told his grandson as much as he thought advisable to tell of his conversation with the Honorable Fletcher Fosdick. At first Albert was inclined to rebel at the idea of permitting his letters to Madeline to be read by the latter's parents, but at length he agreed.

"I'll do it because it may make it easier for her," he said. "She'll have a dreadful time, I suppose, with that unreasonable mother of hers. But, by George, Grandfather," he exclaimed, "isn't she splendid, though!"

"Who? Mrs. Fosdick?"

"No, of course not," indignantly. "Madeline. Isn't she splendid and fine and loyal! I want you to know her, Grandfather, you and Grandmother."

"Um-hm. Well, we'll hope to, some day. Now, son, I'm goin' to ask for another promise. It may seem a hard one to make, but I'm askin' you to make it. I want you to give me your word that, no matter what happens or how long you have to wait, you and Madeline won't get married without tellin' her folks and yours beforehand. You won't run away and marry. Will you promise me that?"

Albert looked at him. This WAS a hard promise to make. In their talks beneath the rainbows, whenever he and Madeline had referred to the future and its doubts, they had always pushed those doubts aside with vague hints of an elopement. If the unreasonableness of parents and grandparents should crowd them too far, they had always as a last resort, the solution of their problem by way of a runaway marriage. And now Captain Zelotes was asking him to give up this last resort.

The captain, watching him keenly, divined what was in his grandson's mind.

"Think it over, Al," he said kindly. "Don't answer me now, but think it over, and to-morrow mornin' tell me how you feel about it." He hesitated a moment and then added: "You know your grandmother and I, we—well, we have maybe cause to be a little mite prejudiced against this elopin' business."

So Albert thought, and the next morning, as the pair were walking together to the office, he spoke his thought. Captain Zelotes had not mentioned the subject.

"Grandfather," said Albert, with some embarrassment, "I'm going to give you that promise."

His grandfather, who had been striding along, his heavy brows drawn together and his glance fixed upon the frozen ground beneath his feet, looked up.

"Eh?" he queried, uncomprehendingly.

"You asked me last night to promise you something, you know. . . . You asked me to think it over. I have, and I'm going to promise you that—Madeline and I won't marry without first telling you."

Captain Zelotes stopped in his stride; then he walked on again.

"Thank you, Al," he said quietly. "I hoped you'd see it that way."

"Yes—yes, I—I do. I don't want to bring any more—trouble of that kind to you and Grandmother. . . . It seems to me that you—that you have had too much already."

"Thank you, son. . . . Much obliged."

The captain's tone was almost gruff and that was his only reference to the subject of the promise; but somehow Albert felt that at that moment he and his grandfather were closer together, were nearer to a mutual understanding and mutual appreciation than they had ever been before.

To promise, however, is one thing, to fulfill the obligation another. As the days passed Albert found his promise concerning letter-writing very, very hard to keep. When, each evening he sat down at the table in his room to pour out his soul upon paper it was a most unsatisfactory outpouring. The constantly enforced recollection that whatever he wrote would be subject to the chilling glance of the eye of Fosdick mater was of itself a check upon the flow. To write a love letter to Madeline had hitherto been a joy, a rapture, to fill pages and pages a delight. Now, somehow, these pages were hard to fill. Omitting the very things you were dying to say, the precious, the intimate things—what was there left? He and she had, at their meetings and in their former correspondence, invented many delightful little pet names for each other. Now those names were taboo; or, at any rate, they might as well be. The thought of Mrs. Fosdick's sniff of indignant disgust at finding her daughter referred to as some one's ownest little rosebud withered that bud before it reached the paper.

And Madeline's letters to him were quite as unsatisfactory. They were lengthy, but oh, so matter of fact! Saharas of fact without one oasis of sentiment. She was well and she had done this and that and had been to see such and such plays and operas. Father was well and very busy. Mother, too, was well, so was Googoo—but these last two bits of news failed to comfort him as they perhaps should. He could only try to glean between the lines, and as Mrs. Fosdick had raked between those lines before him, the gleaning was scant picking indeed.

He found himself growing disconsolate and despondent. Summer seemed ages away. And when at last it should come—what would happen then? He could see her only when properly chaperoned, only when Mother, and probably Googoo, were present. He flew for consolation to the Muse and the Muse refused to console. The poems he wrote were "blue" and despairing likewise. Consequently they did not sell. He was growing desperate, ready for anything. And something came. Germany delivered to our Government its arrogant mandate concerning unlimited submarine warfare. A long-suffering President threw patience overboard and answered that mandate in unmistakable terms. Congress stood at his back and behind them a united and indignant people. The United States declared war upon the Hun.

South Harniss, like every other community, became wildly excited. Captain Zelotes Snow's gray eyes flashed fiery satisfaction. The flags at the Snow place and at the lumber yard flew high night and day. He bought newspapers galore and read from them aloud at meals, in the evenings, and before breakfast. Issachar, as usual, talked much and said little. Laban Keeler's comments were pithy and dryly pointed. Albert was very quiet.

But one forenoon he spoke. Captain Lote was in the inner office, the morning newspaper in his hand, when his grandson entered and closed the door behind him. The captain looked up.

"Well, Al, what is it?" he asked.

Albert came over and stood beside the desk. The captain, after a moment's scrutiny of the young man's face, put down his newspaper.

"Well, Al?" he said, again.

Albert seemed to find it hard to speak.

"Grandfather," he began, "I—I—Grandfather, I have come to ask a favor of you."

The captain nodded, slowly, his gaze fixed upon his grandson's face.

"All right; heave ahead," he said quietly.

"Grandfather, you and I have had a four years' agreement to work together in this office. It isn't up yet, but—but I want to break it. I want you to let me off."

"Humph! . . . Let you off, eh? . . . What for?"

"That's what I came here to tell you. Grandfather, I can't stay here—now. I want to enlist."

Captain Zelotes did not answer. His hand moved upward and pulled at his beard.

"I want to enlist," repeated Albert. "I can't stand it another minute. I must. If it hadn't been for you and our promise and—and Madeline, I think I should have joined the Canadian Army a year or more ago. But now that we have gone into the war, I CAN'T stay out. Grandfather, you don't want me to, do you? Of course you don't."

His grandfather appeared to ponder.

"If you can wait a spell," he said slowly, "I might be able to fix it so's you can get a chance for an officer's commission. I'd ought to have some pull somewheres, seems so."

Albert sniffed impatient disgust. "I don't want to get a commission—in that way," he declared.

"Humph! You'll find there's plenty that do, I shouldn't wonder."

"Perhaps, but I'm not one of them. And I don't care so much for a commission, unless I can earn it. And I don't want to stay here and study for it. I want to go now. I want to get into the thing. I don't want to wait."

Captain Lote leaned forward. His gray eyes snapped.

"Want to fight, do you?" he queried.

"You bet I do!"

"All right, my boy, then go—and fight. I'd be ashamed of myself if I held you back a minute. Go and fight—and fight hard. I only wish to God I was young enough to go with you."

CHAPTER XIII

And so, in this unexpected fashion, came prematurely the end of the four year trial agreement between Albert Speranza and Z. Snow and Co. Of course neither Captain Zelotes nor Albert admitted that it had ended. Each professed to regard the break as merely temporary.

"You'll be back at that desk in a little while, Al," said the captain, "addin' up figgers and tormentin' Issy." And Albert's reply was invariably, "Why, of course, Grandfather."

He had dreaded his grandmother's reception of the news of his intended enlistment. Olive worshiped her daughter's boy and, although an ardent patriot, was by no means as fiercely belligerent as her husband. She prayed each night for the defeat of the Hun, whereas Captain Lote was for licking him first and praying afterwards. Albert feared a scene; he feared that she might be prostrated when she learned that he was to go to war. But she bore it wonderfully well, and as for the dreaded "scene," there was none.

"Zelotes says he thinks it's the right thing for you to do, Albert," she said, "so I suppose I ought to think so, too. But, oh, my dear, DO you really feel that you must? I—it don't seem as I could bear to . . . but there, I mustn't talk so. It ain't a mite harder for me than it is for thousands of women all over this world. . . . And perhaps the government folks won't take you, anyway. Rachel said she read in the Item about some young man over in Bayport who was rejected because he had fat feet. She meant flat feet, I suppose, poor thing. Oh, dear me, I'm laughin', and it seems wicked to laugh a time like this. And when I think of you goin', Albert, I—I . . . but there, I promised Zelotes I wouldn't. . . . And they MAY not take you. . . . But oh, of course they will, of course they will! . . . I'm goin' to make you a chicken pie for dinner to-day; I know how you like it. . . . If only they MIGHT reject you! . . . But there, I said I wouldn't and I won't."

Rachel Ellis's opinion on the subject and her way of expressing that opinion were distinctly her own. Albert arose early in the morning following the announcement of his decision to enter the service. He had not slept well; his mind was too busy with problems and speculations to resign itself to sleep. He had tossed about until dawn and had then risen and sat down at the table in his bedroom to write Madeline of the step he had determined to take. He had not written her while he was considering that step. He felt, somehow, that he alone with no pressure from without should make the decision. Now that it was made, and irrevocably made, she must of course be told. Telling her, however, was not an easy task. He was sure she would agree that he had done the right thing, the only thing, but—

"It is going to be very hard for you, dear," he wrote, heedless of the fact that Mrs. Fosdick's censorious eye would see and condemn the "dear." "It is going to be hard for both of us. But I am sure you will feel as I do that I COULDN'T do anything else. I am young and strong and fit and I am an American. I MUST go. You see it, don't you, Madeline. I can hardly wait until your letter comes telling me that you feel I did just the thing you would wish me to do."

He hesitated and then, even more regardless of the censor, added the quotation which countless young lovers were finding so apt just then:

"I could not love thee, dear, so much,
Loved I not honor more."

So when, fresh from the intimacy of this communication with his adored and with the letter in his hand, he entered the sitting-room at that early hour he was not overjoyed to find the housekeeper there ahead of him. And her first sentence showed that she had been awaiting his coming.

"Good mornin', Albert," she said. "I heard you stirrin' 'round up in your room and I came down here so's you and I could talk together for a minute without anybody's disturbin' us. . . . Humph! I guess likely you didn't sleep any too well last night, did you?"

Albert shook his head. "Not too well, Rachel," he replied.

"I shouldn't wonder. Well, I doubt if there was too much sleep anywheres in this house last night. So you're really goin' to war, are you, Albert?"

"Yes. If the war will let me I certainly am."

"Dear, dear! . . . Well, I—I think it's what Robert Penfold would have done if he was in your place. I've been goin' over it and goin' over it half the night, myself, and I've come to that conclusion. It's goin' to be awful hard on your grandma and grandfather and me and Labe, all us folks here at home, but I guess it's the thing you'd ought to do, the Penfold kind of thing."

Albert smiled. "I'm glad you think so, Rachel," he said.

"Well, I do, and if I'm goin' to tell the truth I might as well say I tried terrible hard to find some good reasons for thinkin' 'twan't. I did SO! But the only good reasons I could scare up for makin' you stay to home was because home was safe and comf'table and where you was goin' wan't. And that kind of reasonin' might do fust-rate for a passel of clams out on the flats, but it wouldn't be much credit to decent, self-respectin' humans. When General Rolleson came to that island and found his daughter and Robert Penfold livin' there in that house made out of pearls he'd built for her—Wan't that him all over! Another man, the common run of man, would have been satisfied to build her a house out of wood and lucky to get that, but no, nothin' would do him but pearls, and if they'd have been di'monds he'd have been better satisfied. Well. . . . Where was I? . . . Oh yes! When General Rolleson came there and says to his daughter, 'Helen, you come home along of me,' and she says, 'No, I shan't leave him,' meanin' Robert Penfold, you understand—When she says that did Robert Penfold say, 'That's the talk! Put that in your pipe, old man, and smoke it?' No, SIR, he didn't! He says, 'Helen, you go straight home along with your pa and work like fury till you find out who forged that note and laid it onto me. You find that out,' he says, 'and then you can come fetch me and not afore.' That's the kind of man HE was! And they sailed off and left him behind."

Albert shook his head. He had heard only about half of the housekeeper's story. "Pretty rough on him, I should say," he commented, absently.

"I GUESS 'twas rough on him, poor thing! But 'twas his duty and so he done it. It was rough on Helen, havin' to go and leave him, but 'twas rougher still on him. It's always roughest, seems to me," she added, "on the ones that's left behind. Those that go have somethin' to take up their minds and keep 'em from thinkin' too much. The ones that stay to home don't have much to do EXCEPT think. I hope you don't get the notion that I feel your part of it is easy, Al. Only a poor, crazy idiot could read the papers these days and feel that any part of this war was EASY! It's awful, but—but it WILL keep you too busy to think, maybe."

"I shouldn't wonder, Rachel. I understand what you mean."

"We're all goin' to miss you, Albert. This house is goin' to be a pretty lonesome place, I cal'late. Your grandma'll miss you dreadful and so will I, but—but I have a notion that your grandpa's goin' to miss you more'n anybody else."

He shook his head. "Oh, not as much as all that, Rachel," he said. "He and I have been getting on much better than we used to and we have come to understand each other better, but he is still disappointed in me. I'm afraid I don't count for much as a business man, you see; and, besides, Grandfather can never quite forget that I am the son of what he calls a Portygee play actor."

Mrs. Ellis looked at him earnestly. "He's forgettin' it better every day, Albert," she said. "I do declare I never believed Capt'n Lote Snow could forget it the way he's doin'. And you—well, you've forgot a whole lot, too. Memory's a good thing, the land knows," she added, sagely, "but a nice healthy forgetery is worth consider'ble—some times and in some cases."

Issachar Price's comments on his fellow employee's decision to become a soldier were pointed. Issy was disgusted.

"For thunder sakes, Al," he demanded, "'tain't true that you've enlisted to go to war and fight them Germans, is it?"

Albert smiled. "I guess it is, Issy," he replied.

"Well, by crimus!"

"Somebody had to go, you see, Is."

"Well, by crimustee!"

"What's the matter, Issy? Don't you approve?"

"Approve! No, by crimus, I don't approve! I think it's a divil of a note, that's what I think."

"Why?"

"WHY? Who's goin' to do the work in this office while you're gone? Labe and me, that's who; and I'll do the heft of it. Slavin' myself half to death as 'tis and now—Oh, by crimustee! This war is a darned nuisance. It hadn't ought to be allowed. There'd ought to be a law against it."

But of all the interviews which followed Albert's decision the most surprising and that which he was the least likely to forget was his interview with Laban Keeler. It took place on the evening of the third day following the announcement of his intention to enlist. All that day, and indeed for several days, Albert had noted in the little bookkeeper certain symptoms, familiar symptoms they were and from experience the young man knew what they portended. Laban was very nervous, his fingers twitched as he wrote, occasionally he rose from his chair and walked up and down the room, he ran his hand through his scanty hair, he was inclined to be irritable—that is, irritable for him. Albert had noted the symptoms and was sorry. Captain Zelotes noted them and frowned and pulled his beard.

"Al," he said to his grandson, "if you can put off goin' up to enlist for a little spell, a few days, I wish you would. Labe's gettin' ready to go on one of his vacations."

Albert nodded. "I'm afraid he is," he said.

"Oh, it's as sartin as two and two makes four. I've lived with him too many years not to know the signs. And I did hope," he added, regretfully, "that maybe he was tryin' to break off. It's been a good long spell, an extry long spell, since he had his last spree. Ah hum! it's a pity a good man should have that weak spot in him, ain't it? But if you could hang around a few more days, while the vacation's goin' on, I'd appreciate it, Al. I kind of hate to be left here alone with nobody but Issachar to lean on. Issy's a good deal like a post in some ways, especially in the makeup of his head, but he's too ricketty to lean on for any length of time."

That evening Albert went to the post-office for the mail. On his way back as he passed the dark corner by the now closed and shuttered moving-picture theater he was hailed in a whisper.

"Al," said a voice, "Al."

Albert turned and peered into the deep shadow of the theater doorway. In the summer this doorway was a blaze of light and gaiety; now it was cold and bleak and black enough. From the shadow a small figure emerged on tiptoe.

"Al," whispered Mr. Keeler. "That's you, ain't it? Yes, yes—yes, yes, yes—I thought 'twas, I thought so."

Albert was surprised. For one thing it was most unusual to see the little bookkeeper abroad after nine-thirty. His usual evening procedure, when not on a vacation, was to call upon Rachel Ellis at the Snow place for an hour or so and then to return to his room over Simond's shoe store, which room he had occupied ever since the building was erected.

There he read, so people said, until eleven sharp, when his lamp was extinguished. During or at the beginning of the vacation periods he usually departed for some unknown destination, destinations which, apparently, varied. He had been seen, hopelessly intoxicated, in Bayport, in Ostable, in Boston, once in Providence. When he returned he never seemed to remember exactly where he had been. And, as most people were fond of and pitied him, few questions were asked.

"Why, Labe!" exclaimed Albert. "Is that you? What's the matter?"

"Busy, are you, Al?" queried Laban. "In a hurry, eh? Are you? In a hurry, Al, eh?"

"Why no, not especially."

"Could you—could you spare me two or three minutes? Two or three minutes—yes, yes? Come up to my room, could you—could you, Al?"

"Yes indeed. But what is it, Labe?"

"I want to talk. Want to talk, I do. Yes, yes, yes. Saw you go by and I've been waitin' for you. Waitin'—yes, I have—yes."

He seized his assistant by the arm and led him across the road toward the shoe store. Albert felt the hand on his arm tremble violently.

"Are you cold, Labe?" he asked. "What makes you shiver so?"

"Eh? Cold? No, I ain't cold—no, no, no. Come, Al, come."

Albert sniffed suspiciously, but no odor of alcohol rewarded the sniff. Neither was there any perfume of peppermint, Mr. Keeler's transparent camouflage at a vacation's beginning. And Laban was not humming the refrain glorifying his "darling hanky-panky." Apparently he had not yet embarked upon the spree which Captain Lote had pronounced imminent. But why did he behave so queerly?

"I ain't the way you think, Al," declared the little man, divining his thought. "I'm just kind of shaky and nervous, that's all. That's all, that's all, that's all. Yes, yes. Come, come! COME!"

The last "come" burst from him in an agony of impatience. Albert hastened up the narrow stairs, Laban leading the way. The latter fumbled with a key, his companion heard it rattling against the keyhole plate. Then the door opened. There was a lamp, its wick turned low, burning upon the table in the room. Mr. Keeler turned it up, making a trembly job of the turning. Albert looked about him; he had never been in that room before.

It was a small room and there was not much furniture in it. And it was a neat room, for the room of an old bachelor who was his own chambermaid. Most things seemed to have places where they belonged and most of them appeared to be in those places. What impressed Albert even more was the number of books. There were books everywhere, in the cheap bookcase, on the pine shelf between the windows, piled in the corners, heaped on the table beside the lamp. They were worn and shabby volumes for the most part, some with but half a cover remaining, some with none. He picked up one of the latter. It was Locke on The Human Understanding; and next it, to his astonishment, was Alice's Adventures in Wonderland.

Mr. Keeler looked over his shoulder and, for an instant, the whimsical smile which was characteristic of him curved his lip.

"Philosophy, Al," he observed. "If Locke don't suit you try the 'mad hatter' feller. I get consider'ble comfort out of the hatter, myself. Do you remember when the mouse was tellin' the story about the three sisters that lived in the well? He said they lived on everything that began with M. Alice says 'Why with an M?' And the hatter, or the March hare, I forget which 'twas, says prompt, 'Why not?' . . . Yes, yes, why not? that's what he said. . . . . There's some philosophy in that, Al. Why does a hen go across the road? Why not? Why is Labe Keeler a disgrace to all his friends and the town he lives in? Why not? . . . Eh? . . . Yes, yes. That's it—why not?"

He smiled again, but there was bitterness and not humor in the smile. Albert put a hand on his shoulder.

"Why, Labe," he asked, in concern, "what is it?"

Laban turned away.

"Don't mind, me, Al," he said, hurriedly. "I mean don't mind if I act funny. I'm—I'm kind of—of—Oh, good Lord A'mighty, DON'T look at me like that! . . . I beg your pardon, Al. I didn't mean to bark like a dog at you. No, I didn't—no, no. Forgive me, will you? Will you, Al, eh?"

"Of course I will. But what is the matter, Labe? Sit down and tell me about it."

Instead of sitting the little bookkeeper began to walk up and down.

"Don't mind me, Al," he said, hurriedly. "Don't mind me. Let me go my own gait. My own gait—yes, yes. You see, Al, I—I'm tryin' to enlist, same as you're goin' to do, and—and MY fight's begun already. Yes indeed—yes, yes—it has so."

Albert was more astonished than ever. There was no smell of alcohol, and Keeler had declared that he had not been drinking; but—

"You're going to ENLIST?" repeated Albert. "YOU? Why, Labe, what—"

Laban laughed nervously. "Not to kill the Kaiser," he replied. "No, no, not that—not exactly. I'd like to, only I wouldn't be much help that way. But—but Al, I—I want to do somethin'. I—I'd like to try to show—I'd like to be an American, a decent American, and the best way to begin, seems to me, is to try and be a man, a decent man. Eh? You understand, I—I—Oh, Lord, what a mess I am makin' of this! I—I—Al," turning and desperately waving his hands, "I'm goin' to try to swear off. Will you help me?"

Albert's answer was enthusiastic. "You bet I will!" he exclaimed. Keeler smiled pathetically.

"It's goin' to be some job, I cal'late," he said. "Some job, yes, yes. But I'm goin' to try it, Al. I read in the papers 'tother day that America needed every man. Then you enlisted, Al,—or you're goin' to enlist. It set me to thinkin' I'd try to enlist, too. For the duration of the war, eh? Yes, yes."

"Good for you, Labe! Bully!"

Laban held up a protesting hand. "Don't hurrah yet, Al," he said. "This ain't the first time I've tried it. I've swore off a dozen times in the last fifteen years. I've promised Rachel and broke the promise over and over again. Broke my promise to her, the best woman in the world. Shows what I am, what sort I am, don't it, Al? Yes, it does,—yes, yes. And she's stuck by me, too, Lord knows why. Last time I broke it I said I'd never promise her again. Bad enough to be a common drunk without bein' a liar—yes, yes. But this is a little different. Seems to me—seems so."

He began his pacing up and down again.

"Seems different, somehow," he went on. "Seems like a new chance. I want to do somethin' for Uncle Sam. I—I'd like to try and enlist for the duration of the war—swear off for that long, anyhow. Then, maybe, I'd be able to keep on for life, you know—duration of Labe Keeler, eh? Yes, yes, yes. But I could begin for just the war, couldn't I? Maybe, 'twould fool me into thinkin' that was easier."

"Of course, Labe. It's a good idea."

"Maybe; and maybe it's a fool one. But I'm goin' to try it. I AM tryin' it, have been all day."

He paused, drew a shaking hand across his forehead and then asked, "Al, will you help me? I asked you up here hopin' you would. Will you, Al, eh? Will you?"

Albert could not understand how he could possibly help another man keep the pledge, but his promise was eagerly given.

"Certainly, Labe," he said.

"Thanks . . . thank you, Al. . . . And now will you do something for me—a favor?"

"Gladly. What is it?"

Laban did not answer at once. He appeared to be on the point of doing so, but to be struggling either to find words or to overcome a tremendous reluctance. When he did speak the words came in a burst.

"Go down stairs," he cried. "Down those stairs you came up. At the foot of 'em, in a kind of cupboard place, under 'em, there's—there probably is a jug, a full jug. It was due to come by express to-day and I cal'late it did, cal'late Jim Young fetched it down this afternoon. I—I could have looked for myself and seen if 'twas there," he added, after a momentary hesitation, "but—but I didn't dare to. I was afraid I'd—I'd—"

"All right, Labe. I understand. What do you want me to do with it if it is there?"

"I want you—I want you to—to—" The little bookkeeper seemed to be fighting another internal battle between inclination and resolution. The latter won, for he finished with, "I want you to take it out back of the buildin' and—and empty it. That's what I want you to do, empty it, Al, every drop. ... And, for the Almighty's sake, go quick," he ordered, desperately, "or I'll tell you not to before you start. Go!"

Albert went. He fumbled in the cupboard under the stairs, found the jug—a large one and heavy—and hastened out into the night with it in his hands. Behind the shoe store, amid a heap of old packing boxes and other rubbish, he emptied it. The process was rather lengthy and decidedly fragrant. As a finish he smashed the jug with a stone. Then he climbed the stairs again.

Laban was waiting for him, drops of perspiration upon his forehead.

"Was—was it there?" he demanded.

Albert nodded.

"Yes, yes. 'Twas there, eh? And did you—did you—?"

"Yes, I did, jug and all."

"Thank you, Al ... thank you ... I—I've been trying to muster up spunk enough to do it myself, but—but I swan I couldn't. I didn't dast to go nigh it ... I'm a fine specimen, ain't I, now?" he added, with a twisted smile. "Some coward, eh? Yes, yes. Some coward."

Albert, realizing a little of the fight the man was making, was affected by it. "You're a brick, Labe," he declared, heartily. "And as for being a coward—Well, if I am half as brave when my turn comes I shall be satisfied."

Laban shook his head. "I don't know how scared I'd be of a German bombshell," he said, "but I'm everlastin' sure I wouldn't run from it for fear of runnin' towards it, and that's how I felt about that jug. ... Yes, yes, yes. I did so ... I'm much obliged to you, Al. I shan't forget it—no, no. I cal'late you can trot along home now, if you want to. I'm pretty safe—for to-night, anyhow. Guess likely the new recruit won't desert afore morning."

But Albert, watching him intently, refused to go.

"I'm going to stay for a while, Labe," he said. "I'm not a bit sleepy, really. Let's have a smoke and talk together. That is, of course, unless you want to go to bed."

Mr. Keeler smiled his twisted smile. "I ain't crazy to," he said. "The way I feel now I'd get to sleep about week after next. But I hadn't ought to keep you up, Al."

"Rubbish! I'm not sleepy, I tell you. Sit down. Have a cigar. Now what shall we talk about? How would books do? What have you been reading lately, Labe?"

They smoked and talked books until nearly two. Then Laban insisted upon his guest departing. "I'm all right, Al" he declared, earnestly. "I am honest—yes, yes, I am. I'll go to sleep like a lamb, yes indeed."

"You'll be at the office in the morning, won't you, Labe?"

The little bookkeeper nodded. "I'll be there," he said. "Got to answer roll call the first mornin' after enlistment. Yes, yes. I'll be there, Al."

He was there, but he did not look as if his indulgence in the lamb-like sleep had been excessive. He was so pale and haggard that his assistant was alarmed.

"You're not sick, are you, Labe?" he asked, anxiously. Laban shook his head.

"No," he said. "No, I ain't sick. Been doin' picket duty up and down the room since half past three, that's all. Um-hm, that's all. Say, Al, if General what's-his-name—er—von Hindenburg—is any harder scrapper than old Field Marshal Barleycorn he's a pretty tough one. Say, Al, you didn't say anything about—about my—er—enlistin' to Cap'n Lote, did you? I meant to ask you not to."

"I didn't, Labe. I thought you might want it kept a secret."

"Um-hm. Better keep it in the ranks until we know how this first—er—skirmish is comin' out. Yes, yes. Better keep it that way. Um-hm."

All day he stuck manfully at his task and that evening, immediately after supper, Albert went to the room over the shoe store, found him there and insisted upon his coming over to call upon Rachel. He had not intended doing so.

"You see, Al," he explained, "I'm—I'm kind of—er—shaky and Rachel will be worried, I'm afraid. She knows me pretty well and she'll cal'late I'm just gettin' ready to—to bust loose again."

Albert interrupted. "No, she won't, Laban," he said. "We'll show her that you're not."

"You won't say anything to her about my—er—enlistin', Al? Don't. No, no. I've promised her too many times—and broke the promises. If anything should come of this fight of mine I'd rather she'd find it out for herself. Better to surprise her than to disapp'int her. Yes, yes, lots better."

Albert promised not to tell Rachel and so Laban made his call. When it was over the young man walked home with him and the pair sat and talked until after midnight, just as on the previous night. The following evening it was much the same, except that, as Mr. Keeler pronounced himself more than usually "shaky" and expressed a desire to "keep movin'," they walked half way to Orham and back before parting. By the end of the week Laban declared the fight won—for the time.

"You've pulled me through the fust tussle, Al," he said. "I shan't desert now, not till the next break-out, anyhow. I cal'late it'll get me harder than ever then. Harder than ever—yes, yes. And you won't be here to help me, neither."

"Never mind; I shall be thinking of you, Labe. And I know you're going to win. I feel it in my bones."

"Um-hm. . . . Yes, yes, yes. . . In your bones, eh? Well, MY bones don't seem to feel much, except rheumatics once in a while. I hope yours are better prophets, but I wouldn't want to bet too high on it. No, I wouldn't—no, no. However, we'll do our best, and they say angels can't do any more—though they'd probably do it in a different way . . . some different. . . . Um-hm. . . . Yes, indeed."

Two letters came to Albert before that week ended. The first was from Madeline. He had written her of his intention to enlist and this was her reply. The letter had evidently been smuggled past the censor, for it contained much which Mrs. Fosdick would have blue-penciled. Its contents were a blend of praise and blame, of exaltation and depression. He was a hero, and so brave, and she was so proud of him. It was wonderful his daring to go, and just what she would have expected of her hero. If only she might see him in his uniform. So many of the fellows she knew had enlisted. They were wonderfully brave, too, although of course nothing like as wonderful as her own etcetera, etcetera. She had seen some of THEM in their uniforms and they were PERFECTLY SPLENDID. But they were officers, or they were going to be. Why wasn't he going to be an officer? It was so much nicer to be an officer. And if he were one he might not have to go away to fight nearly so soon. Officers stayed here longer and studied, you know. Mother had said something about "a common private," and she did not like it. But never mind, she would be just as proud no matter what he was. And she should dream of him and think of him always and always. And perhaps he might be so brave and wonderful that he would be given one of those war crosses, the Croix de Guerre or something. She was sure he would. But oh, no matter what happened, he must not go where it was TOO dangerous. Suppose he should be wounded. Oh, suppose, SUPPOSE he should be killed. What would she do then? What would become of her? MUST he go, after all? Couldn't he stay at home and study or something, for a while, you know? She should be so lonely after he was gone. And so frightened and so anxious. And he wouldn't forget her, would he, no matter where he went? Because she never, never, never would forget him for a moment. And he must write every day. And—

The letter was fourteen pages long.

The other letter was a surprise. It was from Helen. The Reverend Mr. Kendall had been told of Albert's intended enlistment and had written his daughter.

So you are going into the war, Albert (she wrote). I am not surprised because I expected you would do just that. It is what all of us would like to do, I'm sure, and you were always anxious to go, even before the United States came in. So I am writing this merely to congratulate you and to wish you the very best of good luck. Father says you are not going to try for a commission but intend enlisting as a private. I suppose that is because you think you may get to the actual fighting sooner. I think I understand and appreciate that feeling too, but are you sure it is the best plan? You want to be of the greatest service to the country and with your education and brains—This ISN'T flattery, because it is true—don't you think you might help more if you were in command of men? Of course I don't know, being only a girl, but I have been wondering. No doubt you know best and probably it is settled before this; at any rate, please don't think that I intend butting in. "Butting in" is not at all a proper expression for a schoolmarm to use but it is a relief to be human occasionally. Whatever you do I am sure will be the right thing and I know all your friends are going to be very, very proud of you. I shall hear of you through the people at home, I know, and I shall be anxious to hear. I don't know what I shall do to help the cause, but I hope to do something. A musket is prohibitive to females but the knitting needle is ours and I CAN handle that, if I do say it. And I MAY go in for Red Cross work altogether. But I don't count much, and you men do, and this is your day. Please, for the sake of your grandparents and all your friends, don't take unnecessary chances. I can see your face as you read that and think that I am a silly idiot. I'm not and I mean what I say. You see I know YOU and I know you will not be content to do the ordinary thing. We want you to distinguish yourself, but also we want you to come back whole and sound, if it is possible. We shall think of you a great deal. And please, in the midst of the excitement of the BIG work you are doing, don't forget us home folk, including your friend,

HELEN KENDALL.

Albert's feelings when he read this letter were divided. He enjoyed hearing from Helen. The letter was just like herself, sensible and good-humored and friendly. There were no hysterics in it and no heroics but he knew that no one except his grandparents and Rachel and Laban—and, of course, his own Madeline—would think of him oftener or be more anxious for his safety and welfare than Helen. He was glad she was his friend, very glad. But he almost wished she had not written. He felt a bit guilty at having received the letter. He was pretty sure that Madeline would not like the idea. He was tempted to say nothing concerning it in his next letter to his affianced, but that seemed underhanded and cowardly, so he told her. And in her next letter to him Madeline made no reference at all to Helen or her epistle, so he knew she was displeased. And he was miserable in consequence.

But his misery did not last long. The happenings which followed crowded it from his mind, and from Madeline's also, for that matter. One morning, having told no one except his grandfather of his intention, he took the morning train to Boston. When he returned the next day he was Uncle Sam's man, sworn in and accepted. He had passed the physical examination with flying colors and the recruiting officers expressed themselves as being glad to get him. He was home for but one day leave, then he must go to stay. He had debated the question of going in for a commission, but those were the early days of our participation in the war and a Plattsburg training or at least some sort of military education was almost an essential. He did not want to wait; as he had told his grandfather, he wanted to fight. So he enlisted as a private.

And when the brief leave was over he took the train for Boston, no longer Alberto Miguel Carlos Speranza, South Harniss's Beau Brummel, poet and Portygee, but Private Speranza, U.S.A. The farewells were brief and no one cried—much. His grandmother hugged and kissed him, Rachel looked very much as if she wanted to. Laban and Issachar shook hands with him.

"Good luck to you, boy," said Mr. Keeler. "All the luck there is."

"Same to you, old man," replied Albert. Then, in a lower tone, he added, "We'll fight it out together, eh?"

"We'll try. Yes, yes. We'll try. So long, Al."

Issachar struck the reassuring note. "Don't fret about things in the office," he said. "I'll look out for 'em long's I keep my health."

"Be sure and keep that, Issy."

"You bet you! Only thing that's liable to break it down is over-work."

Captain Zelotes said very little. "Write us when you can, Al," he said. "And come home whenever you get leave."

"You may be sure of that, Grandfather. And after I get to camp perhaps you can come and see me."

"Maybe so. Will if I can.... Well, Al, I... I.... Good luck to you, son."

"Thank you, Grandfather."

They shook hands. Each looked as if there was more he would have liked to say but found the saying hard. Then the engine bell rang and the hands fell apart. The little group on the station platform watched the train disappear. Mrs. Snow and Rachel wiped their eyes with their handkerchiefs. Captain Zelotes gently patted his wife's shoulder.

"The team's waitin', Mother," he said. "Labe'll drive you and Rachel home."

"But—but ain't you comin', too, Zelotes?" faltered Olive. Her husband shook his head.

"Not now, Mother," he answered. "Got to go back to the office."

He stood for an instant looking at the faint smear of smoke above the curve in the track. Then, without another word, he strode off in the direction of Z. Snow and Co.'s buildings. Issachar Price sniffed.

"Crimus," he whispered to Laban, as the latter passed him on the way to where Jessamine, the Snow horse, was tied, "the old man takes it cool, don't he! I kind of imagined he'd be sort of shook up by Al's goin' off to war, but he don't seem to feel it a mite."

Keeler looked at him in wonder. Then he drew a long breath.

"Is," he said, slowly, "it is a mighty good thing for the Seven Wise Men of Greece that they ain't alive now."

It was Issachar's turn to stare. "Eh?" he queried. "The Seven Wise Men of Which? Good thing for 'em they ain't alive? What kind of talk's that? Why is it a good thing?"

Laban spoke over his shoulder. "Because," he drawled, "if they was alive now they'd be so jealous of you they'd commit suicide. Yes, they would.... Yes, yes."

With which enigmatical remark he left Mr. Price and turned his attention to the tethered Jessamine.

And then began a new period, a new life at the Snow place and in the office of Z. Snow and Co. Or, rather, life in the old house and at the lumber and hardware office slumped back into the groove in which it had run before the opera singer's son was summoned from the New York school to the home and into the lives of his grandparents. Three people instead of four sat down at the breakfast table and at dinner and at supper. Captain Zelotes walked alone to and from the office. Olive Snow no longer baked and iced large chocolate layer cakes because a certain inmate of her household was so fond of them. Rachel Ellis discussed Foul Play and Robert Penfold with no one. The house was emptier, more old-fashioned and behind the times, more lonely—surprisingly empty and behind the times and lonely.

The daily mails became matters of intense interest and expectation. Albert wrote regularly and of course well and entertainingly. He described the life at the camp where he and the other recruits were training, a camp vastly different from the enormous military towns built later on for housing and training the drafted men. He liked the life pretty well, he wrote, although it was hard and a fellow had precious little opportunity to be lazy. Mistakes, too, were unprofitable for the maker. Captain Lote's eye twinkled when he read that.

Later on he wrote that he had been made a corporal and his grandmother, to whom a major general and a corporal were of equal rank, rejoiced much both at home and in church after meeting was over and friends came to hear the news. Mrs. Ellis declared herself not surprised. It was the Robert Penfold in him coming out, so she said.

A month or two later one of Albert's letters contained an interesting item of news. In the little spare time which military life afforded him he continued to write verse and stories. Now a New York publisher, not one of the most prominent but a reputable and enterprising one, had written him suggesting the collecting of his poems and their publication in book form. The poet himself was, naturally, elated.

"Isn't it splendid!" he wrote. "The best part of it, of course, is that he asked to publish, I did not ask him. Please send me my scrapbook and all loose manuscript. When the book will come out I'm sure I don't know. In fact it may never come out, we have not gotten as far as terms and contracts yet, but I feel we shall. Send the scrapbook and manuscript right away, PLEASE."

They were sent. In his next letter Albert was still enthusiastic.

"I have been looking over my stuff," he wrote, "and some of it is pretty good, if you don't mind my saying so. Tell Grandfather that when this book of mine is out and selling I may be able to show him that poetry making isn't a pauper's job, after all. Of course I don't know how much it will sell—perhaps not more than five or ten thousand at first—but even at ten thousand at, say, twenty-five cents royalty each, would be twenty-five hundred dollars, and that's something. Why, Ben Hur, the novel, you know, has sold a million, I believe."

Mrs. Snow and Rachel were duly impressed by this prophecy of affluence, but Captain Zelotes still played the skeptic.

"A million at twenty-five cents a piece!" exclaimed Olive. "Why, Zelotes, that's—that's an awful sight of money."

Mental arithmetic failing her, she set to work with a pencil and paper and after a strenuous struggle triumphantly announced that it came to two hundred and fifty thousand dollars.

"My soul and body!" she cried. "Two hundred and fifty thousand DOLLARS! My SOUL, Zelotes! Suppose—only suppose Albert's book brought him in as much as that!"

Her husband shook his head. "I can't, Olive," he said, without looking up from his newspaper. "My supposer wouldn't stand the strain."

"But it might, Zelotes, it MIGHT. Suppose it did, what would you say then?"

The captain regarded her over the top of the Transcript. "I shouldn't say a word, Olive," he answered, solemnly. "I should be down sick by the time it got up as far as a thousand, and anything past two thousand you could use to buy my tombstone with.... There, there, Mother," he added, noticing the hurt look on her face, "don't feel bad. I'm only jokin'. One of these days Al's goin' to make a nice, comf'table livin' sellin' lumber and hardware right here in South Harniss. I can SEE that money in the offin'. All this million or two that's comin' from poetry and such is out of sight in the fog. It may be there but—humph! well, I KNOW where Z. Snow and Co. is located."

Olive was not entirely placated. "I must say I think you're awful discouragin' to the poor boy, Zelotes," she said. Her husband put down his paper.

"No, no, I ain't, Mother," he replied, earnestly. "At least I don't mean to be. Way I look at it, this poetry-makin' and writin' yarns and that sort of stuff is just part of the youngster's—er—growin' up, as you might say. Give him time he'll grow out of it, same as I cal'late he will out of this girl business, this—er—Madel—humph—er—ahem.... Looks like a good day to-morrow, don't it."

He pulled up suddenly, and with considerable confusion. He had kept the news of his grandson's infatuation and engagement even from his wife. No one in South Harniss knew of it, no one except the captain. Helen Kendall knew, but she was in Boston.

Rachel Ellis picked up the half knitted Red Cross mitten in her lap. "Well, I don't know whether he's right or you are, Cap'n Lote," she said, with a sigh, "but this I do know—I wish this awful war was over and he was back home again."

That remark ended the conversation. Olive resumed her own knitting, seeing it but indistinctly. Her husband did not continue his newspaper reading. Instead he rose and, saying something about cal'latin' he would go for a little walk before turning in, went out into the yard.

But the war did not end, it went on; so too did the enlisting and training. In the early summer Albert came home for a two days' leave. He was broader and straighter and browner. His uniform became him and, more than ever, the eyes of South Harniss's youthful femininity, native or imported, followed him as he walked the village streets. But the glances were not returned, not in kind, that is. The new Fosdick home, although completed, was not occupied. Mrs. Fosdick had, that summer, decided that her duties as mover in goodness knows how many war work activities prevented her taking her "usual summer rest." Instead she and Madeline occupied a rented villa at Greenwich, Connecticut, coming into town for meetings of all sorts. Captain Zelotes had his own suspicions as to whether war work alone was the cause of the Fosdicks' shunning of what was to have been their summer home, but he kept those suspicions to himself. Albert may have suspected also, but he, too, said nothing. The censored correspondence between Greenwich and the training camp traveled regularly, and South Harniss damsels looked and longed in vain. He saw them, he bowed to them, he even addressed them pleasantly and charmingly, but to him they were merely incidents in his walks to and from the post-office. In his mind's eye he saw but one, and she, alas, was not present in the flesh.

Then he returned to the camp where, later on, Captain Zelotes and Olive visited him. As they came away the captain and his grandson exchanged a few significant words.

"It is likely to be almost any time, Grandfather," said Albert, quietly. "They are beginning to send them now, as you know by the papers, and we have had the tip that our turn will be soon. So—"

Captain Lote grasped the significance of the uncompleted sentence.

"I see, Al," he answered, "I see. Well, boy, I—I—Good luck."

"Good luck, Grandfather."

That was all, that and one more handclasp. Our Anglo-Saxon inheritance descends upon us in times like these. The captain was silent for most of the ride to the railroad station.

Then followed a long, significant interval during which there were no letters from the young soldier. After this a short reassuring cablegram from "Somewhere in France." "Safe. Well," it read and Olive Snow carried it about with her, in the bosom of her gown, all that afternoon and put it upon retiring on her bureau top so that she might see it the first thing in the morning.

Another long interval, then letters, the reassuring but so tantalizingly unsatisfactory letters we American families were, just at that time, beginning to receive. Reading the newspapers now had a personal interest, a terrifying, dreadful interest. Then the packing and sending of holiday boxes, over the contents of which Olive and Rachel spent much careful planning and anxious preparation. Then another interval of more letters, letters which hinted vaguely at big things just ahead.

Then no letter for more than a month.

And then, one noon, as Captain Zelotes returned to his desk after the walk from home and dinner, Laban Keeler came in and stood beside that desk.

The captain, looking up, saw the little bookkeeper's face. "What is it, Labe?" he asked, sharply.

Laban held a yellow envelope in his hand.

"It came while you were gone to dinner, Cap'n," he said. "Ben Kelley fetched it from the telegraph office himself. He—he said he didn't hardly want to take it to the house. He cal'lated you'd better have it here, to read to yourself, fust. That's what he said—yes, yes—that's what 'twas, Cap'n."

Slowly Captain Zelotes extended his hand for the envelope. He did not take his eyes from the bookkeeper's face.

"Ben—Ben, he told me what was in it, Cap'n Lote," faltered Laban. "I—I don't know what to say to you, I don't—no, no."

Without a word the captain took the envelope from Keeler's fingers, and tore it open. He read the words upon the form within.

Laban leaned forward.

"For the Lord sakes, Lote Snow," he cried, in a burst of agony, "why couldn't it have been some darn good-for-nothin' like me instead—instead of him? Oh, my God A'mighty, what a world this is! WHAT a world!"

Still Captain Zelotes said nothing. His eyes were fixed upon the yellow sheet of paper on the desk before him. After a long minute he spoke.

"Well," he said, very slowly, "well, Labe, there goes—there goes Z. Snow and Company."

CHAPTER XIV

The telegram from the War Department was brief, as all such telegrams were perforce obliged to be. The Secretary of War, through his representative, regretted to inform Captain Zelotes Snow that Sergeant Albert Speranza had been killed in action upon a certain day. It was enough, however—for the time quite enough. It was not until later that the little group of South Harniss recovered sufficiently from the stunning effect of those few words to think of seeking particulars. Albert was dead; what did it matter, then, to know how he died?

Olive bore the shock surprisingly well. Her husband's fears for her seemed quite unnecessary. The Captain, knowing how she had idolized her daughter's boy, had dreaded the effect which the news might have upon her. She was broken down by it, it is true, but she was quiet and brave—astonishingly, wonderfully quiet and brave. And it was she, rather than her husband, who played the part of the comforter in those black hours.

"He's gone, Zelotes," she said. "It don't seem possible, I know, but he's gone. And he died doin' his duty, same as he would have wanted to die if he'd known 'twas comin', poor boy. So—so we must do ours, I suppose, and bear up under it the very best we can. It won't be very long, Zelotes," she added. "We're both gettin' old."

Captain Lote made no reply. He was standing by the window of the sitting-room looking out into the wet backyard across which the wind-driven rain was beating in stormy gusts.

"We must be brave, Zelotes," whispered Olive, tremulously. "He'd want us to be and we MUST be."

He put his arm about her in a sudden heat of admiration. "I'd be ashamed not to be after seein' you, Mother," he exclaimed.

He went out to the barn a few moments later and Rachel, entering the sitting-room, found Olive crumpled down in the big rocker in an agony of grief.

"Oh, don't, Mrs. Snow, don't," she begged, the tears streaming down her own cheeks. "You mustn't give way to it like this; you mustn't."

Olive nodded.

"I know it, I know it," she admitted, chokingly, wiping her eyes with a soaked handkerchief. "I shan't, Rachel, only this once, I promise you. You see I can't. I just can't on Zelotes's account. I've got to bear up for his sake."

The housekeeper was surprised and a little indignant.

"For his sake!" she repeated. "For mercy sakes why for his sake? Is it any worse for him than 'tis for you."

"Oh, yes, yes, lots worse. He won't say much, of course, bein' Zelotes Snow, but you and I know how he's planned, especially these last years, and how he's begun to count on—on Albert. . . . No, no, I ain't goin' to cry, Rachel, I ain't—I WON'T—but sayin' his name, you know, kind of—"

"I know, I know. Land sakes, DON'T I know! Ain't I doin' it myself?"

"Course you are, Rachel. But we mustn't when Zelotes is around. We women, we—well, times like these women HAVE to keep up. What would become of the men if we didn't?"

So she and Rachel "kept up" in public and when the captain was present, and he for his part made no show of grief nor asked for pity. He was silent, talked little and to the callers who came either at the house or office was uncomplaining.

"He died like a man," he told the Reverend Mr. Kendall when the latter called. "He took his chance, knowin' what that meant—"

"He was glad to take it," interrupted the minister. "Proud and glad to take it."

"Sartin. Why not? Wouldn't you or I have been glad to take ours, if we could?"

"Well, Captain Snow, I am glad to find you so resigned."

Captain Zelotes looked at him. "Resigned?" he repeated. "What do you mean by resigned? Not to sit around and whimper is one thing—any decent man or woman ought to be able to do that in these days; but if by bein' resigned you mean I'm contented to have it so—well, you're mistaken, that's all."

Only on one occasion, and then to Laban Keeler, did he open his shell sufficiently to give a glimpse of what was inside. Laban entered the inner office that morning to find his employer sitting in the desk chair, both hands jammed in his trousers' pockets and his gaze fixed, apparently, upon the row of pigeon-holes. When the bookkeeper spoke to him he seemed to wake from a dream, for he started and looked up.

"Cap'n Lote," began Keeler, "I'm sorry to bother you, but that last carload of pine was—"

Captain Zelotes waved his hand, brushing the carload of pine out of the conversation.

"Labe," he said, slowly, "did it seem to you that I was too hard on him?"

Laban did not understand. "Hard on him?" he repeated. "I don't know's I just get—"

"Hard on Al. Did it seem to you as if I was a little too much of the bucko mate to the boy? Did I drive him too hard? Was I unreasonable?"

The answer was prompt. "No, Cap'n Lote," replied Keeler.

"You mean that?... Um-hm.... Well, sometimes seems as if I might have been. You see, Labe, when he first come I—Well, I cal'late I was consider'ble prejudiced against him. Account of his father, you understand."

"Sartin. Sure. I understand."

"It took me a good while to get reconciled to the Portygee streak in him. It chafed me consider'ble to think there was a foreign streak in our family. The Snows have been straight Yankee for a good long while.... Fact is, I—I never got really reconciled to it. I kept bein' fearful all the time that that streak, his father's streak, would break out in him. It never did, except of course in his poetry and that sort of foolishness, but I was always scared 'twould, you see. And now—now that this has happened I—I kind of fret for fear that I may have let my notions get ahead of my fair play. You think I did give the boy a square deal, Labe?"

"Sure thing, Cap'n."

"I'm glad of that.... And—and you cal'late he wasn't—wasn't too prejudiced against me? I don't mean along at first, I mean this last year or two."

Laban hesitated. He wished his answer to be not an overstatement, but the exact truth.

"I think," he said, with emphasis, "that Al was comin' to understand you better every day he lived, Cap'n. Yes, and to think more and more of you, too. He was gettin' older, for one thing—older, more of a man—yes, yes."

Captain Zelotes smiled sadly. "He was more boy than man by a good deal yet," he observed. "Well, Labe, he's gone and I'm just beginnin' to realize how much of life for me has gone along with him. He'd been doin' better here in the office for the last two or three years, seemed to be catchin' on to business better. Didn't you think so, Labe?"

"Sartin. Yes indeed. Fust-rate, fust-rate."

"No, not first-rate. He was a long ways from a business man yet, but I did think he was doin' a lot better. I could begin to see him pilotin' this craft after I was called ashore. Now he's gone and . . . well, I don't see much use in my fightin' to keep it afloat. I'm gettin' along in years—and what's the use?"

It was the first time Laban had ever heard Captain Zelotes refer to himself as an old man. It shocked him into sharp expostulation.

"Nonsense!" he exclaimed. "You ain't old enough for the scrap heap by a big stretch. And besides, he made his fight, didn't he? He didn't quit, Al didn't, and he wouldn't want us to. No sir-ee, he wouldn't! No, sir, no! . . . I—I hope you'll excuse me, Cap'n Lote. I—declare it must seem to you as if I was talkin' pretty fresh. I swan I'm sorry. I am so . . . sorry; yes, yes, I be."

The captain was not offended. He waved the apologies aside.

"So you think it's worth while my fightin' it out, do you, Labe?" he asked, reflectively.

"I—I think it's what you ought to do anyhow, whether it's worth while or not. The whole world's fightin'. Uncle Sam's fightin'. Al was fightin'. You're fightin'. I'm fightin'. It's a darn sight easier to quit, a darn sight, but—but Al didn't quit. And—and we mustn't—not if we can help it," he added, drawing a hand across his forehead.

His agitation seemed to surprise Captain Zelotes. "So all hands are fightin', are they, Labe," he observed. "Well, I presume likely there's some truth in that. What's your particular fight, for instance?"

The little bookkeeper looked at him for an instant before replying. The captain's question was kindly asked, but there was, or so Laban imagined, the faintest trace of sarcasm in its tone. That trace decided him. He leaned across the desk.

"My particular fight?" he repeated. "You—you want to know what 'tis, Cap'n Lote? All right, all right, I'll tell you."

And without waiting for further questioning and with, for him, surprisingly few repetitions, he told of his "enlistment" to fight John Barleycorn for the duration of the war. Captain Zelotes listened to the very end in silence. Laban mopped his forehead with a hand which shook much as it had done during the interview with Albert in the room above the shoe store.

"There—there," he declared, in conclusion, "that's my fight, Cap'n Lote. Al and I, we—we kind of went into it together, as you might say, though his enlistin' was consider'ble more heroic than mine—yes indeed, I should say so . . . yes, yes, yes. But I'm fightin' too . . . er . . . I'm fightin' too."

Captain Zelotes pulled his beard.

"How's the fight goin', Labe?" he asked, quietly.

"Well—well, it's kind of—kind of spotty, as you might say. There's spots when I get along fairly smooth and others when—well, when it's pretty rough goin'. I've had four hard spots since Al went away, but there's two that was the hardest. One was along Christmas and New Year time; you know I 'most generally had one of my—er—spells along about then. And t'other is just now; I mean since we got word about—about Al. I don't suppose likely you surmised it, Cap'n, but—but I'd come to think a lot of that boy—yes, I had. Seems funny to you, I don't doubt, but it's so. And since the word come, you know—I—I—well, I've had some fight, some fight. I—I don't cal'late I've slept more'n four hours in the last four nights—not more'n that, no. Walkin' helps me most, seems so. Last night I walked to West Orham."

"To West Orham! You WALKED there? Last NIGHT?"

"Um-hm. Long's I can keep walkin' I—I seem to part way forget—to forget the stuff, you know. When I'm alone in my room I go 'most crazy—pretty nigh loony. . . . But there! I don't know why I got to talkin' like this to you, Cap'n Lote. You've got your troubles and—"

"Hold on, Labe. Does Rachel know about your fight?"

"No. No, no. Course she must notice how long I've been—been straight, but I haven't told her. I want to be sure I'm goin' to win before I tell her. She's been disappointed times enough before, poor woman. . . . There, Cap'n Lote, don't let's talk about it any more. Please don't get the notion that I'm askin' for pity or anything like that. And don't think I'm comparin' what I call my fight to the real one like Al's. There's nothin' much heroic about me, eh? No, no, I guess not. Tell that to look at me, eh?"

Captain Zelotes rose and laid his big hand on his bookkeeper's shoulder.

"Don't you believe it, Labe," he said. "I'm proud of you. . . . And, I declare, I'm ashamed of myself. . . . Humph! . . . Well, to-night you come home with me and have supper at the house."

"Now, now, Cap'n Lote—"

"You do as I tell you. After supper, if there's any walkin' to be done—if you take a notion to frog it to Orham or San Francisco or somewheres—maybe I'll go with you. Walkin' may be good for my fight, too; you can't tell till you try. . . . There, don't argue, Labe. I'm skipper of this craft yet and you'll obey my orders; d'you hear?"

The day following the receipt of the fateful telegram the captain wrote a brief note to Fletcher Fosdick. A day or two later he received a reply. Fosdick's letter was kindly and deeply sympathetic. He had been greatly shocked and grieved by the news.

Young Speranza seemed to me, (he wrote) in my one short interview with him, to be a fine young fellow. Madeline, poor girl, is almost frantic. She will recover by and by, recovery is easier at her age, but it will be very, very hard for you and Mrs. Snow. You and I little thought when we discussed the problem of our young people that it would be solved in this way. To you and your wife my sincerest sympathy. When you hear particulars concerning your grandson's death, please write me. Madeline is anxious to know and keeps asking for them. Mrs. Fosdick is too much concerned with her daughter's health to write just now, but she joins me in sympathetic regards.

Captain Zelotes took Mrs. Fosdick's sympathy with a grain of salt. When he showed this letter to his wife he, for the first time, told her of the engagement, explaining that his previous silence had been due to Albert's request that the affair be kept a secret for the present. Olive, even in the depth of her sorrow, was greatly impressed by the grandeur of the alliance.

"Just think, Zelotes," she exclaimed, "the Fosdick girl—and our Albert engaged to marry her! Why, the Fosdicks are awful rich, everybody says so. Mrs. Fosdick is head of I don't know how many societies and clubs and things in New York; her name is in the paper almost every day, so another New York woman told me at Red Cross meetin' last summer. And Mr. Fosdick has been in politics, way up in politics."

"Um-hm. Well, he's reformed lately, I understand, so we mustn't hold that against him."

"Why, Zelotes, what DO you mean? How can you talk so? Just think what it would have meant to have our Albert marry a girl like Madeline Fosdick."

The captain put his arm about her and gently patted her shoulder.

"There, there, Mother," he said, gently, "don't let that part of it fret you."

"But, Zelotes," tearfully, "I don't understand. It would have been such a great thing for Albert."

"Would it? Well, maybe. Anyhow, there's no use worryin' about it now. It's done with—ended and done with . . . same as a good many other plans that's been made in the world."

"Zelotes, don't speak like that, dear, so discouraged. It makes me feel worse than ever to hear you. And—and he wouldn't want you to, I'm sure."

"Wouldn't he? No, I cal'late you're right, Mother. We'll try not to."

Other letters came, including one from Helen. It was not long. Mrs. Snow was a little inclined to feel hurt at its brevity. Her husband, however, did not share this feeling.

"Have you read it carefully, Mother?" he asked.

"Of course I have, Zelotes. What do you mean?"

"I mean—well, I tell you, Mother, I've read it three time. The first time I was like you; seemed to me as good a friend of Al and of us as Helen Kendall ought to have written more than that. The second time I read it I begun to wonder if—if—"

"If what, Zelotes?"

"Oh, nothin', Mother, nothin'. She says she's comin' to see us just as soon as she can get away for a day or two. She'll come, and when she does I cal'late both you and I are goin' to be satisfied."

"But why didn't she WRITE more, Zelotes? That's what I can't understand."

Captain Zelotes tugged at his beard reflectively. "When I wrote Fosdick the other day," he said, "I couldn't write more than a couple of pages. I was too upset to do it. I couldn't, that's all."

"Yes, but you are Albert's grandfather."

"I know. And Helen's always . . . But there, Mother, don't you worry about Helen Kendall. I've known her since she was born, pretty nigh, and *I* tell you she's all RIGHT."

Fosdick, in his letter, had asked for particulars concerning Albert's death. Those particulars were slow in coming. Captain Zelotes wrote at once to the War Department, but received little satisfaction. The Department would inform him as soon as it obtained the information. The name of Sergeant Albert Speranza had been cabled as one of a list of fatalities, that was all.

"And to think," as Rachel Ellis put it, "that we never knew that he'd been made a sergeant until after he was gone. He never had time to write it, I expect likely, poor boy."

The first bit of additional information was furnished by the press. A correspondent of one of the Boston dailies sent a brief dispatch to his paper describing the fighting at a certain point on the Allied front. A small detachment of American troops had taken part, with the French, in an attack on a village held by the enemy. The enthusiastic reporter declared it to be one of the smartest little actions in which our soldiers had so far taken part and was eloquent concerning the bravery and dash of his fellow countrymen. "They proved themselves," he went on, "and French officers with whom I have talked are enthusiastic. Our losses, considering the number engaged, are said to be heavy. Among those reported as killed is Sergeant Albert Speranza, a Massachusetts boy whom American readers will remember as a writer of poetry and magazine fiction. Sergeant Speranza is said to have led his company in the capture of the village and to have acted with distinguished bravery." The editor of the Boston paper who first read this dispatch turned to his associate at the next desk.

"Speranza? . . . Speranza?" he said aloud. "Say, Jim, wasn't it Albert Speranza who wrote that corking poem we published after the Lusitania was sunk?"

Jim looked up. "Yes," he said. "He has written a lot of pretty good stuff since, too. Why?"

"He's just been killed in action over there, so Conway says in this dispatch."

"So? . . . Humph! . . . Any particulars?"

"Not yet. 'Distinguished bravery,' according to Conway. Couldn't we have something done in the way of a Sunday special? He was a Massachusetts fellow."

"We might. We haven't a photograph, have we? If we haven't, perhaps we can get one."

The photograph was obtained—bribery and corruption of the Orham photographer—and, accompanied by a reprint of the Lusitania poem, appeared in the "Magazine Section" of the Sunday newspaper. With these also appeared a short notice of the young poet's death in the service of his country.

That was the beginning. At the middle of that week Conway sent another dispatch. The editor who received it took it into the office of the Sunday editor.

"Say," he said, "here are more particulars about that young chap Speranza, the one we printed the special about last Sunday. He must have been a corker. When his lieutenant was put out of business by a shrapnel this Speranza chap rallied the men and jammed 'em through the Huns like a hot knife through butter. Killed the German officer and took three prisoners all by himself. Carried his wounded lieutenant to the rear on his shoulders, too. Then he went back into the ruins to get another wounded man and was blown to slivers by a hand grenade. He's been cited in orders and will probably be decorated by the French—that is, his memory will be. Pretty good for a poet, I'd say. No 'lilies and languors' about that, eh?"

The Sunday editor nodded approval.

"Great stuff!" he exclaimed. "Let me have that dispatch, will you, when you've finished. I've just discovered that this young Speranza's father was Speranza, the opera baritone. You remember him? And his mother was the daughter of a Cape Cod sea captain. How's that? Spain, Cape Cod, opera, poetry and the Croix de Guerre. And have you looked at the young fellow's photograph? Combination of Adonis and 'Romeo, where art thou.' I've had no less than twenty letters about him and his poetry already. Next Sunday we'll have a special 'as is.' Where can I get hold of a lot of his poems?"

The "special as was" occupied an entire page. A reporter had visited South Harniss and had taken photographs of the Snow place and some of its occupants. Captain Zelotes had refused to pose, but there was a view of the building and yards of "Z. Snow and Co." with the picturesque figure of Mr. Issachar Price tastefully draped against a pile of boards in the right foreground. Issy had been a find for the reporter; he supplied the latter with every fact concerning Albert which he could remember and some that he invented on the spur of the moment. According to Issy, Albert was "a fine, fust-class young feller. Him and me was like brothers, as you might say. When he got into trouble, or was undecided or anything, he'd come to me for advice and I always gave it to him. Land, yes! I always give to Albert. No matter how busy I was I always stopped work to help HIM out." The reporter added that Mr. Price stopped work even while speaking of it.

The special attracted the notice of other newspaper editors. This skirmish in which Albert had taken so gallant part was among the first in which our soldiers had participated. So the story was copied and recopied. The tale of the death of the young poet, the "happy warrior," as some writer called him, was spread from the Atlantic to the Pacific and from Canada to the Gulf. And just at this psychological moment the New York publisher brought out the long deferred volume. The Lances of Dawn, Being the Collected Poems of Albert M. C. Speranza, such was its title.

Meanwhile, or, rather, within the week when the Lances of Dawn flashed upon the public, Captain Zelotes received a letter from the captain of Albert's regiment in France. It was not a long letter, for the captain was a busy man, but it was the kindly, sympathetic letter of one who was, literally, that well-advertised combination, an officer and a gentleman. It told of Albert's promotion to the rank of sergeant, "a promotion which, had the boy been spared, would, I am sure, have been the forerunner of others." It told of that last fight, the struggle for the village, of Sergeant Speranza's coolness and daring and of his rush back into the throat of death to save a wounded comrade.

The men tell me they tried to stop him (wrote the captain). He was himself slightly wounded, he had just brought Lieutenant Stacey back to safety and the enemy at that moment was again advancing through the village. But he insisted upon going. The man he was trying to rescue was a private in his company and the pair were great friends. So he started back alone, although several followed him a moment later. They saw him enter the ruined cottage where his friend lay. Then a party of the enemy appeared at the corner and flung grenades. The entire side of the cottage which he had just entered was blown in and the Germans passed on over it, causing our men to fall back temporarily. We retook the place within half an hour. Private Kelly's body—it was Private Kelly whom Sergeant Speranza was attempting to rescue—was found and another, badly disfigured, which was at first supposed to be that of your grandson. But this body was subsequently identified as that of a private named Hamlin who was killed when the enemy first charged. Sergeant Speranza's body is still missing, but is thought to be buried beneath the ruins of the cottage. These ruins were subsequently blown into further chaos by a high explosive shell.

Then followed more expressions of regret and sympathy and confirmation of the report concerning citation and the war cross. Captain Lote read the letter at first alone in his private office. Then he brought it home and gave it to his wife to read. Afterward he read it aloud to Mrs. Ellis and to Laban, who was making his usual call in the Snow kitchen.

When the reading was ended Labe was the first to speak. His eyes were shining.

"Godfreys!" he exclaimed. "Godfreys, Cap'n Lote!"

The captain seemed to understand.

"You're right, Labe," he said. "The boy's made us proud of him. . . . Prouder than some of us are of ourselves, I cal'late," he added, rising and moving toward the door.

"Sho, sho, Cap'n, you mustn't feel that way. No, no."

"Humph! . . . Labe, I presume likely if I was a pious man, one of the old-fashioned kind of pious, and believed the Almighty went out of his way to get square with any human bein' that made a mistake or didn't do the right thing—if I believed that I might figger all this was a sort of special judgment on me for my prejudices, eh?"

Mr. Keeler was much disturbed.

"Nonsense, nonsense, Cap'n Lote!" he protested. "You ain't fair to yourself. You never treated Al anyhow but just honest and fair and square. If he was here now instead of layin' dead over there in France, poor feller, he'd say so, too. Yes, he would. Course he would."

The captain made no reply, but walked from the room. Laban turned to Mrs. Ellis.

"The old man broods over that," he said. "I wish. . . . Eh? What's the matter, Rachel? What are you lookin' at me like that for?"

The housekeeper was leaning forward in her chair, her cheeks flushed and her hands clenched.

"How do you know he's dead?" she asked, in a mysterious whisper.

"Eh? How do I know who's dead?"

"Albert. How do you know he's dead?"

Laban stared at her.

"How do I know he's DEAD!" he repeated. "How do I know—"

"Yes, yes, yes," impatiently; "that's what I said. Don't run it over three or four times more. How do you know Albert's dead?"

"Why, Rachel, what kind of talk's that? I know he's dead because the newspapers say so, and the War Department folks say so, and this cap'n man in France that was right there at the time, HE says so. All hands say so—yes, yes. So don't—"

"Sh! I don't care if they all say so ten times over. How do they KNOW? They ain't found him dead, have they? The report from the War Department folks was sent when they thought that other body was Albert's. Now they know that wasn't him. Where is he?"

The Portygee | 229

"Why, under the ruins of that cottage. 'Twas all blown to pieces and most likely—"

"Um-hm. There you are! 'Most likely!' Well, I ain't satisfied with most likelys. I want to KNOW."

"But—but—"

"Laban Keeler, until they find his body I shan't believe Albert's dead."

"But, Rachel, you mustn't try to deceive yourself that way. Don't you see—"

"No, I don't see. Labe, when Robert Penfold was lost and gone for all them months all hands thought he was dead, didn't they? But he wasn't; he was on that island lost in the middle of all creation. What's to hinder Albert bein' took prisoner by those Germans? They came back to that cottage place after Albert was left there, the cap'n says so in that letter Cap'n Lote just read. What's to hinder their carryin' Al off with 'em? Eh? What's to hinder?"

"Why—why, nothin', I suppose, in one way. But nine chances out of ten—"

"That leaves one chance, don't it. I ain't goin' to give up that chance for—for my boy. I—I—Oh, Labe, I did think SO much of him."

"I know, Rachel, I know. Don't cry any more than you can help. And if it helps you any to make believe—I mean to keep on hopin' he's alive somewheres—why, do it. It won't do any harm, I suppose. Only I wouldn't hint such a thing to Cap'n Lote or Olive."

"Of course not," indignantly. "I ain't quite a fool, I hope. . . . And I presume likely you're right, Laban. The poor boy is dead, probably. But I—I'm goin' to hope he isn't, anyhow, just to get what comfort I can from it. And Robert Penfold did come back, you know."

For some time Laban found himself, against all reason, asking the very question Rachel had asked: Did they actually KNOW that Albert was dead? But as the months passed and no news came he ceased to ask it. Whenever he mentioned the subject to the housekeeper her invariable reply was: "But they haven't found his body, have they?" She would not give up that tenth chance. As she seemed to find some comfort in it he did not attempt to convince her of its futility.

And, meanwhile The Lances of Dawn, Being the Collected Poems of Albert M. C. Speranza was making a mild sensation. The critics were surprisingly kind to it. The story of the young author's recent and romantic death, of his gallantry, his handsome features displayed in newspapers everywhere, all these helped toward the generous welcome accorded the little volume. If the verses were not inspired—why, they were at least entertaining and pleasant. And youth, high-hearted youth sang on every page. So the reviewers were kind and forbearing to the poems themselves, and, for the sake of the dead soldier-poet, were often enthusiastic. The book sold, for a volume of poems it sold very well indeed.

At the Snow place in South Harniss pride and tears mingled. Olive read the verses over and over again, and wept as she read. Rachel Ellis learned many of them by heart, but she, too, wept as she recited them to herself or to Laban. In the little bookkeeper's room above Simond's shoe store The Lances of Dawn lay under the lamp upon the center table as before a shrine. Captain Zelotes read the verses. Also he read all the newspaper notices which, sent to the family by Helen Kendall, were promptly held before his eyes by Olive and Rachel. He read the publisher's advertisements, he read the reviews. And the more he read the more puzzled and bewildered he became.

"I can't understand it, Laban," he confided in deep distress to Mr. Keeler. "I give in I don't know anything at all about this. I'm clean off soundin's. If all this newspaper stuff is so Albert was right all the time and I was plumb wrong. Here's this feller," picking up a clipping from the desk, "callin' him a genius and 'a gifted youth' and the land knows what. And every day or so I get a letter from somebody I never heard of tellin' me what a comfort to 'em those poetry pieces of his are. I don't understand it, Labe. It worries me. If all this is true then—then I was all wrong. I tried to keep him from makin' up poetry, Labe—TRIED to, I did. If what these folks say is so somethin' ought to be done to me. I—I—by thunder, I don't know's I hadn't ought to be hung! . . . And yet—and yet, I did what I thought was right and did it for the boy's sake . . . And—and even now I—I ain't sartin I was wrong. But if I wasn't wrong then this is . . . Oh, I don't know, I don't know!"

And not only in South Harniss were there changes of heart. In New York City and at Greenwich where Mrs. Fosdick was more than ever busy with war work, there were changes. When the newspaper accounts of young Speranza's heroic death were first published the lady paid little attention to them. Her daughter needed all her care just then—all the care, that is, which she could spare from her duties as president of this society and corresponding secretary of that. If her feelings upon hearing the news could have been analyzed it is probable that their larger proportion would have been a huge sense of relief. THAT problem was solved, at all events. She was sorry for poor Madeline, of course, but the dear child was but a child and would recover.

But as with more and more intensity the limelight of publicity was turned upon Albert Speranza's life and death and writing, the wife of the Honorable Fletcher Fosdick could not but be impressed. As head of several so-called literary societies, societies rather neglected since the outbreak of hostilities, she had made it her business to hunt literary lions. Recently it was true that military lions—Major Vermicelli of the Roumanian light cavalry, or Private Drinkwater of the Tank Corps—were more in demand than Tagores, but, as Mrs. Fosdick read of Sergeant Speranza's perils and poems, it could not help occurring to her that here was a lion both literary and martial. Decidedly she had not approved of her daughter's engagement to that lion, but now the said lion was dead, which rendered him a perfectly harmless yet not the less fascinating animal. And then appeared The Lances of Dawn and Mrs. Fosdick's friends among the elect began to read and talk about it.

It was then that the change came. Those friends, one by one, individuals judiciously chosen, were told in strict confidence of poor Madeline's romantic love affair and its tragic ending. These individuals, chosen judiciously as has been stated, whispered, also in strict confidence, the tale to other friends and acquaintances. Mrs. Fosdick began to receive condolences on her daughter's account and on her own. Soon she began to speak publicly of "My poor, dear daughter's dead fiance. Such a loss to American literature. Sheer genius. Have you read the article in the Timepiece? Madeline, poor girl, is heartbroken, naturally, but very proud, even in the midst of her grief. So are we all, I assure you."

She quoted liberally from The Lances of Dawn. A copy specially bound, lay upon her library table. Albert's photograph in uniform, obtained from the Snows by Mr. Fosdick, who wrote for it at his wife's request, stood beside it. To callers and sister war workers Mrs. Fosdick gave details of the hero's genius, his bravery, his devotion to her daughter. It was all so romantic and pleasantly self-advertising—and perfectly safe.

Summer came again, the summer of 1918. The newspapers now were gravely personal reading to millions of Americans. Our new army was trying its metal on the French front and with the British against the vaunted Hindenburg Line. The transports were carrying thousands on every trip to join those already "over there." In South Harniss and in Greenwich and New York, as in every town and city, the ordinary summer vacations and playtime occupations were forgotten or neglected and war charities and war labors took their place. Other soldiers than Sergeant Speranza were the newspaper heroes now, other books than The Lances of Dawn talked about.

As on the previous summer the new Fosdick cottage was not occupied by its owners. Mrs. Fosdick was absorbed by her multitudinous war duties and her husband was at Washington giving his counsel and labor to the cause. Captain Zelotes bought to his last spare dollar of each successive issue of Liberty Bonds, and gave that dollar to the Red Cross or the Y. M. C. A.; Laban and Rachel did likewise. Even Issachar Price bought Thrift Stamps and exhibited them to anyone who would stop long enough to look.

"By crimus," declared Issy, "I'm makin' myself poor helpin' out the gov'ment, but let 'er go and darn the Kaiser, that's my motto. But they ain't all like me. I was down to the drug store yesterday and old man Burgess had the cheek to tell me I owed him for some cigars I bought—er—last fall, seems to me 'twas. I turned right around and looked at him—'I've got my opinion,' says I, 'of a man that thinks of cigars and such luxuries when the country needs every cent. What have you got that gov'ment poster stuck up on your wall for?' says I. 'Read it,' I says. 'It says' '"Save! Save! Save!"' don't it? All right. That's what I'M doin'. I AM savin'.' Then when he was thinkin' of somethin' to answer back I walked right out and left him. Yes sir, by crimustee, I left him right where he stood!"

August came; September—the Hindenburg Line was broken. Each day the triumphant headlines in the papers were big and black and also, alas, the casualty lists on the inside pages long and longer. Then October. The armistice was signed. It was the end. The Allied world went wild, cheered, danced, celebrated. Then it sat back, thinking, thanking God, solemnly trying to realize that the killing days, the frightful days of waiting and awful anxiety, were over.

And early in November another telegram came to the office of Z. Snow and Co. This time it came, not from the War Department direct, but from the Boston headquarters of the American Red Cross.

And this time, just as on the day when the other fateful telegram came, Laban Keeler was the first of the office regulars to learn its contents. Ben Kelley himself brought this message, just as he had brought that telling of Albert Speranza's death. And the usually stolid Ben was greatly excited. He strode straight from the door to the bookkeeper's desk.

"Is the old man in, Labe?" he whispered, jerking his head toward the private office, the door of which happened to be shut.

Laban looked at him over his spectacles. "Cap'n Lote, you mean?" he asked. "Yes, he's in. But he don't want to be disturbed—no, no. Goin' to write a couple of important letters, he said. Important ones. . . . Um-hm. What is it, Ben? Anything I can do for you?"

Kelley did not answer that question. Instead he took a telegram from his pocket.

"Read it, Labe," he whispered. "Read it. It's the darndest news—the—the darnedest good news ever you heard in your life. It don't seem as if it could be, but, by time, I guess 'tis. Anyhow, it's from the Red Cross folks and they'd ought to know."

Laban stared at the telegram. It was not in the usual envelope; Kelley had been too anxious to bring it to its destination to bother with an envelope.

"Read it," commanded the operator again. "See if you think Cap'n Lote ought to have it broke easy to him or—or what? Read it, I tell you. Lord sakes, it's no secret! I hollered it right out loud when it come in over the wire and the gang at the depot heard it. They know it and it'll be all over town in ten minutes. READ IT."

Keeler read the telegram. His florid cheeks turned pale.

"Good Lord above!" he exclaimed, under his breath.

"Eh? I bet you! Shall I take it to the cap'n? Eh? What do you think?"

"Wait. . . . Wait . . . I—I—My soul! My soul! Why . . . It's—it's true. . . . And Rachel always said . . . Why, she was right . . . I . . ."

From without came the sound of running feet and a series of yells.

"Labe! Labe!" shrieked Issy. "Oh, my crimus! . . . Labe!"

He burst into the office, his eyes and mouth wide open and his hands waving wildly.

"Labe! Labe!" he shouted again. "Have you heard it? Have you? It's true, too. He's alive! He's alive! He's alive!"

Laban sprang from his stool. "Shut up, Is!" he commanded. "Shut up! Hold on! Don't—"

"But he's alive, I tell you! He ain't dead! He ain't never been dead! Oh, my crimus! . . . Hey, Cap'n Lote! HE'S ALIVE!"

Captain Zelotes was standing in the doorway of the private office. The noise had aroused him from his letter writing.

"Who's alive? What's the matter with you this time, Is?" he demanded.

"Shut up, Issy," ordered Laban, seizing the frantic Mr. Price by the collar. "Be still! Wait a minute."

"Be still? What do I want to be still for? I cal'late Cap'n Lote'll holler some, too, when he hears. He's alive, Cap'n Lote, I tell ye. Let go of me, Labe Keeler! He's alive!"

"Who's alive? What is it? Labe, YOU answer me. Who's alive?"

Laban's thoughts were still in a whirl. He was still shaking from the news the telegraph operator had brought. Rachel Ellis was at that moment in his mind and he answered as she might have done.

"Er—er—Robert Penfold," he said.

"Robert PENFOLD! What—"

Issachar could hold in no longer.

"Robert Penfold nawthin'!" he shouted. "Who in thunder's he? 'Tain't Robert Penfold nor Robert Penholder neither. It's Al Speranza, that's who 'tis. He ain't killed, Cap'n Lote. He's alive and he's been alive all the time."

Kelley stepped forward.

"Looks as if 'twas so, Cap'n Snow," he said. "Here's the telegram from the Red Cross."

CHAPTER XV

There was nothing miraculous about it. That is to say, it was no more of a miracle than hundreds of similar cases in the World War. The papers of those years were constantly printing stories of men over whose supposed graves funeral sermons had been preached, to whose heirs insurance payments had been made, in whose memory grateful communities had made speeches and delivered eulogiums—the papers were telling of instance after instance of those men being discovered alive and in the flesh, as casuals in some French hospital or as inmates of German prison camps.

Rachel Ellis had asked what was to hinder Albert's having been taken prisoner by the Germans and carried off by them. As a matter of fact nothing had hindered and that was exactly what had happened. Sergeant Speranza, wounded by machine gun fire and again by the explosion of the grenade, was found in the ruins of the cottage when the detachment of the enemy captured it. He was conscious and able to speak, so instead of being bayonetted was carried to the rear where he might be questioned concerning the American forces. The questioning was most unsatisfactory to the Prussian officers who conducted it. Albert fainted, recovered consciousness and fainted again. So at last the Yankee swine was left to die or get well and his Prussian interrogators went about other business, the business of escaping capture themselves. But when they retreated the few prisoners, mostly wounded men, were taken with them.

Albert's recollections of the next few days were hazy and very doubtful. Pain, pain and more pain. Hours and hours—they seemed like years—of jolting over rough roads. Pawing-over by a fat, bearded surgeon, who may not have been intentionally brutal, but quite as likely may. A great desire to die, punctuated by occasional feeble spurts of wishing to live. Then more surgical man-handling, more jolting—in freight cars this time—a slow, miserable recovery, nurses who hated their patients and treated them as if they did, then, a prison camp, a German prison camp. Then horrors and starvation and brutality lasting many months. Then fever.

He was wandering in that misty land between this world and the next when, the armistice having been signed, an American Red Cross representative found him. In the interval between fits of delirium he told this man his name and regiment and, later, the name of his grandparents. When it seemed sure that he was to recover the Red Cross representative cabled the facts to this country. And, still later, those facts, or the all-important fact that Sergeant Albert M. C. Speranza was not dead but alive, came by telegraph to Captain Zelotes Snow of South Harniss. And, two months after that, Captain Zelotes himself, standing on the wharf in Boston and peering up at a crowded deck above him, saw the face of his grandson, that face which he had never expected to see again, looking eagerly down upon him.

A few more weeks and it was over. The brief interval of camp life and the mustering out were things of the past. Captain Lote and Albert, seated in the train, were on their way down the Cape, bound home. Home! The word had a significance now which it never had before. Home!

Albert drew a long breath. "By George!" he exclaimed. "By George, Grandfather, this looks good to me!"

It might not have looked as good to another person. It was raining, the long stretches of salt marsh were windswept and brown and bleak. In the distance Cape Cod Bay showed gray and white against a leaden sky. The drops ran down the dingy car windows.

Captain Zelotes understood, however. He nodded.

"It used to look good to me when I was bound home after a v'yage," he observed. "Well, son, I cal'late your grandma and Rachel are up to the depot by this time waitin' for you. We ain't due for pretty nigh an hour yet, but I'd be willin' to bet they're there."

Albert smiled. "My, I do want to see them!" he said.

"Shouldn't wonder a mite if they wanted to see you, boy. Well, I'm kind of glad I shooed that reception committee out of the way. I presumed likely you'd rather have your first day home to yourself—and us."

"I should say so! Newspaper reporters are a lot of mighty good fellows, but I hope I never see another one. . . . That's rather ungrateful, I know," he added, with a smile, "but I mean it—just now."

He had some excuse for meaning it. The death of Albert Speranza, poet and warrior, had made a newspaper sensation. His resurrection and return furnished material for another. Captain Zelotes was not the only person to meet the transport at the pier; a delegation of reporters was there also. Photographs of Sergeant Speranza appeared once more in print. This time, however, they were snapshots showing him in uniform, likenesses of a still handsome, but less boyish young man, thinner, a scar upon his right cheek, and the look in his eyes more serious, and infinitely older, the look of one who had borne much and seen more. The reporters found it difficult to get a story from the returned hero. He seemed to shun the limelight and to be almost unduly modest and retiring, which was of itself, had they but known it, a transformation sufficiently marvelous to have warranted a special "Sunday special."

"Will not talk about himself," so one writer headed his article. Gertie Kendrick, with a brand-new ring upon her engagement finger, sniffed as she read that headline to Sam Thatcher, who had purchased the ring. "Al Speranza won't talk about himself!" exclaimed Gertie. "Well, it's the FIRST time, then. No wonder they put it in the paper."

But Albert would not talk, claiming that he had done nothing worth talking about, except to get himself taken prisoner in almost his first engagement. "Go and ask some of the other fellows aboard here," he urged. "They have been all through it." As he would not talk the newspaper men were obliged to talk for him, which they did by describing his appearance and his manner, and by rehashing the story of the fight in the French village. Also, of course, they republished some of his verses. The Lances of Dawn appeared in a special edition in honor of its author's reappearance on this earth.

"Yes sir," continued Captain Zelotes, "the reception committee was consider'ble disappointed. They'd have met you with the Orham band if they'd had their way. I told 'em you'd heard all the band music you wanted in camp, I guessed likely, and you'd rather come home quiet. There was goin' to be some speeches, too, but I had them put off."

"Thanks, Grandfather."

"Um-hm. I had a notion you wouldn't hanker for speeches. If you do Issy'll make one for you 'most any time. Ever since you got into the papers Issy's been swellin' up like a hot pop-over with pride because you and he was what he calls chummies. All last summer Issachar spent his evenin's hangin' around the hotel waitin' for the next boarder to mention your name. Sure as one did Is was ready for him. 'Know him?' he'd sing out. 'Did I know Al Speranza? ME? Well, now say!—' And so on, long as the feller would listen. I asked him once if he ever told any of 'em how you ducked him with the bucket of water. He didn't think I knew about that and it kind of surprised him, I judged."

Albert smiled. "Laban told you about it, I suppose," he said. "What a kid trick that was, wasn't it?"

The captain turned his head and regarded him for an instant. The old twinkle was in his eye when he spoke.

"Wouldn't do a thing like that now, Al, I presume likely?" he said. "Feel a good deal older now, eh?"

Albert's answer was seriously given.

"Sometimes I feel at least a hundred and fifty," he replied.

"Humph! . . . Well, I wouldn't feel like that. If you're a hundred and fifty I must be a little older than Methuselah was in his last years. I'm feelin' younger to-day, younger than I have for quite a spell. Yes, for quite a spell."

His grandson put a hand on his knee. "Good for you, Grandfather," he said. "Now tell me more about Labe. Do you know I think the old chap's sticking by his pledge is the bulliest thing I've heard since I've been home."

So they talked of Laban and of Rachel and of South Harniss happenings until the train drew up at the platform of that station. And upon that platform stepped Albert to feel his grandmother's arms about him and her voice, tremulous with happiness, at his ear. And behind her loomed Mrs. Ellis, her ample face a combination of smiles and tears, "all sunshine and fair weather down below but rainin' steady up aloft," as Captain Lote described it afterwards. And behind her, like a foothill in the shadow of a mountain, was Laban. And behind Laban—No, that is a mistake—in front of Laban and beside Laban and in front of and beside everyone else when opportunity presented was Issachar. And Issachar's expression and bearings were wonderful to see. A stranger, and there were several strangers amid the group at the station, might have gained the impression that Mr. Price, with of course a very little help from the Almighty, was responsible for everything.

"Why, Issy!" exclaimed Albert, when they shook hands. "You're here, too, eh?"

Mr. Price's already protuberant chest swelled still further. His reply had the calmness of finality.

"Yes, sir," said Issy, "I'm here. 'Who's goin' to look out for Z. Snow and Co. if all hands walks out and leaves 'em?' Labe says. 'I don't know,' says I, 'and I don't care. I'm goin' to that depot to meet Al Speranzy and if Z. Snow and Co. goes to pot while I'm gone I can't help it. I have sacrificed,' I says, 'and I stand ready to sacrifice pretty nigh everything for my business, but there's limits and this is one of 'em. I'm goin' acrost to that depot to meet him,' says I, 'and don't you try to stop me, Labe Keeler.'"

"Great stuff, Is!" said Albert, with a laugh. "What did Labe say to that?"

"What was there for him to say? He could see I meant it. Course he hove out some of his cheap talk, but it didn't amount to nothin'. Asked if I wan't goin' to put up a sign sayin' when I'd be back, so's to ease the customers' minds. 'I don't know when I'll be back,' I says. 'All right,' says he, 'put that on the sign. That'll ease 'em still more.' Just cheap talk 'twas. He thinks he's funny, but I don't pay no attention to him."

Others came to shake hands and voice a welcome. The formal reception, that with the band, had been called off at Captain Zelotes's request, but the informal one was, in spite of the rain, which was now much less heavy, quite a sizable gathering.

The Reverend Mr. Kendall held his hand for a long time and talked much, it seemed to Albert that he had aged greatly since they last met. He wandered a bit in his remarks and repeated himself several times.

"The poor old gentleman's failin' a good deal, Albert," said Mrs. Snow, as they drove home together, he and his grandparents, three on the seat of the buggy behind Jessamine. "His sermons are pretty tiresome nowadays, but we put up with 'em because he's been with us so long. . . . Ain't you squeezed 'most to death, Albert? You two big men and me all mashed together on this narrow seat. It's lucky I'm small. Zelotes ought to get a two-seated carriage, but he won't."

"Next thing I get, Mother," observed the captain, "will be an automobile. I'll stick to the old mare here as long as she's able to navigate, but when she has to be hauled out of commission I'm goin' to buy a car. I believe I'm pretty nigh the last man in this county to drive a horse, as 'tis. Makes me feel like what Sol Dadgett calls a cracked teapot—a 'genuine antique.' One of these city women will be collectin' me some of these days. Better look out, mother."

Olive sighed happily. "It does me good to hear you joke again, Zelotes," she said. "He didn't joke much, Albert, while—when we thought you—you—"

Albert interrupted in time to prevent the threatened shower.

"So Mr. Kendall is not well," he said. "I'm very sorry to hear it."

"Of course you would be. You and he used to be so friendly when Helen was home. Oh, speakin' of Helen, she IS comin' home in a fortni't or three weeks, so I hear. She's goin' to give up her teachin' and come back to be company for her father. I suppose she realizes he needs her, but it must be a big sacrifice for her, givin' up the good position she's got now. She's such a smart girl and such a nice one. Why, she came to see us after the news came—the bad news—and she was so kind and so good. I don't know what we should have done without her. Zelotes says so too, don't you, Zelotes?"

Her husband did not answer. Instead he said: "Well, there's home, Al. Rachel's there ahead of us and dinner's on the way, judgin' by the smoke from the kitchen chimney. How does the old place look to you, boy?"

Albert merely shook his head and drew a long breath, but his grandparents seemed to be quite satisfied.

There were letters and telegrams awaiting him on the table in the sitting-room. Two of the letters were postmarked from a town on the Florida coast. The telegram also was from that same town.

"*I* had one of those things," observed Captain Zelotes, alluding to the telegram. "Fosdick sent me one of those long ones, night-letters I believe they call 'em. He wants me to tell you that Mrs. Fosdick is better and that they cal'late to be in New York before very long and shall expect you there. Of course you knew that, Al, but I presume likely the main idea of the telegram was to help say, 'Welcome home' to you, that's all."

Albert nodded. Madeline and her mother had been in Florida all winter. Mrs. Fosdick's health was not good. She declared that her nerves had given way under her frightful responsibilities during the war. There was, although it seems almost sacrilege to make such a statement, a certain similarity between Mrs. Fletcher Fosdick and Issachar Price. The telegram was, as his grandfather surmised, an expression of welcome and of regret that the senders could not be there to share in the reception. The two letters which accompanied it he put in his pocket to read later on, when alone. Somehow he felt that the first hours in the old house belonged exclusively to his grandparents. Everything else, even Madeline's letters, must take second place for that period.

Dinner was, to say the least, an ample meal. Rachel and Olive had, as Captain Lote said, "laid themselves out" on that dinner. It began well and continued well and ended best of all, for the dessert was one of which Albert was especially fond. They kept pressing him to eat until Laban, who was an invited guest, was moved to comment.

"Humph!" observed Mr. Keeler. "I knew 'twas the reg'lar program to kill the fatted calf when the prodigal got home, but I see now it's the proper caper to fat up the prodigal to take the critter's place. No, no, Rachel, I'd like fust-rate to eat another bushel or so to please you, but somethin'—that still, small voice we're always readin' about, or somethin'—seems to tell me 'twouldn't be good jedgment.... Um-hm.... 'Twouldn't be good jedgment. ... Cal'late it's right, too.... Yes, yes, yes."

"Now, Cap'n Lote," he added, as they rose from the table, "you stay right to home here for the rest of the day. I'll hustle back to the office and see if Issy's importance has bust his b'iler for him. So-long, Al. See you pretty soon. Got some things to talk about, you and I have. . . . Yes, yes."

Later, when Rachel was in the kitchen with the dishes, Olive left the sitting room and reappeared with triumph written large upon her face. In one hand she held a mysterious envelope and in the other a book. Albert recognized that book. It was his own, The Lances of Dawn. It was no novelty to him. When first the outside world and he had reopened communication, copies of that book had been sent him. His publisher had sent them, Madeline had sent them, his grandparents had sent them, comrades had sent them, nurses and doctors and newspaper men had brought them. No, The Lances of Dawn was not a novelty to its author. But he wondered what was in the envelope.

Mrs. Snow enlightened him. "You sit right down now, Albert," she said. "Sit right down and listen because I've got somethin' to tell you. Yes, and somethin' to show you, too. Here! Stop now, Zelotes! You can't run away. You've got to sit down and look on and listen, too."

Captain Zelotes smiled resignedly. There was, or so it seemed to his grandson, an odd expression on his face. He looked pleased, but not altogether pleased. However, he obeyed his wife's orders and sat.

"Stop, look and listen," he observed. "Mother, you sound like a railroad crossin'. All right, here I am. Al, the society of 'What did I tell you' is goin' to have a meetin'."

His wife nodded. "Well," she said, triumphantly, "what DID I tell you? Wasn't I right?"

The captain pulled his beard and nodded.

"Right as right could be, Mother," he admitted. "Your figgers was a few hundred thousand out of the way, maybe, but barrin' that you was perfectly right."

"Well, I'm glad to hear you say so for once in your life. Albert," holding up the envelope, "do you know what this is?"

Albert, much puzzled, admitted that he did not. His grandmother put down the book, opened the envelope and took from it a slip of paper.

"And can you guess what THIS is?" she asked. Albert could not guess.

"It's a check, that's what it is. It's the first six months' royalties, that's what they call 'em, on that beautiful book of yours. And how much do you suppose 'tis?"

Albert shook his head. "Twenty-five dollars?" he suggested jokingly.

"Twenty-five dollars! It's over twenty-five HUNDRED dollars. It's twenty-eight hundred and forty-three dollars and sixty-five cents, that's what it is. Think of it! Almost three thousand dollars! And Zelotes prophesied that 'twouldn't be more than—"

Her husband held up his hand. "Sh-sh! Sh-sh, Mother," he said. "Don't get started on what I prophesied or we won't be through till doomsday. I'll give in right off that I'm the worst prophet since the feller that h'isted the 'Fair and Dry' signal the day afore Noah's flood begun. You see," he explained, turning to Albert, "your grandma figgered out that you'd probably clear about half a million on that book of poetry, Al. I cal'lated 'twan't likely to be much more'n a couple of hundred thousand, so—"

"Why, Zelotes Snow! You said—"

"Yes, yes. So I did, Mother, so I did. You was right and I was wrong. Twenty-eight hundred ain't exactly a million, Al, but it's a darn sight more than I ever cal'lated you'd make from that book. Or 'most anybody else ever made from any book, fur's that goes," he added, with a shake of the head. "I declare, I—I don't understand it yet. And a poetry book, too! Who in time BUYS 'em all? Eh?"

Albert was looking at the check and the royalty statement.

"So this is why I couldn't get any satisfaction from the publisher," he observed. "I wrote him two or three times about my royalties, and he put me off each time. I began to think there weren't any."

Captain Zelotes smiled. "That's your grandma's doin's," he observed. "The check came to us a good while ago, when we thought you was—was—well, when we thought—"

"Yes. Surely, I understand," put in Albert, to help him out.

"Yes. That's when 'twas. And Mother, she was so proud of it, because you'd earned it, Al, that she kept it and kept it, showin' it to all hands and—and so on. And then when we found out you wasn't—that you'd be home some time or other—why, then she wouldn't let me put it in the bank for you because she wanted to give it to you herself. That's what she said was the reason. I presume likely the real one was that she wanted to flap it in my face every time she crowed over my bad prophesyin', which was about three times a day and four on Sundays."

"Zelotes Snow, the idea!"

"All right, Mother, all right. Anyhow, she got me to write your publisher man and ask him not to give you any satisfaction about those royalties, so's she could be the fust one to paralyze you with 'em. And," with a frank outburst, "if you ain't paralyzed, Al, I own up that *I* am. Three thousand poetry profits beats me. *I* don't understand it."

His wife sniffed. "Of course you don't," she declared. "But Albert does. And so do I, only I think it ought to have been ever and ever so much more. Don't you, yourself, Albert?"

The author of The Lances of Dawn was still looking at the statement of its earnings.

"Approximately eighteen thousand sold at fifteen cents royalty," he observed. "Humph! Well, I'll be hanged!"

"But you said it would be twenty-five cents, not fifteen," protested Olive. "In your letter when the book was first talked about you said so."

Albert smiled. "Did I?" he observed. "Well, I said a good many things in those days, I'm afraid. Fifteen cents for a first book, especially a book of verse, is fair enough, I guess. But eighteen thousand SOLD! That is what gets me."

"You mean you think it ought to be a lot more. So do I, Albert, and so does Rachel. Why, we like it a lot better than we do David Harum. That was a nice book, but it wasn't lovely poetry like yours. And David Harum sold a million. Why shouldn't yours sell as many? Only eighteen thousand—why are you lookin' at me so funny?"

Her grandson rose to his feet. "Let's let well enough alone, Grandmother," he said. "Eighteen thousand will do, thank you. I'm like Grandfather, I'm wondering who on earth bought them."

Mrs. Snow was surprised and a little troubled.

"Why, Albert," she said, "you act kind of—kind of queer, seems to me. You talk as if your poetry wasn't beautiful. You know it is. You used to say it was, yourself."

He interrupted her. "Did I, Grandmother?" he said. "All right, then, probably I did. Let's walk about the old place a little. I want to see it all. By George, I've been dreaming about it long enough!"

There were callers that afternoon, friends among the townsfolk, and more still after supper. It was late—late for South Harniss, that is—when Albert, standing in the doorway of the bedroom he nor they had ever expected he would occupy again, bade his grandparents good night. Olive kissed him again and again and, speech failing her, hastened away down the hall. Captain Zelotes shook his hand, opened his mouth to speak, shut it again, repeated both operations, and at last with a brief, "Well, good night,

Al," hurried after his wife. Albert closed the door, put his lamp upon the bureau, and sat down in the big rocker.

In a way the night was similar to that upon which he had first entered that room. It had ceased raining, but the wind, as on that first night, was howling and whining about the eaves, the shutters rattled and the old house creaked and groaned rheumatically. It was not as cold as on that occasion, though by no means warm. He remembered how bare and comfortless he had thought the room. Now it looked almost luxurious. And he had been homesick, or fancied himself in that condition. Compared to the homesickness he had known during the past eighteen months that youthful seizure seemed contemptible and quite without excuse. He looked about the room again, looked long and lovingly. Then, with a sigh of content, drew from his pocket the two letters which had lain upon the sitting-room table when he arrived, opened them and began to read.

Madeline wrote, as always, vivaciously and at length. The maternal censorship having been removed, she wrote exactly as she felt. She could scarcely believe he was really going to be at home when he received this, at home in dear, quaint, queer old South Harniss. Just think, she had not seen the place for ever and ever so long, not for over two years. How were all the funny, odd people who lived there all the time? Did he remember how he and she used to go to church every Sunday and sit through those dreadful, DREADFUL sermons by that prosy old minister just as an excuse for meeting each other afterward? She was SO sorry she could not have been there to welcome her hero when he stepped from the train. If it hadn't been for Mother's poor nerves she surely would have been. He knew it, didn't he? Of course he did. But she should see him soon "because Mother is planning already to come back to New York in a few weeks and then you are to run over immediately and make us a LONG visit. And I shall be so PROUD of you. There are lots of Army fellows down here now, officers for the most part. So we dance and are very gay—that is, the other girls are; I, being an engaged young lady, am very circumspect and demure, of course. Mother carries The Lances about with her wherever she goes, to teas and such things, and reads aloud from it often. Captain Blanchard, he is one of the family's officer friends, is crazy about your poetry, dear. He thinks it WONDERFUL. You know what *I* think of it, don't you, and when I think that *I* actually helped you, or played at helping you write some of it!

"And I am WILD to see your war cross. Some of the officers here have them—the crosses, I mean—but not many. Captain Blanchard has the military medal, and he is almost as modest about it as you are about your decoration. I don't see how you CAN be so modest. If *I* had a Croix de

Guerre I should want EVERY ONE to know about it. At the tea dance the other afternoon there was a British major who—"

And so on. The second letter was really a continuation of the first. Albert read them both and, after the reading was finished, sat for some time in the rocking chair, quite regardless of the time and the cold, thinking. He took from his pocketbook a photograph, one which Madeline had sent him months before, which had reached him while he lay in the French hospital after his removal from the German camp. He looked at the pretty face in the photograph. She looked just as he remembered her, almost exactly as she had looked more than two years before, smiling, charming, carefree. She had not, apparently, grown older, those age-long months had not changed her. He rose and regarded his own reflection in the mirror of the bureau. He was surprised, as he was constantly being surprised, to see that he, too, had not changed greatly in personal appearance.

He walked about the room. His grandmother had told him that his room was just as he had left it. "I wouldn't change it, Albert," she said, "even when we thought you—you wasn't comin' back. I couldn't touch it, somehow. I kept thinkin', 'Some day I will. Pretty soon I MUST.' But I never did, and now I'm so glad."

He wandered back to the bureau and pulled open the upper drawers. In those drawers were so many things, things which he had kept there, either deliberately or because he was too indolent to destroy them. Old dance cards, invitations, and a bundle of photographs, snapshots. He removed the rubber band from the bundle and stood looking them over. Photographs of school fellows, of picnic groups, of girls. Sam Thatcher, Gertie Kendrick— and Helen Kendall. There were at least a dozen of Helen.

One in particular was very good. From that photograph the face of Helen as he had known it four years before looked straight up into his— clear-eyed, honest, a hint of humor and understanding and common-sense in the gaze and at the corners of the lips. He looked at the photograph, and the photograph looked up at him. He had not seen her for so long a time. He wondered if the war had changed her as it had changed him. Somehow he hoped it had not. Change did not seem necessary in her case.

There had been no correspondence between them since her letter written when she heard of his enlistment. He had not replied to that because he knew Madeline would not wish him to do so. He wondered if she ever thought of him now, if she remembered their adventure at High Point light. He had thought of her often enough. In those days and nights of horror in the prison camp and hospital he had found a little relief, a little solace in lying with closed eyes and summoning back from memory the things of home and the faces of home. And her face had been one of these. Her face and those of his grandparents and Rachel and Laban, and visions of the old house and the rooms—they were the substantial things to cling to and he had clung to them. They WERE home. Madeline—ah! yes, he had longed for her and dreamed of her, God knew, but Madeline, of course, was different.

He snapped the rubber band once more about the bundle of photographs, closed the drawer and prepared for bed.

For the two weeks following his return home he had a thoroughly good time. It was a tremendous comfort to get up when he pleased, to eat the things he liked, to do much or little or nothing at his own sweet will. He walked a good deal, tramping along the beach in the blustering wind and chilly sunshine and enjoying every breath of the clean salt air. He thought much during those solitary walks, and at times, at home in the evenings, he would fall to musing and sit silent for long periods. His grandmother was troubled.

"Don't it seem to you, Zelotes," she asked her husband, "as if Albert was kind of discontented or unsatisfied these days? He's so—so sort of fidgety. Talks like the very mischief for ten minutes and then don't speak for half an hour. Sits still for a long stretch and then jumps up and starts off walkin' as if he was crazy. What makes him act so? He's kind of changed from what he used to be. Don't you think so?"

The captain patted her shoulder. "Don't worry, Mother," he said. "Al's older than he was and what he's been through has made him older still. As for the fidgety part of it, the settin' down and jumpin' up and all that, that's the way they all act, so far as I can learn. Elisha Warren, over to South Denboro, tells me his nephew has been that way ever since he got back. Don't fret, Mother, Al will come round all right."

"I didn't know but he might be anxious to see—to see her, you know."

"Her? Oh, you mean the Fosdick girl. Well, he'll be goin' to see her pretty soon, I presume likely. They're due back in New York 'most any time now, I believe. . . . Oh, hum! Why in time couldn't he—"

"Couldn't he what, Zelotes?"

"Oh, nothin', nothin'."

The summons came only a day after this conversation. It came in the form of another letter from Madeline and one from Mrs. Fosdick. They were, so the latter wrote, back once more in their city home, her nerves, thank Heaven, were quite strong again, and they were expecting him, Albert, to come on at once. "We are all dying to see you," wrote Mrs. Fosdick. "And poor, dear Madeline, of course, is counting the moments."

"Stay as long as you feel like, Al," said the captain, when told of the proposed visit. "It's the dull season at the office, anyhow, and Labe and I can get along first-rate, with Issy to superintend. Stay as long as you want to, only—"

"Only what, Grandfather?"

"Only don't want to stay too long. That is, don't fall in love with New York so hard that you forget there is such a place as South Harniss."

Albert smiled. "I've been in places farther away than New York," he said, "and I never forgot South Harniss."

"Um-hm. . . . Well, I shouldn't be surprised if that was so. But you'll have better company in New York than you did in some of those places. Give my regards to Fosdick. So-long, Al."

CHAPTER XVI

The Fosdick car was at the Grand Central Station when the Knickerbocker Limited pulled in. And Madeline, a wonderfully furred and veiled and hatted Madeline, was waiting there behind the rail as he came up the runway from the train. It was amazing the fact that it was really she. It was more amazing still to kiss her there in public, to hold her hand without fear that some one might see. To—

"Shall I take your bags, sir?"

It was the Fosdick footman who asked it. Albert started guiltily. Then he laughed, realizing that the hand-holding and the rest were no longer criminal offenses. He surrendered his luggage to the man. A few minutes later he and Madeline were in the limousine, which was moving rapidly up the Avenue. And Madeline was asking questions and he was answering and—and still it was all a dream. It COULDN'T be real.

It was even more like a dream when the limousine drew up before the door of the Fosdick home and they entered that home together. For there was Mrs. Fosdick, as ever majestic, commanding, awe-inspiring, the same Mrs. Fosdick who had, in her letter to his grandfather, written him down a despicable, underhanded sneak, here was that same Mrs. Fosdick—but not at all the same. For this lady was smiling and gracious, welcoming him to her home, addressing him by his Christian name, treating him kindly, with almost motherly tenderness. Madeline's letters and Mrs. Fosdick's own letters received during his convalescence abroad had prepared him, or so he had thought, for some such change. Now he realized that he had not been prepared at all. The reality was so much more revolutionary than the anticipation that he simply could not believe it.

But it was not so very wonderful if he had known all the facts and had been in a frame of mind to calmly analyze them. Mrs. Fletcher Fosdick was a seasoned veteran, a general who had planned and fought many hard campaigns upon the political battlegrounds of women's clubs and societies of various sorts. From the majority of those campaigns she had emerged victorious, but her experiences in defeat had taught her that the next best thing to winning is to lose gracefully, because by so doing much which appears to be lost may be regained. For Albert Speranza, bookkeeper and would-be poet of South Harniss, Cape Cod, she had had no use whatever as a prospective son-in-law. Even toward a living Albert Speranza, hero and newspaper-made genius, she might have been cold. But when that hero and genius was, as she and every one else supposed, safely and satisfactorily dead and out of the way, she had seized the opportunity to bask in the radiance of his memory. She had talked Albert Speranza and read Albert Speranza and boasted of Albert Speranza's engagement to her daughter before the world. Now that the said Albert Speranza had been inconsiderate enough to "come alive again," there was but one thing for her to do—that is, to make the best of it. And when Mrs. Fletcher Fosdick made the best of anything she made the very best.

"It doesn't make any difference," she told her husband, "whether he really is a genius or whether he isn't. We have said he is and now we must keep on saying it. And if he can't earn his salt by his writings—which he probably can't—then you must fix it in some way so that he can make-believe earn it by something else. He is engaged to Madeline, and we have told every one that he is, so he will have to marry her; at least, I see no way to prevent it."

"Humph!" grunted Fosdick. "And after that I'll have to support them, I suppose."

"Probably—unless you want your only child to starve."

"Well, I must say, Henrietta—"

"You needn't, for there is nothing more TO say. We're in it and, whether we like it or not, we must make the best of it. To do anything now except appear joyful about it would be to make ourselves perfectly ridiculous. We can't do that, and you know it."

Her husband still looked everything but contented.

"So far as the young fellow himself goes," he said, "I like him, rather. I've talked with him only once, of course, and then he and I weren't agreeing exactly. But I liked him, nevertheless. If he were anything but a fool poet I should be more reconciled."

He was snubbed immediately. "THAT," declared Mrs. Fosdick, with decision, "is the only thing that makes him possible."

So Mrs. Fosdick's welcome was whole-handed if not whole-hearted. And her husband's also was cordial and intimate. The only member of the Fosdick household who did not regard the guest with favor was Googoo. That aristocratic bull-pup was still irreconcilably hostile. When Albert attempted to pet him he appeared to be planning to devour the caressing hand, and when rebuked by his mistress retired beneath a davenport, growling ominously. Even when ignominiously expelled from the room he growled and cast longing backward glances at the Speranza ankles. No, Googoo did not dissemble; Albert was perfectly sure of his standing in Googoo's estimation.

Dinner that evening was a trifle more formal than he had expected, and he was obliged to apologize for the limitations of his wardrobe. His dress suit of former days he had found much too dilapidated for use. Besides, he had outgrown it.

"I thought I was thinner," he said, "and I think I am. But I must have broadened a bit. At any rate, all the coats I left behind won't do at all. I shall have to do what Captain Snow, my grandfather, calls 'refit' here in New York. In a day or two I hope to be more presentable."

Mrs. Fosdick assured him that it was quite all right, really. Madeline asked why he didn't wear his uniform. "I was dying to see you in it," she said. "Just think, I never have."

Albert laughed. "You have been spared," he told her. "Mine was not a triumph, so far as fit was concerned. Of course, I had a complete new rig when I came out of the hospital, but even that was not beautiful. It puckered where it should have bulged and bulged where it should have been smooth."

Madeline professed not to believe him.

"Nonsense!" she declared. "I don't believe it. Why, almost all the fellows I know have been in uniform for the past two years and theirs fitted beautifully."

"But they were officers, weren't they, and their uniforms were custom made."

"Why, I suppose so. Aren't all uniforms custom made?"

Her father laughed. "Scarcely, Maddie," he said. "The privates have their custom-made by the mile and cut off in chunks for the individual. That was about it, wasn't it, Speranza?"

"Just about, sir."

Mrs. Fosdick evidently thought that the conversation was taking a rather low tone. She elevated it by asking what his thoughts were when taken prisoner by the Germans. He looked puzzled.

"Thoughts, Mrs. Fosdick?" he repeated. "I don't know that I understand, exactly. I was only partly conscious and in a good deal of pain and my thoughts were rather incoherent, I'm afraid."

"But when you regained consciousness, you know. What were your thoughts then? Did you realize that you had made the great sacrifice for your country? Risked your life and forfeited your liberty and all that for the cause? Wasn't it a great satisfaction to feel that you had done that?"

Albert's laugh was hearty and unaffected. "Why, no," he said. "I think what I was realizing most just then was that I had made a miserable mess of the whole business. Failed in doing what I set out to do and been taken prisoner besides. I remember thinking, when I was clear-headed enough to think anything, 'You fool, you spent months getting into this war, and then got yourself out of it in fifteen minutes.' And it WAS a silly trick, too."

Madeline was horrified.

"What DO you mean?" she cried. "Your going back there to rescue your comrade a silly trick! The very thing that won you your Croix de Guerre?"

"Why, yes, in a way. I didn't save Mike, poor fellow—"

"Mike! Was his name Mike?"

"Yes; Michael Francis Xavier Kelly. A South Boston Mick he was, and one of the finest, squarest boys that ever drew breath. Well, poor Mike was dead when I got to him, so my trip had been for nothing, and if he had been alive I could not have prevented his being taken. As it was, he was dead and I was a prisoner. So nothing was gained and, for me, personally, a good deal was lost. It wasn't a brilliant thing to do. But," he added apologetically, "a chap doesn't have time to think collectively in such a scrape. And it was my first real scrap and I was frightened half to death, besides."

"Frightened! Why, I never heard anything so ridiculous! What—"

"One moment, Madeline." It was Mrs. Fosdick who interrupted. "I want to ask—er—Albert a question. I want to ask him if during his long imprisonment he composed—wrote, you know. I should have thought the sights and experiences would have forced one to express one's self—that is, one to whom the gift of expression was so generously granted," she added, with a gracious nod.

Albert hesitated.

"Why, at first I did," he said. "When I first was well enough to think, I used to try to write—verses. I wrote a good many. Afterwards I tore them up."

"Tore them up!" Both Mrs. and Miss Fosdick uttered this exclamation.

"Why, yes. You see, they were such rot. The things I wanted to write about, the things *I* had seen and was seeing, the—the fellows like Mike and their pluck and all that—well, it was all too big for me to tackle. My jingles sounded, when I read them over, like tunes on a street piano. *I couldn't do it.* A genius might have been equal to the job, but I wasn't."

Mrs. Fosdick glanced at her husband. There was something of alarmed apprehension in the glance. Madeline's next remark covered the situation. It expressed the absolute truth, so much more of the truth than even the young lady herself realized at the time.

"Why, Albert Speranza," she exclaimed, "I never heard you speak of yourself and your work in that way before. Always—ALWAYS you have had such complete, such splendid confidence in yourself. You were never afraid to attempt ANYTHING. You MUST not talk so. Don't you intend to write any more?"

Albert looked at her. "Oh, yes, indeed," he said simply. "That is just what I do intend to do—or try to do."

That evening, alone in the library, he and Madeline had their first long, intimate talk, the first since those days—to him they seemed as far away as the last century—when they walked the South Harniss beach together, walked beneath the rainbows and dreamed. And now here was their dream coming true.

Madeline, he was realizing it as he looked at her, was prettier than ever. She had grown a little older, of course, a little more mature, but surprisingly little. She was still a girl, a very, very pretty girl and a charming girl. And he—

"What are you thinking about?" she demanded suddenly.

He came to himself. "I was thinking about you," he said. "You are just as you used to be, just as charming and just as sweet. You haven't changed."

She smiled and then pouted.

"I don't know whether to like that or not," she said. "Did you expect to find me less—charming and the rest?"

"Why, no, of course not. That was clumsy on my part. What I meant was that—well, it seems ages, centuries, since we were together there on the Cape—and yet you have not changed."

She regarded him reflectively.

"You have," she said.

"Have what?"

"Changed. You have changed a good deal. I don't know whether I like it or not. Perhaps I shall be more certain by and by. Now show me your war cross. At least you have brought that, even if you haven't brought your uniform."

He had the cross in his pocket-book and he showed it to her. She enthused over it, of course, and wished he might wear it even when in citizen's clothes. She didn't see why he couldn't. And it was SUCH a pity he could not be in uniform. Captain Blanchard had called the evening before, to see Mother about some war charities she was interested in, and he was still in uniform and wearing his decorations, too. Albert suggested that probably Blanchard was still in service. Yes, she believed he was, but she could not see why that should make the difference. Albert had BEEN in service.

He laughed at this and attempted to explain. She seemed to resent the attempt or the tone.

"I do wish," she said almost pettishly, "that you wouldn't be so superior."

He was surprised. "Superior!" he repeated. "Superior! I? Superiority is the very least of my feelings. I—superior! That's a joke."

And, oddly enough, she resented that even more. "Why is it a joke?" she demanded. "I should think you had the right to feel superior to almost any one. A hero—and a genius! You ARE superior."

However, the little flurry was but momentary, and she was all sweetness and smiles when she kissed him good night. He was shown to his room by a servant and amid its array of comforts—to him, fresh from France and the camp and his old room at South Harniss, it was luxuriously magnificent—he sat for some time thinking. His thoughts should have been happy ones, yet they were not entirely so. This is a curiously unsatisfactory world, sometimes.

The next day he went shopping. Fosdick had given him a card to his own tailor and Madeline had given him the names of several shops where, so she declared, he could buy the right sort of ties and things. From the tailor's Albert emerged looking a trifle dazed; after a visit to two of the shops the dazed expression was even more pronounced. His next visits were at establishments farther downtown and not as exclusive. He returned to the Fosdick home feeling fairly well satisfied with the results achieved. Madeline, however, did not share his satisfaction.

"But Dad sent you to his tailor," she said. "Why in the world didn't you order your evening clothes there? And Brett has the most stunning ties. Every one says so. Instead you buy yours at a department store. Now why?"

He smiled. "My dear girl," he said, "your father's tailor estimated that he might make me a very passable dress suit for one hundred and seventy-five dollars. Brett's ties were stunning, just as you say, but the prices ranged from five to eight dollars, which was more stunning still. For a young person from the country out of a job, which is my condition at present, such things may be looked at but not handled. I can't afford them."

She tossed her head. "What nonsense!" she exclaimed. "You're not out of a job, as you call it. You are a writer and a famous writer. You have written one book and you are going to write more. Besides, you must have made heaps of money from The Lances. Every one has been reading it."

When he told her the amount of his royalty check she expressed the opinion that the publisher must have cheated. It ought to have been ever and ever so much more than that. Such wonderful poems!

The next day she went to Brett's and purchased a half dozen of the most expensive ties, which she presented to him forthwith.

"There!" she demanded. "Aren't those nicer than the ones you bought at that old department store? Well, then!"

"But, Madeline, I must not let you buy my ties."

"Why not? It isn't such an unheard-of thing for an engaged girl to give her fiance a necktie."

"That isn't the idea. I should have bought ties like those myself, but I couldn't afford them. Now for you to—"

"Nonsense! You talk as if you were a beggar. Don't be so silly."

"But, Madeline—"

"Stop! I don't want to hear it."

She rose and went out of the room. She looked as if she were on the verge of tears. He felt obliged to accept the gift, but he disliked the principle of the things as much as ever. When she returned she was very talkative and gay and chatted all through luncheon. The subject of the ties was not mentioned again by either of them. He was glad he had not told her that his new dress suit was ready-made.

While in France, awaiting his return home, he had purchased a ring and sent it to her. She was wearing it, of course. Compared with other articles of jewelry which she wore from time to time, his ring made an extremely modest showing. She seemed quite unaware of the discrepancy, but he was aware of it.

On an evening later in the week Mrs. Fosdick gave a reception. "Quite an informal affair," she said, in announcing her intention. "Just a few intimate friends to meet Mr. Speranza, that is all. Mostly lovers of literature—discerning people, if I may say so."

The quite informal affair looked quite formidably formal to Albert. The few intimate friends were many, so it seemed to him. There was still enough of the former Albert Speranza left in his make-up to prevent his appearing in the least distressed or ill at ease. He was, as he had always been when in the public eye, even as far back as the school dancing-classes with the Misses Bradshaw's young ladies, perfectly self-possessed, charmingly polite, absolutely self-assured. And his good looks had not suffered during his years of imprisonment and suffering. He was no longer a handsome boy, but he was an extraordinarily attractive and distinguished man.

Mrs. Fosdick marked his manner and appearance and breathed a sigh of satisfaction. Madeline noted them. Her young friends of the sex noted them and whispered and looked approval. What the young men thought does not matter so much, perhaps. One of these was the Captain Blanchard, of whom Madeline had written and spoken. He was a tall, athletic chap, who looked well in his uniform, and whose face was that of a healthy, clean-living and clean-thinking young American. He and Albert shook hands and looked each other over. Albert decided he should like Blanchard if he knew him better. The captain was not talkative; in fact, he seemed rather taciturn. Maids and matrons gushed when presented to the lion of the evening. It scarcely seemed possible that they were actually meeting the author of The Lances of Dawn. That wonderful book! Those wonderful poems! "How CAN you write them, Mr. Speranza?" "When do your best inspirations come, Mr. Speranza?" "Oh, if I could write as you do I should walk on air." The matron who breathed the last-quoted ecstasy was distinctly weighty; the mental picture of her pedestrian trip through the atmosphere was interesting. Albert's hand was patted by the elderly spinsters, young women's eyes lifted soulful glances to his.

It was the sort of thing he would have revelled in three or four years earlier. Exactly the sort of thing he had dreamed of when the majority of the poems they gushed over were written. It was much the same thing he remembered having seen his father undergo in the days when he and the opera singer were together. And his father had, apparently, rather enjoyed it. He realized all this—and he realized, too, with a queer feeling that it should be so, that he did not like it at all. It was silly. Nothing he had written warranted such extravagances. Hadn't these people any sense of proportion? They bored him to desperation. The sole relief was the behavior of the men, particularly the middle-aged or elderly men, obviously present through feminine compulsion. They seized his hand, moved it up and down with a pumping motion, uttered some stereotyped prevarications about their pleasure at meeting him and their having enjoyed his poems very much, and then slid on in the direction of the refreshment room.

And Albert, as he shook hands, bowed and smiled and was charmingly affable, found his thoughts wandering until they settled upon Private Mike Kelly and the picturesque language of the latter when he, as sergeant, routed him out for guard duty. Mike had not gushed over him nor called him a genius. He had called him many things, but not that.

He was glad indeed when he could slip away for a dance with Madeline. He found her chatting gaily with Captain Blanchard, who had been her most recent partner. He claimed her from the captain and as he led her out to the dance floor she whispered that she was very proud of him. "But I DO wish YOU could wear your war cross," she added.

The quite informal affair was the first of many quite as informally formal. Also Mrs. Fosdick's satellites and friends of the literary clubs and the war work societies seized the opportunity to make much of the heroic author of The Lances of Dawn. His society was requested at teas, at afternoon as well as evening gatherings. He would have refused most of these invitations, but Madeline and her mother seemed to take his acceptance for granted; in fact, they accepted for him. A ghastly habit developed of asking him to read a few of his own poems on these occasions. "PLEASE, Mr. Speranza. It will be such a treat, and such an HONOR." Usually a particular request was made that he read "The Greater Love." Now "The Greater Love" was the poem which, written in those rapturous days when he and Madeline first became aware of their mutual adoration, was refused by one editor as a "trifle too syrupy." To read that sticky effusion over and over again became a torment. There were occasions when if a man had referred to "The Greater Love," its author might have howled profanely and offered bodily violence. But no men ever did refer to "The Greater Love."

On one occasion when a sentimental matron and her gushing daughter had begged to know if he did not himself adore that poem, if he did not consider it the best he had ever written, he had answered frankly. He was satiated with cake and tea and compliments that evening and recklessly truthful. "You really wish to know my opinion of that poem?" he asked. Indeed and indeed they really wished to knew just that thing. "Well, then, I think it's rot," he declared. "I loathe it."

Of course mother and daughter were indignant. Their comments reached Madeline's ear. She took him to task.

"But why did you say it?" she demanded. "You know you don't mean it."

"Yes, I do mean it. It IS rot. Lots of the stuff in that book of mine is rot. I did not think so once, but I do now. If I had the book to make over again, that sort wouldn't be included."

She looked at him for a moment as if studying a problem.

"I don't understand you sometimes," she said slowly. "You are different. And I think what you said to Mrs. Bacon and Marian was very rude."

Later when he went to look for her he found her seated with Captain Blanchard in a corner. They were eating ices and, apparently, enjoying themselves. He did not disturb them. Instead he hunted up the offended Bacons and apologized for his outbreak. The apology, although graciously accepted, had rather wearisome consequences. Mrs. Bacon declared she knew that he had not really meant what he said.

"I realize how it must be," she declared. "You people of temperament, of genius, of aspirations, are never quite satisfied, you cannot be. You are always trying, always seeking the higher attainment. Achievements of the past, though to the rest of us wonderful and sublime, are to you—as you say, 'rot.' That is it, is it not?" Albert said he guessed it was, and wandered away, seeking seclusion and solitude. When the affair broke up he found Madeline and Blanchard still enjoying each other's society. Both were surprised when told the hour.

CHAPTER XVII

So the first three weeks of his proposed month's visit passed and the fourth began. And more and more his feelings of dissatisfaction and uneasiness increased. The reasons for those feelings he found hard to define. The Fosdicks were most certainly doing their best to make him comfortable and happy. They were kind—yes, more than kind. Mr. Fosdick he really began to like. Mrs. Fosdick's manner had a trace of condescension in it, but as the lady treated all creation with much the same measure of condescension, he was more amused than resentful. And Madeline—Madeline was sweet and charming and beautiful. There was in her manner toward him, or so he fancied, a slight change, perhaps a change a trifle more marked since the evening when his expressed opinion of "The Greater Love" had offended her and the Bacons. It seemed to him that she was more impatient, more capricious, sometimes almost overwhelming him with attention and tenderness and then appearing to forget him entirely and to be quite indifferent to his thoughts and opinions. Her moods varied greatly and there were occasions when he found it almost impossible to please her. At these times she took offense when no offense was intended and he found himself apologizing when, to say the least, the fault, if there was any, was not more than half his. But she always followed those moods with others of contrition and penitence and then he was petted and fondled and his forgiveness implored.

These slight changes in her he noticed, but they troubled him little, principally because he was coming to realize the great change in himself. More and more that change was forcing itself upon him. The stories and novels he had read during the first years of the war, the stories by English writers in which young men, frivolous and inconsequential, had enlisted and fought and emerged from the ordeal strong, purposeful and "made-over"—those stories recurred to him now. He had paid little attention to the "making-over" idea when he read those tales, but now he was forced to believe there might be something in it. Certainly something, the three years or the discipline and training and suffering, or all combined, had changed him. He was not as he used to be. Things he liked very much he no longer liked at all. And where, oh where, was the serene self-satisfaction which once was his?

The change must be quite individual, he decided. All soldiers were not so affected. Take Blanchard, for instance. Blanchard had seen service, more and quite as hard fighting as he had seen, but Blanchard was, to all appearances, as light-hearted and serene and confident as ever. Blanchard was like Madeline; he was much the same now as he had been before the war. Blanchard could dance and talk small talk and laugh and enjoy himself. Well, so could he, on occasions, for that matter, if that had been all. But it was not all, or if it was why was he at other times so discontented and uncomfortable? What was the matter with him, anyway?

He drew more and more into his shell and became more quiet and less talkative. Madeline, in one of her moods, reproached him for it.

"I do wish you wouldn't be grumpy," she said.

They had been sitting in the library and he had lapsed into a fit of musing, answering her questions with absentminded monosyllables. Now he looked up.

"Grumpy?" he repeated. "Was I grumpy? I beg your pardon."

"You should. You answered every word I spoke to you with a grunt or a growl. I might as well have been talking to a bear."

"I'm awfully sorry, dear. I didn't feel grumpy. I was thinking, I suppose."

"Thinking! You are always thinking. Why think, pray? . . . If I permitted myself to think, I should go insane."

"Madeline, what do you mean?"

"Oh, nothing. I'm partially insane now, perhaps. Come, let's go to the piano. I feel like playing. You don't mind, do you?"

That evening Mrs. Fosdick made a suggestion to her husband.

"Fletcher," she said, "I am inclined to think it is time you and Albert had a talk concerning the future. A business talk, I mean. I am a little uneasy about him. From some things he has said to me recently I gather that he is planning to earn his living with his pen."

"Well, how else did you expect him to earn it; as bookkeeper for the South Harniss lumber concern?"

"Don't be absurd. What I mean is that he is thinking of devoting himself to literature exclusively. Don't interrupt me, please. That is very beautiful and very idealistic, and I honor him for it, but I cannot see Madeline as an attic poet's wife, can you?"

"I can't, and I told you so in the beginning."

"No. Therefore I should take him to one side and tell him of the opening in your firm. With that as a means of keeping his feet on the ground his brain may soar as it likes, the higher the better."

Mr. Fosdick, as usual, obeyed orders and that afternoon Albert and he had the "business talk." Conversation at dinner was somewhat strained. Mr. Fosdick was quietly observant and seemed rather amused about something. His wife was dignified and her manner toward her guest was inclined to be abrupt. Albert's appetite was poor. As for Madeline, she did not come down to dinner, having a headache.

She came down later, however. Albert, alone in the library, was sitting, a book upon his knees and his eyes fixed upon nothing in particular, when she came in.

"You are thinking again, I see," she said.

He had not heard her enter. Now he rose, the book falling to the floor.

"Why—why, yes," he stammered. "How are you feeling? How is your head?"

"It is no worse. And no better. I have been thinking, too, which perhaps explains it. Sit down, Albert, please. I want to talk with you. That is what I have been thinking about, that you and I must talk."

She seated herself upon the davenport and he pulled forward a chair and sat facing her. For a moment she was silent. When she did speak, however, her question was very much to the point.

"Why did you say 'No' to Father's offer?" she asked. He had been expecting this very question, or one leading up to it. Nevertheless, he found answering difficult. He hesitated, and she watched him, her impatience growing.

"Well?" she asked.

He sighed. "Madeline," he said, "I am afraid you think me very unreasonable, certainly very ungrateful."

"I don't know what to think about you. That is why I feel we must have this talk. Tell me, please, just what Father said to you this afternoon."

"He said—well, the substance of what he said was to offer me a position in his office, in his firm."

"What sort of a position?"

"Well, I—I scarcely know. I was to have a desk there and—and be generally—ornamental, I suppose. It was not very definite, the details of the position, but—"

"The salary was good, wasn't it?"

"Yes; more than good. Much too good for the return I could make for it, so it seemed to me."

"And your prospects for the future? Wasn't the offer what people call a good opportunity?"

"Why, yes, I suppose it was. For the right sort of man it would have been a wonderful opportunity. Your father was most kind, most generous, Madeline. Please don't think I am not appreciative. I am, but—"

"Don't. I want to understand it all. He offered you this opportunity, this partnership in his firm, and you would not accept it? Why? Don't you like my father?"

"Yes, I like him very much."

"Didn't you," with the slightest possible curl of the lip, "think the offer worthy of you? . . . Oh, I don't mean that! Please forgive me. I am trying not to be disagreeable. I—I just want to understand, Albert, that's all."

He nodded. "I know, Madeline," he said. "You have the right to ask. It wasn't so much a question of the offer being worthy of me as of my being worthy the offer. Oh, Madeline, why should you and I pretend? You know why Mr. Fosdick made me that offer. It wasn't because I was likely to be worth ten dollars a year to his firm. In Heaven's name, what use would I be in a stockbroker's office, with my make-up, with my lack of business ability? He would be making a place for me there and paying me a high salary for one reason only, and you know what that is. Now don't you?"

She hesitated now, but only for an instant. She colored a little, but she answered bravely.

"I suppose I do," she said, "but what of it? It is not unheard of, is it, the taking one's prospective son-in-law into partnership?"

"No, but—We're dodging the issue again, Madeline. If I were likely to be of any help to your father's business, instead of a hindrance, I might perhaps see it differently. As it is, I couldn't accept unless I were willing to be an object of charity."

"Did you tell Father that?"

"Yes."

"What did he say?"

"He said a good deal. He was frank enough to say that he did not expect me to be of great assistance to the firm. But I might be of SOME use—he didn't put it as baldly as that, of course—and at all times I could keep on with my writing, with my poetry, you know. The brokerage business should not interfere with my poetry, he said; your mother would scalp him if it did that."

She smiled faintly. "That sounds like dad," she commented.

"Yes. Well, we talked and argued for some time on the subject. He asked me what, supposing I did not accept this offer of his, my plans for the future might be. I told him they were pretty unsettled as yet. I meant to write, of course. Not poetry altogether. I realized, I told him, that I was not a great poet, a poet of genius."

Madeline interrupted. Her eyes flashed.

"Why do you say that?" she demanded. "I have heard you say it before. That is, recently. In the old days you were as sure as I that you were a real poet, or should be some day. You never doubted it. You used to tell me so and I loved to hear you."

Albert shook his head. "I was sure of so many things then," he said. "I must have been an insufferable kid."

She stamped her foot. "It was less than three years ago that you said it," she declared. "You are not so frightfully ancient now.... Well, go on, go on. How did it end, the talk with Father, I mean?"

"I told him," he continued, "that I meant to write and to earn my living by writing. I meant to try magazine work—stories, you know—and, soon, a novel. He asked if earning enough to support a wife on would not be a long job at that time. I said I was afraid it might, but that that seemed to me my particular game, nevertheless."

She interrupted again. "Did it occur to you to question whether or not that determination of yours was quite fair to me?" she asked.

"Why—why, yes, it did. And I don't know that it IS exactly fair to you. I—"

"Never mind. Go on. Tell me the rest. How did it end?"

"Well, it ended in a sort of flare-up. Mr. Fosdick was just a little bit sarcastic, and I expressed my feelings rather freely—too freely, I'm afraid."

"Never mind. I want to know what you said."

"To be absolutely truthful, then, this is what I said: I said that I appreciated his kindness and was grateful for the offer. But my mind was made up. I would not live upon his charity and draw a large salary for doing nothing except be a little, damned tame house-poet led around in leash and exhibited at his wife's club meetings.... That was about all, I think. We shook hands at the end. He didn't seem to like me any the less for . . . Why, Madeline, have I offended you? My language was pretty strong, I know, but—"

She had bowed her head upon her arms amid the sofa cushions and was crying. He sprang to his feet and bent over her.

"Why, Madeline," he said again, "I beg your pardon. I'm sorry—"

"Oh, it isn't that," she sobbed. "It isn't that. I don't care what you said."

"What is it, then?"

She raised her head and looked at him.

"It is you," she cried. "It is myself. It is everything. It is all wrong. I—I was so happy and—and now I am miserable. Oh—oh, I wish I were dead!"

She threw herself upon the cushions again and wept hysterically. He stood above her, stroking her hair, trying to soothe her, to comfort her, and all the time he felt like a brute, a heartless beast. At last she ceased crying, sat up and wiped her eyes with her handkerchief.

"There!" she exclaimed. "I will not be silly any longer. I won't be! I WON'T! . . . Now tell me: Why have you changed so?"

He looked down at her and shook his head. He was conscience-stricken and fully as miserable as she professed to be.

"I don't know," he said. "I am older and—and—and I DON'T see things as I used to. If that book of mine had appeared three years ago I have no doubt I should have believed it to be the greatest thing ever printed. Now, when people tell me it is and I read what the reviewers said and all that, I—I DON'T believe, I KNOW it isn't great—that is, the most of it isn't. There is some pretty good stuff, of course, but—You see, I think it wasn't the poems themselves that made it sell; I think it was all the fool tommyrot the papers printed about me, about my being a hero and all that rubbish, when they thought I was dead, you know. That—"

She interrupted. "Oh, don't!" she cried. "Don't! I don't care about the old book. I'm not thinking about that. I'm thinking about you. YOU aren't the same—the same toward me."

"Toward you, Madeline? I don't understand what you mean."

"Yes, you do. Of course you do. If you were the same as you used to be, you would let Father help you. We used to talk about that very thing and—and you didn't resent it then."

"Didn't I? Well, perhaps I didn't. But I think I remember our speaking sometimes of sacrificing everything for each other. We were to live in poverty, if necessary, and I was to write, you know, and—"

"Stop! All that was nonsense, nonsense! you know it."

"Yes, I'm afraid it was."

"You know it was. And if you were as you used to be, if you—"

"Madeline!"

"What? Why did you interrupt me?"

"Because I wanted to ask you a question. Do you think YOU are exactly the same—as you used to be?"

"What do you mean?"

"Haven't YOU changed a little? Are you as sure as you were then—as sure of your feeling toward me?"

She gazed at him, wide-eyed. "WHAT do you mean?"

"I mean ARE you sure? It has seemed to me that perhaps—I was out of your life for a long time, you know, and during a good deal of that time it seemed certain that I had gone forever. I am not blaming you, goodness knows, but—Madeline, isn't there—Well, if I hadn't come back, mightn't there have been some one—else?"

She turned pale.

"What do—" she stammered, inarticulate. "Why, why—"

"It was Captain Blanchard, wasn't it?"

The color came back to her cheeks with a rush. She blushed furiously and sprang to her feet.

"How—how can you say such things!" she cried. "What do you mean? How DARE you say Captain Blanchard took advantage of—How—how DARE you say I was not loyal to you? It is not true. It is not true. I was. I am. There hasn't been a word—a word between us since—since the news came that you were—I told him—I said—And he has been splendid! Splendid! And now you say—Oh, what AM I saying? What SHALL I do?"

She collapsed once more among the cushions. He leaned forward.

"My dear girl—" he began, but she broke in.

"I HAVEN'T been disloyal," she cried. "I have tried—Oh, I have tried so hard—"

"Hush, Madeline, hush. I understand. I understand perfectly. It is all right, really it is."

"And I should have kept on trying always—always."

"Yes, dear, yes. But do you think a married life with so much trying in it likely to be a happy one? It is better to know it now, isn't it, a great deal better for both of us? Madeline, I am going to my room. I want you to think, to think over all this, and then we will talk again. I don't blame you. I don't, dear, really. I think I realize everything—all of it. Good night, dear."

He stooped and kissed her. She sobbed, but that was all. The next morning a servant came to his room with a parcel and a letter. The parcel was a tiny one. It was the ring he had given her, in its case. The letter was short and much blotted. It read:

Dear Albert:

I have thought and thought, as you told me to, and I have concluded that you were right. It IS best to know it now. Forgive me, please, PLEASE. I feel wicked and horrid and I HATE myself, but I think this is best. Oh, do forgive me. Good-by.

MADELINE.

His reply was longer. At its end he wrote:

Of course I forgive you. In the first place there is nothing to forgive. The unforgivable thing would have been the sacrifice of your happiness and your future to a dream and a memory. I hope you will be very happy. I am sure you will be, for Blanchard is, I know, a fine fellow. The best of fortune to you both.

The next forenoon he sat once more in the car of the morning train for Cape Cod, looking out of the window. He had made the journey from New York by the night boat and had boarded the Cape train at Middleboro. All the previous day, and in the evening as he tramped the cold wind-swept deck of the steamer, he had been trying to collect his thoughts, to readjust them to the new situation, to comprehend in its entirety the great change that had come in his life. The vague plans, the happy indefinite dreams, all the rainbows and roses had gone, shivered to bits like the reflection in a broken mirror. Madeline, his Madeline, was his no longer. Nor was he hers. In a way it seemed impossible.

He tried to analyze his feelings. It seemed as if he should have been crushed, grief-stricken, broken. He was inclined to reproach himself because he was not. Of course there was a sadness about it, a regret that the wonder of those days of love and youth had passed. But the sorrow was not bitter, the regret was but a wistful longing, the sweet, lingering fragrance of a memory, that was all. Toward her, Madeline, he felt—and it surprised him, too, to find that he felt—not the slightest trace of resentment. And more surprising still he felt none toward Blanchard. He had meant what he said in his letter, he wished for them both the greatest happiness.

And—there was no use attempting to shun the fact—his chief feeling, as he sat there by the car window looking out at the familiar landscape, was a great relief, a consciousness of escape from what might have been a miserable, crushing mistake for him and for her. And with this a growing sense of freedom, of buoyancy. It seemed wicked to feel like that. Then it came to him, the thought that Madeline, doubtless, was experiencing the same feeling. And he did not mind a bit; he hoped she was, bless her!

A youthful cigar "drummer," on his first Down-East trip, sat down beside him.

"Kind of a flat, bare country, ain't it?" observed the drummer, with a jerk of his head toward the window. "Looks bleak enough to me. Know anything about this neck of the woods, do you?"

Albert turned to look at him.

"Meaning the Cape?" he asked.

"Sure."

"Indeed I do. I know all about it."

"That so! Say, you sound as if you liked it."

Albert turned back to the window again.

"Like it!" he repeated. "I love it." Then he sighed, a sigh of satisfaction, and added: "You see, I BELONG here."

His grandparents and Rachel were surprised when he walked into the house that noon and announced that he hoped dinner was ready, because he was hungry. But their surprise was more than balanced by their joy. Captain Zelotes demanded to know how long he was going to stay.

"As long as you'll have me, Grandfather," was the answer.

"Eh? Well, that would be a consider'ble spell, if you left it to us, but I cal'late that girl in New York will have somethin' to say as to time limit, won't she?"

Albert smiled. "I'll tell you about that by and by," he said.

He did not tell them until that evening after supper. It was Friday evening and Olive was going to prayer-meeting, but she delayed "putting on her things" to hear the tale. The news that the engagement was off and that her grandson was not, after all, to wed the daughter of the Honorable Fletcher Fosdick, shocked and grieved her not a little.

"Oh, dear!" she sighed. "I suppose you know what's best, Albert, and maybe, as you say, you wouldn't have been happy, but I DID feel sort of proud to think my boy was goin' to marry a millionaire's daughter."

Captain Zelotes made no comment—then. He asked to be told more particulars. Albert described the life at the Fosdick home, the receptions, his enforced exhibitions and readings. At length the recital reached the point of the interview in Fosdick's office.

"So he offered you to take you into the firm—eh, son?" he observed.

"Yes, sir."

"Humph! Fosdick, Williamson and Hendricks are one of the biggest brokerage houses goin', so a good many New Yorkers have told me."

"No doubt. But, Grandfather, you've had some experience with me as a business man; how do you think I would fit into a firm of stockbrokers?"

Captain Lote's eye twinkled, but he did not answer the question. Instead he asked:

"Just what did you give Fosdick as your reason for not sayin' yes?"

Albert laughed. "Well, Grandfather," he said, "I'll tell you. I said that I appreciated his kindness and all that, but that I would not draw a big salary for doing nothing except to be a little, damned tame house-poet led around in leash and shown off at his wife's club meetings."

Mrs. Snow uttered a faint scream. "Oh, Albert!" she exclaimed. She might have said more, but a shout from her husband prevented her doing so.

Captain Zelotes had risen and his mighty hand descended with a stinging slap upon his grandson's shoulder.

"Bully for you, boy!" he cried. Then, turning to Olive, he added, "Mother, I've always kind of cal'lated that you had one man around this house. Now, by the Lord A'Mighty, I know you've got TWO!"

Olive rose. "Well," she declared emphatically, "that may be; but if both those men are goin' to start in swearin' right here in the sittin' room, I think it's high time SOMEBODY in that family went to church."

So to prayer meeting she went, with Mrs. Ellis as escort, and her husband and grandson, seated in armchairs before the sitting room stove, both smoking, talked and talked, of the past and of the future—not as man to boy, nor as grandparent to grandson, but for the first time as equals, without reservations, as man to man.

CHAPTER XVIII

The next morning Albert met old Mr. Kendall. After breakfast Captain Zelotes had gone, as usual, directly to the office. His grandson, however, had not accompanied him.

"What are you cal'latin' to do this mornin', Al?" inquired the captain.

"Oh, I don't know exactly, Grandfather. I'm going to look about the place a bit, write a letter to my publishers, and take a walk, I think. You will probably see me at the office pretty soon. I'll look in there by and by."

"Ain't goin' to write one or two of those five hundred dollar stories before dinner time, are you?"

"I guess not, sir. I'm afraid they won't be written as quickly as all that."

Captain Lote shook his head. "Godfreys!" he exclaimed; "it ain't the writin' of 'em I'd worry about so much as the gettin' paid for 'em. You're sure that editor man ain't crazy, you say?"

"I hope he isn't. He seemed sane enough when I saw him."

"Well, I don't know. It's live and learn, I suppose, but if anybody but you had told me that magazine folks paid as much as five hundred dollars a piece for yarns made up out of a feller's head without a word of truth in 'em, I'd — well, I should have told the feller that told me to go to a doctor right off and have HIS head examined. But — well, as 'tis I cal'late I'd better have my own looked at. So long, Al. Come in to the office if you get a chance."

He hurried out. Albert walked to the window and watched the sturdy figure swinging out of the yard. He wondered if, should he live to his grandfather's age, his step would be as firm and his shoulders as square.

Olive laid a hand on his arm.

"You don't mind his talkin' that way about your writin' those stories, do you, Albert?" she asked, a trace of anxiety in her tone. "He don't mean it, you know. He don't understand it — says he don't himself — but he's awful proud of you, just the same. Why, last night, after you and he had finished talkin' and he came up to bed — and the land knows what time of night or mornin' THAT was — he woke me out of a sound sleep to tell me about that New York magazine man givin' you a written order to write six stories for his magazine at five hundred dollars a piece. Zelotes couldn't seem to get over it. 'Think of it, Mother,' he kept sayin'. 'Think of it! Pretty nigh twice what I pay as good a man as Labe Keeler for keepin' books a whole year. And Al says he ought to do a story every forni't. I used to jaw his head off, tellin' him he was on the road to starvation and all that. Tut, tut, tut! Mother, I've waited a long time to say it, but it looks as if you married a fool.' . . . That's the way he talked, but he's a long ways from bein' a fool, your grandfather is, Albert."

Albert nodded. "No one knows that better than I," he said, with emphasis.

"There's one thing," she went on, "that kind of troubled me. He said you was goin' to insist on payin' board here at home. Now you know this house is yours. And we love to—"

He put his arm about her. "I know it, Grandmother," he broke in, quickly. "But that is all settled. I am going to try to make my own living in my own way. I am going to write and see what I am really worth. I have my royalty money, you know, most of it, and I have this order for the series of stories. I can afford to pay for my keep and I shall. You see, as I told Grandfather last night, I don't propose to live on his charity any more than on Mr. Fosdick's."

She sighed.

"So Zelotes said," she admitted. "He told me no less than three times that you said it. It seemed to tickle him most to death, for some reason, and that's queer, too, for he's anything but stingy. But there, I suppose you can pay board if you want to, though who you'll pay it to is another thing. *I* shan't take a cent from the only grandson I've got in the world."

It was while on his stroll down to the village that Albert met Mr. Kendall. The reverend gentleman was plodding along carrying a market basket from the end of which, beneath a fragment of newspaper, the tail and rear third of a huge codfish drooped. The basket and its contents must have weighed at least twelve pounds and the old minister was, as Captain Zelotes would have said, making heavy weather of it. Albert went to his assistance.

"How do you do, Mr. Kendall," he said; "I'm afraid that basket is rather heavy, isn't it. Mayn't I help you with it?" Then, seeing that the old gentleman did not recognize him, he added, "I am Albert Speranza."

Down went the basket and the codfish and Mr. Kendall seized him by both hands.

"Why, of course, of course," he cried. "Of course, of course. It's our young hero, isn't it. Our poet, our happy warrior. Yes,—yes, of course. So glad to see you, Albert. . . . Er . . . er . . . How is your mother?"

"You mean my grandmother? She is very well, thank you."

"Yes—er—yes, your grandmother, of course. . . . Er . . . er. . . . Did you see my codfish? Isn't it a magnificent one. I am very fond of codfish and we almost never have it at home. So just now, I happened to be passing Jonathan Howes'—he is the—er—fishdealer, you know, and . . . Jonathan is a very regular attendant at my Sunday morning services. He is—is. . . . Dear me. . . . What was I about to say?"

Being switched back to the main track by Albert he explained that he had seen a number of cod in Mr. Howes' possession and had bought this specimen. Howes had lent him the basket.

"And the newspaper," he explained; adding, with triumph, "I shall dine on codfish to-day, I am happy to say." Judging by appearances he might dine and sup and breakfast on codfish and still have a supply remaining. Albert insisted on carrying the spoil to the parsonage. He was doing nothing in particular and it would be a pleasure, he said. Mr. Kendall protested for the first minute or so but then forgot just what the protest was all about and rambled garrulously on about affairs in the parish. He had failed in other faculties, but his flow of language was still unimpeded. They entered the gate of the parsonage. Albert put the basket on the upper step.

"There," he said; "now I must go. Good morning, Mr. Kendall."

"Oh, but you aren't going? You must come in a moment. I want to give you the manuscript of that sermon of mine on the casting down of Baal, that is the one in which I liken the military power of Germany to the brazen idol which. . . . Just a moment, Albert. The manuscript is in my desk and. . . . Oh, dear me, the door is locked. . . . Helen, Helen!"

He was shaking the door and shouting his daughter's name. Albert was surprised and not a little disturbed. It had not occurred to him that Helen could be at home. It is true that before he left for New York his grandmother had said that she was planning to return home to be with her father, but since then he had heard nothing more concerning her. Neither of his grandparents had mentioned her name in their letters, nor since his arrival the day before had they mentioned it. And Mr. Kendall had not spoken of her during their walk together. Albert was troubled and taken aback. In one way he would have liked to meet Helen very much indeed. They had not met since before the war. But he did not, somehow, wish to meet her just then. He did not wish to meet anyone who would speak of Madeline, or ask embarrassing questions. He turned to go.

"Another time, Mr. Kendall," he said. "Good morning."

But he had gone only a few yards when the reverend gentleman was calling to him to return.

"Albert! Albert!" called Mr. Kendall.

He was obliged to turn back, he could do nothing else, and as he did so the door opened. It was Helen who opened it and she stood there upon the threshold and looked down at him. For a moment, a barely perceptible interval, she looked, then he heard her catch her breath quickly and saw her put one hand upon the door jamb as if for support. The next, and she was running down the steps, her hands outstretched and the light of welcome in her eyes.

"Why, Albert Speranza!" she cried. "Why, ALBERT!"

He seized her hands. "Helen!" he cried, and added involuntarily, "My, but it's good to see you again!"

She laughed and so did he. All his embarrassment was gone. They were like two children, like the boy and girl who had known each other in the old days.

"And when did you get here?" she asked. "And what do you mean by surprising us like this? I saw your grandfather yesterday morning and he didn't say a word about your coming."

"He didn't know I was coming. I didn't know it myself until the day before. And when did you come? Your father didn't tell me you were here. I didn't know until I heard him call your name."

He was calling it again. Calling it and demanding attention for his precious codfish.

"Yes, Father, yes, in a minute," she said. Then to Albert, "Come in. Oh, of course you'll come in."

"Why, yes, if I won't be interfering with the housekeeping."

"You won't. Yes, Father, yes, I'm coming. Mercy, where did you get such a wonderful fish? Come in, Albert. As soon as I get Father's treasure safe in the hands of Maria I'll be back. Father will keep you company. No, pardon me, I am afraid he won't, he's gone to the kitchen already. And I shall have to go, too, for just a minute. I'll hurry."

She hastened to the kitchen, whither Mr. Kendall, tugging the fish basket, had preceded her. Albert entered the little sitting-room and sat down in a chair by the window. The room looked just as it used to look, just as neat, just as homelike, just as well kept. And when she came back and they began to talk, it seemed to him that she, too, was just as she used to be. She was a trifle less girlish, more womanly perhaps, but she was just as good to look at, just as bright and cheerful and in her conversation she had the same quietly certain way of dealing directly with the common-sense realities and not the fuss and feathers. It seemed to him that she had not changed at all, that she herself was one of the realities, the wholesome home realities, like Captain Zelotes and Olive and the old house they lived in. He told her so. She laughed.

"You make me feel as ancient as the pyramids," she said.

He shook his head. "I am the ancient," he declared. "This war hasn't changed you a particle, Helen, but it has handed me an awful jolt. At times I feel as if I must have sailed with Noah. And as if I had wasted most of the time since."

She smiled. "Just what do you mean by that?" she asked.

"I mean—well, I don't know exactly what I do mean, I guess. I seem to have an unsettled feeling. I'm not satisfied with myself. And as I remember myself," he added, with a shrug, "that condition of mind was not usual with me."

She regarded him for a moment without speaking, with the appraising look in her eyes which he remembered so well, which had always reminded him of the look in his grandfather's eyes, and which when a boy he resented so strongly.

"Yes," she said slowly, "I think you have changed. Not because you say you feel so much older or because you are uneasy and dissatisfied. So many of the men I talked with at the camp hospital, the men who had been over there and had been wounded, as you were, said they felt the same way. That doesn't mean anything, I think, except that it is dreadfully hard to get readjusted again and settle down to everyday things. But it seems to me that you have changed in other ways. You are a little thinner, but broader, too, aren't you? And you do look older, especially about the eyes. And, of course—well, of course I think I do miss a little of the Albert Speranza I used to know, the young chap with the chip on his shoulder for all creation to knock off."

"Young jackass!"

"Oh, no indeed. He had his good points. But there! we're wasting time and we have so much to talk about. You—why, what am I thinking of! I have neglected the most important thing in the world. And you have just returned from New York, too. Tell me, how is Madeline Fosdick?"

"She is well. But tell me about yourself. You have been in all sorts of war work, haven't you. Tell me about it."

"Oh, my work didn't amount to much. At first I 'Red Crossed' in Boston, then I went to Devens and spent a long time in the camp hospital there."

"Pretty trying, wasn't it?"

"Why—yes, some of it was. When the 'flu' epidemic was raging and the poor fellows were having such a dreadful time it was bad enough. After that I was sent to Eastview. In the hospital there I met the boys who had been wounded on the other side and who talked about old age and dissatisfaction and uneasiness, just as you do. But MY work doesn't count. You are the person to be talked about. Since I have seen you you have become a famous poet and a hero and—"

"Don't!"

She had been smiling; now she was very serious.

"Forgive me, Albert," she said. "We have been joking, you and I, but there was a time when we—when your friends did not joke. Oh, Albert, if you could have seen the Snow place as I saw it then. It was as if all the hope and joy and everything worth while had been crushed out of it. Your grandmother, poor little woman, was brave and quiet, but we all knew she was trying to keep up for Captain Zelotes' sake. And he—Albert, you can scarcely imagine how the news of your death changed him. . . . Ah! well, it was a hard time, a dreadful time for—for every one."

She paused and he, turning to look at her, saw that there were tears in her eyes. He knew of her affection for his grandparents and theirs for her. Before he could speak she was smiling again.

"But now that is all over, isn't it?" she said. "And the Snows are the happiest people in the country, I do believe. AND the proudest, of course. So now you must tell me all about it, about your experiences, and about your war cross, and about your literary work—oh, about everything."

The all-inclusive narrative was not destined to get very far. Old Mr. Kendall came hurrying in, the sermon on the casting down of Baal in his hand. Thereafter he led, guided, and to a large extent monopolized the conversation. His discourse had proceeded perhaps as far as "Thirdly" when Albert, looking at his watch, was surprised to find it almost dinner time. Mr. Kendall, still talking, departed to his study to hunt for another sermon. The young people said good-by in his absence.

"It has been awfully good to see you again, Helen," declared Albert. "But I told you that in the beginning, didn't I? You seem like—well, like a part of home, you know. And home means something to me nowadays."

"I'm glad to hear you speak of South Harniss as home. Of course I know you don't mean to make it a permanent home—I imagine Madeline would have something to say about that—but it is nice to have you speak as if the old town meant something to you."

He looked about him.

"I love the place," he said simply.

"I am glad. So do I; but then I have lived here all my life. The next time we talk I want to know more about your plans for the future—yours and Madeline's, I mean. How proud she must be of you."

He looked up at her; she was standing upon the upper step and he on the walk below.

"Madeline and I—" he began. Then he stopped. What was the use? He did not want to talk about it. He waved his hand and turned away.

After dinner he went out into the kitchen to talk to Mrs. Ellis, who was washing dishes. She was doing it as she did all her share of the housework, with an energy and capability which would have delighted the soul of a "scientific management" expert. Except when under the spell of a sympathetic attack Rachel was ever distinctly on the job.

And of course she was, as always, glad to see her protege, her Robert Penfold. The proprietary interest which she had always felt in him was more than ever hers now. Had not she been the sole person to hint at the possibility of his being alive, when every one else had given him up for dead? Had not she been the only one to suggest that he might have been taken prisoner? Had SHE ever despaired of seeing him again—on this earth and in the flesh? Indeed, she had not; at least, she had never admitted it, if she had. So then, hadn't she a RIGHT to feel that she owned a share in him? No one ventured to dispute that right.

She turned and smiled over one ample shoulder when he entered the kitchen.

"Hello," she hailed cheerfully. "Come callin', have you, Robert—Albert, I mean? It would have been a great help to me if you'd been christened Robert. I call you that so much to myself it comes almost more natural than the other. On account of you bein' so just like Robert Penfold in the book, you know," she added.

"Yes, yes, of course, Rachel, I understand," put in Albert hastily. He was not in the mood to listen to a dissertation on a text taken from Foul Play. He looked about the room and sighed happily.

"There isn't a speck anywhere, is there?" he observed. "It is just as it used to be, just as I used to think of it when I was laid up over there. When I wanted to try and eat a bit, so as to keep what strength I had, I would think about this kitchen of yours, Rachel. It didn't do to think of the places where the prison stuff was cooked. They were not—appetizing."

Mrs. Ellis nodded. "I presume likely not," she observed. "Well, don't tell me about 'em. I've just scrubbed this kitchen from stem to stern. If I heard about those prison places, I'd feel like startin' right in and scrubbin' it all over again, I know I should. . . . Dirty pigs! I wish I had the scourin' of some of those Germans! I'd—I don't know as I wouldn't skin 'em alive."

Albert laughed. "Some of them pretty nearly deserved it," he said.

Rachel smiled grimly. "Well, let's talk about nice things," she said. "Oh, Issy Price was here this forenoon; Cap'n Lote sent him over from the office on an errand, and he said he saw you and Mr. Kendall goin' down street together just as he was comin' along. He hollered at you, but you didn't hear him. 'Cordin' to Issachar's tell, you was luggin' a basket with Jonah's whale in it, or somethin' like that."

Albert described his encounter with the minister. Rachel was much interested.

"Oh, so you saw Helen," she said. "Well, I guess she was surprised to see you."

"Not more than I was to see her. I didn't know she was in town. Not a soul had mentioned it—you nor Grandfather nor Grandmother."

The housekeeper answered without turning her head. "Guess we had so many things to talk about we forgot it," she said. "Yes, she's been here over a week now. High time, from what I hear. The poor old parson has failed consider'ble and Maria Price's housekeepin' and cookin' is enough to make a well man sick—or wish he was. But he'll be looked after now. Helen will look after him. She's the most capable girl there is in Ostable County. Did she tell you about what she done in the Red Cross and the hospitals?"

"She said something about it, not very much."

"Um-hm. She wouldn't, bein' Helen Kendall. But the Red Cross folks said enough, and they're sayin' it yet. Why—"

She went on to tell of Helen's work in the Red Cross depots and in the camp, and hospitals. It was an inspiring story.

"There they was," said Rachel, "the poor things, just boys most of 'em, dyin' of that dreadful influenza like rats, as you might say. And, of course it's dreadful catchin', and a good many was more afraid of it than they would have been of bullets, enough sight. But Helen Kendall wa'n't afraid—no, siree! Why—"

And so on. Albert listened, hearing most of it, but losing some as his thoughts wandered back to the Helen he had known as a boy and the Helen he had met that forenoon. Her face, as she had welcomed him at the parsonage door—it was surprising how clearly it showed before his mind's eye. He had thought at first that she had not changed in appearance. That was not quite true—she had changed a little, but it was merely the fulfillment of a promise, that was all. Her eyes, her smile above a hospital bed—he could imagine what they must have seemed like to a lonely, homesick boy wrestling with the "flu."

"And, don't talk!" he heard the housekeeper say, as he drifted out of his reverie, "if she wa'n't popular around that hospital, around both hospitals, fur's that goes! The patients idolized her, and the other nurses they loved her, and the doctors—"

"Did they love her, too?" Albert asked, with a smile, as she hesitated.

She laughed. "Some of 'em did, I cal'late," she answered. "You see, I got most of my news about it all from Bessie Ryder, Cornelius Ryder's niece, lives up on the road to the Center; you used to know her, Albert. Bessie was nursin' in that same hospital, the one Helen was at first. 'Cordin' to her, there was some doctor or officer tryin' to shine up to Helen most of the time. When she was at Eastview, so Bessie heard, there was a real big-bug in the Army, a sort of Admiral or Commodore amongst the doctors he was, and HE was trottin' after her, or would have been if she'd let him. 'Course you have to make some allowances for Bessie—she wouldn't be a Ryder if she didn't take so many words to say so little that the truth gets stretched pretty thin afore she finished—but there must have been SOMETHIN' in it. And all about her bein' such a wonderful nurse and doin' so much for the Red Cross I KNOW is true.... Eh? Did you say anything, Albert?"

Albert shook his head. "No, Rachel," he replied. "I didn't speak."

"I thought I heard you or somebody say somethin'. I—Why, Laban Keeler, what are you doin' away from your desk this time in the afternoon?"

Laban grinned as he entered the kitchen.

"Did I hear you say you thought you heard somebody sayin' somethin', Rachel?" he inquired. "That's queer, ain't it? Seemed to me *I* heard somebody sayin' somethin' as I come up the path just now. Seemed as if they was sayin' it right here in the kitchen, too. 'Twasn't your voice, Albert, and it couldn't have been Rachel's, 'cause she NEVER talks—'specially to you. It's too bad, the prejudice she's got against you, Albert," he added, with a wink.

"Um-hm, too bad—yes, 'tis—yes, yes."

Mrs. Ellis sniffed.

"And that's what the newspapers in war time used to call—er—er—oh, dear, what was it?—camel—seems's if 'twas somethin' about a camel—"

"Camouflage?" suggested Albert.

"That's it. All that talk about me is just camouflage to save him answerin' my question. But he's goin' to answer it. What are you doin' away from the office this time in the afternoon, I want to know?"

Mr. Keeler perched his small figure on the corner of the kitchen table.

"Well, to tell you the truth, Rachel," he said solemnly. "I'm here to do what the folks in books call demand an explanation. You and I, Rachel, are just as good as engaged to be married, ain't we? I've been keepin' company with you for the last twenty, forty or sixty years, some such spell as that. Now, just as I'm gettin' used to it and beginnin' to consider it a settled arrangement, as you may say, I come into this house and find you shut up in the kitchen with another man. Now, what—"

The housekeeper advanced toward him with the dripping dishcloth.

"Laban Keeler," she threatened, "if you don't stop your foolishness and answer my question, I declare I'll—"

Laban slid from his perch and retired behind the table.

"Another man," he repeated. "And SOME folks—not many, of course, but some—might be crazy enough to say he was a better-lookin' man than I am. Now, bein' ragin' jealous,—All right, Rachel, all right, I surrender. Don't hit me with all those soapsuds. I don't want to go back to the office foamin' at the mouth. The reason I'm here is that I had to go down street to see about the sheathin' for the Red Men's lodge room. Issy took the order, but he wasn't real sure whether 'twas sheathin' or scantlin' they wanted, so I told Cap'n Lote I'd run down myself and straighten it out. On the way back I saw you two through the window and I thought I'd drop in and worry you. So here I am."

Mrs. Ellis nodded. "Yes," she sniffed. "And all that camel—camel—Oh, DEAR, what DOES ail me? All that camel—No use, I've forgot it again."

"Never mind, Rachel," said Mr. Keeler consolingly. "All the—er—menagerie was just that and nothin' more. Oh, by the way, Al," he added, "speakin' of camels—don't you think I've done pretty well to go so long without any—er—liquid nourishment? Not a drop since you and I enlisted together.... Oh, she knows about it now," he added, with a jerk of his head in the housekeeper's direction. "I felt 'twas fairly safe and settled, so I told her. I told her. Yes, yes, yes. Um-hm, so I did."

Albert turned to the lady.

"You should be very proud of him, Rachel," he said seriously. "I think I realize a little something of the fight he has made, and it is bully. You should be proud of him."

Rachel looked down at the little man.

"I am," she said quietly. "I guess likely he knows it."

Laban smiled. "The folks in Washington are doin' their best to help me out," he said. "They're goin' to take the stuff away from everybody so's to make sure *I* don't get any more. They'll probably put up a monument to me for startin' the thing; don't you think they will, Al? Eh? Don't you, now?"

Albert and he walked up the road together. Laban told a little more of his battle with John Barleycorn.

"I had half a dozen spells when I had to set my teeth, those I've got left, and hang on," he said. "And the hangin'-on wa'n't as easy as stickin' to fly-paper, neither. Honest, though, I think the hardest was when the news came that you was alive, Al. I—I just wanted to start in and celebrate. Wanted to whoop her up, I did." He paused a moment and then added, "I tried whoopin' on sass'parilla and vanilla sody, but 'twa'n't satisfactory. Couldn't seem to raise a real loud whisper, let alone a whoop. No, I couldn't—no, no."

Albert laughed and laid a hand on his shoulder. "You're all right, Labe," he declared. "I know you, and I say so."

Laban slowly shook his head. His smile, as he answered, was rather pathetic.

"I'm a long, long ways from bein' all right, Al," he said. "A long ways from that, I am. If I'd made my fight thirty year ago, I might have been nigher to amountin' to somethin'.... Oh, well, for Rachel's sake I'm glad I've made it now. She's stuck to me when everybody would have praised her for chuckin' me to Tophet. I was readin' one of Thackeray's books t'other night—Henry Esmond, 'twas; you've read it, Al, of course; I was readin' it t'other night for the ninety-ninth time or thereabouts, and I run across the place where it says it's strange what a man can do and a woman still keep thinkin' he's an angel. That's true, too, Al. Not," with the return of the slight smile, "that Rachel ever went so far as to call me an angel. No, no. There's limits where you can't stretch her common-sense any farther. Callin' me an angel would be just past the limit. Yes, yes, yes. I guess SO."

They spoke of Captain Zelotes and Olive and of their grief and discouragement when the news of Albert's supposed death reached them.

"Do you know," said Labe, "I believe Helen Kendall's comin' there for a week did 'em more good than anything else. She got away from her soldier nursin' somehow—must have been able to pull the strings consider'ble harder'n the average to do it—and just came down to the Snow place and sort of took charge along with Rachel. Course she didn't live there, her father thought she was visitin' him, I guess likely, but she was with Cap'n Lote and Olive most of the time. Rachel says she never made a fuss, you understand, just was there and helped and was quiet and soft-spoken and capable and—and comfortin', that's about the word, I guess. Rachel always thought a sight of Helen afore that, but since then she swears by her."

That evening—or, rather, that night, for they did not leave the sitting room until after twelve—Mrs. Snow heard her grandson walking the floor of his room, and called to ask if he was sick.

"I'm all right, Grandmother," he called in reply. "Just taking a little exercise before turning in, that's all. Sorry if I disturbed you."

The exercise was, as a matter of fact, almost entirely mental, the pacing up and down merely an unconscious physical accompaniment. Albert Speranza was indulging in introspection. He was reviewing and assorting his thoughts and his impulses and trying to determine just what they were and why they were and whither they were tending. It was a mental and spiritual picking to pieces and the result was humiliating and in its turn resulted in a brand-new determination.

Ever since his meeting with Helen, a meeting which had been quite unpremeditated, he had thought of but little except her. During his talk with her in the parsonage sitting room he had been—there was no use pretending to himself that it was otherwise—more contented with the world, more optimistic, happier, than he had been for months, it seemed to him for years. Even while he was speaking to her of his uneasiness and dissatisfaction he was dimly conscious that at that moment he was less uneasy and less dissatisfied, conscious that the solid ground was beneath his feet at last, that here was the haven after the storm, here was—

He pulled up sharply. This line of thought was silly, dangerous, wicked. What did it mean? Three days before, only three days, he had left Madeline Fosdick, the girl whom he had worshiped, adored, and who had loved him. Yes, there was no use pretending there, either; he and Madeline HAD loved each other. Of course he realized now that their love had nothing permanently substantial about it. It was the romance of youth, a dream which they had shared together and from which, fortunately for both, they had awakened in time. And of course he realized, too, that the awakening had begun long, long before the actual parting took place. But nevertheless only three days had elapsed since that parting, and now—What sort of a man was he?

Was he like his father? Was it what Captain Zelotes used to call the "Portygee streak" which was now cropping out? The opera singer had been of the butterfly type—in his later years a middle-aged butterfly whose wings creaked somewhat—but decidedly a flitter from flower to flower. As a boy, Albert had been aware, in an uncertain fashion, of his father's fondness for the sex. Now, older, his judgment of his parent was not as lenient, was clearer, more discerning. He understood now. Was his own "Portygee streak," his inherited temperament, responsible for his leaving one girl on a Tuesday and on Friday finding his thoughts concerned so deeply with another?

Well, no matter, no matter. One thing was certain—Helen should never know of that feeling. He would crush it down, he would use his commonsense. He would be a decent man and not a blackguard. For he had had his chance and had tossed it away. What would she think of him now if he came to her after Madeline had thrown him over—that is what Mrs. Fosdick would say, would take pains that every one else should say, that Madeline had thrown him over—what would Helen think of him if he came to her with a second-hand love like that?

And of course she would not think of him as a lover at all. Why should she? In the boy and girl days she had refused to let him speak of such a thing. She was his friend, a glorious, a wonderful friend, but that was all, all she ever dreamed of being.

Well, that was right; that was as it should be. He should be thankful for such a friend. He was, of course. And he would concentrate all his energies upon his work, upon his writing. That was it, that was it. Good, it was settled!

So he went to bed and, eventually, to sleep.

CHAPTER XIX

While dressing in the cold light of dawn his perturbations of the previous night appeared in retrospect as rather boyish and unnecessary. His sudden and unexpected meeting with Helen and their talk together had tended to make him over-sentimental, that was all. He and she were to be friends, of course, but there was no real danger of his allowing himself to think of her except as a friend. No, indeed. He opened the bureau drawer in search of a tie, and there was the package of "snapshots" just where he had tossed them that night when he first returned home after muster-out. Helen's photograph was the uppermost. He looked at it—looked at it for several minutes. Then he closed the drawer again and hurriedly finished his dressing. A part, at least, of his resolve of the night before had been sound common-sense. His brain was suffering from lack of exercise. Work was what he needed, hard work.

So to work he went without delay. A place to work in was the first consideration. He suggested the garret, but his grandmother and Rachel held up their hands and lifted their voices in protest.

"No, INDEED," declared Olive. "Zelotes has always talked about writin' folks and poets starvin' in garrets. If you went up attic to work he'd be teasin' me from mornin' to night. Besides, you'd freeze up there, if the smell of moth-balls didn't choke you first. No, you wait; I've got a notion. There's that old table desk of Zelotes' in the settin' room. He don't hardly ever use it nowadays. You take it upstairs to your own room and work in there. You can have the oil-heater to keep you warm."

So that was the arrangement made, and in his own room Albert sat down at the battered old desk, which had been not only his grandfather's but his great-grandfather's property, to concentrate upon the first of the series of stories ordered by the New York magazine. He had already decided upon the general scheme for the series. A boy, ragamuffin son of immigrant parents, rising, after a wrong start, by sheer grit and natural shrewdness and ability, step by step to competence and success, winning a place in and the respect of a community. There was nothing new in the idea itself. Some things his soldier chum Mike Kelley had told him concerning an uncle of his—Mike's—suggested it. The novelty he hoped might come from the incidents, the various problems faced by his hero, the solution of each being a step upward in the latter's career and in the formation of his character. He wanted to write, if he could, the story of the building of one more worth-while American, for Albert Speranza, like so many others set to thinking by the war and the war experiences, was realizing strongly that the gabbling of a formula and the swearing of an oath of naturalization did not necessarily make an American. There were too many eager to take that oath with tongue in cheek and knife in sleeve. Too many, for the first time in their lives breathing and speaking as free men, thanks to the protection of Columbia's arm, yet planning to stab their protectress in the back.

So Albert's hero was to be an American, an American to whom the term meant the highest and the best. If he had hunted a lifetime for something to please and interest his grandfather he could not have hit the mark nearer the center. Cap'n Lote, of course, pretended a certain measure of indifference, but that was for Olive and Rachel's benefit. It would never do for the scoffer to become a convert openly and at once. The feminine members of the household clamored each evening to have the author read aloud his day's installment. The captain sniffed.

"Oh, dear, dear," with a groan, "now I've got to hear all that made-up stuff that happened to a parcel of made-up folks that never lived and never will. Waste of time, waste of time. Where's my Transcript?"

But it was noticed—and commented upon, you may be sure—by his wife and housekeeper that the Transcript was likely to be, before the reading had progressed far, either in the captain's lap or on the floor. And when the discussion following the reading was under way Captain Zelotes' opinions were expressed quite as freely as any one's else. Laban Keeler got into the habit of dropping in to listen.

One fateful evening the reading was interrupted by the arrival of Mr. Kendall. The reverend gentleman had come to make a pastoral call. Albert's hero was in the middle of a situation. The old clergyman insisted upon the continuation of the reading. It was continued and so was the discussion following it; in fact, the discussion seemed likely to go on indefinitely, for the visitor showed no inclination of leaving. At ten-thirty his daughter appeared to inquire about him and to escort him home. Then he went, but under protest. Albert walked to the parsonage with them.

"Now we've started somethin'," groaned the captain, as the door closed. "That old critter'll be cruisin' over here six nights out of five from now on to tell Al just how to spin those yarns of his. And he'll talk—and talk—and talk. Ain't it astonishin' how such a feeble-lookin' craft as he is can keep blowin' off steam that way and still be able to navigate."

His wife took him to task. "The idea," she protested, "of your callin' your own minister a 'critter'! I should think you'd be ashamed. . . . But, oh, dear, I'm afraid he WILL be over here an awful lot."

Her fears were realized. Mr. Kendall, although not on hand "six nights out of five," as the captain prophesied, was a frequent visitor at the Snow place. As Albert's story-writing progressed the discussions concerning the growth and development of the hero's character became more and more involved and spirited. They were for the most part confined, when the minister was present, to him and Mrs. Snow and Rachel. Laban, if he happened to be there, sat well back in the corner, saying little except when appealed to, and then answering with one of his dry, characteristic observations. Captain Lote, in the rocker, his legs crossed, his hand stroking his beard, and with the twinkle in his eyes, listened, and spoke but seldom. Occasionally, when he and his grandson exchanged glances, the captain winked, indicating appreciation of the situation.

"Say, Al," he said, one evening, after the old clergyman had departed, "it must be kind of restful to have your work all laid out for you this way. Take it to-night, for instance; I don't see but what everything's planned for this young feller you're writin' about so you nor he won't have to think for yourselves for a hundred year or such matter. Course there's some little difference in the plans. Rachel wants him to get wrecked on an island or be put in jail, and Mother, she wants him to be a soldier and a poet, and Mr. Kendall thinks it's high time he joined the church or signed the pledge or stopped swearin' or chewin' gum."

"Zelotes, how ridiculous you do talk!"

"All right, Mother, all right. What strikes me, Al, is they don't any of 'em stop to ask you what YOU mean to have him do. Course I know 'tain't any of your business, but still—seems 's if you might be a little mite interested in the boy yourself."

Albert laughed. "Don't worry, Grandfather," he said. "I'm enjoying it all very much. And some of the suggestions may be just what I'm looking for."

"Well, son, we'll hope so. Say, Labe, I've got a notion for keepin' the minister from doin' all the talkin.' We'll ask Issy Price to drop in; eh?"

Laban shook his head. "I don't know, Cap'n Lote," he observed. "Sounds to me a good deal like lettin' in a hurricane to blow out a match with. . . . Um-hm. Seems so to me. Yes, yes."

Mr. Kendall's calls would have been more frequent still had Helen not interfered. Very often, when he came she herself dropped in a little later and insisted upon his making an early start for home. Occasionally she came with him. She, too, seemed much interested in the progress of the stories, but she offered few suggestions. When directly appealed to, she expressed her views, and they were worth while.

Albert was resolutely adhering to his determination not to permit himself to think of her except as a friend. That is, he hoped he was; thoughts are hard to control at times. He saw her often. They met on the street, at church on Sunday—his grandmother was so delighted when he accompanied her to "meeting" that he did so rather more frequently, perhaps, than he otherwise would—at the homes of acquaintances, and, of course, at the Snow place. When she walked home with her father after a "story evening" he usually went with them as additional escort.

She had not questioned him concerning Madeline since their first meeting that morning at the parsonage. He knew, therefore, that some one—his grandmother, probably—had told her of the broken engagement. When they were alone together they talked of many things, casual things, the generalities of which, so he told himself, a conversation between mere friends was composed. But occasionally, after doing escort duty, after Mr. Kendall had gone into the house to take his "throat medicine"—a medicine which Captain Zelotes declared would have to be double-strength pretty soon to offset the wear and tear of the story evenings—they talked of matters more specific and which more directly concerned themselves. She spoke of her hospital work, of her teaching before the war, and of her plans for the future. The latter, of course, were very indefinite now.

"Father needs me," she said, "and I shall not leave him while he lives."

They spoke of Albert's work and plans most of all. He began to ask for advice concerning the former. When those stories were written, what then? She hoped he would try the novel he had hinted at.

"I'm sure you can do it," she said. "And you mustn't give up the poems altogether. It was the poetry, you know, which was the beginning."

"YOU were the beginning," he said impulsively. "Perhaps I should never have written at all if you hadn't urged me, shamed me out of my laziness."

"I was a presuming young person, I'm afraid," she said. "I wonder you didn't tell me to mind my own business. I believe you did, but I wouldn't mind."

June brought the summer weather and the summer boarders to South Harniss. One of the news sensations which came at the same time was that the new Fosdick cottage had been sold. The people who had occupied it the previous season had bought it. Mrs. Fosdick, so rumor said, was not strong and her doctors had decided that the sea air did not agree with her.

"Crimustee!" exclaimed Issachar, as he imparted the news to Mr. Keeler, "if that ain't the worst. Spend your money, and a pile of money, too, buyin' ground, layin' of it out to build a house on to live in, then buildin' that house and then, by crimus, sellin' it to somebody else for THEM to live in. That beats any foolishness ever come MY way."

"And there's some consider'ble come your way at that, ain't they, Is?" observed Laban, busy with his bookkeeping.

Issachar nodded. "You're right there has," he said complacently. "I . . . What do you mean by that? Tryin' to be funny again, ain't you?"

Albert heard the news with a distinct feeling of relief. While the feeling on his part toward Madeline was of the kindliest, and Madeline's was, he felt sure, the same toward him, nevertheless to meet her day after day, as people must meet in a village no bigger than South Harniss, would be awkward for both. And to meet Mrs. Fosdick might be more awkward still. He smiled as he surmised that the realization by the lady of that very awkwardness was probably responsible for the discovery that sea air was not beneficial.

The story-writing and the story evenings continued. Over the fourth story in the series discussion was warm, for there were marked differences of opinion among the listeners. One of the experiences through which Albert had brought his hero was that of working as general assistant to a sharp, unscrupulous and smooth-tongued rascal who was proprietor of a circus sideshow and fake museum. He was a kind-hearted swindler, but one who never let a question of honesty interfere with the getting of a dollar. In this fourth story, to the town where the hero, now a man of twenty-five, had established himself in business, came this cheat of other days, but now he came as a duly ordained clergyman in answer to the call of the local church. The hero learned that he had not told the governing body of that church of his former career. Had he done so, they most certainly would not have called him. The leading man in that church body was the hero's patron and kindest friend. The question: What was the hero's duty in the matter?

Of course the first question asked was whether or not the ex-sideshow proprietor was sincerely repentant and honestly trying to walk the straight path and lead others along it. Albert replied that his hero had interviewed him and was satisfied that he was; he had been "converted" at a revival and was now a religious enthusiast whose one idea was to save sinners.

That was enough for Captain Zelotes.

"Let him alone, then," said the captain. "He's tryin' to be a decent man. What do you want to do? Tell on him and have him chucked overboard from one church after another until he gets discouraged and takes to swindlin' again?"

Rachel Ellis could not see it that way.

"If he was a saved sinner," she declared, "and repentant of his sins, then he'd ought to repent 'em out loud. Hidin' 'em ain't repentin'. And, besides, there's Donald's (Donald was the hero's name) there's Donald's duty to the man that's been so good to him. Is it fair to that man to keep still and let him hire a minister that, like as not, will steal the collection, box and all, afore he gets through? No, sir, Donald ought to tell THAT man, anyhow."

Olive was pretty dubious about the whole scheme. She doubted if anybody connected with a circus COULD ever become a minister.

"The whole—er—er—trade is so different," she said.

Mr. Kendall was not there that evening, his attendance being required at a meeting of the Sunday School teachers. Helen, however, was not at that meeting and Captain Zelotes declared his intention of asking her opinion by telephone.

"She'll say same as I do—you see if she don't," he declared. When he called the parsonage, however, Maria Price answered the phone and informed him that Helen was spending the evening with old Mrs. Crowell, who lived but a little way from the Snow place. The captain promptly called up the Crowell house.

"She's there and she'll stop in here on her way along," he said triumphantly. "And she'll back me up—you see."

But she did not. She did not "back up" any one. She merely smiled and declared the problem too complicated to answer offhand.

"Why don't you ask Albert?" she inquired. "After all, he is the one who must settle it eventually."

"He won't tell," said Olive. "He's real provokin', isn't he? And now you won't tell, either, Helen."

"Oh, I don't know—yet. But I think he does."

Albert, as usual, walked home with her.

"How are you going to answer your hero's riddle?" she asked.

"Before I tell you, suppose you tell me what your answer would be."

She reflected. "Well," she said, "it seems to me that, all things being as they are, he should do this: He should go to the sideshow man—the minister now—and have a very frank talk with him. He should tell him that he had decided to say nothing about the old life and to help him in every way, to be his friend—provided that he keep straight, that is all. Of course more than that would be meant, the alternative would be there and understood, but he need not say it. I think that course of action would be fair to himself and to everybody. That is my answer. What is yours?"

He laughed quietly. "Just that, of course," he said. "You would see it, I knew. You always see down to the heart of things, Helen. You have the gift."

She shook her head. "It didn't really need a gift, this particular problem, did it?" she said. "It is not—excuse me—it isn't exactly a new one."

"No, it isn't. It is as old as the hills, but there are always new twists to it."

"As there are to all our old problems."

"Yes. By the way, your advice about the ending of my third story was exactly what I needed. The editor wrote me he should never have forgiven me if it had ended in any other way. It probably WOULD have ended in another way if it hadn't been for you. Thank you, Helen."

"Oh, you know there was really nothing to thank me for. It was all you, as usual. Have you planned the next story, the fifth, yet?"

"Not entirely. I have some vague ideas. Do you want to hear them?"

"Of course."

So they discussed those ideas as they walked along the sidewalk of the street leading down to the parsonage. It was a warm evening, a light mist, which was not substantial enough to be a fog, hanging low over everything, wrapping them and the trees and the little front yards and low houses of the old village in a sort of cozy, velvety, confidential quiet. The scent of lilacs was heavy in the air.

They both were silent. Just when they had ceased speaking neither could have told. They walked on arm in arm and suddenly Albert became aware that this silence was dangerous for him; that in it all his resolves and brave determinations were melting into mist like that about him; that he must talk and talk at once and upon a subject which was not personal, which—

And then Helen spoke.

"Do you know what this reminds me of?" she said. "All this talk of ours? It reminds me of how we used to talk over those first poems of yours. You have gone a long way since then."

"I have gone to Kaiserville and back."

"You know what I mean. I mean your work has improved wonderfully. You write with a sure hand now, it seems to me. And your view is so much broader."

"I hope I'm not the narrow, conceited little rooster I used to be. I told you, Helen, that the war handed me an awful jolt. Well, it did. I think it, or my sickness or the whole business together, knocked most of that self-confidence of mine galley-west. For so much I'm thankful."

"I don't know that I am, altogether. I don't want you to lose confidence in yourself. You should be confident now because you deserve to be. And you write with confidence, or it reads as if you did. Don't you feel that you do, yourself? Truly, don't you?"

"Well, perhaps, a little. I have been at it for some time now. I ought to show some progress. Perhaps I don't make as many mistakes."

"I can't see that you have made any."

"I have made one . . . a damnable one."

"Why, what do you mean?"

"Oh, nothing. I didn't mean to say that. . . . Helen, do you know it is awfully good of you to take all this interest in me—in my work, I mean. Why do you do it?"

"Why?"

"Yes, why?"

"Why, because—Why shouldn't I? Haven't we always talked about your writings together, almost since we first knew each other? Aren't we old friends?"

There it was again—friends. It was like a splash of cold water in the face, at once awakening and chilling. Albert walked on in silence for a few moments and then began speaking of some trivial subject entirely disconnected with himself or his work or her. When they reached the parsonage door he said good night at once and strode off toward home.

Back in his room, however, he gave himself another mental picking to pieces. He was realizing most distinctly that this sort of thing would not do. It was easy to say that his attitude toward Helen Kendall was to be that of a friend and nothing more, but it was growing harder and harder to maintain that attitude. He had come within a breath that very night of saying what was in his heart.

Well, if he had said it, if he did say it—what then? After all, was there any real reason why he should not say it? It was true that he had loved, or fancied that he loved, Madeline, that he had been betrothed to her—but again, what of it? Broken engagements were common enough, and there was nothing disgraceful in this one. Why not go to Helen and tell her that his fancied love for Madeline had been the damnable mistake he had confessed making. Why not tell her that since the moment when he saw her standing in the doorway of the parsonage on the morning following his return from New York he had known that she was the only woman in the world for him, that it was her image he had seen in his dreams, in the delirium of fever, that it was she, and not that other, who—

But there, all this was foolishness, and he knew it. He did not dare say it. Not for one instant had she, by speech or look or action, given him the slightest encouragement to think her feeling for him was anything but friendship. And that friendship was far too precious to risk. He must not risk it. He must keep still, he must hide his thoughts, she must never guess. Some day, perhaps, after a year or two, after his position in his profession was more assured, then he might speak. But even then there would be that risk. And the idea of waiting was not pleasant. What had Rachel told him concerning the hosts of doctors and officers and generals who had been "shining up" to her. Some risk there, also.

Well, never mind. He would try to keep on as he had been going for the present. He would try not to see her as frequently. If the strain became unbearable he might go away somewhere—for a time.

He did not go away, but he made it a point not to see her as frequently. However, they met often even as it was. And he was conscious always that the ice beneath his feet was very, very thin.

One wonderful August evening he was in his room upstairs. He was not writing. He had come up there early because he wished to think, to consider. A proposition had been made to him that afternoon, a surprising proposition—to him it had come as a complete surprise—and before mentioning it even to his grandparents he wished to think it over very carefully.

About ten o'clock his grandfather called to him from the foot of the stairs and asked him to come down.

"Mr. Kendall's on the phone," said Captain Zelotes. "He's worried about Helen. She's up to West Harniss sittin' up along of Lurany Howes, who's been sick so long. She ain't come home, and the old gentleman's frettin' about her walkin' down from there alone so late. I told him I cal'lated you'd just as soon harness Jess and drive up and get her. You talk with him yourself, Al."

Albert did and, after assuring the nervous clergyman that he would see that his daughter reached home safely, put on his hat and went out to the barn. Jessamine was asleep in her stall. As he was about to lead her out he suddenly remembered that one of the traces had broken that morning and Captain Zelotes had left it at the harness-maker's to be mended. It was there yet. The captain had forgotten the fact, and so had he. That settled the idea of using Jessamine and the buggy. Never mind, it was a beautiful night and the walk was but little over a mile.

When he reached the tiny story-and-a-half Howes cottage, sitting back from the road upon the knoll amid the tangle of silverleaf sprouts, it was Helen herself who opened the door. She was surprised to see him, and when he explained his errand she was a little vexed.

"The idea of Father's worrying," she said. "Such a wonderful night as this, bright moonlight, and in South Harniss, too. Nothing ever happens to people in South Harniss. I will be ready in a minute or two. Mrs. Howes' niece is here now and will stay with her until to-morrow. Then her sister is coming to stay a month. As soon as I get her medicine ready we can go."

The door of the tiny bedroom adjoining the sitting room was open, and Albert, sitting upon the lounge with the faded likeness of a pink dog printed on the plush cover, could hear the querulous voice of the invalid within. The widow Howes was deaf and, as Laban Keeler described it, "always hollered loud enough to make herself hear" when she spoke. Helen was moving quietly about the sick room and speaking in a low tone. Albert could not hear what she said, but he could hear Lurania.

"You're a wonder, that's what you be," declared the latter, "and I told your pa so last time he was here. 'She's a saint,' says I, 'if ever there was one on this earth. She's the nicest, smartest, best-lookin' girl in THIS town and . . .' eh?"

There had been a murmur, presumably of remonstrance, from Helen.

"Eh?"

Another murmur.

"EH? WHO'D you say was there?"

A third murmur.

"WHO? . . . Oh, that Speranzy one? Lote Snow's grandson? The one they used to call the Portygee? . . . Eh? Well, all right, I don't care if he did hear me. If he don't know you're nice and smart and good-lookin', it's high time he did."

Helen, a trifle embarrassed but laughing, emerged a moment later, and when she had put on her hat she and Albert left the Howes cottage and began their walk home. It was one of those nights such as Cape Codders, year-rounders or visitors, experience three or four times during a summer and boast of the remainder of the year. A sky clear, deep, stretched cloudless from horizon to horizon. Every light at sea or on shore, in cottage window or at masthead or in lighthouse or on lightship a twinkling diamond point. A moon, apparently as big as a barrel-head, hung up in the east and below it a carpet of cold fire, of dancing, spangled silver spread upon the ocean. The sound of the surf, distant, soothing; and for the rest quiet and the fragrance of the summer woods and fields.

They walked rather fast at first and the conversation was brisk, but as the night began to work its spell upon them their progress was slower and there were intervals of silence of which neither was aware. They came to the little hill where the narrow road from West Harniss comes to join the broader highway leading to the Center. There were trees here, a pine grove, on the landward side, and toward the sea nothing to break the glorious view.

Helen caught her breath. "Oh, it is beautiful, beautiful!" she said.

Albert did not answer. "Why don't you talk?" she asked. "What are you thinking about?"

He did not tell her what he was thinking about. Instead, having caught himself just in time, he began telling her of what he had been thinking when his grandfather called him to the telephone.

"Helen," he said, "I want to ask your advice. I had an astonishing proposal made to me this afternoon. I must make a decision, I must say yes or no, and I'm not sure which to say."

She looked up at him inquiringly.

"This afternoon," he went on, "Doctor Parker called me into his office. There was a group of men there, prominent men in politics from about the country; Judge Baxter from Ostable was there, and Captain Warren from South Denboro, and others like them. What do you suppose they want me to do?"

"I can't imagine."

"They offer me the party nomination for Congress from this section. That is, of course, they want me to permit my name to stand and they seem sure my nomination will be confirmed by the voters. The nomination, they say, is equivalent to election. They seem certain of it. . . . And they were insistent that I accept."

"Oh—oh, Albert!"

"Yes. They said a good many flattering things, things I should like to believe. They said my war record and my writing and all that had made me a prominent man in the county—Please don't think I take any stock in that—"

"But *I* do. Go on."

"Well, that is all. They seemed confident that I would make a good congressman. I am not so sure. Of course the thing . . . well, it does tempt me, I confess. I could keep on with my writing, of course. I should have to leave the home people for a part of the year, but I could be with them or near them the rest. And . . . well, Helen, I—I think I should like the job. Just now, when America needs Americans and the thing that isn't American must be fought, I should like—if I were sure I was capable of it—"

"Oh, but you are—you ARE."

"Do you really think so? Would you like to have me try?"

He felt her arm tremble upon his. She drew a long breath.

"Oh, I should be so PROUD!" she breathed.

There was a quiver in her voice, almost a sob. He bent toward her. She was looking off toward the sea, the moonlight upon her face was like a glory, her eyes were shining—and there were tears in them. His heart throbbed wildly.

"Helen!" he cried. "Helen!"

She turned and looked up into his face. The next moment her own face was hidden against his breast, his arms were about her, and . . . and the risk, the risk he had feared to take, was taken.

They walked home after a time, but it was a slow, a very slow walk with many interruptions.

"Oh, Helen," he kept saying, "I don't see how you can. How can you? In spite of it all. I—I treated you so badly. I was SUCH an idiot. And you really care? You really do?"

She laughed happily. "I really do . . . and . . . and I really have, all the time."

"Always?"

"Always."

"Well—well, by George! And . . . Helen, do you know I think—I think I did too—always—only I was such a young fool I didn't realize it. WHAT a young fool I was!"

"Don't say that, dear, don't. . . . You are going to be a great man. You are a famous one already; you are going to be great. Don't you know that?"

He stooped and kissed her.

"I think I shall have to be," he said, "if I am going to be worthy of you."

CHAPTER XX

Albert, sitting in the private office of Z. Snow and Co., dropped his newspaper and looked up with a smile as his grandfather came in. Captain Zelotes' florid face was redder even than usual, for it was a cloudy day in October and blowing a gale.

"Whew!" puffed the captain, pulling off his overcoat and striding over to warm his hands at the stove; "it's raw as January comin' over the tops of those Trumet hills, and blowin' hard enough to part your back hair, besides. One time there I didn't know but I'd have to reef, cal'late I would if I'd known how to reef an automobile."

"Is the car running as well as ever?" asked Albert.

"You bet you! Took all but two of those hills on full steam and never slowed down a mite. Think of goin' to Trumet and back in a forenoon, and havin' time enough to do the talkin' I went to do besides. Why, Jess would have needed the whole day to make the down cruise, to say nothin' of the return trip. Well, the old gal's havin' a good rest now, nothin' much to do but eat and sleep. She deserves it; she's been a good horse for your grandma and me."

He rubbed his hands before the stove and chuckled.

"Olive's still scared to death for fear I'll get run into, or run over somebody or somethin'," he observed. "I tell her I can navigate that car now the way I used to navigate the old President Hayes, and I could do that walkin' in my sleep. There's a little exaggeration there," he added, with a grin. "It takes about all my gumption when I'm wide awake to turn the flivver around in a narrow road, but I manage to do it. . . . Well, what are you doin' in here, Al?" he added. "Readin' the Item's prophesy about how big your majority's goin' to be?"

Albert smiled. "I dropped in here to wait for you, Grandfather," he replied. "The novel-writing mill wasn't working particularly well, so I gave it up and took a walk."

"To the parsonage, I presume likely?"

"Well, I did stop there for a minute or two."

"You don't say! I'm surprised to hear it. How is Helen this mornin'? Did she think you'd changed much since you saw her last night?"

"I don't know. She didn't say so if she did. She sent her love to you and Grandmother—"

"What she had left over, you mean."

"And said to tell you not to tire yourself out electioneering for me. That was good advice, too. Grandfather, don't you know that you shouldn't motor all the way to Trumet and back a morning like this? I'd rather—much rather go without the votes than have you do such things."

Captain Zelotes seated himself in his desk chair.

"But you ain't goin' to do without 'em," he chuckled. "Obed Nye—he's chairman of the Trumet committee—figgers you'll have a five-to-one majority. He told me to practice callin' you 'the Honorable' because that's what you'd be by Tuesday night of week after next. And next winter Mother and I will be takin' a trip to Washin'ton so as to set in the gallery and listen to you makin' speeches. We'll be some consider'ble proud of you, too, boy," he added, with a nod.

His grandson looked away, out of the window, over the bleak yard with its piles of lumber. The voice of Issacher raised in expostulation with the driver of Cahoon's "truck-wagon" could be faintly heard.

"I shall hate to leave you and Grandmother and the old place," he said. "If I am elected—"

"WHEN you're elected; there isn't any 'if.'"

"Well, all right. I shall hate to leave South Harniss. Every person I really care for will be here. Helen—and you people at home."

"It's too bad you and Helen can't be married and go to Washin'ton together. Not to stay permanent," he added quickly, "but just while Congress is in session. Your grandma says then she'd feel as if you had somebody to look after you. She always figgers, you know, that a man ain't capable of lookin' out for himself. There'd ought to be at least one woman to take care of him, see that he don't get his feet wet and goes to meetin' reg'lar and so on; if there could be two, so much the better. Mother would have made a pretty good Mormon, in some ways."

Albert laughed. "Helen feels she must stay with her father for the present," he said. "Of course she is right. Perhaps by and by we can find some good capable housekeeper to share the responsibility, but not this winter. IF I am sent to Washington I shall come back often, you may be sure."

"When ARE you cal'latin' to be married, if that ain't a secret?"

"Perhaps next spring. Certainly next fall. It will depend upon Mr. Kendall's health. But, Grandfather, I do feel rather like a deserter, going off and leaving you here—"

"Good Lord! You don't cal'late I'M breakin' down, runnin' strong to talk and weakenin' everywhere else, like old Minister Kendall, do you?"

"Well, hardly. But . . . well, you see, I have felt a little ungrateful ever since I came back from the war. In a way I am sorry that I feel I must give myself entirely to my writing—and my political work. I wish I might have gone on here in this office, accepted that partnership you would have given me—"

"You can have it yet, you know. Might take it and just keep it to fall back on in case that story-mill of yours busts altogether or all hands in Ostable County go crazy and vote the wrong ticket. Just take it and wait. Always well to have an anchor ready to let go, you know."

"Thanks, but that wouldn't be fair. I wish I MIGHT have taken it— for your sake. I wish for your sake I were so constituted as to be good for something at it. Of course I don't mean by that that I should be willing to give up my writing—but—well, you see, Grandfather, I owe you an awful lot in this world . . . and I know you had set your heart on my being your partner in Z. Snow and Co. I know you're disappointed."

Captain Lote did not answer instantly. He seemed to be thinking. Then he opened a drawer in his desk and took out a box of cigars similar to those he had offered the Honorable Fletcher Fosdick on the occasion of their memorable interview.

"Smoke, Al?" he asked. Albert declined because of the nearness to dinner time, but the captain, who never permitted meals or anything else to interfere with his smoking, lighted one of the cigars and leaned back in his chair, puffing steadily.

"We-ll, Al," he said slowly, "I'll tell you about that. There was a time— I'll own up that there was a time when the idea you wasn't goin' to turn out a business man and the partner who would take over this concern after I got my clearance papers was a notion I wouldn't let myself think of for a minute. I wouldn't THINK of it, that's all. But I've changed my mind about that, as I have about some other things." He paused, tugged at his beard, and then added, "And I guess likely I might as well own up to the whole truth while I'm about it: I didn't change it because I wanted to, but because I couldn't help it—'twas changed for me."

He made this statement more as if he were thinking aloud than as if he expected a reply. A moment later he continued.

"Yes, sir," he said, "'twas changed for me. And," with a shrug, "I'd rather prided myself that when my mind was made up it stayed that way. But—but, well, consarn it, I've about come to the conclusion that I was a pig-headed old fool, Al, in some ways."

"Nonsense, Grandfather. You are the last man to—"

"Oh, I don't mean a candidate for the feeble-minded school. There ain't been any Snows put there that I can remember, not our branch of 'em, anyhow. But, consarn it, I—I—" he was plainly finding it hard to express his thought, "I—well, I used to think I knew consider'ble, had what I liked to think was good, hard sense. 'Twas hard enough, I cal'late—pretty nigh petrified in spots."

Albert laid a hand on his knee.

"Don't talk like that," he replied impulsively. "I don't like to hear you."

"Don't you? Then I won't. But, you see, Al, it bothers me. Look how I used to talk about makin' up poetry and writin' yarns and all that. Used to call it silliness and a waste of time, I did—worse names than that, generally. And look what you're makin' at it in money, to say nothin' of its shovin' you into Congress, and keepin' the newspapers busy printin' stuff about you.... Well, well," with a sigh of resignation, "I don't understand it yet, but know it's so, and if I'd had my pig-headed way 'twouldn't have been so. It's a dreadful belittlin' feelin' to a man at my time of life, a man that's commanded ten-thousand-ton steamers and handled crews and bossed a business like this. It makes him wonder how many other fool things he's done.... Why, do you know, Al," he added, in a sudden burst of confidence, "I was consider'ble prejudiced against you when you first came here."

He made the statement as if he expected it to come as a stunning surprise. Albert would not have laughed for the world, nor in one way did he feel like it, but it was funny.

"Well, perhaps you were, a little," he said gravely. "I don't wonder."

"Oh, I don't mean just because you was your father's son. I mean on your own account, in a way. Somehow, you see, I couldn't believe—eh? Oh, come in, Labe! It's all right. Al and I are just talkin' about nothin' in particular and all creation in general."

Mr. Keeler entered with a paper in his hand.

"Sorry to bother you, Cap'n Lote," he said, "but this bill of Colby and Sons for that last lot of hardware ain't accordin' to agreement. The prices on those butts ain't right, and neither's those half-inch screws. Better send it back to em, eh?"

Captain Zelotes inspected the bill.

"Humph!" he grunted. "You're right, Labe. You generally are, I notice. Yes, send it back and tell 'em—anything you want to."

Laban smiled. "I want to, all right," he said. "This is the third time they've sent wrong bills inside of two months. Well, Al," turning toward him, "I cal'late this makes you kind of homesick, don't it, this talk about bills and screws and bolts and such? Wa'n't teasin' for your old job back again, was you, Al? Cal'late he could have it, couldn't he, Cap'n? We'll need somebody to heave a bucket of water on Issy pretty soon; he's gettin' kind of pert and uppish again. Pretty much so. Yes, yes, yes."

He departed, chuckling. Captain Zelotes looked after him. He tugged at his beard.

"Al," he said, "do you know what I've about made up my mind to do?"

Albert shook his head.

"I've about made up my mind to take Labe Keeler into the firm of Z. Snow and Co. YOU won't come in, and," with a twinkle, "I need somebody to keep my name from gettin' lonesome on the sign."

Albert was delighted.

"Bully for you, Grandfather!" he exclaimed. "You couldn't do a better thing for Labe or for the firm. And he deserves it, too."

"Ye-es, I think he does. Labe's a mighty faithful, capable feller, and now that he's sworn off on those vacations of his he can be trusted anywheres. Yes, I've as good as made up my mind to take him in. Of course," with the twinkle in evidence once more, "Issachar'll be a little mite jealous, but we'll have to bear up under that as best we can."

"I wonder what Labe will say when you tell him?"

"He'll say yes. I'll tell Rachel first and she'll tell him to say it. And then I'll tell 'em both I won't do it unless they agree to get married. I've always said I didn't want to die till I'd been to that weddin'. I want to hear Rachel tell the minister she'll 'obey' Labe. Ho, ho!"

"Do you suppose they ever will be married?"

"Why, yes, I kind of think so. I shouldn't wonder if they would be right off now if it wasn't that Rachel wouldn't think of givin' up keepin' house for your grandmother. She wouldn't do that and Labe wouldn't want her to. I've got to fix that somehow. Perhaps they could live along with us. Land knows there's room enough. They're all right, those two. Kind of funny to look at, and they match up in size like a rubber boot and a slipper, but I declare I don't know which has got the most common-sense or the biggest heart. And 'twould be hard to tell which thinks the most of you, Al. . . . Eh? Why, it's after half-past twelve o'clock! Olive'll be for combin' our topknots with a belayin' pin if we keep her dinner waitin' like this."

As they were putting on their coats the captain spoke again.

"I hadn't finished what I was sayin' to you when Labe came in," he observed. "'Twasn't much account; just a sort of confession, and they say that's good for the soul. I was just goin' to say that when you first came here I was prejudiced against you, not only because your father and I didn't agree, but because he was what he was. Because he was—was—"

Albert finished the sentence for him.

"A Portygee," he said.

"Why, yes, that's what I called him. That's what I used to call about everybody that wasn't born right down here in Yankeeland. I used to be prejudiced against you because you was what I called a half-breed. I'm sorry, Al. I'm ashamed. See what you've turned out to be. I declare, I—"

"Shh! shh! Don't, Grandfather. When I came here I was a little snob, a conceited, insufferable little—"

"Here, here! Hold on! No, you wa'n't, neither. Or if you was, you was only a boy. I was a man, and I ought to—"

"No, I'm going to finish. Whatever I am now, or whatever I may be. I owe to you, and to Grandmother, and Rachel and Laban—and Helen. You made me over between you. I know that now."

They walked home instead of riding in the new car. Captain Zelotes declared he had hung on to that steering wheel all the forenoon and he was afraid if he took it again his fingers would grow fast to the rim. As they emerged from the office into the open air, he said:

"Al, regardin' that makin'-over business, I shouldn't be surprised if it was a kind of—er—mutual thing between you and me. We both had some prejudices to get rid of, eh?"

"Perhaps so. I'm sure I did."

"And I'm sartin sure I did. And the war and all that came with it put the finishin' touches to the job. When I think of what the thousands and thousands of men did over there in those hell-holes of trenches, men with names that run all the way from Jones and Kelly to—er—"

"Speranza."

"Yes, and Whiskervitch and the land knows what more. When I think of that I'm ready to take off my hat to 'em and swear I'll never be so narrow again as to look down on a feller because he don't happen to be born in Ostable County. There's only one thing I ask of 'em, and that is that when they come here to live—to stay—under our laws and takin' advantage of the privileges we offer 'em—they'll stop bein' Portygees or Russians or Polacks or whatever they used to be or their folks were, and just be Americans—like you, Al."

"That's what we must work for now, Grandfather. It's a big job, but it must be done."

They walked on in silence for a time. Then the captain said:

"It's a pretty fine country, after all, ain't it, Albert?"

Albert looked about him over the rolling hills, the roofs of the little town, the sea, the dunes, the pine groves, the scene which had grown so familiar to him and which had become in his eyes so precious.

"It is MY country," he declared, with emphasis.

His grandfather caught his meaning.

"I'm glad you feel that way, son," he said, "but 'twasn't just South Harniss I meant then. I meant all of it, the whole United States. It's got its faults, of course, lots of 'em. And if I was an Englishman or a Frenchman I'd probably say it wasn't as good as England or France, whichever it happened to be. That's all right; I ain't findin' any fault with 'em for that—that's the way they'd ought to feel. But you and I, Al, we're Americans. So the rest of the world must excuse us if we say that, take it by and large, it's a mighty good country. We've planned for it, and worked for it, and fought for it, and we know. Eh?"

"Yes. We know."

"Yes. And no howlin', wild-eyed bunch from somewhere else that haven't done any of these things are goin' to come here and run it their way if we can help it—we Americans; eh?"

Alberto Miguel Carlos Speranza, American, drew a long breath.

"No!" he said, with emphasis.

"You bet! Well, unless I'm mistaken, I smell salt fish and potatoes, which, accordin' to Cape Cod notion, is a good American dinner. I don't know how you feel, Al, but I'm hungry."